Ashes on His Boot

Acknowledgements

Some of this story is fiction. Much, however, is historical fact, a result of painstaking research by my co-author and good friend, Howard Carman. Howard provided insights, details and kept me moving forward in writing this story of an unsung hero of the West.

We were influenced in our storytelling by *Empire of the Summer Moon* by S. C. Gwynne and *The Texas Rangers: A Century of Frontier Defense* by Walter Prescott Webb, two notable historical accounts of the period. Both documentary works are recommended for those who would like to understand more about the real American West of the 19th Century.

In June 2013, Howard and I were introduced to Charlotte Cook at the St. Petersburg, FL Historical Novel Society Meeting. She agreed, somewhat reluctantly, to be our editor, and her help was indispensable. You'll enjoy evidence of Charlotte's motto throughout this work of fiction: "Writers come to an empty page with a full mind. Readers come to a full page with an empty mind."

Our copy editors, Nancy and Bill Montwieler of Washington, DC, plowed through the finished manuscript with uncommon diligence and great patience. They made sure the facts were indeed facts, that we'd written so readers could truly understand the story, and that we'd not used too many Tennessee and Texas colloquialisms. Final editing and overall design was provided via the creative work of *Reelfoot Publishing*.

Lastly, we are indebted to two gentlemen, both noted historians and authors, who took time to read parts of the story and offer valuable feedback. Dr. James E. Crisp, Professor of History at NC State University, set us straight about the relationship between Jack Hays and Andrew Jackson, and Jack W. London critiqued our point of narration and made sure we refrained from misstating the early history of the San Antonio area.

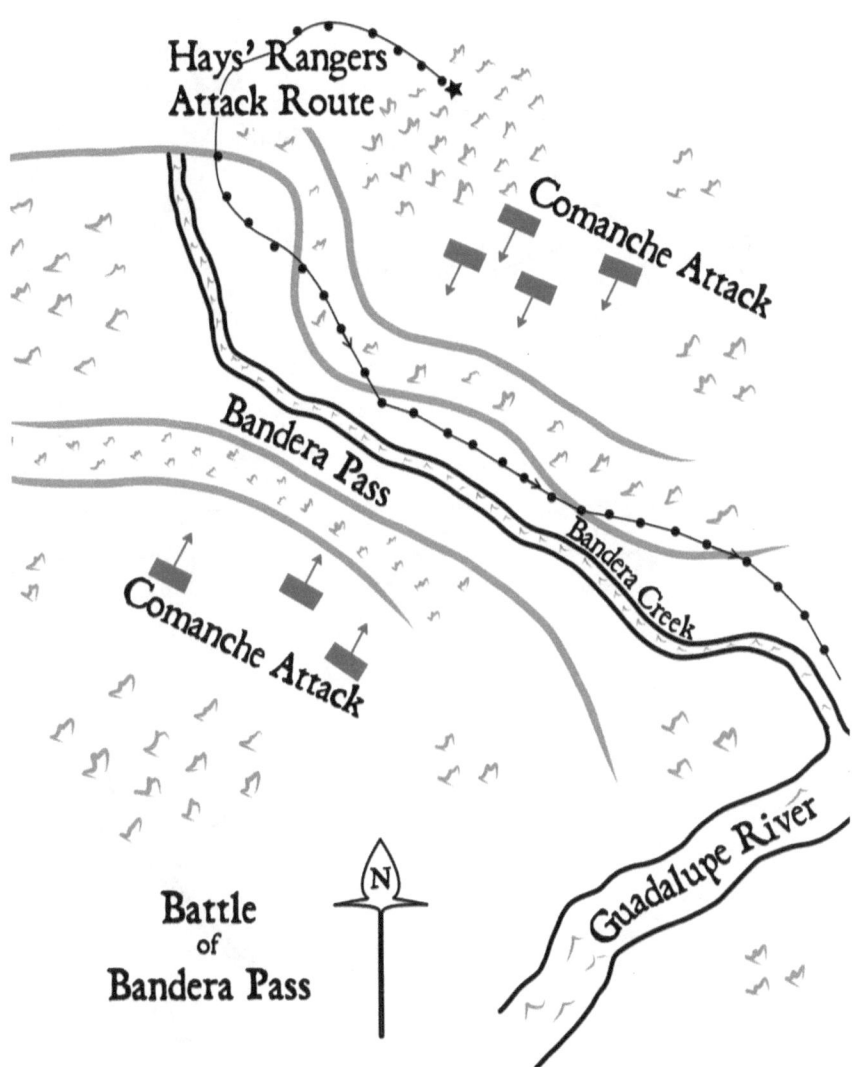

Hays' Rangers
Attack Route

Comanche Attack

Bandera Pass

Bandera Creek

Comanche Attack

N

Battle
of
Bandera Pass

Guadalupe River

7

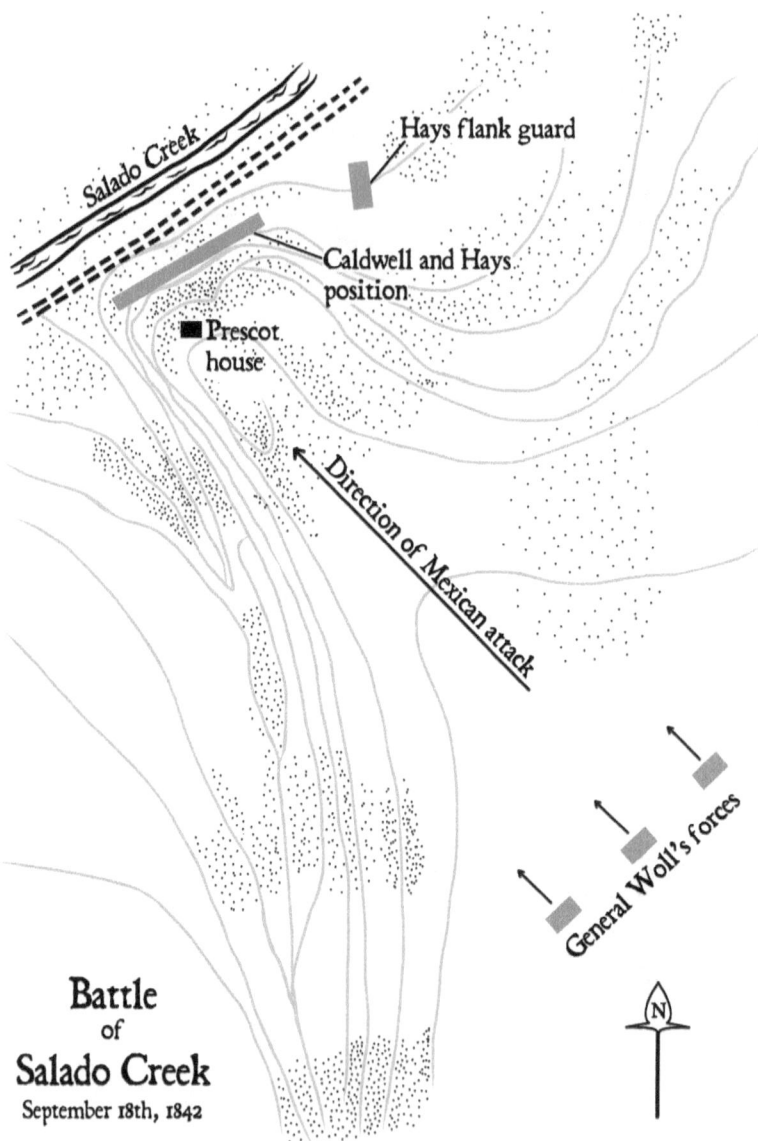

Hays flank guard

Caldwell and Hays
position

Salado Creek

Prescot
house

Direction of Mexican attack

General Woll's forces

N

Battle
of
Salado Creek
September 18th, 1842

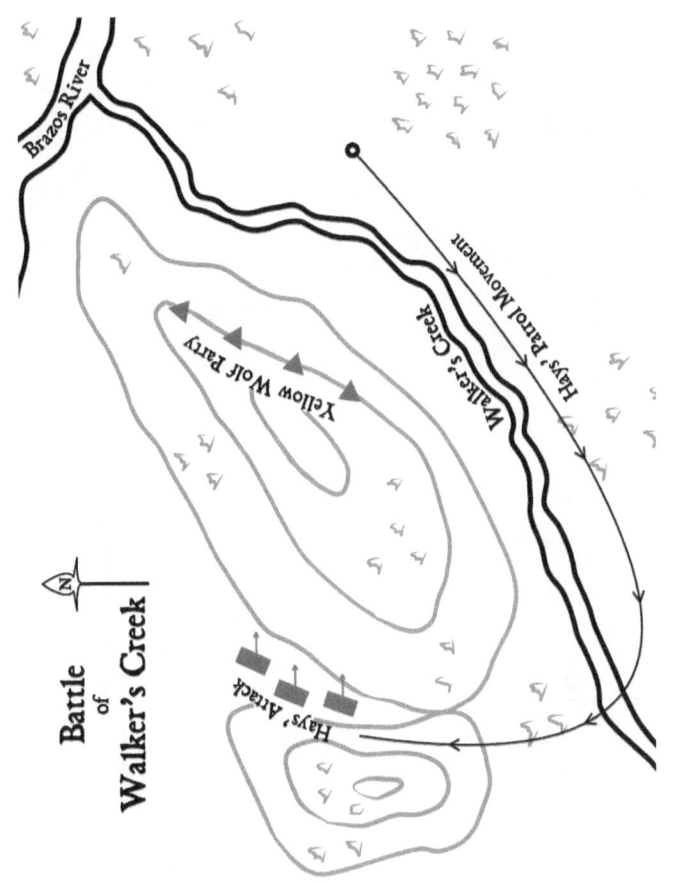

Battle
of
Walker's Creek

Brazos River

Walker's Creek

Hays' Patrol Movement

Yellow Wolf Party

Hays' Attack

N

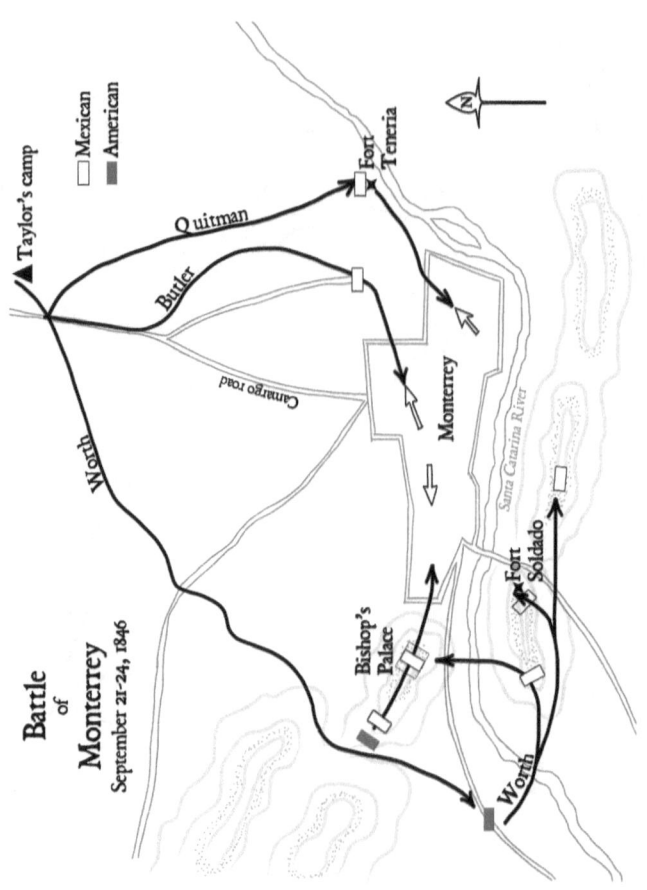

Battle
of
Monterrey
September 21–24, 1846

☐ Mexican
■ American

▲ Taylor's camp

Quitman

Butler

Worth

Camargo road

Fort
Teneria

Monterrey

Santa Catarina River

Bishop's
Palace

Fort
Soldado

Worth

N

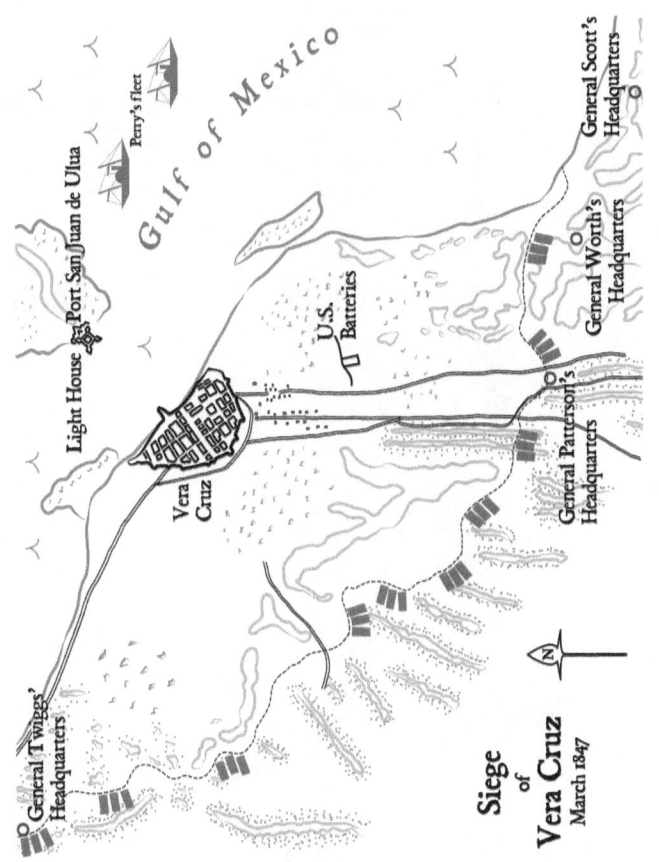

Siege
of
Vera Cruz
March 1847

Gulf of Mexico

Perry's fleet

Light House

Port San Juan de Ulua

Vera Cruz

U.S. Batteries

General Scott's Headquarters

General Worth's Headquarters

General Patterson's Headquarters

General Twiggs' Headquarters

N

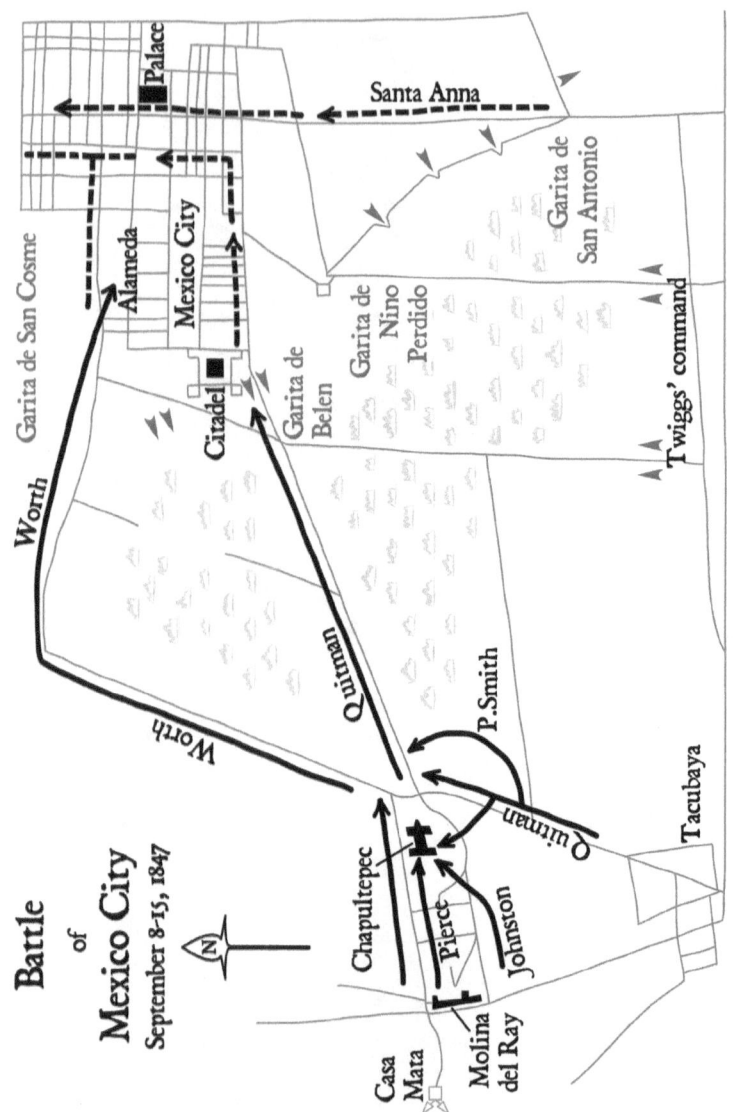

Battle
of
Mexico City
September 8–15, 1847

N

Casa Mata

Molina del Ray

Chapultepec

Pierce

Johnston

P. Smith

Quitman

Quitman

Tacubaya

Worth

Quitman

Citadel

Garita de Belen

Garita de Nino Perdido

Garita de San Antonio

Twiggs' command

Worth

Garita de San Cosme

Alameda

Mexico City

Palace

Santa Anna

"Some say Virginia is the mother of Texas. We never knew who the father was, but we kinda suspected Tennessee." ~ *Tex Ritter, noted country musician and native Texan*

PART ONE

The People - Numunuh

"My people have never first drawn a bow or fired a gun against the Whites. It was you who sent out the first soldier, and we who sent out the second."

Ten Bears, a Yamparika Comanche Chief, speaking at the October 1867 Medicine Lodge Councils Treaty Conference, Fort Leavenworth, Kansas.

Chapter One

Nashville to Nacogdoches – April 1836

"Name's Jack. Jack Hays." The young man shouted, his high-pitched voice challenging the tavern noise. "I'm from Nashville."

Jack Hays laid his room key on the bar and fingered a shot of whiskey. He'd pushed back the brim of his weathered, wide-brimmed hat so he could see the face of the taller man standing next to him. The owner of the Goins Inn and Drinking Establishment was fifty, maybe a little older, and he wore good city clothes, so he'd obviously made money in life. William Goins wasn't White, but he wasn't a Negro, either. Leastways not the kind Jack had known back in Tennessee. But the man did have kinky, sort of grayish hair, so there was some black blood in him from somewhere.

Goins was a Freeman, for sure. So why did he own slaves? Jack was pretty sure Mr. Goins was a slaver. One of the barefoot Negro boys in the man's service had taken Jack's horse down to the smithy just after he rode in. Clear as could be, Texas was new territory. Lots of surprises out here. Might be less people, but there were more kinds of them. Even the whiskey tasted different. Tennessee corn whiskey didn't burn from gum to gut like this East Texas piss did.

The barkeep's sunken eyes and thin lips had tired wrinkle lines all around. Jack had noticed that when the man was up close and pouring his first shot. Everybody else in the place looked weather-beaten and wore down, too. Sort of like those old oaks around his great aunt's mansion back in Nashville.

The longer he stood at the bar rail, the noisier the place got. Jack chewed bits of buffalo jerky, sipped at a second whiskey and peered around the dimly lit saloon. William Goins, he'd said to call him Willie, leaned against the bar and surveyed his patrons. The tavern owner had kept his eye on that same table in the corner all night. Much of the loudest talking and commotion was coming from over there.

Three rough-looking men sat in the half-light of an oil lamp with a fourth hulking, barrel-chested fellow. The big man was standing now, pouring more whiskey. A scraggly, red beard covered the jaw of his large, pockmarked face. His soiled black mariner's cap was pulled down hard, flattening a reddish, dusty mop of hair. A red-and-white bandana sagged around his thick neck. He'd jammed a massive flintlock pistol with a heart-shaped handle into his dirty shirtwaist. Wide, black suspenders over a half-open shirt strained against the weight of the pistol to hold up the man's sagging, gray breeches.

The crowd and the racket made Jack a little jumpy. Open land and being outdoors alone was sure as hell better than this. He sipped his whiskey and listened to Goins try to talk past the laughter and shouting. From what Jack could make out, the big man in the corner was some Swedish drifter named Sven "Big Red" Olafsson. According to the proprietor, the Swede and his boys never caused the saloon any trouble and always had cash from somewhere. But they were known to be more than a nuisance to many of the good people of Nacogdoches.

"I just come here to Texas." Jack Hays shouted, "Hoping maybe to help folks like Colonel Crockett and General Sam Houston have done." He was getting hoarse trying to tell his story over the din. "Guess I missed the real fight'n. But as a fact, I'm on to find General Houston, wherever he's at. Got the wants and means to be of help wherever I'm called on."

Jack drew the front of his unbuttoned oilskin duster aside and patted a flintlock pistol in the waist of his leather leggings. He smiled at Willie Goins, his youthful grey eyes wide, but serious. He might have just turned nineteen, but Jack Hays hadn't ridden all this way without purpose.

"Got a letter of introduction, too. For Gen'ral Sam." Jack explained. "Letter's from Mr., I mean President Andrew Jackson. He's married to my kin, Miz Rachel Jackson. Maybe his say-so'll be enough for the General, then I can stay a spell and sign on with the military."

Goins stared at him. Was he doubting Jack's story? The inn owner might've been ready to say something, but a gravelly snarl erupted from the Swede's table in the far corner, hushing the tavern. A chair clattered to the floor. The big ugly one was standing, his sleeves rolled past his elbows and one hand on his pistol handle. He stretched out the other muscular arm and waggled a meaty hand in Jack's direction.

"Hey Willie. Willie Goins. You gottdam' half-nigger." The Swede bellowed, "Why, I declare, you got a new little buddy there? Dat little shit gonna be new mascot for da bar?"

Olafsson was pointing his sausage of an index finger at Jack. The Swede's boys chuckled, but no sound came from the rest of the smoke-filled room. Men stopped playing cards. Jittery. Listening. Waiting. Everybody expected the newcomer to respond. To say or do something. An ominous, stony silence hung over the place.

Jack turned from the bar to fully face Olafsson, then leaned back and took a deep breath. He pushed the brim of his hat further up to get a better look at the man. Damn near twice his size, by God. Jack's long trail duster was still open so the Swede could plainly see his weapon.

Eyes narrowing, Olafsson howled, "Sonny! Oh, sonny boy, you got no gottdam business come in here with a gun like dat. You maybe hurt yourself."

His mouth curled into a sneering smile. The Goliath stepped away from his table and ambled toward the bar. Jack hoped he signaled no hint of fear. Staring, he waited with both arms outstretched along the rail. The Swede was even bigger now that he was coming into better light.

"Mr. Hays. Uh, Mr. Hays, don't mind Mr. Olafsson there," Goins spoke up, waving one hand in the plodding Swede's direction. "He's somewhat the legend 'round these parts. He's got Viking in his blood. Makes him want to take charge of everything and everybody." Goins turned away from Jack and shouted toward the Swede. "Big Red, why don't you just sit back down over there? I'll have the barkeep bring you and your boys a round on the house."

"Shut your hole, Willie," Olafsson barked. "I maybe do that after I get me a look on baby boy's flintlock. Don't think he needs such big gun near bad as I do." Olafsson patted his own pistol and growled. "Why…. Why, I bet his lil ass fly clean over da bar he try to shoot that thing."

Olafsson, close now, whisked a broad knife from somewhere behind his back. Shit, the Swede was quicker than he looked. The point waved near Hays' face. Jack flinched once, then took in the man's every move. Couldn't ignore that blade, even for a split second.

"Now come on, lil boy," Big Red warned. "Gimme dat gun 'fore you get yourself killed."

Jack kept his voice low and even. "Mister, you are truly about the ugliest, stinkin'est thing on two legs I ever laid eyes on. For sure, you're the most ill-tempered." He tipped his head in William Goins' direction, then barked again. "I believe you owe Mr. Goins here an apology."

The Swede's left eyelid twitched over a bloodshot eye. He stepped back and lowered the knife. His pox-scarred brow wrinkled.

Would the big man lunge or maybe slash at him? Hays tensed and touched his flintlock handle. He challenged the Swede again.

"As for me…. If you want my gun so bad, you'll just have to take it."

Now Olafsson's ears turned crimson. He blinked rapidly, as if to clear some pesky gnat from his eyes. The man sure hadn't been around this kind of backtalk. The giant's breathing shortened as his chest heaved.

"And you?" Jack pressed on. "You with no more'n that ol' dull knife you're wavin', and that sissy-man's pistol stuck down where your balls oughta be? Well, that just ain't gonna happen, now is it?"

Olafsson's forehead flashed purple and immediately beaded sweat. He lunged and thrust the knife toward Jack's throat while his other hand fished for Hays' pistol. Jack parried the knife thrust and ducked to one side, drawing his flintlock in one fluid motion. He'd sidestepped Olafsson's clumsy assault. Jack's half-empty shot glass spilled whiskey across the bar and bounced to the floor next to the Swede's still spinning knife. Jack now held the muzzle of his double-cocked pistol inches from the man's meaty face.

The Swede, breathless, his crooked eyes bulging, slowly leaned back against the bar and clung to the brass rail. Jack Hays glared, his pistol closer now to the big man's chin. That heart-shaped gun handle still stuck out of the Swede's belt.

Two metal-on-metal clicks came from somewhere to Jack's right. He glanced over his shoulder, then snapped back to Olafsson. No move. The bartender had aimed a double-cocked Kentucky long-rifle at the Swede's accomplices. They stood ready with hands on undrawn pistols. Saloon patrons shuffled and scattered. Chairs clattered over as several men scuttered out. Others ducked down and lay flat, many hiding under their tables.

"Gentlemen, I reckon it's time for you to head out." Goins spoke up, glancing first at Big Red, then at his three comrades across the room. "No need to concern yourselves with settling up now. Just get-on gone."

Big Red muttered something under his breath, maybe in Swedish. He bent and snatched at his fallen cap. Jack kicked the big man's knife out of reach with one flick of his boot toe and moved the flint cock of his weapon to its safety position. Then he eased his sidearm back into his trouser waist. Had his attacker had enough?

Olafsson straightened. A one-sided grin warped his sweaty face. Damn, that big flintlock was now in one of his dirty, fat hands, a metallic double click and the muzzle pointed at Jack's face.

Shoot the Swede or die.

In one lightning motion, Jack pulled his pistol, touch-fingered the trigger and stroked the filed-down flint cock with his other open hand. Noise. Thunder. A shattering crack-crack ripped through the tense, silent bar. Not one shot, but two.

Sparks, fire and smoke trailed the heavy, forty-four caliber ball from Jack's weapon. Olafsson's shot passed Jack's ear and shattered bottles and a mirror behind the bar. Jack's round slammed into the Swede's barrel chest. The giant's massive red head and heavy arms snapped forward. He was lifted from the floor and flung backward. His skull struck the floor first with a dull crack and splintered boards. His body thudded into a heap, scattering dust and board fragments.

The barman kept his rifle trained on Big Red's boys. Silence. Jack Hays slowly lowered his flintlock, then turned and nodded a wordless apology to William Goins. He stared down at the big Swede. Blood from the chest wound pooled under his body, and wisps of smoke rose from scorch marks on Olafsson's reddening shirt.

Murmurs broke the stillness, then the chatter of tavern patrons returned. Ale tins and whiskey glasses clinked. Men relit cigars. Some raised drinks or doffed their hat in salute to Jack. Big Sven Olafsson was dead. The man sure as hell wouldn't bother anyone else.

Jack checked his pistol flint, then tamped black powder down the still-warm barrel and rammed a patch-wrapped ball home. He had to be reloaded and ready – could be more trouble soon. After one more quick look around and another nod to his host, Hays stepped away from the bar and strode the stairs two at a time to his room. Once inside, he turned the heavy iron key to lock the door and wedged a rough bench from the foot of the bed against the door handle. Jack sat on the bed and grappled with the reality of what he'd done. He was alive, but he'd just killed a man. Anyway, provoked or not, the bastard had aimed to do him in.

Jack let his breath settle to its natural rhythm. His ears were ringing. After a time, he stretched out with his boots still on and his reloaded flintlock close by. No sense being unprepared for a midnight encounter with Big Red's boys.

• • •

"Last anybody saw of 'em," William Goins bragged, "The Swede's boys were high-tailing it down El Camino Real, looking for the fastest way out of town."

Jack sat beside Nacogdoches Mayor Adolphus Sterne at breakfast and listened to William Goins recount the previous night's events. The Mayor fiddled with his pocket watch. Hays sat silent and downcast, only half-listening. He'd barely slept, partly from fear, but mostly from remorse. Jack had been in fights plenty of times before – threatened by drunken Cherokees, facing down horse thieves and the like – but he'd never killed a man.

"Son, you must, and you will, get past this moment. Schnell, quickly." Mayor Sterne declared in his distinct German accent. "Our town, all of us, we see you as...as some kind of liberator. Perhaps we can make you sheriff, no?"

The Mayor went through the insults and intimidations Big Red and his cohorts had put the good folks of Nacogdoches through over the last few months. Guess it was good riddance, as far as most were concerned. But Jack was not planning on staying around. He had to make General Sam's acquaintance, maybe even join up with the new Rangers he'd heard about.

His second and last evening in town was "Jack Hays Night" at Mayor Sterne's house. People said the place was the town's finest residence, but the outside was just an ordinary white-framed structure with a long-railed porch. Inside was a different story. More than a hundred candles flickered in two crystal chandeliers suspended over a massive oak dining table. Oil paintings hung on every wall. Silverware, glass and fine china surrounded Jack at the table. More eating tools than he knew what to do with, really. Felt almost like he was back in Nashville at his Great Aunt Rachel's mansion. But even there, when Andrew Jackson was home, he'd never seen this many happy people eating, drinking and celebrating.

After dinner, Jack sipped at a German brandy, so strong and acidic he needed ale to wash the stuff down. He half-listened to Adolphus Sterne's speech. Something about him being the third Tennessean honored with an official dinner at the mayor's residence. Jack was in good company. Congressman David Crockett and General Sam Houston had been the other two.

The next morning, Jack sat astride a fresh local mount, a mustang. Willie Goins had suggested he ride a smaller, faster pony out here on the frontier. Jack trotted along El Camino Real, headed west out of Nacogdoches. He wore new, knee-high black boots and slung a finely tooled pommel bag over the horn of his Spanish saddle – all gifts of Mayor Sterne.

Had the whole damned town turned out today? Hats, scarves and hands waved as the townspeople cheered and applauded. Jack tipped his freshly dusted hat to the crowd. His head hurt, probably from the brandy, but he smiled anyway.

Even though Jack regretted killing the big Swede, life felt pretty good right now. Big Red's pistol ball that broke so much glass over Goins' bar, the thing could have gotten him. But it hadn't. Could life keep going that well?

Chapter Two

Finding General Sam - late April 1836

Jack pushed the new pony hard and rode southwest until a half moon rose in the evening sky. Days were already hot in Texas territory, but nights cooled down quickly. By the time Jack had eaten and bedded down, he needed his blanket and trail duster for cover.

His pony had watered back at a small stream. Now, tethered to a mesquite bush, the saddled animal nibbled sparse greens off the underbrush. Supper for Jack had been bull cheese and hardtack, and he washed it down with half his second canteen of water. No campfire. Might be warmer and drive off four-legged prowlers, but fires also attracted the unwelcome two-legged bastards.

Last evening, back in Nacogdoches, Adolphus Sterne had said General Houston would be somewhere in Washington town or nearby Nolansville. Jack would be riding again before daybreak, headed for Washington-on-the-Brazos. He aimed to find the General.

By mid-afternoon the next day, Jack tied his lathered mount to the rail in front of the Fanthorpe Inn, the main stagecoach stop on the outskirts of Nolansville. He'd ridden most of the way at a gallop. These mustangs didn't need much caring for, and they sure liked to run. Jack's pony could go further on less feed and water than any horse he'd ever ridden. Being small and slight of build himself, Jack reckoned he and his mustang matched up pretty good. Plus, he was born to run, too.

Hays, with his pommel bag slung over one shoulder, took three stairs in two strides onto the spacious, white-railed wooden porch. He pushed through the oak-and-glass front door of the inn. High ceilings trapped most of the spring heat in the gathering room. Hotter here than back home. Flies were already buzzin' around. Heat wouldn't keep him from his search, but the stickiness and damned flies were hard to ignore.

The staircases to the balcony at one end were curved and had steps covered in expensive-looking red carpet. Hadn't seen anything like that since Nashville. A thin, spectacled girl in a pink-and-white dress sat at a small, cluttered desk shuffling papers. She neither acknowledged nor greeted him when he walked up. That loose dress and those white polkadots, now that reminded him of Aunt Rachel, for sure.

"Excuse me, Ma'am," Jack said, doffing his hat, polite as possible. "Name's Hays. Jack Hays. I'm lookin' for Gen'ral Sam Houston."

The girl looked up and gave a one-sided sneer punctuated by several missing teeth. She said something, but her voice was weak and hard to understand. After some time and effort, she'd made it clear that Jack had to pay in silver coin if he wanted a night's lodging. He obliged, and she handed over a heavy, worn key. The girl pushed her thick glasses further up her sliver of a nose and stared at Jack like he oughtn't be there.

"Thar ye be. Y'all's got a room. Got plenty anyways this time a year." The girl spoke loud and slow, maybe to make sure he was listening. "And you? Best y'all hush up 'bout Gen'ral Sam. We don't never tell nobody where he be."

"Time-to-time," she continued, "He stay with us here at the inn. I cain't say he come 'ner gone a'ready, 'cause you got no concern to be inquirin'. Less'n he knows you, ain't likely to see you noways."

Jack had had enough. Where the hell was the owner? Somebody more forthcoming and hospitable to a paying guest than this halfwit desk clerk? He persisted, persuaded. In the end, Jack prevailed on her to fetch the inn's owner.

• • •

Jack followed the lanky, balding Henry Fanthorpe onto the wide veranda. A small, olive-skinned porter with a stained khaki apron struggled to keep up, then veered off down the front steps toward Hays' pony. Fanthorpe led Jack around the east corner of the inn and continued along the side porch. Jack tried to adjust his eyes to the shade. A man sitting alone with one stretched leg stirred off in the distance.

The man's black, bushy eyebrows widened and his forehead pushed into a scowl at Jack's approach. The fellow probably would've rather been left undisturbed to enjoy the afternoon shade. He wore a dark blue military jacket trimmed in gold braid, unbuttoned and open to the heat. Underneath was a starched white shirt and black tie, and Jack now saw that the man's outstretched leg favored a heavily wrapped ankle splint protruding from his gray military trousers.

"General Sam, this here's a fellow Tennessean," the innkeeper announced. "Name's Hays. John Coffee Hays. Young man says he come all the way from Nashville and brought you a private message from President Jackson hisself."

As best as he knew how, Jack Hays stood at rigid attention in front of the man he'd ridden weeks to meet. The General fixed his gaze on him for a spell, then un-furrowed his brow and dismissed Fanthorpe with a nod and the wave of an upraised hand.

Houston reached for a tin flask on the table next to him and took a long sip, grimacing all the while. The General was younger than Hays had imagined, but damn, he looked just as weary as everybody else in Texas. Had that ankle been hurt in the San Jacinto battle? What was in the flask? Whiskey? No, most likely laudanum - for the pain.

"Take it easy, boy," Houston spoke, his voice both gentle and clear with authority. "You liable to pass out if you keep them knees locked together like that. Sit. Your ass ain't too saddle sore to sit, is it?"

Hays snatched off his hat, opened his trail duster and hastened to a seat in the rocker next to Houston. He pushed with his boot heel and slid the rocker around some so he could see the General better. He tried to breathe. How had movin' a chair gotten him this much out of wind?

"Now, let me see that paper you carryin'," Houston ordered. "You claimin' it was written by Andy Jackson?"

Jack fumbled and fished a thin, oilskin-wrapped packet out of his shirt. His fingers trembled when he handed over the pouch. He couldn't remember ever being this nervous.

"You're his wife's kin?" The General asked. "Andy Jackson and Miz Rachel took you in as an orphan, that right?"

Hays nodded, still too hesitant to speak. Houston unfolded the packet and laid the oilskin wrapper aside. He studied the two papers. Sweat beaded on Jack's forehead. He dabbed at it with a loose bandana.

Houston stared at Jack and grumbled, "Had some disagreements with Andy Jackson myself. Hard man to like sometimes."

The General cleared his throat and began reading, first Andrew Jackson's letter, then Adolphus Sterne's glowing commendation. Hays shifted side-to-side, not at all comfortable. The chair squeaked with every move. He stopped moving and began rolling his hat brim with both hands, trying to collect himself. Houston quit reading and glared at him with one dark eyebrow raised.

"Sir, I," Jack stammered. "I go by the name of Jack. Jack Hays, that is. I really appreciate…"

Houston waved his free hand and stopped Hays in mid-sentence. Agonizing minutes passed as Jack sat motionless and rigid. Eventually, Houston looked up and stared straight into Hays' wide-open eyes.

"Sir, as you can see from… " Hays managed to lower his voice a bit.

Houston waved again, one palm in the air that demanded silence. The General sipped from his flask and sighed. He rubbed his propped leg. Jack still couldn't tell what happened to that ankle. Horse accident? Musket ball? Gout, maybe? Whiskey sure as hell wouldn't help the gout none.

"Son, rest easy now," Sam Houston said. "I already knew who you were 'fore I even read President Jackson's letter."

Houston smiled. Must've liked what he'd read. But he said he knew of him before. How? The General waved Nacogdoches Mayor Sterne's letter in the air between them.

"Is this all true?" The General asked. "Did you actually do what Mayor Sterne says here you did?"

Hays nodded. The General shook his head and glanced down at the floor, then looked up and took another long, deliberate pull off his flask. Jack was expected to do more than nod now. He had to say something.

"Yessir, yes Sir." Jack said, "Afraid so. Not much choice in the matter. That Swedish feller, he was wound up tight as a cheap watch. When I heard his flint cock set, I figured it was time I got to him 'fore he got to me."

The General pulled a kerchief and wiped his brow. He looked Jack up and down then fixed unblinking eyes on the flintlock pistol stuck in Hays' trouser waist.

"Everybody in town seemed right happy about how it all come about," Hays went on. "Had a hard time gettin' outta Nacogdoches. Lots of waves and smiles from folks," Jack looked down at his new boots, still embarrassed, maybe a little ashamed of what he'd done. "And I got me a present or two from the Mayor to boot."

"Jack Hays," the General said. "Son, you might've got to Texas too late for the war with Santa Anna," He rested a hand on Jack's shoulder. "But there's plenty of fightin' left. We got Comanche, we got highwaymen, common horse thieves and the damnable Mexicans. Hell, even el Henerale Santa Anna, before all's said and done."

Hays' steel-gray eyes locked on Houston's. Was he about to

get a lecture on fightin'? Or maybe the General did have a real job for him.

"I want you and me to sit down tonight." Houston stretched his leg. "We'll talk about it all at supper. I got somethin' in mind for you that'll be just what you come to Texas for. I'm eatin' early, though. Come down to my table 'bout sunset, all right?"

Hays nodded agreement and stood, sensing he'd been dismissed. Jack finally felt his body relax. Sure had been nervous about his first meeting with General Sam Houston.

• • •

Hays trailed the waiter over to the General's table on the other side of the small dining room. Sam Houston sipped at his tin of ale and motioned Hays into the chair opposite him. A full ale sat on the blue-and-white checkered tablecloth at Jack's seat.

Hays hung his gray hat on his chair post, then sat and turned to face his host. Houston lifted his ale tin and looked Jack in the eye. A toast. Jack raised his tin mug in a return salute. The brew was bitter, but at least it was cool. Jack drank deeply before he put it down. Damn, he had a powerful thirst. Been through a lot to get to this moment.

A heaped pile of chitlins scrambled into eggs was put in front of Jack, along with corn grits, bitter steamed greens and thick slabs of toasted bread. General Houston stirred a spoon of molasses into his grits. Houston's idea of supper seemed more like a Tennessee country breakfast, not the evening meal Hays had expected. But he ate and sipped, and he responded when addressed.

Houston warned him between forkfuls about drifters, highwaymen, Indians and Mexicans. For strangers, best shoot first and talk later was his fork-waving advice. Jack listened to the General's pointed, colorful commentary, mainly about war with the

Mexicans and problems with Indians. Through the whole evening, the man hadn't gotten out that small medicine flask. Why not?

The General finished off his second full plate, then wiped his chin and peered into his empty ale tin. A bony hand went up to signal the waiter. Houston bent down stiffly, reached into a heavy, well-worn leather case on the floor beside him, and drew out Hays' oilskin letter pouch, along with a scrawled sheet of paper.

"Jack Hays," Sam Houston said, handing him the pouch and paper. "This here's my personal order to you, plus your letters from Gen'ral, er, President Jackson and Mayor Sterne. You do read awright, don't you, son?"

Hays nodded and took the packet. Sure he could read and write. After all, he'd been trained for land surveyin' back home.

Houston went on. "Well, all my scribblin' says you are to proceed on to Goliad, Texas tomorrow. Little over 200 miles of hard ridin', mostly south a' here. Once there, you'll report to Lieutenant Deaf Smith of the Texas Rangers."

Hays took it all in, straight-faced. Inside, he felt the adrenalin rush. The excitement. He'd made it. Jack was joinin' the fight.

"Lieutenant's real name's Erasmus, but we call him Deaf. Some boys say Deef." Houston intoned, his voice full of emotion and respect. "He cain't hear goddamn thunder no more. He was a sapper for me in the war, and a damn good one." Houston used his bandana to wipe his face. "Lit one too many kegs 'a black powder, I reckon."

Black powder? Went deaf? Strange way to fight a war. It was one thing to get bad ears from cannon fire, but settin' off black powder close by, that was crazy.

"Helluva fightin' fellow. But ol' Deef's headin' a burial detail right now." Houston looked down. "More'n three hundred good men murdered by that little Mexican bastard, Santa Anna."

Hold on. Wait a minute. This didn't sound like fighting. Not how Jack had pictured his first duty in Texas. Was he headed to a Ranger unit run by a deaf man to do nothing but bury a pile of dead folks?

"Mexicanos burned the bodies. Left 'em stacked like firewood outside town. Worse'n the damned Comanche. Both of 'em, Comanche and Mexicans, ain't nothin' but enemies. Enemies of Texas." Houston brightened, then finished, "Goliad. Fort Defiance. It'll be your first assignment. I expect, though, you'll find more to do than just bury folks. Leastways our folks, before long."

General Sam Houston stood, a little unsteady at first. Dinner and the briefing were done. Hays bolted up from his seat and hurried to aid Houston, as did the waiter, but the General waved them off and straightened, erect and soldierly.

Favoring his bad ankle, Sam Houston fetched his white hat from the chair post. He gripped the ornate wood-and-silver cane and adjusted the brim of his hat, ready to leave. Jack turned and faced the General, having to look up a bit to be eye-to-eye.

"General Houston," Jack spoke, thoughtful. "I am much in your debt for dinner and all. And for the Rangerin' order, too. You can be sure I'll do my part and more." Hays extended his hand. "I'll represent the Rangers well, whatever I'm called on to do. You don't have to worry 'bout me and fightin'."

Hays kept his eyes on the General. Sam Houston took Jack's hand and smiled. The General had long, thin hands with a lot of callouses. Jack Hays couldn't tell from the handshake just what the General thought of him. Didn't matter much, though. The evening was over, and Jack Hays was now a Texas Ranger by personal order of General Sam Houston. He couldn't ask for more than that.

Chapter Three

On to Goliad - April 1836

Three days out of Nolansville, near a rough trail deeply rutted from spring rains and wagon traffic, Jack made camp. The Guadalupe River roared in shallow rapids upstream, but it was calm here where he'd stopped for the night. Early tomorrow he'd come out of the mesquite thicket and swim his pony across.

Trail riding in Texas was a hell of a lot different from Tennessee. More wide open and flatter the further south and west you rode. Almost no forests, just scrub brush, mesquite and live oaks. And no cover to speak of, except along the few creeks and rivers he'd crossed. Thick marsh grass and reeds grew there, along with plenty of critters, snakes and such. He'd seen few people, mostly just settler families on scattered farms and one or two isolated hamlets. Texas had miles of land to be surveyed one of these days, for certain.

Where had all the ruts in the trail come from? There'd been only two wagons – one a finely outfitted dry goods trader, the other a real pale migrant family. They spoke some language he'd not been able to make out. Both were headed in the opposite direction from him. Wouldn't there have to be more than two wagons to make all those ruts?

A desolate place, this here Texas. He'd been given good well water by a Spanish – or more likely Mexican – ranch hand at one of the homesteads. Jack had filled both canteens, but he'd gotten nothing else from anybody.

No Indians so far. At least no Indians that he'd seen. People or no people, desolate or not, he had a mission to tend to. An order straight from Sam Houston himself. He slept lightly.

At dawn the next morning, Jack swam the fast-moving current of the Guadalupe alongside his pony. He climbed into the saddle as soon as he found footing and rode up the southwest bank, soaked to his neck. The pony shook its head and snorted repeatedly to rid itself of the wetness. Jack checked his pistols inside his oilskin duster to make sure they'd remained dry.

Some distance away, two riders appeared, headed at a gallop in his direction. Jack reckoned they were still maybe half-a-mile upstream. He reined in his pony and stayed in the morning shadows near the line of low pecan trees along the river. They kept coming, spurring their horses and riding hell-for-leather straight at him. The two were damned-well up to mischief of some kind. Not Indians, for sure. They had to be highwaymen, and they'd spotted him. Jack was not about to give up the almost sixty dollars in gold pieces and silver coins he'd stuffed deep into the lining of his new pommel bag. That was his life savings. In such instances, best shoot first, General Sam had said.

Jack unhooked the bag flap and hoisted the heavier of his two flintlocks. He half-cocked the pistol, then spurred his pony hard and charged the two highwaymen, thundering at the riders through the prairie grass. From the way they reined up, his move had surprised them. Jack slid from his mount's back and clung to the saddle horn from the right side, mostly shielded by his galloping pony. He crossed his left leg behind his right knee and pushed hard, jamming his right boot tighter into the stirrup. The two highwaymen fired on him as the gap narrowed. Both shots missed high and wide.

Jack cocked his flintlock full and took jostling aim. He fired over his empty saddle at the closer of the two riders. The shot caught the man in the shoulder and toppled him head-over-boot, one foot still caught in the stirrup. The marauder's mount bolted to the left and thundered away, its rider little more than a rag doll flopping and bouncing against the hardpan. Mushrooming dust trailed the pair through the underbrush and over the ridge.

Hays came erect in his saddle and wheeled his pony. He stashed the spent pistol, then grabbed his other flintlock, galloping hard at the second rider. The dark, bearded man had drawn a long saber of some kind and rode scowling and screaming toward him.

Jack fired. Dust flew from the man's jacket. His attacker lost his blade into the air and grabbed his chest. Grimacing through his dark beard, the second highwayman pulled up short, his mount rearing to a skidding halt. Sagging rider and frenzied horse turned tail and fled from the fight, disappearing over the low ridge-line. No blood that Jack could see, but his shot sure as hell had found its mark.

Jack reined his pony to a pawing stop and reloaded the second pistol. Flintlock still at the ready, he held his hat on and bent down from the saddle to have a closer look at a grayish, short-billed sea cap laying on the trail. A cap very much like the ones Big Red's boys had worn.

• • •

Once in Goliad, Jack Hays had no trouble finding the encampment of the Texas Ranger burial detail. Houston had told him the camp was where three roads came together, right where most of Colonel Fannin's Texas detachment had been murdered on Santa Anna's personal order.

Dirty, off-white tents rustled in the wind in crooked rows just beyond the entrance to Fort Defiance. The sun warmed the air, but the stink of death fouled the April breeze and made it hard to breathe. The choking odor of burned and rotting flesh even managed to work its way through the bandana Jack had pulled over his nose and mouth as he rode.

Hays dismounted, still holding the kerchief over his face, and stared up at the blue-and-white one-star flag of the Republic of Texas. He was for sure in a foreign country. The stink and that flag proved it. Hellfire, this was a strange place all right.

Jack tied his horse near the flagpole and walked toward the

largest tent. A sullen, slouching cavalryman he guessed to be the guard responded to his question about Lieutenant Smith. Two muttered words and one finger pointed Jack through the tent flap. The trooper was the first person Jack had heard a word from in days.

Lieutenant Erasmus Smith sat behind his crude board of a desk near the rear of the tent. He looked up when Hays entered, and put hard eyes on Jack as he saluted, announced his name and handed over his orders from Sam Houston. Smith's blue militia jacket looked much like General Houston's, apart from the single brass bar on each shoulder where Houston's stars had been. Any further similarity to military dress ended with the jacket.

Plain to see, Smith wasn't too interested in him. Not today, leastways. The Ranger Lieutenant had those same tired eyes as the barkeep back in Nacogdoches. Seemed wore out. Deaf Smith put all Jack's papers aside without even so much as a grunt.

"Boy, you got a bedroll." the Lieutenant shouted. "Put it and the rest of your tack on down the tent row." Smith waved an arm in the air. "Empty cot's down there somewheres."

Jack waited for more, shifting nervously. There had to be a rank. An assignment. He'd not just joined the Texas Rangers, Gen'ral Houston had said he was going to the Rangers' best unit. Wasn't much, so far.

"Supper's at sunset." His commander said. "Cider and biscuits sunup tomorrow. Burial detail's all day after that. Horse corral's by the creek."

Deaf Smith wasn't only hard of hearing, he wasn't much of a talker either. No more orders from his commander. Jack saluted as best he knew how, then turned and took his leave.

• • •

The days and nights in Goliad pressed down hard on Jack. They were always hot and sticky, but the duty was worse than the heat. The burial detail sickened him. Pissed him off. He'd never in his nineteen years seen this much death piled up, not even at hog butchering time back home. This was a hell of an initiation, for sure. Anyway, he'd do what he had to and not fret too much these first few weeks.

"Deef's Devils," they called themselves. Lieutenant Smith's company of Texas Rangers. Hard to believe what he'd heard General Sam say about these men blooding themselves well and proud against the Mexicans at San Jacinto. They might've fought well, but they sure as shit weren't much to look at.

He liked their war cry, though. "Remember Goliad! Remember the Alamo!" Jack would most surely never forget Goliad. And he'd see the Alamo soon enough. Probably pretty lucky he'd missed that fight. Two hundred or so murdered in San Antone before Sam Houston had kicked the Mexicans' asses at San Jacinto, and that had been just a few weeks before he arrived.

• • •

Jack Hays rode north with "Deef's Devils" toward San Antonio de Béxar. He still had the smell of death in his clothes. They all did. But bad smell and all, Jack was finally headed for excitement. Deaf Smith rode at the head of the column, going home to what General Sam had said was a wife and four children. Lieutenant Smith looked even more bone tired when he'd passed Jack on the trail than he did weeks ago when Jack had first reported in.

Before long, Jack would stand inside the Alamo Mission. Maybe he'd get somebody to show him where Congressman Crockett had died. And one day, if he was lucky, he'd face General Santa Anna. Then he'd do the deed and even the damned score with that little

Mexican.

A curious and talkative Indian scout rode beside Jack part of the way. Hays reckoned him to be about his own age. The scout sat sinewy and proud in a Spanish-looking saddle. What he wore was truly something to behold, especially for an Indian. Head-to-toe, a fine, near-white, fringed deerskin, but without beads or decoration. A black bandana protected his forehead and tied his long, black hair down his back. He sure wasn't like the Cherokee and Choctaw Jack had known back in Tennessee.

The young Indian had a full quiver of arrows and a short hunting bow slung across his back, plus a fine Jaeger rifle tucked in a quick-draw saddle holster at the back of his leg. Hays guessed the fellow knew how to use both equally well. Andrew Jackson had shared a story with Jack long ago about the Jaeger. He'd been up against the weapon in the 1812 War. German-made, deadly accurate and reliable, the rifle had been the British Infantry's standard weapon.

"I am called Flacco the Younger," the Indian remarked. "In my Lipan band, I am chief. So, OK you call me Chief Flacco." Flacco continued, not waiting for a response. "We Lipans part of famous Apache People. Everybody know Apache here. We good people. Not enemy to you White Face."

Maybe not warring Indians, the Lipans, but Flacco couldn't possibly be their main chief. He was just too damn young. Besides, if he was Chief, he wouldn't be out here dressed halfway like David Crockett, sittin' in a fancy saddle, packin' a fancy rifle and ridin' with Texas Rangers.

Flacco was full of questions for Jack. He just never shut up. Most Indians Jack had come across were not this noisy. And for somebody so young, Flacco sure seemed to have been around. He'd had more'n his share of ups-and-downs. Who knew how much of it was truth, though.

"Why so many Tennessee White Faces come to Texas?" Flacco asked. And before Jack could answer, "You really know famous General Sam?"

When Jack didn't talk, Flacco seemed to take his silence in stride. Maybe because he was used to not being quiet, not being listened to. The young Indian gave a lot of opinions and simply asked a different question if he got no answer.

"You ride like Apache, not like White Face soldier. How you anyway get Indian pony?" Flacco went on...and on and on. "You kill Comanche and take pony? Mucho good, if Comanche die. They kill Apache people. They kill Tonkawa people. Take our land. Comanche shit, you know. They just shit!"

Jack hoped the young Apache was half as good at tracking as he was at talking. Eventually, Jack asked questions. The "Chief" gave long, often angry answers. All Indians called themselves "The People," he was told. Flacco's people, the Lipans, had another name for the Numunuh bands in Texas. They were called "Ku-man-shee," the Apache and Ute word for "enemy."

"Ku-man-shee always like fight. Kill everybody." Flacco wailed. "Always kill all men, everywhere. Take my Peoples' land. Take White Faces' land. Mexicanos' land, too."

"They come down sneaky from great cold North, long time back." Flacco continued. "Comanche coward. Not like cold weather. Move all tribe. Make women and children move tipis and do all work. Comanche man no farm. Only hunt. Only kill."

Then Flacco announced his warning. "But Comanche very clever tradesman. First time, Comanche happy to trade buffalo skin and meat for whiskey and gun. Maybe horses, too. Not enough whiskey and guns come, so clever Comanche now take women and children. Can trade for much more whiskey and gun."

Flacco still wasn't finished.

"And long as Comanche take woman and child, why not take horse, too?" Flacco patted his pony and stared straight ahead as they rode. "Comanche take everybody horse. Comanche ride good. Shoot much arrow quick from horse." Flacco pointed at Hays' flintlock. "White Face gun slow. One shot, bang. Comanche quicker. Arrow, arrow, arrow. Kill White Face reloading every time."

Jack Hays liked this young Indian, despite his talking and talking. Couldn't quite put his finger on it all yet, but Jack was sure Flacco's coal-black eyes held no fear. And the Indian wasn't tired of fighting. Not by a long shot.

Chapter Four

San Antonio de Béxar - early May 1836

Jack Hays woke from his third damp night in the Ranger camp on the outskirts of San Antonio. A beetle crawled across the tent canvas above him. Somewhere, he heard a bugle sound. Could be reveille, but a few notes were definitely wrong.

The early morning sun warmed Jack when he stepped outside. A thick carpet of cobalt blue buffalo clover and flame red indian paintbrush lined the well-worn wagon path between the tent rows. Jack washed up near the mess tent and hurried through the loose flap for a tin of watered-down cider. Even with such foul stuff to drink first thing in the morning, San Antone was a lot better than Goliad.

Quickened steps got Jack to his first duty meeting in San Antonio. He stepped in past the splintered wooden doors of the Alamo Mission and looked up through the few remaining charred rafters toward a cloudless, blue sky. No wonder somebody had made the Texas Republic flag sky-blue.

Damn, the smell of burnt wood and powder was strong as hell, and the stench of death, while fainter than in Goliad, still fouled the quiet of the old mission. The battle had taken away Colonel Crockett, Jim Bowie and a lot of other good men only a few months earlier. Jack jarred himself back to the moment and looked for his commander, Lieutenant Smith. He found him in his temporary office in one small corner at the rear of the mission.

"Set yourself, son." Erasmus Smith motioned toward a rough cane chair. "I'm finished in a bit. Just readin' about an Indian war party. Big one. Maybe more'n a hundred."

Hays took a chair. My God, there were now two bars on Deaf Smith's epaulets. Somebody, General Houston maybe, had promoted him from lieutenant to captain. And just since they'd gotten in from Goliad.

"Raidin' party's Comanche, maybe some Wichitas and Caddo," Smith almost shouted. "They was north a' here and ridin' east, day before yesterday. Probably headed for Fort Parker, 'bout a hundred mile northeast."

Hays thought back to some of his trail talk with Flacco. Sounded familiar. Would the whole Ranger company be going after these bastards? Whose squad would he be in? He might be getting some action out of this after all.

"Ol' John Parker's a stubborn sonofabitch." Smith spoke like he wanted the whole camp to hear. "Built hisself a sizable fort and armed everybody around him. Then he pretty much dared anybody, be they red devils, Mexicanos or highwayman. Daren't try running 'em off the land they're farmin'." Smith sighed. "Wouldn't want to be part of his flock, myself."

The Ranger captain picked up what looked like the orders Hays had received from Sam Houston. Jack shifted, trying to get comfortable in his chair. Captain Smith sure hadn't talked this much before. Being home or getting promoted must've loosened his tongue.

"John Coffee Hays, is it?" Deaf Smith kept up in his loud voice. "Who the hell hung that 'coffee' moniker on you, anyway?"

Jack shrugged without responding. How many times had he been asked that question? And how could a man named "Erasmus," then nicknamed "Deaf," consider a name like Coffee to be odd? Why should Jack have to talk the truth about his middle name over and over anyway? He kept his tongue.

Smith shuffled papers and eyed Jack. "Names don't matter a damn, I guess. Lemme see.... Based on General Houston's writin' and Mayor Sterne's say-so, you can sure as hell take care of yourself in a fight."

Hays nodded. Ol' Deaf Captain Smith ought to get on with things. Didn't the man already say they had Comanche to worry about, maybe Mexicans to boot? For sure more highwaymen were runnin' loose. Where was this discussion going?

"So, I been thinkin' about all this," Smith said. "And you, you bein' sent to my care…. You listenin' boy?"

Hays flinched and snapped his gaze back to the Captain. Now they just might be gettin' to the point.

"Here's what we're gonna do." Smith frowned. "I'm givin' you the rank of sergeant in this here company, right here and now. You goin' to be in charge of weapons and tactics."

Sergeant? In charge of weapons? Tactics? Yes, Jack was good with a gun and could ride a horse as well as anybody, and he knew attacking was better'n defending. But this sounded like a lot of responsibility and a rank he'd not had a chance to earn yet.

Smith's next words were another surprise. "Seems you already made the acquaintance of one of my Apache scouts, Chief Flacco. Indian says he likes you. Told me so in no uncertain words. Lots of words." The Captain smiled for the first time. "That's good. He don't like most us White men."

Sure had taken a long time for Captain Smith to get to the meat of Jack's assignment. Not so sure he and Flacco would get along, though. Probably needed to hear more about just what his commander had in mind.

"So that means," Smith said, a little softer now, "Chief Flacco's gonna be your 'shadow man.' You'll not so much as take a piss 'ner shit without him at your back. Got that?"

Jack nodded. So, the Captain trusted the young Indian. Guess Flacco as his number one man was a good enough start.

"Now to our most serious business, killin' Comanche." Smith rolled out a crude map. "You'll be next out on long range patrol. Ride outta here no later'n a week from tomorrow."

The new captain moved a shaky finger across the paper. Jack saw where he was headed. Definitely "Comancheria," as people called it. Even said so on the map.

"You'll move north fifty, maybe sixty mile," Smith ordered.

"Then the same east, patrollin' back here. Gonna be you and your Indian and a squad of regulars." Smith waved another paper at Hays. "Want you to scout out this here Comanche war party report. Just scoutin', you hear?"

Hays mostly understood, but he felt more nervous now. He had to find the right men and train 'em, and he had to do it in a week's time. Get everybody workin' together. Get 'em prepared for the fight of their lives.

"No fightin'," Smith ordered. "Less'n you have to. To break contact."

"And boy," Deaf Smith handed Jack the fistful of papers. "If you can read more'n a map, then study all this and git to work, dammit. Pick any seven 'er eight 'a my men. Get fixed up with a small supply wagon or a couple 'a pack horses. Tell the men what they gotta do."

"That's all. Git now, boy." Smith yelled in Jack's direction. "I want you and your party alive and back here with Redskin news in no more'n a fortnight."

The Captain waved a half-knuckle salute as a dismissal. Jack slapped on his wide-brimmed hat, then snapped to a rigid stance and rendered his commander a two-fingered salute. He'd just turned on his heel and headed for the door when his head finally cleared. My God, he was taking men to war. He about-faced.

"Cap'n, pardon the interruption." Jack said. "Meant to say it awready. Congratulations on gettin' promoted." Then Hays stood at ease and smiled. "And just one more thing, sir. We won't be needin' supply wagons nor pack horses. Gonna be travellin' light. Not taking the whole damn Ranger camp with us."

Smith looked at him like he wasn't there, then a puzzled half-smiling gaze. Man knew a lot about war fighting. Gen'ral Sam had told Jack that much. Smith had a family, though. Used to living indoors, mostly. Having a hot supper and a bed or a cot for sleep. Rangers hunting the enemy didn't need all that. Couldn't afford it, neither.

"No tents. No fires." Hays went on. "Just two pommel bags each and more flintlock pistols, extra powder and galena. Maybe two or three good Jaeger rifles like that Indian's got. Couple more sabers and some real sharp knives."

Deaf Smith's eyes told Jack all he needed to know. The man thought he was plum daft. Well, maybe he was, but Jack knew how to stay alive out in the open. Draggin' a bunch of home comforts along sure as hell wouldn't help.

"For chow, just takin' some hardtack and bull cheese." Jack kept on, louder. "Uh, guess that last one's called jerky here in Texas. We'll also need two canteens each for water."

"Goddamnit, I heard you, boy." Smith said loudly. "Spite a' my nickname, I ain't full deaf, you know. Don't ask me no more." The Captain ordered. "What I can spare, quartermaster'll issue. Go tell him all that crap. Now git."

Hays took his leave. Seemed to Jack like the man just didn't believe him. But hellfire, this warn't much more than huntin' bear back home. You didn't go after bear with a whole raft of wagons, pack horses and such. You took what you needed to eat and drink, something to put your head on at night, and what little else you needed to live long enough to sneak up and kill the goddamn bear. Didn't need wagons and shit to bear hunt, nor to kill Indians.

• • •

In the early afternoon, Jack found Chief Flacco alone and working near a tree line beyond the last tent row. He figured Flacco had been told of his new assignment, maybe even before Captain Smith had told Jack. The Indian threw a broad knife again and again at a makeshift target propped against a live oak trunk. Pretty damned accurate and deadly with that knife throwin'.

The Indian turned to face him. "Sergeant Jack, I think you

find me already quick. You and me good team. Teach Comanche not mess with Rangers." Flacco stabbed his knife at the air. "What you want I do first?"

Jack knew he didn't have much time. He needed men he could whip into shape and hit the trail. Flacco had to know who was good with a gun, who could ride and shoot, and who wouldn't mind sleeping in the bush night after night.

"Flacco. Uh, Chief," Jack still stumbled a bit over the title. "Find me boys who can shoot on the move, fight with their bare hands, and don't need fancy food nor drink. Not prone to carousin' around, neither." Jack went on. "They got to have no fear. Not even of th' Evil One hisself."

The Indian nodded. Flacco said nothing. Made no sound. But he grinned. Now that was more Indian-like. The Chief bowed, arms extended and palms up, then scurried off, Jack hoped, to find some boys who wanted to fight.

Less than an hour later, he was back and standing straight and proud at Jack's open tent.

"Sergeant Jack," Chief Flacco was excited. "Four White Faces and one Mexicano will join Hays' Rangers. Mexicano good boy. Three White Faces good, too." Flacco caught his breath, frowned and went on. "One White boy, Iverson, bad. He volunteer, but Iverson lazy, no-good bone picker. Only like Rangers for money, whiskey and women."

Jack Hays had seen Trooper Theodore "Tojo" Iverson more than once at Goliad, but he'd never talked to him. Even so, he was pretty certain Flacco had him pegged. Hard to fathom why Iverson would want to be part of Hays' Ranger patrol. Reckon he'd have to see what this fellow was all about.

"Chief," Jack Hays said. "Iverson's yours to shape up. And we still got to have two more for the scouting party. You know what we need. Men that listen more'n they talk."

Flacco looked like he had an idea. This new, quieter Apache was more to Jack's liking. The Chief was talking only when he had something to say, and he got to the point fast.

"O'Keefe boys we need." Flacco surmised. "They not older than you and me, Sergeant Jack. Real good with pistol and musket, too. Run fast, like deer. Always like fight. Fight with everybody, every day. Eat mostly mush and jerky. They say mush is hasty pudding."

"But boys drink mucho beer." Talkative Flacco was back. "No water, no whiskey. They not like 'no beer rule' by Sergeant Jack."

Hays stopped Flacco. Whatever their ilk, they should be recruited. He'd work around the beer problem. One more thing Jack wanted to know, could the O'Keefe brothers ride? Flacco thought not, but he'd have them ready anyway for Sergeant Jack's powwow in the afternoon.

· · ·

Jack Hays stood on an empty crate and addressed seven heavily armed, slouching men. No uniforms. One of the O'Keefe's wore a pair of striped pajama pants tucked into high boots. Some had clean shaven faces, others scraggly beards. Broad hats, a sombrero, a couple of short-billed caps, even a wrapped scarf and one black headband covered each of the seven heads. They were a rough looking bunch. If they could fight, Jack didn't care.

"Fellers, y'all got pistols or muskets? Enough powder, wad and galena? Everbody's got a knife, hardtack and bull, uh…jerky?" Jack glanced around, "And water too, right?"

Nods of agreement came, along with a mumble or two. Looked like the boys were nervous. Maybe they didn't know what was next.

"In about an hour," Jack went on. "Soon as it's dusk, we all headin' outta San Antone. Two night's and day's foot patrol. No horses." Surprised faces. Jack went on. "Patrol by night, sleep by day with gear on. We packin' everything we need on us."

"Y'all know out there's Comanche country," Jack said, more stern now. "Might be trainin', but we gonna need a watch ever' mornin'. Chief here," Jack pointed to Flacco and ordered. "He's sayin' who gets that duty."

He finished. "So that's it. All of you be right here at sunset, ready to go. Anybody got questions, complaints?"

Silence. No telling what was going on in their heads right about now. Jack stepped down and strode back to his tent. An hour later, he led them out of garrison on foot, single file and spread ten yards apart. He'd learned a lot about how Indians fought and why Rangers had had problems dealing with Comanche battle tactics so far. Flacco had seen to that. Now the time had come to teach these men what he knew.

· · ·

The shake down patrol went well the first night. Jack had the squad make camp and lie low, concealed till late afternoon the next day. The second night, he went man-to-man on the march to make certain they kept their tactical spread and moved silent as possible. Jack taught his squad how to see better at night by looking off-center. He made damned sure they conserved water. So far, so good.

The squad camped the second morning in a sizable grove of live oaks. Jack wrapped his duster tight and lay down. He was exhausted, but he was satisfied with their progress. Filtered sun came at him through the sparse tree canopy after a passing shower had cooled the air. Jack dozed off, then quickly came awake after half-hearing soft footsteps.

"Sergeant Jack," Flacco whispered, touching his commander's shoulder. "Sergeant Jack, you come now. Come quick. Mucho bad medicine. You come."

Hays shook off the sleep. What the hell had gone wrong. He

bounced up and stared, then rubbed his eyes and blinked at his Apache scout as he hastened to follow.

Flacco motioned, palm down, for Jack to walk low and soft toward the tree line. Ahead, Jack saw the sentry, Tojo Iverson, not moving, hat off, musket in his lap, and his back resting against a live oak. Iverson's legs were stretched straight out. His boots were off and lying to one side.

Jack approached him and leaned down for a closer look. His sentry was sound asleep. Scrawled in mud across Iverson's forehead, plain as day, was a big "X."

Hays pulled his pistol, gripped the barrel, then swung the handle in a blow against Iverson's head. The wood-on-bone thud was loud enough to wake some of the squad. Bits of the dried mud on the scrawny boy's forehead flew off. Iverson came awake, startled, then grabbed at his head with both hands.

"He's all yours, Chief." Hays ordered. "Truss this piece of shit up and lead him home. Man's lucky he's still got his scalp. Guess we all are." Jack glared at Tojo Iverson. "Mister, you won't be Rangerin' with us no more."

The squad was awake now, everyone standing around. No doubt Jack had everyone's full attention. Iverson stayed down in the dirt and rubbed his temple. He held his head in one hand and picked at the leftover mud with the other.

"Fellers, this trooper's real fortunate." Hays waved the handle of his pistol at Iverson. "Fact is, we all are. We're all still breathin', in spite of him. He shoulda died today for what he done."

"Gents, here's my new standin' order," Jack made sure everybody was listening. "Anybody else that me or Chief catch sleepin' on watch, we'll slit his throat front to back. No questions asked. No quarter. You boys got that?" Silence. So Jack growled again. "That clear?"

Foot shuffling. Otherwise, silence. To a man, the new Ranger squad nodded their understanding and began milling around and fidgeting with their gear. Flacco busied himself securing his prisoner as Jack had ordered.

Late in the afternoon, Sergeant Jack Hays led his squad back into the Ranger camp. Flacco brought up the rear, leading the lanky, bound-up Iverson by a heavy rope around the prisoner's neck.

"Chief Flacco," Jack made sure everyone within earshot could hear. "Take the prisoner to the stockade. He's Cap'n Smith's problem now. Rest of you take the night off. Mess tent's got grub and ale. Be here on the quad with your mounts and arms at sun-up tomorrow and ready to ride."

• • •

Hays assembled his squad shortly after daybreak and led them to the edge of the encampment. He and the Chief sat side-by-side on their ponies and studied the line of seven mounted men. Iverson was gone. Overnight, Flacco had recruited a second Apache scout, "Red Wing," a boy who couldn't have been older than fifteen.

The rest, except for Jaime Esteban, were the White boys who'd volunteered: Stimson, Halvorsen, Haynes and the O'Keefes. The O'Keefes insisted they were English immigrants and could ride, but Jack bet the brothers were Irish and had never been near a damned horse. Well, whatever the O'Keefe boys were, he judged they could take care of themselves in a scrape.

"Awright, men, listen up." Hays made his voice as command-like as possible. "Y'all look downfield there." Jack gestured toward five posts in a long row, a hundred feet apart. Each post had several hay-filled bags tied to it. "Chief Flacco's gonna give you the idea what this is all about."

Flacco kicked his mount and galloped toward the first post. The scout drew the long-barreled Jaeger rifle from his saddle holster and, weapon snugged to his shoulder, double-cocked and took his shot. A straw-filled bag flew apart, scattering its insides to the wind.

Still at full gallop, the Chief stowed the rifle and weaved left, guiding his pony with his knees. Flacco snapped his bow around, then slotted and quickly launched an arrow that struck and buried to the feathers in a bag on the second post. Seconds later, bags on the last three posts had been similarly through-shot. A satisfied Chief Flacco then trotted back and edged his pony in beside Hays in front of the squad.

"OK, who's next?" Hays asked. "Volunteers?"

Jaime Esteban, the squad's only Mexican, spurred his horse and rode hard at the first post. Jack couldn't believe the boy took off with no warning. Esteban drew a curved, gleaming saber and slashed the first bag cleanly from its mounting. He stashed the saber and drew, cocked and fired his flintlock on the second post. An eruption of scattering hay and dust lifted into the air. The bag on post three was pierced by a quick throw of a wide knife, but the Mexican's second knife missed the fourth mark, instead skewering deep into the mounting post beneath the targeted hay bag. For the last post, still riding hard, Esteban pulled a second flintlock and destroyed the target. He turned his mount and trotted back toward the squad line. The way Jack looked at it, the boy had five kills, just as Flacco had done.

Others also fared well on the course. Denny O'Keefe, the young, pajama-clad boy, had fallen from his pony midway toward the first post, but he somehow managed to pull his musket and a pistol with him to the dust. After scrambling to his feet, Denny took the first target with his pistol, then shouldered his musket quick as lightning and, with a loud crack of fire, struck the second post. Next, a raving madman, he charged the third post with a long knife. Jack ordered him back to the line, yelling loud as he could. The big Irish boy had spunk. As Jack had suspected though, the O'Keefe brothers were terrible horsemen.

• • •

Hays gathered his squad late on day two of mounted drills. Every man in the squad was sweaty and caked with dust. Jack had spent the second afternoon drilling them on the sidesaddle attack technique. Red Wing, the new Indian, got it. Flacco did not. The only other squad member who'd mastered the maneuver was Jaime Esteban.

Jack eyed each of his men in turn. "Fellers, time's almost here. Tomorrow we head out after Comanche. We had a little fun and did a lot of hard work these last few days, but I got just one more little trick for y'all."

Groans and grumbles came from most. Jack dug deep in one pocket and held up a silver coin. He tossed the small silver piece into the dirt.

"Now this here's a money maker, boys." Jack shouted from his prancing horse. "How many think I can pick that five cent piece outta the dirt at full gallop?" No hands came up. Jack went on. "I'll bet anybody here I fetch it on the first try. If I don't, beer's on me. If I do, beer's on you. Awright?"

Nods of most heads showed the challenge had been accepted. Jack reined around and readied his pony. Close by, a young woman stood, a silent observer. She had a bouquet of daisies in her hands. Looked to Jack like she'd been picking wildflowers, and he'd stopped her in her tracks. Was she curious to see what he and his boys were up to?

The gal was damned good-looking. She had on a long white dress and had tied a red scarf around the crown of a broad straw hat. Her shiny black hair matched her cinched-up belt and a pair of expensive-looking boots. Jack trotted past her on his pony and tipped his hat as politely as he could. He'd need to do this coin trick perfect if he was to keep his boys' eyes on him and not her.

Jack galloped downfield, turned, then charged back toward the squad and the young woman. Coming into his sidesaddle position as he rode, head down with dust and black hat flying, Jack bent to the dirt and plucked the silver coin between two fingers, then raised the prize over his head.

Rousing cheers and applause erupted from his squad. Jack galloped past, catching the young woman's eye. She smiled, then turned and walked away toward the hamlet of San Antonio, waving her flowers in farewell.

Chapter Five

The First Patrol - May 1836

The air was hot and sticky again on the morning of day ten just northwest of San Antonio. At dawn, Jack had ordered Chief Flacco and Red Wing to move ahead of the rest of the Ranger squad to find a spot for the patrol to rest. Now he surveyed what they'd found, a thicket of live oaks and low mesquite bushes near a small, fast-running creek.

The ground between the trees and brush was overgrown with thick grasses and reeds. Messy, but good cover for the time they'd be there. Some spots were matted down, maybe from earlier travelers. Deer? Indians? Mexican deserters? Just when the rest of the squad caught up, Hays spotted his two Indian scouts on foot near a clump of mesquite.

"Sergeant Jack," Flacco called, waving. "Here. See. Pony shit from Comanche."

Flacco pointed to what looked to be scant evidence of horse dung, but from the large Comanche war party? The area had been picked almost clean.

"This be Comanche, all right." Flacco insisted. "They ride fast. Always leave shit behind. Mucho braves here, maybe more than two hundred, I think."

"How long ago?" Jack asked, wondering whether Flacco was certain or just anxious.

Red Wing interrupted. "Two sun and moon, maybe three. Chief Flacco correct. Many light pony tracks. No travois. This some big war party."

Red Wing hadn't uttered a word in any language till now. The boy spoke pretty good English. A good recruit by Flacco. How did Red Wing know so much already?

Hays ordered the squad to dismount and get under some shade for rest. Still saddled, their ponies were watered and tied to nearby mesquite bushes. The animals nibbled quietly at the greenery.

Jack's men dropped for sleep, some on oilskins, others on dusty blankets. Their pommel bags were suitable pillows. Not soft, but the bags kept their side arms close. Jack could see the training was working.

Denny O'Keefe and John "Rusty" Stimson drew the watch for the morning. Hays' eyes followed both men as they moved toward the perimeter. They stayed low and took separate paths. Good, they'd remembered his instructions. Jack turned and settled himself on the ground. He needed some sleep.

• • •

"Sergeant. Sergeant Jack, you gotta wake up," Stimson shook him and whispered. "There's a pile a' Indians comin' our way. Denny's out there yet. Got 'em in his sights."

"Get your ass back out there," Hays whispered, suddenly awake. "And signal Denny not, I repeat, not to fire till he hears us firin'. Got that?"

Stimson acknowledged and scuttled off. Hays touched Flacco on the shoulder. No need, the Chief was awake. Hays and Flacco roused the rest of the squad.

No noise so far. Good. Horses stirred, but made no snorts or whinnies. Men moved low to their assigned firing positions. All faced the clearing with their backs to the muddy creek bank. Nobody would surprise them from the rear, nor would the squad retreat. They were committed to battle.

Jack eyed the enemy. Many carried long feathered lances. Bows with full arrow quivers were slung across mostly bare backs, and some warriors' legs were covered with fringed, leather trousers.

Their faces were painted black and red. Some were bare headed. Others wore a buffalo horn headdress or skullcap with three or four feathers. All rode confident and proud. Jack counted twenty warriors in total. They were close, but not quite close enough.

"Comanche wear war paint. Come here, want water." Flacco whispered to Jack. "Maybe last from big party gone east. We make sure these not go further. Kill now, I think."

Jack nodded. He drew one pistol and hunkered in the tall, thick grass at the edge of the clearing. He waited as long as he dared, then full-cocked his pistol. Very little sound.

Chief Flacco and Red Wing snugged double-cocked rifles against their shoulders and took aim down the barrels. The rest of the squad readied their weapons as they'd been drilled to do. Jack raised his free arm.

He held tight until he was sure the lead warrior was still headed straight for the creek through the opening in the live oaks. They had to be almost on top of Stimson and O'Keefe by now. Hays dropped his arm and fired his first pistol.

The morning quiet abruptly shattered with synchronous cracks, smoke, fire and echoing thunder. Flintlock pistols, muskets and rifles blasted lead. The galena balls whizzed and zipped through thick brush and grass and thumped into their human targets. With breechclouts and fringed legs flailing, five Comanche braves thudded onto the hardpan in clouds of dust.

Jack's eyes fixed on a sixth brave. He'd been hit heavy in his mid-section, but he somehow straightened his body and turned his pony to retreat. The rest of the war party saw the gut-shot brave and their dead comrades in the dirt. They reined up short to regroup.

Seconds later the Comanche rallied, shrieked their war whoops and charged. War-painted, wildly feathered braves brought arrows to bows and launched salvos into the Rangers' thick grass and mesquite cover.

"Here they come, boys!" Jack Hays yelled. "Make every shot count!"

Arrows swished past him and ricocheted in three directions off the high, thick grass. The war party drew up short again. Chief Flacco had been right; riding into this underbrush was hard. Take that, you devils. Jack Hays' campsite was a well-protected ambush spot.

More arrows rained in. One hit Eddie Halvorsen with a shot through his thigh that buried the shaft almost to the fletching. Halvorsen glanced down at the blood. Maybe it didn't hurt that much. The boy ignored the protruding shaft and busied himself with his gun again.

Jack reloaded while Halvorsen cocked his weapon and fired next to him. Eddie took a warrior out with a single shot to the head. The boy could still aim and shoot straight, in spite of that arrow.

An idea formed then struck Jack. He grabbed Jaime Esteban who'd crouched nearby and pulled the young Mexican running and stumbling by one arm toward the ponies. The two mounted up amidst Jack's shouted instructions and a third assault by the Comanche war party. The Indians were met first by the deafening roar from another Ranger volley out of the grasses.

Jack and the Mexican pounded out of the woods, the ponies galloping with their riders hanging side saddle. Hays and Esteban fired into the charging Comanche flanks and knocked down two more of the horsemen. Jack slowed his pony to reload both flintlocks. He knew he and his squad had their enemy dead to rights, but he sure as hell wished they had extra pistols already loaded and at the ready.

Esteban's pony took an arrow in its midsection and reared violently, unhorsing Jaime just as arrows hissed overhead. Jack wanted to pursue one group of retreating braves, but he wheeled and rode hard to hoist up a sweating, grit-covered Jaime Esteban behind him instead.

Hays glanced toward the four Comanche riders disappearing over a hillock. Probably wouldn't be back. He turned and watched the remaining skirmish from a distance. The rest of the warriors charged again.

The Comanche launched flurries of arrows, shouted their death cries and jumped from their ponies into the head-high grass swinging war clubs and axes. Jack heard the cries, grunts and shouts coming from the deep shade. The tall grasses shook and waved. Life and death was being waged with his boys in there.

Jack needed to get back into the fight, and quick. He kicked his pony with Esteban still clinging to him and rode straight for the ruckus. Seconds later, the air in and around the grasses and bushes near the stream fell quiet, as if there'd never even been a fight.

Hays and Esteban dismounted and found Rusty Stimson pacing the battleground. Fresh carnage. Not like Goliad. Hays counted fourteen Comanche bodies flattening the thick grasses and dotting the clearing just beyond. Could any of them be older than him? Jack reckoned not. War was a young man's business.

A deafening, thunderous single crack echoed somewhere behind Jack and startled him back to the present. Jack wheeled around with his pistol re-drawn and double-cocked. Jaime Esteban had put down his wounded pony and now chased after a riderless Comanche mount.

Dumb. Real dumb, boy. Esteban should've rounded up the new pony first and warned everyone that he was gonna shoot his pony. Good way to end up just another dead Mexican.

Jack shook off the scare and drew in a couple of deep breaths. He spotted Flacco and Red Wing a little further out – the two Apaches were straddled over corpses, harvesting scalps. Disgusting. But Indians had their traditions.

Bobby Haynes was dead. Jack stared down at the arrow buried between the boy's shoulder blades, and somehow the scene didn't look real. Haynes had been one of the first to sign on for the mission. Jack remembered him saying he wanted to even the score "with the damnable savages that gutted my brother." Haynes' dead hand clutched a feathered war axe. The metal blade was bloody.

"Sergeant Jack," Rusty Stimson muttered close by, his wild

eyes now meeting Jack's. "A'fore he died, I saw Bobby pull two a them bastards down from their horses. He grabbed one's axe there and split both their devil-painted heads. Like he was crackin' a gourd or a pun'kin."

Hays heard the killing lust in the boy's husky voice. He saw the tears mixed with dirt that muddied his cheeks. So this was what Andrew Jackson had seen and felt, what he had talked to Jack about back in Nashville when he was a boy. His men's "will to kill" in the war with the damned British.

Red Wing treated Eddie Halvorsen's wound. Hays tried not to look. The young scout broke the arrow off near the fletching and pulled the shaft out forward by the point. The boy screamed mightily, but he'd ride and fight again when he'd been bandaged up.

Jack Hays led his men down to the creek where they laid Ranger Robert E. Haynes in a shallow grave on the bank. Before the muddy dirt and stones were piled on, Jack put a small blue flag of the new Texas Republic on the boy's chest. Some men stood and leaned on muskets, others sat on their ponies. Ranger sergeant Jack Hays removed his hat. The other men followed his lead, doffing hats and caps, unwrapping bandanas and head rags. Jack bowed his head.

"Fellers, let's pray for Bobby."

Chapter Six

Fort Parker - May 1836

Buffalo Hump knelt on one deerskin-clad knee, low enough that the edge of his beaded leather vest touched the grass and earth. Eagle feathers plaited into the ponytail down the Chief's neck and back showed his rank and power. Black-and-white war paint covered his face. He stretched out and steadied himself on one muscular, tattooed forearm, his wrist guarded by a copper and leather band. His other arm extended flat in the buffalo grass, fingers curled around his feathered war spear. Comfort came from fingering the long, carved shaft.

The Penateka Chief squinted at the fields outside the fort from his position just below the crest of the ridge-line. White Faces, six men, sometimes more, tall and pale, worked the crops with some kind of long-handled shovels. He studied the scene framed by the long, spiked wooden wall of the fort. Buffalo Hump gripped his war lance. Could the White Faces take the same comfort from their thin shovel handles?

Wagon tracks ran from the Chief's position down the hill and through the field to a pair of heavy doors at the midpoint of a distant wall. The White Faces had built watchtowers at both ends of the long wall. One had movement inside. Buffalo Hump was careful to put every possible detail into his thoughts. Leave nothing to chance.

White Face Parker had seized Numunuh land and taken wood for his fort. Said the land was his. Worse, this White God preacher had harbored rebel Texas militia. Parker had challenged Numunuh with soldiers. Buffalo Hump would end this occupation. He would eliminate this threat.

Earlier, Buffalo Hump had directed the four hundred

warriors from his raiding party into position. Almost a hundred were braves of his band, the Penatekas. They lay concealed near the fort. He'd ordered the chiefs of the other bands to take their war parties and surround every farm nearby. All were ready. The hour was near. A full moon would rise tonight. Summer Moon. The Blood Moon of his people.

The War Chief swallowed his bitter taste of anger. White Faces – young, healthy men and women – came and went in the field. His only daughter would not walk any fields again. Never bring him a grandchild. She and many other Numunuh had been ravaged, not by war, but by these White Demons' pox. Her death had been agonizing, not just for her, but for Buffalo Hump and the entire village. More reason for vengeance. Punishment.

The waves of afternoon heat distorted the shapes of the White Faces. The rains had not come, so now they labored to save their new plantings. These interlopers had no true understanding of the workings of the Great Mystery. Because of their trespass, everybody suffered from no water, Numunuh and White Faces alike.

Soon enough, the White Face men here would all die. Buffalo Hump would take their scalps to make sure no White Face spirits would reside in the After Life. Their women and children would live on to join his Penateka band. At least the young, healthy ones would. His village would grow stronger, and the rains would come.

• • •

Buffalo Hump made his way back to the main war party to wait for the shadows of evening. Most of the raiders lay concealed below the ridge-line. The Chief found shade and sat cross-legged. A young brave Buffalo Hump recognized from his rear party approached, a sweating, nervous warrior clad only in a breechclout. The boy was missing his buffalo skull headgear and vest, nor did he carry a war lance or bow.

"Paraibo, my chief, I make no excuse. We failed." The young brave, Mo'pie, addressed Buffalo Hump. "We were ambushed seeking water. Devil Rangers, they used new tactics. Ghost ponies. Curses from the Spirit World. Many fire sticks. Only we four are left from eighteen." Mo'pie waved toward the three braves behind him. "We saw nothing. Heard nothing. Smelled no White Face before they attacked. They may come here."

Mo'pie told him of gunfire from the very bellies of riderless horses. Buffalo Hump sat silent. Mo'pie and the other three from his rear guard swore they'd been tricked by magic from the White Face cavalry.

Buffalo Hump stood and faced Mo'pie. This ghost pony and fire stick story was nothing more than the White Face learning the Comanche way of launching arrows from under the horse's neck, except the enemy had used pistols, maybe a rifle. The ambush from the tall grasses by the creek had been well planned. The chief gave grudging credit to whoever had led the White Face soldiers.

Buffalo Hump spoke in a low and even voice. "Mo'pie, how many of these Devils did you encounter? How many of their scalps decorate your loins? You say you make no excuse, yet you tell nothing but tales, my young brave. Where are your fallen brothers?"

"Paraibo, none live." Mo'pie responded with no emotion. "Five or six I saw fall in the open. All fought well. They died honorably in the fields and grasses as they killed our enemy." The young warrior turned his eyes and looked down. "There was no time for cave burying, not even for laying stones. We took no White Face scalps."

Fourteen seasoned warriors murdered by some Texas army. Who were these new troublesome people? These Rangers? Buffalo Hump would do something about them soon.

First, though, what must he do about Mo'pie and his three companions? They had failed. Lacked Puha. No Numunuh should run from combat as these boys had done. Shamefully, they had not cared for their dead brothers. Killed no enemy. Brought no scalps. Now Mo'pie and the other three would pay for their failure. Buffalo Hump's duty was to see that honor was restored.

"Mo'pie, my young warrior," Buffalo Hump whispered. "Take your three companions and cleanse your spirits." He handed Mo'pie a long stick with a white cloth tied at the top. "Find your lost Puha. Go. Remain unarmed. Wear white painted faces. Summon the devils from the fort to talk." Then a reprimand. "And Mo'pie, before I am signaled to join you, be certain that the White Face preacher, Parker, their paraibo, is present."

• • •

At sunset, Buffalo Hump took his position again below the crest of the hillock. Light from the orange sun behind him faded on the bare backs of Mo'pie and the other three warriors. The peace party walked unarmed. Not even a small knife shared between them. Mo'pie carried the white cloth parley flag. The four Comanche braves stopped on the path. The white banner waved back and forth in the light wind. Their forms diminished against the massive presence of Fort Parker as they continued forward again. Their moccasins stirred puffs of tan dust. Dust was sacred – the origins of his People.

Some minutes later, one of the huge wooden doors moved and a young White Face poked his head out. Then the gate swung wide and a single person walked toward Buffalo Hump's warriors. The braves stood their ground.

The White Face was not the Elder Parker. Too young. This was a mere boy with blond hair. He wore black trousers held with black strings stretched over a white cloth that included arms. Mo'pie had the same cloth tied to his parley pole. The blond boy held both arms out. No fire stick, but maybe a hidden knife?

Heads bobbed as the blond boy and Mo'pie talked. The

parley lasted too many minutes. Buffalo Hump wanted to act. Blond boy turned around and went back inside the fort. The gate stood open. More minutes passed. The evening grew darker now with more long shadows. Not easy to see.

The boy finally came back with another White Face. He also had blond hair. Brothers? More talk. Arms waved and pointed. White Faces always wanted talk, but never with truth. Buffalo Hump kept rock-still, waiting, but his patience waned.

Now Mo'pie raised his peace pole high and moved it up and down. The signal for Buffalo Hump's time, but still no Paraibo Parker. The Penateka Chief stood and started down the long slope to the parley. He left his war lance beside the wagon path. He did not wipe away his black war paint.

• • •

"My name is Benjamin Parker," the older man-boy said to Buffalo Hump. "And this here's Silas, my brother."

So these were Paraibo Parker's sons? Younger blond boy, Silas, he made a frightened face. He knew he might die soon. The Chief saw no such fear in the speaking one, Benjamin. So the White Face chief had sent his boys out to face the unknown. This Parker man would sacrifice his children. His sons. Where was his honor?

"We come, I come, to speak only with Elder Parker." Buffalo Hump used his few White Face words, even the right title for Paraibo Parker. This was the right moment to put his battle plan in motion. "If there is peace between us.... If wood camp stays," the Chief gestured toward Fort Parker, "I discuss only with Parker chief."

"I'm real sorry, but our Pa's not here," The one called Benjamin replied. His voice sounded calm. "But we can all talk, peaceable like, out here, maybe. Just till he gets back."

The boy looked around, then looked down. He did not look

in Buffalo Hump's eyes. He was lying. He was stalling. Buffalo Hump smelled death. His daughter had died bravely. Suffered the White Face's pox. These two would die now. And once Buffalo Hump found him, their father would die, too. There was no bravery or honorable life in lies.

The Old Parker must be inside, cowering behind women and children. Or had he already run away by some hidden gate or tunnel to the creek? Maybe this was a trap or an ambush the White Faces had set? Could there be White Face Rangers hidden inside about to attack? No matter, the Penateka Chief's plan was in place. The Great Summer Raid would begin now.

Buffalo Hump rolled his eyes upward into his forehead behind wide-open lids. He hardened his face like stone. An ear-splitting, whooping scream erupted from deep within him.

Buffalo Hump grasped the hilt of the knife slung low in his belt. A metallic zing-swish then a soft crunch sounded as the Chief slit through Benjamin Parker's throat directly at his Adam's apple. A wheeze of air mixed with red wetness spilled from the severed windpipe where knife had met neck bone. The boy's stunned eyes swelled in surprise. Whatever words were on his lips were swallowed in a head-bobbing, blood-frothing gurgle. His slack body slumped forward into the dirt and began puddling red into the soft earth around his head. The first Parker was dead before the echo of Buffalo Hump's war whoop fell away.

A broad, heavy knife slammed Buffalo Hump in his beaded vest, but the weapon hit flat and clattered to the ground. Silas Parker had missed his only chance. He turned and ran. Mo'pie retrieved the knife and flung it deep into the back of the retreating Parker boy. Buffalo Hump thrust his own bloody knife up into the evening air. His second war whoop broke the eerie silence once again.

Prone in the surrounding fields, Caddo archers and ax-wielding Penatekas rose as one and took up the charge. Mo'pie and his three weaponless, penitent braves led the dash for the gates. Buffalo Hump straddled Silas Parker and sliced away a clod of his scalp, then ran after his war party. His triumph over White Face Parker and his band was coming soon.

Mo'pie and the others were in the shadow of the fort and wrestled to push open one of the heavy gates. Screams echoed. Gunshots from above crackled and filled the darkening sky. The struggle echoed all along the spiked walls of Fort Parker.

The Chief caught up with Mo'Pie and ran beside the charging warriors through the gates. A sudden thud and the back half of Mo'pie's head fell away, struck by a heavy musket ball. Red and gray brain matter sprayed, carrying the brave's last thoughts into the wind past Buffalo Hump. The Chief ran on, leading the charge and pressing the attack into the heart of the fort.

In minutes, burning cabins and smoldering ramparts torched by Buffalo Hump's raiding party lit the open space in the center of Fort Parker. The cries of women and children mixed with animal noises and filled the surrounding night. Buffalo Hump ordered them all herded together through the open gates, the only light provided by a brilliant full moon. Now he would find the White Face Parker and bring justice.

• • •

Buffalo Hump tied the naked man to four stakes, spread-eagled and face-up on the ground. The Penateka Chief stood over him with his skinning knife in one hand, ready. The White Face paraibo squirmed and moaned, but no words could come through his gag. The gray-haired Parker squaw, his warriors had told him she was called Rachel, was also gagged and tied to a chair, fully clothed. The Chief had positioned her in the flickering light so she could watch the proceedings. Buffalo Hump felt the edge of his knife with one thumb.

"Elder Parker," Buffalo Hump addressed the chalk-white,

balding figure lying face up. "What you thought? No need to make parley with lowly Comanche Paraibo? Not greet peaceful visitor? Now I say you will talk no more. You will walk no more."

Buffalo Hump explained the ritual evenly, and Elder Parker tried to cower. The bound man's eyes begged because his gagged mouth could not. The Chief's eyes met John Parker's without expression. Muffled screams came from the Parker squaw. Her chair thumped the ground. The staked-down man twisted and strained against his bonds.

"Elder Parker has no courage, so no need for man parts." Buffalo Hump pointed his knife at Parker's exposed crotch. The captive Parker writhed. His chest heaved and noises came from his throat. Buffalo Hump gripped the knife tighter then moved closer to his prisoner's head.

"You show no honor of me," Buffalo Hump shouted. "So I take scalp while you still live." He waved the knife in a circle around Parker's quivering head. "You never follow me into After Life."

With one practiced motion, Buffalo Hump sliced away a clump of Parker's skin and knots of hair, then stood erect. He tied the howling man's balding scalp to his belt and set to work between Parker's naked legs. Seconds later, the Chief turned away to walk the grounds of the burning fort, leaving the nightmarish shrieks behind him. The screams lowered and became muffled, but many more, higher-pitched moans added to the chaos. This suffering noise would go on a long time.

How did these foolish intruders think they could take Numunuh land? What gave them any right to invade the plains and foul the sacred ground that belonged to his people? Land that fed buffalo and deer and was home to soaring eagles and ravens? They had offended the Great Mystery and brought pestilence and death to his people. The punishment the Chief had dealt was fair.

Buffalo Hump looked back once more toward the bound-up Parkers and shook his head, then he strode out through the fallen, smoldering gates. Bright moonlight fell on the Chief's bare shoulders and washed over the three eagle feathers in his plaited hair. Here his task was finished, but one battle – even a Numunuh victory as big as this one – must be followed by others. Buffalo Hump resolved to gather all the bands on the High Plain and lead them against the White Faces in Texas.

• • •

At mid-morning, Buffalo Hump's war party gathered and made camp while he surveyed the spoils from the fort invasion. They had taken fire sticks and many horses. Live pigs were slung across the horses' backs. Many captives, young women and children, promised good medicine for his people's future. The Chief had seen several adult women he approved of for his band.

One girl-child from the fort was called Cynthia Parker. She was only nine or ten years of age, still too young for obedience lessons, but she was already strong and defiant and would make a good gift to Iron Jacket someday – a White squaw for Iron Jacket's son, Peta Nokona. Tribute for success in last night's raids.

"Bring the two women I saw by the creek," Buffalo Hump ordered. "Mother and daughter Pierce, I believe they are called. The loud, kicking ones." He stamped his war lance on the turf. "Time for burial ceremony."

Two terrified young women, mother and daughter, were brought to him. Buffalo Hump had ordered them fed, watered and dressed properly in long, fringed deerskin dresses. Earlier, the striking mother and daughter had been stripped naked and subjected to their first lesson: ritual intercourse with one of Buffalo Hump's braves. The Chief showed a friendly face when they were paraded to him.

"You are now of my band. You are Penateka women," Buffalo Hump said in English. "Today is for learning our ways. Now, second lesson." The Chief turned and announced to his warriors in their dialect. "Time for burial. Bring our brother, Mo'pie."

Buffalo Hump, clad ceremonially in fringed leggings and his white beaded vest, grasped his war lance and lowered the point to the earth. He traced a semi-circle in the dirt. Heads bowed and warriors moved to encircle the chief. One brave took the two women from the center to their place outside the solemn assembly.

A single pony bearing a blanket-wrapped body was led into the center of the circle where the Chief now stood alone. Buffalo Hump raised his eyes toward the two women outside the circle. They looked bewildered. Crazed. New outlander women always did.

Buffalo Hump waved the lance again and Mo'pie's comrades placed his body on the soft ground. Without expression or comment, the Chief bent down and laid small fetishes on Mo'pie's beaded vest. The young brave still had his scalp, at least all that had not been blown off by the fatal shot. He had redeemed himself in battle. The Chief laid a long, beaded pipe alongside Mo'pie's body, cradling the object in the crook of his arm.

"Our brother," Buffalo Hump intoned as he stood up, "will have a safe journey and peace in the After Life. His medicine was good. Mo'pie did not suffer old man's pains while he lived with us."

Buffalo Hump gazed around, then fixed his eyes again on the two new women. The afternoon sun faded behind gathering clouds. An anvil-shaped thunderhead towered in the distance, mushrooming, bright with lightning and making a low rumbling thunder. This was indeed good medicine.

"Mo'pie can meet a new brother there," the Chief said with certainty in his voice. "One young White Face Parker looked upon me with no fear in his eyes. I did not take his scalp. He can share the Great Mystery with Mo'pie."

Buffalo Hump stepped aside and motioned the mother and daughter into the circle. A strong gust of wind blew the Chief's leg fringes, and thunder echoed louder and closer. He was pleased that the Great Mystery might bless his people with rain.

Kati and Marianne Pierce already knew their task. They

hoisted heavy stones and piled them carefully around and on top of Mo'pie's body. Another introduction to the Penateka band.

Chapter Seven

Hill Country Hostages - August 1836

Three months had passed since the great Comanche Massacre at Fort Parker. Captain Erasmus Smith's company had been ordered into the field late in July by General Sam Houston. The last two nights, Jack Hays' squad had camped with the rest of Smith's unit on an open higher plain in the hill country northwest of San Antonio.

The Rangers had been guaranteed safe passage by the Comanche for their special mission. Jack was nervous anyway. He paced the open area just west of the main campsite. The early morning sun was already oppressive.

"Make damn sure that table and them barrels sit in the clear," Jack ordered. "Way out there in the middle of the field. Cap'n says everthing's got to be just so before these bastards will even show up to talk, much less do any hostage trading."

Trooper Eddie Halvorsen and the O'Keefe boys followed Jack's orders. They lined up wide boards on empty wooden barrels. The rest of his squad came with more barrels and set them around the makeshift table.

Jack constructed a white flag that he tied to a sharpened tent pole, then jammed the end into the ground next to the table. Why talk? Why bargain with a bunch of savages who wanted only to trade horses and money for White women? Oughta just shoot 'em – all the Comanche – when they showed up.

Jack yelled an order to his Lipan scouts. "Chief Flacco, Red Wing, take the horses we brought for trade and wait in the tree line."

No sense pissing off the Comanche more by having Apaches visible near the trading table, according to Cap'n Smith. Jack had left Jaime Esteban back in San Antone, too. Didn't want to rub Buffalo

Hump's boys' noses in the fact that Mexicans and Tejanos worked together in the Rangers.

One more thing, though. Why the hell had General Sam ordered some mulatto woman brought all the way from Morgan's Point down on Galveston Bay for this parley? Supposedly some kind of Indian expert or Comanche talker named Emily West. Jack doubted the woman would be that useful today.

"Cap'n Smith," Hays reported. "We got it all ready. Ain't a single Indian in sight, though. So far, this whole goddamn thing stinks like…like…" Jack raised a hand to his hat. "You want me to fetch that West lady from her tent? She ready for this?"

Deaf Smith snapped the latch on a small box of silver coins and tucked the container under one arm, Then he closed his tent flaps and glanced at his pocket watch. Did Smith think the Comanche might be late for their own damned party? Jack walked a step to the rear of his commander down the path toward the last tent in the row. At least from behind, Deaf Smith couldn't read the frustration on his face.

"Sergeant Hays," Captain Smith shouted, turning his head. "Gen'ral Sam personally ordered the West woman to be here, just like us." Smith's upper lip curled. "Main reason is, she speaks Comanche lingo, so the bastards cain't put nothin' over on us. Second, she ain't White, so the fuckin' Redskins are more likely to trust her. Least that's what the General thinks. And he's the one knows her."

Hays stopped in his tracks behind Captain Smith. The woman stood outside, tying her tent flaps shut. She was a couple of inches taller than Jack and had smooth, olive skin and blue-green, oval eyes. Her dark, straight hair was pulled back under an expensive-looking broad-brimmed leather hat. A bright green scarf hung at her long neck. She wore an open black leather vest with silver conchos. The woman could've been William Goins' daughter, the best looking female Jack had seen in quite a while.

Damned if Miss West didn't have a McKenzie flintlock stuffed into those leather pants, too. Jack would've admired her beauty more, but he was distracted by that pistol. The same heart-shaped handle as Big Red's weapon. Wonder if she'd ever fired the thing? He'd like to have seen that.

"Captain Smith," The woman spoke, her voice soft as velvet, "My thanks for the accommodations. I hope the trouble of all this will prove worthwhile to Texas."

She smiled. Jack Hays smiled back and tilted his head. Smith frowned.

"Miss West," Captain Smith spoke, softer than normal. "This here's Sergeant Hays. Jack Hays."

Jack nodded. He touched his hat brim and tried not to smile any more. Emily West was looking him over, for sure.

Smith continued. "Him and his squad, they're going to be your personal protection while we talk with the Comanche."

West extended her hand. Her palm felt as calloused as Jack recalled Sam Houston's was. A lot prettier, though.

"Sergeant, I am pleased to make your acquaintance," Emily West said. Her eyes were big and serious, with a deep twinkle. "I heard you've already had a run in or two with the Indians we're dealing with."

"Just one skirmish, Ma'am," Jack responded. "Turned out okay for us Rangers. Hopin' today's not another one, though."

The pounding thumps of running feet interrupted Jack. Chief Flacco dashed toward him across the open field with both arms waving in the humid air.

"Captain, Sergeant Jack, they…" Flacco stammered. "The Comanche come. Red Wing hear pony feet, maybe twenty riders. Half mile now."

The young Indian's chest heaved from the long run in the morning heat. He glanced from Jack to Deaf Smith and nodded, but did not acknowledge Emily West's presence.

"Let's get on with it," Deaf Smith ordered. "Chief, you only come with horses if I give you the signal."

Flacco nodded and ran back toward the trees. Jack squinted in the bright sun toward the ridge-line. He hoped the scouts were right about the Comanche peace party.

• • •

A dust cloud formed on the hill crest. Jack stood at the end of the barrel table next to Emily West with Smith directly to her right. He counted a little more than twenty bronzed, bareback horsemen riding toward them. Red Wing's estimate had been close.

The Indian party slowed to a trot. All of the young, stern-faced braves had weapons. Bows with quivers full of arrows were slung across their backs, some had muskets, and all appeared to have knives in their belts. The leader carried a feathered lance with a white flag fluttering from the blunted shaft. The flag matched the face paint of the entire party. Hays had been this close to Comanche already, but never peaceably.

The warriors flanked two blond, long-skirted women riders. Hard to tell they were White, except for their hair. Once they got closer, the younger of the two showed small scars on her face. She was already spoken for in the Penateka village. Flacco had said ownership marks like these could make for a hard trade.

Three braves dismounted and ambled toward the table. The lead Indian had inscribed a thin, jagged blue lightning bolt across his white-painted forehead, a sign of tribal rank and power. Eagle feathers in his hair blew in the light breeze. Jack was itchy.

Open, beaded vests draped the upper torsos of all three warriors. They walked in high-top moccasins and wore long-fringed leggings, not breechclouts. The leader carried the blunted lance with the white flag upright. They'd dressed for peace. A good sign, if it was true.

The three negotiators carried broad-bladed knives, but no other weapons. They placed them one-by-one on the table opposite the three flintlocks that belonged to Jack, Emily West and Captain Smith. The rest of the Comanche party and the two captive women stayed back nearer the ridge-line, astride their ponies.

Jack Hays glanced down. Three flintlock pistols on the table, loaded, not cocked, with muzzles pointed toward the Comanche. And three gleaming knives pointed in his direction from the Comanche side. How many scalps had those taken over the years?

West sat in the center on the Texas side with Hays and Captain Smith flanking her. The lightning bolt brave, apparently the spokesman, sat across the table facing her flanked by his two bare-chested Penateka braves.

He broke the silence. "I am Kablito. I bring you greetings to our land and wishes for health from Buffalo Hump, Chief of all Penateka."

Captain Smith spoke for the Texans, and the palaver started. Frustrating minutes, then more than an hour passed. The sun and the August humidity pressed down. Jack lifted his hat and wiped his brow with a bright bandana. The Comanche did not sweat. Neither did the bastards blink. They looked to be not human at all.

. . .

"So, Tejas friends," Kablito spoke, his palms turned up. "There is agreement on the mother for you. We keep daughter."

Deaf Smith nodded. Jack couldn't believe his Captain. The man was willing to let the young girl go back with these savages? Hays shook his head. West didn't react.

Kablito ignored Jack. "We take ten ponies and one hundred silver pieces. You get Mother Pierce. Daughter stay with Chief Buffalo Hump. Stay with Penateka."

"Penateka brothers," West spoke her first words. Comanche talk? Jack didn't understand. "It is bad medicine to separate mother and daughter. Both must come back to us."

The three braves looked toward each other, then from West to Captain Smith. Dammit all, until now everything had been clear and in English. What the hell had she said in Comanche? And why now? From the looks on the Comanche faces, she was sure saying something that was not in the original plan.

"Your Paraibo, Buffalo Hump," West continued in their language. "Knows well the value of family. Could your Chief have sent you to trade women like animals? Such behavior does not make for peace."

More bad looks from the Comanche. The leader stared at Emily West, wide-eyed. Matters didn't look very good at all. The other two Indians now seemed confused. They shifted on their barrel stools and leaned forward toward their knives.

Emily West's hand moved toward her flintlock, maybe an inch. Why? Why the devil had she done that? The Comanche leader, Kablito, laid one hand on his knife, covering the blade.

This crazy woman was going to get them all killed. Jack could take down one Indian before West or any of the three savages could finish their moves, but after that? Twenty braves stood armed and ready less than a hundred yards away on the other side with no fear of death.

On Jack's side of the parley, thirty hot, dusty Rangers stood the same distance behind him, locked and loaded. Flacco and Red Wing hid in the tree line with rifles ready. Out here in the sun, everybody was wound up tight. One mistake or false move and they'd have a bloodbath on their hands. Things were restlessly quiet now. No more words from either West or Kablito.

My God, the heat. Jack's mouth and lips were parched. Still, nobody moved. A horse whinnied from the tree line. The only other sound Jack could hear was his pulse pounding in his ears.

"We just here for trading. Peace business, Yellow Woman." Kablito broke the uneasy, overheated silence in broken English. He spread both hands palms up on the table. "No war today. Maybe another day better."

He smiled and looked Emily West up and down. Jack tensed even more. Been in lots of uncomfortable circumstances, but never in such a fix as this one. What the hell could he come up with to ease things up?

"New bargain." Kablito looked first to Smith, then to Hays. "Rangers take Pierce mother and daughter, we take ten ponies and Yellow Woman." Kablito gestured with his hand toward Emily West. "She not White Face, anyway. Yellow Woman be happier with Numunuh."

Hays grimaced, then stared at a wide-eyed Emily West. Her hand still rested near her pistol. Seemed like the woman had just gotten a lot whiter. Jack leaned in and put one hand over Emily's hand and squeezed tight. Leastways now she couldn't shoot the damned Indian.

"Afraid not, Chief." Jack Hays spoke, still looking at Emily. "Already took this squaw for myself some time ago."

West turned and looked at Jack. He stared as romantically as he could. He kept his hand snug over hers. Jack felt the woman relax, then she smiled.

• • •

Sunset in the hill country heralded a cooler, welcome breeze from the northwest. Astride his pony, Hays escorted the Comanche party away from the Ranger campsite. Kati Pierce, the daughter, rode with the band as they passed her mother. Marianne Pierce sat cross-legged in the grass at the edge of the woods. Hays had ordered her held there, watched by Flacco and Red Wing. The mother did not look to her daughter. What in God's name could the two Pierce women be thinking?

Near the crest of the ridge, the peace party halted. Hays faced

Kablito and rested one hand across his saddle. The Comanche laid his lance across his pony's back. The white flag was gone and rawhide held a metal point where the flag had been.

"Tell your Chief, Buffalo Hump," Jack said, "that we appreciate his peace offerings. Returning the woman."

"Maybe another day," Kablito replied, open hand raised, "you meet Buffalo Hump, face-on-face. Maybe talk peace. Maybe not."

Hays tipped his hat and eased back in his saddle. Kablito kneed his pony around. Had the Indian smiled? Kablito jabbed his lance point at the air. A shrill cry not unlike like an eagle's scream came from the young Comanche's throat as he galloped to the head of his party. The braves turned and kicked at their ponies, the young Pierce girl in their midst. The Comanche band galloped over the hill crest and out of view.

Jack reined his mount, turned and headed in the opposite direction toward the double line of white tents and blue Texas flag. Emily West sat in front of her tent with her hat in her lap. She waved the hat when Jack rode by. He gripped the brim of his hat in a salute and rode on.

Emily West wasn't any prettier than the young woman he remembered from that coin trick afternoon back in San Antone, but something about her sure could turn a man's head. Wait a minute. Why the hell was he all of a sudden thinkin' about all these women all the time? He ought to be wondering what General Sam was going to say about this mission.

PART TWO

The Weapon

"God made all men. Samuel Colt made all men equal."

American frontier saying - late 1800s

Chapter Eight

New York to Hartford - Early 1839

Twenty-five year old entrepreneur Samuel Colt took the two steps down from a liveried carriage and into the winter chill. He hastened across the northbound train platform, a leather valise in one gloved hand. Harlem was the newest and northernmost stop on the New York-Stamford run. Samuel Colt liked the new station. Harlem was closer to his offices in town and was a progressive, culturally mixed part of the city. Too bad he had business up in Connecticut. He'd rather be here sampling the evening pleasures.

A harsh north wind watered Colt's eyes. Snow stung his exposed cheeks above a well-trimmed beard. Another Nor'easter, the third one of the winter, fluttered his silk scarf behind him and knifed through the long, light wool coat that covered his white linen shirt, black cravat and matching wool vest. He might be stylish, but not dressed for this winter storm. Next time he'd wear a heavier coat and wrap his ears in a woolen scarf.

The relative protection of the last open passenger car beckoned, and Sam Colt rushed for the entry door. He glanced sideways and caught the eye of a striking, equally stylish young woman. High cheekbones, smooth olive skin and blue-green eyes punctuated the young woman's angular face. A green wool scarf wrapped her head and black hair. The red wool greatcoat draped over what he could see of her matching velvet dress and down to black leather boots. Elegant. And the attire had been well chosen for protection from the bitter weather. Still, she shivered and clutched herself, waiting on the platform near the car.

Once inside, Sam found the New York-Stamford train packed. Winter body smells oppressed the close quarters. He took the last aisle seat and gazed down the crowded entryway. The striking, darkly exotic woman pushed her way along the aisle, drawing long looks from other travelers as she approached. Who could this person be? Where was she from? Why travel alone?

The woman reached the only open spot, a window seat a row ahead of Samuel Colt and across the aisle. She wrestled a carpetbag into the overhead rack. The portly, rough-dressed man on the aisle turned his head, raised an eyebrow and glared up at her. He shifted his sizable frame and used one stocky leg to block the woman's passage to the open spot.

"Find another seat," the man barked. "I'll not share a journey with a Colored."

"And I, sir," the woman responded, looking down, "am loathe to be in the company of such rudeness and lack of couth. But I shall have that window seat."

She nudged at the man's outstretched leg with her knee. Samuel Colt surveyed the aisle, front-to-rear. Was the lady to have no official assistance? Where was the conductor? Should he intervene?

"If my presence would so offend you," she persisted, one stylish boot still shoved against the man's calf. "Perhaps someone will trade seats. That would relieve us both of a burdensome presence."

Still no train official had appeared for the pointed exchange. Samuel Colt took his opportunity. The young entrepreneur rose and stepped into the aisle. He moved forward, valise in hand, and stood next to the woman.

"Sir," Samuel Colt first addressed the seated man. Then he

turned. "And Madam. Permit me to resolve the dilemma. I'd be pleased to share the journey to Stamford with the lady. Would the gentleman kindly remove himself to my earlier place yonder on the bench?"

Sam gestured toward his now-empty seat. The stout fellow was silent, looking up at him. Then the man stood, frowned, and grabbed a worn carpetbag. He shuffled wordlessly past Colt, back one row. The woman smiled and, at Samuel Colt's direction, took the window seat.

Metal-to-metal clanked when the train car shuddered, jostling Colt as he tried to sit. A distant shrill whistle confirmed that the journey to Stamford was underway. Sam's seat companion adjusted her green scarf, turned up her coat collar and gazed out the window. The train wheezed from the station into the snowy countryside north of New York City.

Minutes passed. Samuel Colt was mesmerized. The young woman's appearance was hypnotic. He had to find out more about her.

Colt cleared his throat and spoke. "M'lady, you look quite familiar. Surely we've met before."

She turned, head erect, and locked fiery green eyes on his. Unsmiling, she pulled the scarf away, shaking her head till thick hair fell loose. The woman ran long, elegant fingers with manicured nails through the shiny black mass and turned her collar down.

"Come, come," the woman replied. "You have been quite gallant, the perfect gentleman till now. Should you be English, you could be Robin Hood. Yet you are such a clumsy flirt. From what obscure Victorian woodland might you hail, sir?"

The woman's voice was as husky and smooth as the velvet she wore. Colt flinched, caught off-guard by her verbal sparring. The accent, what was it? Saint Domingue? Canary Islands? He doffed his beaver skin top hat and fumbled the heavy pelt to his side. He needed a moment to recover, but smiled.

"Hartford, Ma'am," Colt replied. "Hartford, Connecticut,

that is. Though I once spent a year in England and am just returned from Scotland. As for you, our paths have indeed crossed somewhere. That's fact, not flirting."

"So then, you have been in the Texas Republic," the woman said, chin upturned. She kept eye contact, unblinking. "Aiding the new country? Or perhaps you work in the city. You've seen me in New York?"

"Certainly not in Texas," Colt replied. "I've never been west, but I'd like to go. Texas and its plight as an independent republic are of particular interest to me." The eyes of his seat companion brightened. "Presently, though, I have a small weapons manufacturing plant in New Jersey. Business takes me into the city often, to a trading office on Broadway."

"My name is Samuel Colt," he said. "I'm an engineer and inventor, but a man regrettably forced by skeptics to produce and market his own considerable innovations."

"I am pleased to make your acquaintance, Mr. Colt," The woman spoke with a slight Latin lisp, Castilian probably. "My name is Emily West, of late a New Yorker, but I consider myself more a Tejano. Tell me about some of your inventions, particularly your weapons, if they are not some deeply held secret."

Samuel Colt sensed heat welling into his face and ears. Emily West - her name matched neither her looks nor demeanor. She might say she was Texan, but culturally the woman had to be old family Caribbean Spanish, maybe Creole French, perhaps even Mexican aristocracy.

Whoever the hell she was, the woman had no idea just how good he was at inventing things. Moreover, she likely had no understanding of weapons of war. Or did she? Only one way to find out. Colt retrieved a hard leather case from his valise, clicked the latch open and put the contents on his lap. The young woman looked down at the heavy pistol, then back to Colt and smiled. Emily West approved.

"My latest development." Colt touched the long barrel and

gleaming cylinder. "This is a five-shot repeating pistol, a device that will change warfare forever."

She stared, eyes wide. Had he shocked her delicate sensibilities? She'd probably never seen such a weapon. He'd surely offended her.

"My sincere apologies, madam." Colt said, nodding. "Such hardware should not be of concern to women of your background and station."

"You apparently know nothing of women like me, Mr. Colt," West snapped back. Her voice had a hard edge. "Though I crave civility, I've seen more than my share of conflict. I have smelled death and endured the company of warlords and pirates. We frontier women, we may dress and conduct ourselves as the weaker sex when in your civilization, but on the open sea and in the wilds of Texas, I and countless others could have benefitted more than once from such a weapon. May I examine it closer?"

Colt handed over the pistol, expecting his new acquaintance to struggle with its heft. Instead, she took a firm, two-handed grip on the bone handle. West had held more than one pistol in those elegant hands before. And the questions she posed – caliber, cocking, firing and how quickly reloading might be accomplished. This woman knew her guns.

"Miss West," Colt queried. "Are you, as I am, bound for New Haven with the Overland coach tomorrow? Or does your journey only take you as far as Stamford?"

Emily West handed the weapon back to him. "I am indeed bound for New Haven in the morning. And if we are to share the coach tomorrow, perhaps we can continue our conversation. I can tell you why your repeating device there interests me, if it truly works. If nothing else, we shall relieve ourselves of some of the journey's boredom."

"Madam, I would be delighted," Colt said. "And my repeater pistol most certainly works. Meanwhile, would you permit me to introduce you to Webb's Tavern this evening, the best eating establishment in Stamford? Our discussion can already continue there. Shall we meet in the gathering room of the inn at seven?"

Emily West hesitated, then gave Colt a thin smile and an affirmative nod. Good, he'd surprised her. But before he could say more, West put her coat collar up and turned back to the window. Their train conversation was apparently finished. Colt put the pistol away and pondered what specific circumstance might have required this woman to know weaponry. Maybe she'd tell him later.

Chapter Nine

A Family Affair - Early 1839

Sam Colt sat opposite his dinner guest at a small table and turned to glance out one partly shuttered window of the old but stylish Stamford Tavern. A howling wind blew new snow into drifts, obstructing his view of carriages and riders on the cobblestone street. Colt returned his attention to Emily West and dabbed a napkin at the corner of his mouth. They'd shared a hearty meat pie, warm fruit and cream. Emily's coal-black hair fell loose over a draped green-and-gray shoulder wrap. Sam permitted himself a small cigar while she sipped at her glass of wine.

Emily's story had been straightforward and plausible. She was born in the northeast, probably Connecticut, the illicit child of a free woman of Color, and the woman's employer. She'd described her early struggles as a Colored and later, her harrowing experiences in the Texas war for independence. She'd been captured at Morgan's Point by Santa Anna's forces just before the Battle of San Jacinto. Then she'd spent time as the Mexican General's personal prisoner. She had successfully spied for General Houston and relayed valuable tactical information back to the Texas militia before she escaped.

West had shown Sam a handwritten document guaranteeing her safe passage as a hero of the Texas revolution. In the paper, Emily was described as "a notable citizen of the new Republic." The document was signed "Samuel Houston, General, Republic of Texas Militia."

She told him, too, about the Comanche hostage negotiations in Texas. But that had been more than two years ago. What had she been doing since then back here in the Northeast? And why the family quest now?

"Your exploits, Emily.... May I call you Emily?" Sam said,

noting a slight nod of approval from his companion. "Your exploits make my life seem dull by comparison. One would never have guessed that the beautiful woman whose company I share is a friend of Sam Houston, has escaped the clutches of General Santa Anna and once worked to free women hostages from Indian savages. You are truly Amazonian."

"Amazonian?" Emily West looked down at her glass. "Nothing of the sort, Mr. Colt. The war with Mexico ended well for the Republic. I had little to do with that, and I remain dismayed over my biggest failure, not gaining the young Pierce woman's release. It pains me to think about what that poor girl and others like her may endure these days as victims of such exploitation. Quite barbaric."

"I know nothing of Indian culture, savage or otherwise," Colt replied. "Especially the Comanche. But I doubt they ever intended to release the girl. And as you said, it was fortunate for you, my dear, that the young Ranger sergeant was quick-witted."

The warmth of the candlelit tavern and the excellent meal had relaxed Sam Colt. Emily's beauty was as intoxicating as the wine, her aloofness a challenge. He reached for her arm. She flinched and raised one hand in his direction, palm up.

"Come now," West admonished. "Let us keep this evening to business. My interest in you, Samuel Colt, extends only to tools of war. I have had quite enough romance already in my life."

Chastened and sobered, Sam considered his next move. He had business with the Eli Whitney Company in New Haven. Emily West was on some family mission to the city. She seemed genuinely interested in the Colt repeater. If her exploits were as she'd told him, she could be useful to the Colt Arms Company. After all, he was an inventor, not a salesman. But this woman's beauty alone would gain an audience anywhere. Perhaps she was his best hope for marketing Colt repeating pistols. A plan began to take shape in Sam Colt's mind.

"Fine then." Colt shrugged off West's personal rebuff. "Perhaps I can assist you, Emily, or rather I should say, Miss West, in your personal quest in New Haven. And might you return the favor by further enlightening me as to arms sales opportunities in Texas?" He pulled a small notebook from his coat pocket. "Do you need information, contacts, official assistance in New Haven?"

"Thank you very much, Mr. Colt." Emily West smiled. "I meant no disrespect, but I am quite tired. Perhaps as I suggested on the train, we may discuss all this more in the carriage on our way to New Haven tomorrow."

• • •

Coat collar turned up against the bitter wind, Sam Colt stood the next morning and faced a taller man in a long hooded cloak near the open door of the Overland coach. Emily, bundled against the cold in her red wool coat, held Sam's arm and stood close and as protected by his frame as she could. Colt's repeating pistol was visible, cradled against his thigh in a leather holster. Weak sunlight glinted off the hammer.

"Sir," Sam Colt bellowed at the man. "Have you the slightest notion whom you offend with your crass objections? My traveling companion is a hero of the Texas War for Independence. Neither her race nor her free status is your affair. I dare say that she, nay we, now have no intention of sharing a coach with the likes of you."

His adversary had a long, angular face with well-trimmed mutton-chops along an iron jaw. A gold-lamé vest covered his broad chest under a brown waistcoat and open winter cloak. But no weapon was visible.

Despite the man's size and seeming irritation, he put a hand to his hat then doffed it in token that he had understood his personal peril. He brought the hat down to his side.

"Now, now," the man said in a voice barely above a whisper. "No call for that. I am unarmed." He bowed, turning both palms out. "My apologies to the young woman. I am inconvenienced by the delay, but you have admirably made your point, sir."

The man donned his hat and backed away. Sam rested one hand on his pistol handle, eyeing his opponent who turned and took the snowy steps of the inn two at a time. Colt felt the tight grip Emily kept on his arm. Warm, even affectionate.

"Seems that gentleman has poor eyesight," Colt said gaily as he turned to Emily. "And no taste in women. But he does have an appreciation for fine hardware."

Emily smiled. Sam Colt reveled in the moment. Would he have shot the insolent bastard? Probably not. Didn't matter now, though.

Colt stroked his trimmed beard. "Madam, I have once again peaceably defended your honor. So you shall have to wait another day to find out just how well the Paterson Colt would have performed had I not been so persuasive." He patted the holster.

Colt kept Emily's arm snugged in his and guided her to the waiting coach. Their luggage had been loaded. There was freight, but no other passengers. The coach and two drivers were theirs alone for the journey.

Samuel Colt had hoped to be in New Haven by mid-afternoon, but heavy wagon traffic on the partly frozen roads between Stamford and New Haven had left deep ruts that slowed their carriage. The city was in twilight and lamplighters were about their work when the driver reined in the team in front of their lodging. After a hasty dismount from the carriage, Colt ushered Emily West up a flight of stone steps and through the main door of the fashionable Eaton Hotel On The Green.

The slow trip had at least given Samuel Colt more time to examine Emily West's professional attributes. The woman indeed knew weapons and could handle herself in tough situations. He was convinced of that. So, despite the absence of any mutual attraction shown by Emily so far, she should be one hell of a business asset. He'd scribbled a note for the carriage driver to deliver to Nathaniel Miller of the Eli Whitney Company, post haste. Colt wanted to advise

Miller that Emily would be joining them for dinner tonight as his new assistant. All that Emily needed to know was that they'd be dining this evening with an important business associate, one who could ensure production of his weapons in suitable quantities to make both him and her rich.

• • •

Less than an hour later, Samuel Colt crossed The Green, trudging through drifting snow with Emily West tight on his arm. He pushed open the heavy door of "Fin and Fowl," New Haven's best known eating and drinking establishment. Smells of fresh roasted game and potatoes met his nose, mixing with the odor of burning wood from the massive stone fireplace. Colt peered around in the thin light for Nathaniel Miller. He spotted the short, balding Whitney executive seated at a private table near the fireplace, sipping from an ornate pewter mug.

Sam handed his top hat to the innkeeper and helped Emily West with her heavy coat. Once their outerwear was taken care of, he guided her toward the fireplace and past tables of other dinner patrons. Nathaniel Miller waved one arm and jumped to his feet, stumbling over a chair leg and spilling ale from his mug. My God, now the man stared as though he'd seen a ghost.

Nathaniel Miller barely looked at Sam. Instead, he surveyed Emily West, wide-eyed, head to toe. She stared back, tight-lipped and speechless. Had Sam missed something about his dinner guests? Did they already know each other?

"Nathaniel Miller, Sir," Samuel Colt announced in his most confident manner, "May I present Miss Emily West, my weapons assistant?" Sam turned to Emily. "Miss West, this is the President of the Eli Whitney Arms Company, Mr. Nathaniel Miller."

West nodded slightly without smiling. Miller remained

standing and turned his head, chin down, away from West toward the fireplace. He dabbed with his napkin at the small pool of spilled ale on the table. What in Heaven's name could this possibly be about? Seconds dragged by.

"Mr. Colt," Emily West put her hand on Sam's arm and broke the silence. She was formal, cold. "A most unfortunate circumstance, one that none of us would have supposed, nor certainly could have ever predicted." She sighed and stared at Nathaniel Miller. "Mr. Miller probably suspects, as do I, that he and I are…well…we are related. Siblings separated shortly after my birth, so one story goes. He being the legitimate son, and I the bastard daughter." She shook her head. "A considerable embarrassment would be afforded to the Millers and the Whitneys were my existence, my heritage, ever revealed in the lofty social circles of New Haven."

Silence hung over the table until Nathaniel Miller turned and faced Sam Colt.

"Such is indeed the nature of coincidence, Mr. Colt," Nathaniel Miller blurted. "The woman's admission I believe is quite accurate. This development, as you can see, is extraordinary. I'm afraid that Miss West being in your employ would make any further collaboration between us impossible. I shall be in contact within a fortnight as to the termination of our weapons agreement. Meanwhile, this entire encounter, I insist, must not go beyond the three of us."

Without further acknowledging Emily or shaking hands with Samuel Colt, Miller made for the tavern door, snatching his topcoat and hat from the rack as he went. He brushed past the innkeeper and vanished into the cold of the New Haven evening. Samuel Colt stared at Emily West, dumbfounded.

Chapter Ten

The Problem with Pistols - Early March 1839

Morning sun peeked through low clouds and dirty workshop windows. Dull, yellow light reflected off a half-empty whiskey glass in Sam Colt's hand. He stood in his small, cluttered Paterson factory building surrounded by gun parts and rough sketches of weaponry scattered across his work surface. Frustration balled his free hand into a white-knuckled fist. Sam put down the glass and tightened the other hand into a second fist, then slammed both together and down on the workbench.

Across the table, Emily West flinched. She sighed and met Sam's grim look. A thin smile formed, breaking the straight line of her lips. Sam couldn't return the smile, pretend forgiveness, or show understanding. He had too damned much frustration built-up inside.

"Mr. Colt." West spoke, looking down at the oil-stained floor. "I am truly sorry I wasn't forthright when you first told me about your benefactor in New Haven."

Emily shook her head. That long, shiny black hair swirled around her elegant neck. Sam Colt thought back to the dinner meeting, then the official rejection notice. Nathaniel Miller had flatly refused to fund any further repeating pistol work. Sam had not been surprised, not after the earlier episode. But the rejection had left him stranded again for materials and tooling. Now, without enough personal cash or hard assets to meet his commitments, he'd be hard pressed to succeed, especially in this cramped warehouse.

Sam Colt had dreamed of skilled workmen, twenty or thirty of them side-by-side, assembling interchangeable parts into identical weapons. Production runs of hundreds of pistols a week. That would have been possible at the Whitney Arms Works. Now, he still needed to assemble and ship enough weapons to meet his first, albeit tentative, contracts with the South Carolina and Florida militias. Plus, Sam had to address the Texas inquiry for up to 200 repeating pistols for Sam Houston's new Gulf of Mexico navy.

Was his now dire circumstance the fault of the young woman standing in his workshop, the woman he'd introduced to Nathaniel Miller as his new business partner? There had to be more. Events like this were not necessarily bad omens. Sam Colt knew he was a lucky person. Must be a good reason, some quirk of fate, behind Emily West's intrusion into his life.

Still, some things about Emily West just didn't add up. She and Nathaniel Miller were siblings? Maybe. But why take the name West? Besides, before calling herself West, she'd also told him she'd been a Morgan. And what about all that time in Texas? Was the Sam Houston endorsement letter even real? Most important, was she truly good with a gun?

"I'll survive," Sam broke his silence, still frowning, "without either Miller's backing or his production capacity." He poured more whiskey into his glass. "Life presents us with such dilemmas for a reason. We shall, with time and diligence, determine the facts. Let truth prevail." A heavy sigh, then finally a thin smile. "And you may yet prove your worth to my enterprise, Miss West."

Emily West frowned. Sam took a sip of whiskey. He wasn't going to let her off so easy. The woman was in his debt. Sam Colt was determined to turn this disaster to his advantage.

"The next step in the process, Madame," Colt announced, "is to determine your proficiency with my invention." He lifted a pistol from the table. "Shall we get on with the evaluation?"

• • •

The early afternoon sun had driven the clouds away and now warmed Sam's back. A westerly breeze blew across the firing line.

Sam Colt stood near Emily West. She was motionless, dressed in leathers, hands protected by heavy foundry gloves with the thumbs and fingertips cut away. Colt's carriage and his driver, their lone observer, waited some distance to the rear.

Sam put the pistol on a small stand next to a container of lead balls, wads, a powder horn and percussion caps. Emily peered down range from under the visor of a leather helmet fashioned to protect her head, ears and neck. Sam had dressed the same as a precaution, except for the gloves. He pointed to a stack of three empty powder kegs, her target, some forty yards away in front of a high dirt berm.

"Tell me something before we begin the weapons evaluation." Colt reached for the handgun on the stand. "Just how would you instruct the South Carolina militia to properly load and fire a new Paterson Colt five-shot pistol?"

He handed her the heavy, matte-finished weapon, with its gleaming cylindrical chamber and maple handle. West took the pistol in both hands and gripped it tightly. She cocked the hammer back one click.

"Hammer at half-cock, rotate the cylinder," she announced, continuing the loading sequence. "Chamber twenty-four grains of black powder, insert the wad and seat it, drop the thirty-six caliber ball into the chamber and seat it." She rammed the first lead ball home. "Last, seat a percussion cap on the chamber nipple. Repeat for the other four cylinders." She clicked the cylinder to the next empty chamber. "Except, we'll leave the percussion cap off the last one, for safety."

She finished loading all five chambers, then glanced up at Sam and smiled. Sam Colt kept a straight face and nodded his approval. He needed to stay professional. But God, the woman was striking, even under all that heavy leather gear. He stepped back two paces.

"Excellent, Emily," Colt gushed. "You may fully cock your weapon and fire four shots when ready."

Sam pulled a watch from his coat. The other hand covered his ear closest to West. The three-pound pistol issued a thunderous, crackling report. Heavy metal kicked upward in her gloved hands, accompanied by a flash at the percussion cap. The bottom keg partly splintered, as if struck by an invisible axe. A shower of wood fragments flew backward toward the berm. The two kegs above teetered, then came to rest, still upright in the stack.

She used the recoil to let the pistol continue its upward path. The spent percussion cap slipped off the nipple and fell to the ground. West brought the weapon down to eye level. She double-cocked the hammer again, arms extended but not locked, as Sam had instructed. She aimed at the wobbling kegs. A wispy plume of smoke from the gun barrel floated off to West's right.

Three more rounds echoed and whined down range in less time than Sam Colt could take a breath. The first struck the center keg, splitting it in half. The top keg tipped and clattered downward as the second of her three shots shattered one disc-shaped end in mid-air. West's last shot kicked up a plume of dust on the berm, striking behind the target area above the broken pile of kegs. Colt drew in his breath, held it and glanced at his watch.

Three kills out of four shots at forty yards in less than a minute. One hell of a performance. The woman knew her guns. And his invention was working even better than he'd hoped.

"God in Heaven," Sam Colt shouted, exhaling. "That, Madam, was quite the exhibition. I have indeed hired well." He recovered his professional demeanor. "Now, quickly reload and fire at will."

Colt stared at his watch. Emily worked through the reloading process a second time, took her two-handed firing stance and fired the next round. The impact of the massive ball lifted half of one of the remaining keg sides high in the air, sailing, end-over-end, several feet down range. According to Colt's watch, the elapsed time from the start of reload to firing that round was less than two minutes.

West cocked, aimed and fired a second round. This time there was almost no fire or recoil, and no indication of any hit on the target. Big trouble. Colt's breath caught. Too little fire and smoke. Not good. Not good at all. He should've warned her about breech and muzzle blockage. Sam had to stop her before she fired again.

"Cease fire," Sam shouted. Then again, louder. "Cease Fire!"

He dashed forward. West's eyes narrowed as she cocked the Paterson Colt. Too efficient. Oh God, she was too quick. The woman had no idea what could happen next. The damned pistol would explode. She pointed the muzzle at the remains of a target keg laying sideways on the ground. Sam lunged for her arm, shielding his eyes and groping for his protégé. Damnation.

A violent blast. The pistol barrel fractured, banana-peeling razor edged metal strips outward. Concussive pressure hammered Sam's ears. Wild, uncontrolled recoil threw Emily backward and separated her from the weapon. Frame, handle and cylinder soared from an expanding cloud of smoke and fire that fouled the spring air.

Colt caught West when her body slammed into his, the impact felling them both. Air whooshed out of his lungs. Stunned, ears ringing, Sam tried to roll her to one side. Blood covered Emily's face and head. He snatched at the smoldering foundry gloves and headgear. Metal shards festooned one sleeve of her leather jacket. The pistol cylinder thudded somewhere behind him and discharged more rounds, spraying metal and dirt around the field.

Sam Colt raised his head and shouted for his carriage. One arm pawed the air, motioning for the driver. No time to dally. The Paterson Colt had experienced its first massive test failure, and Emily West was the weapon's first serious casualty.

• • •

A white-coated attendant wheeled Emily away from the drab, two-story hospital. One of her arms was in a sling, and her head had bandages down to one eye. Samuel Colt took Emily West's free arm and ushered her out of the wheelchair. She stepped up and into his enclosed, black lacquered carriage. The attendant handed over Emily's personal belongings. Sam closed the carriage door and settled into the red leather seat across from his injured assistant. He covered her lap with a blanket. She was lucky, only one night in that God-forsaken infirmary. Nothing was broken, as far as Sam knew, and her vision had not been affected.

"Emily, my.... My thanks to God." Sam blurted his first words as the carriage shook and lurched away from the hospital, "We, you.... We both are quite fortunate. I'm to understand, uh, that is the doctor says, the burns to your hands and face are superficial. The foundry gloves and headgear did their job."

Why the hell had he not given Emily more instruction on the weapon? Sam Colt had known the risks. Last year he'd almost lost an arm in the same kind of blowback explosion. Better not to talk about that now. A bit late for such confessions.

"Your two fingers were severely dislocated, not broken," Colt opined. "The doctor was able to...to put them back. But you'll still wear the splint and sling for some days. Could be weeks."

Only the soft click of well-shod horses on cobblestone and the repeated squeaking of one warped wheel intruded on the silence in Samuel Colt's carriage. Emily turned from her gaze out the carriage window and looked down. Sam waited. Minutes passed, an eternity before Emily looked up and locked her eyes on his.

"I am well aware, Sam Colt," West's husky voice washed over him, "that the doctor straightened the dislocated fingers. He did that before the ether really took effect. And...and it all still hurts like hell, I must say." She grimaced, touched bandages on her forehead, then gave a lopsided smile. "Even so, I was indeed fortunate. What happened? You must tell me. Was it my fault?"

Colt responded. "First let me express my sincere apologies. And, no...no, the mishap was not of your making." He shook his head and reached one hand out for hers. "The second shot after reload ignited weakly. Most likely a bad percussion cap." Emily let her free hand rest in his. "That round, I'm certain, still fouled the barrel when you fired again. So the third ball and propellant had nowhere to go, except outward and rearward."

Emily West removed her hand and folded her free arm under the sling. She turned quiet, then dozed off. Carriage motions jostled Sam Colt, wide-eyed, in his seat. He looked at her and smiled his relief. She slept.

This accident could not thwart his plans and dreams of a new weapon. A pistol that afforded the ultimate battlefield advantage - rapid, accurate firepower. First matter of business, though, was to make matters right with his new associate, Emily West. Keep her committed to him and his project. She knew how to use guns. With that and her uncommon beauty, she ought to be able to sell them.

He had inventory, more than two hundred complete pistols, plus enough parts for another hundred or so. Better inspect that supply of percussion caps, for sure. Just as soon as he could get Emily West fit to travel, she was bound for South Carolina and Florida. And when he'd met those commitments, maybe they'd head for Texas together. Emily would bring home the cash, wherever they went.

Chapter Eleven

Carolina Conflict - Spring and Summer 1839

A bouquet of daisies on the linen-draped table separated Samuel Colt and Emily West. She sipped vintage Dom Perignon, while the staff of the Windust prepared dinner table side. Sam Colt gazed at his protégé. Barely three weeks since the accident, but he'd brought Emily to downtown New York for meetings with critical suppliers to the Paterson Arms Company. As far as Sam was concerned, dining at Windust this evening was a celebration of Emily's remarkable recovery and her assistance with the negotiations.

He'd been around attractive, strong women before. Had sometimes enjoyed their intimacy. Sam had even fallen for such women more than once. But something about Emily was different. She was half-white. Primal, in a sense. Yet intelligent and quite shrewd. She could never be subjugated. The waiter jarred Colt from his frustrated reverie with their entrees.

Emily West grasped her knife and fork. "Mr. Colt, how did the recent tests of the new firing mechanism go? You know better than I that we need to deliver the South Carolina order soon."

She cut into her veal and smiled, then put down her utensils. More on her mind than dinner? Sam held his knife and fork, waiting. He was famished.

"Then too, the guns for Florida." She persisted. "For the Seminole war. What about that order?"

Sam Colt stared down at his food. Ever the businesswoman, ever the warrior. Sam looked up at Emily again. Her burns were healing well, but patches of redness still marked her face and bare arms. They had to be painful. Even with the bandages gone, she'd need at least another month before he could dispatch her on the South Carolina mission. Sam took a bite and put down his knife and fork, dabbing the napkin at his bearded chin.

"Miss West. For God's sake, Emily," he spoke with his most serious demeanor, "last week I implemented the improvements we tested. I'll have eighty, maybe a hundred refurbished revolvers for South Carolina ready within the month." He put out one hand. "We can address Florida when South Carolina is done. At least then I'll have something more, more money at least, in this empty hand."

Sam Colt hoped he didn't show his discouragement. He considered the private letters he'd exchanged with Millard Luke Bonham, state senator and head of the South Carolina Militia Procurement Committee. The politician had claimed official reluctance to consummate the arms deal. Bonham's stated concern? The new weapon had never been in federal military use, an arguable mandate under the Militia Act of 1808.

Sam had countered that President Jackson had personally approved the Paterson Colt. From Sam's perspective, nothing more than petty squabbling between generals had blocked the procurement. Damn it all, the South Carolina Congressman already knew all this, just more political maneuvering and bickering to try and land a better deal.

Sam had advised Bonham that he was sending his personal envoy to deliver the weapons, perform training and collect payment. He'd sent Emily's official credentials to Senator Bonham. The Senator had acquiesced, agreed to meet with her and complete the transaction, subject to final demonstration of the Colt pistol's function and use.

Sending a woman, a Colored at that, to a Southern state to sell arms and ammunition, to train openly bigoted White boys in the use of tools of war? Then she was to collect payment and return north? Hers was one hell of a tall order, and an abundant risk, even for someone like Emily West.

• • •

The small booster steam engine on the "Jersey" fired up for the voyage to Charleston. Smoke billowed from a vertical stack amidships. Two burly, off-duty New York policemen in Sam Colt's temporary employ struggled to secure almost three hundred pounds of weapons – four wooden crates – in the ship's hold.

"Captain Willmott," Sam Colt addressed the ship's captain. "May I present my assistant, Miss Emily West."

Edmund Willmott, graying hair and muttonchops framing a round, ruddy face, swept off his gold braided black-billed cap and bowed. The short, stocky ships' captain with a bulbous red nose wore a double-breasted white jacket and black trousers. His bow to West was enough to be proper, not quite enough to show full respect for Emily's position with the Colt Arms Company.

"Miss West," Sam spoke, eyes fixed on Captain Willmott, "Is to be treated as my personal representative aboard your vessel. She is on an authorized mission for the Colt Arms Company to deliver a substantial quantity of weapons and ammunition to the militia of South Carolina."

Captain Willmott nodded and droned his response, "I assure you, sir, Miss West shall be accorded every courtesy while aboard this vessel, and every safeguard shall be undertaken for your shipment." The Captain bowed a bit further this time, waving his cap. "Miss West will be offered a seat next to me at the captain's table each evening. My engineering officer will attend her whenever she is on deck." He smiled openly at Emily, then turned back to Sam, serious. "Neither racial innuendos nor spurious remarks as to an unaccompanied woman will be tolerated on my ship."

Colt smiled and shook the Captain's hand. Things were in order. He'd reviewed Willmott's history before booking the journey. Besides, Emily could call on the two New York policemen traveling with her if needed. And, as a last line of defense, she had a newly upgraded Paterson Colt in her valise. Emily would be fine.

"Bon voyage, Emily." Samuel Colt said and tipped his newest beaver pelt hat. "Safe journey. I'm certain you'll be successful. And by the time you return," he added, "I'll have completed the assembly of at least another hundred weapons for either Florida or Texas."

"Samuel Colt," Emily responded, her eyes moist and piercing, "I'll miss New York. You as well. Charleston is a great city, but I've never been comfortable there. And don't worry about the South Carolina Militia matter. In a few weeks, you shall have your money. Ample funds for ongoing production."

They'd have money if the woman could work her charms on that bastard, Millard Bonham. He'd find pleasure in that. But the congressman was a sleazy character. A bit of a lecher, a bigot who might feel entitled to take liberties with an attractive mulatto woman. No matter, Emily was strong. Wouldn't take anybody's guff. Emily West could handle a tough situation. And besides, she was delivering his revolutionary repeater pistols. The South Carolina Militia could ill afford to reject them.

A smile from Emily broke the seriousness of the moment. Colt moved in to give his employee a farewell kiss, just for luck. Emily West turned her head and his pursed lips landed on one cheek. Colt reddened, then turned and shook hands with the two policemen in her entourage. Overhead, a shrill steam whistle blew a single alert, announcing the ship's impending departure. He needed to leave. Sam Colt waved goodbye with his hat and headed down the gangplank.

• • •

Sam Colt had the morning to himself and welcomed the quiet. One shipment of cylinders was missing. Two workers hadn't shown up at six o'clock on the assembly line. The constable had them in jail. Something about a bar brawl the evening before.

No news from Emily either. She should be in the thick of

training the South Carolina militia about now. Sam had difficulty imagining just how Emily might have gone about her mission, but she was a resourceful sort. She'd be fine.

Noise erupted in the hallway. Some kind of altercation? What the bloody hell?

A thud and Emily West crashed through his half-open office door, mayhem or worse flashing in her green eyes. Sam Colt bounced to his feet. Emily's lethal side was on full display. The desk clutter piled in front of Sam offered no protection. What the hell? God, she'd not even been three weeks away in South Carolina.

"You, Samuel Colt," she shouted, her gloved hand in a tight fist. "You are a conniving, low-life, despicable sonofabitch. You dispatched me to do the undoable. To…to prostitute myself with some thick-headed, fat, racist pig!"

West moved in and leaned across his desk. The sweep of her hand sent a pistol hammer and spring sailing into the wall. Sam Colt put both hands in the air.

"For what?" She shouted. "To sell a few pistols? Make you a little money?"

Sam Colt came around his desk. "Emily, my God, what happened? What could have gone awry?" He extended one hand toward a chair. "Please, please sit down. I can explain whatever you've encountered. We can get past whatever happened."

Well, he'd certainly miscalculated this time. What had Millard Bonham said? What prurient moves had he, or someone, made that had set the woman into a rage that lasted the entire boat trip back? Better not ask for details.

Did she still have the pistols and ammunition? Damn it, man, that wasn't the priority right now.

Sam tried to grasp Emily's arm. He moved a chair toward her. West spun and shoved him away with both hands. She lifted the shopworn piece of furniture. By Heaven, the woman was strong. Emily tossed the chair clattering and skidding across the room. Old wood shattered. Bits of cane flew in all directions. Emily West crossed her arms and glared, then paced left and right in front of Sam.

"You...you," West stammered, uncrossing her arms and waving them. "You purposely did not give me all the facts! Caution me about the risks! Like sending men on a suicide mission without telling them!"

"No, Emily, no." Samuel Colt shot back. "I told you all I knew. We both knew the task wouldn't be easy. We agreed on that much before you left." He pulled over a second chair. "Please, sit down and hear me out. We can still get this done."

West kicked the chair away. "People have used me to dubious advantage, but none...never more deviously than you." Her green eyes glared. "First you tried to kill me with that damnable contraption, then you dispatched me to South Carolina where you knew I'd fail." She threw up her arms. "And you've still not paid me a cent! Your...your 'slave girl.' We are done, Mister Colt. Done. Finished."

Emily West turned away. One fashionable boot heel dug into the floor planking when she pivoted and stormed for the door. Her ankle-length skirt swirled and rustled. God, the woman was beautiful, even outraged. Sam's rickety oak office door slammed behind her. The dry, poorly varnished wood splintered with a short, loud crack. A brass knob slipped from the inside socket and fell, wobbling slowly across the floor. The tarnished hardware rolled to rest at his feet.

Sam Colt stared at the half-open door. She'd be back as soon as she settled down. They had unfinished business.

Chapter Twelve

Pistols for the Botanist - January 1840

Hard to believe she'd let Samuel Colt talk her into coming back to work for the Colt Arms Company. He'd sounded pathetic and desperate, and, after all, Emily did need the money. When this stint with Colonel Bayley and his raggedy-assed Florida regiment was done, she'd better be well rewarded for putting up with such bumpkins and bastards. These Floridians made people in Texas, if Emily could ever get back to them, seem easy to deal with.

She'd waited a long time for a day like this. Ten dusty, unshaven men stood on the firing line, a double arms' length separating each one. The Florida militiamen wore planters' dress, square-cut white or tan shirts stuffed into pantaloons or trousers. White belts crossed their chests under dark-colored, open vests. Some wore straw hats. Others, cloth foraging caps. All wore crude, unpolished shoes or boots. Today, each man held a loaded, half-cocked Paterson Colt revolver in one hand, pointed down range. Emily West, in leather pants, polished riding boots and white blouse, her eyes shaded by a broad-brimmed straw hat, paced the line five yards behind the squad. Emily's hard work, all the sacrifice, would start to pay off if these men could be trained.

"Ready and steady on the line." West shouted, looking left to right. "Remember the drill. If you hear 'cease fire,' that by God means no more shooting."

She took a breath. Were they ready? Was she capable of controlling this rabble?

"On my command of 'fire at will'," Emily announced. "You are to fully cock and discharge your first five rounds, exchange cylinders from your pouches and engage the targets with another five rounds. Understood?"

One or two nods, but more side-to-side head shakes and grumbling came from the hard-faced, sullen troops. She eyed their firing positions, pacing left then right along the silent, rag-tag line. Only two of the men had paid Emily any attention at all when she'd shown them the firing and reloading process and given the safety talk. Even those two had mostly leered, looking her up and down. They'd been openly insulting, practically undressed her with their eyes.

"Missy, you don't worry none 'bout me and my boys," Corporal Johnny Edwards, the squad leader, had said through broken yellow teeth and cracked lips. "We been shootin' Redskins and runaway niggers a long time." He'd waved his new Paterson Colt in her face. "You ever git tired a' playing with these here toy pistols, I'll let you play with a real gun, pretty girl."

Emily came back to the present. "Gentlemen," Why the hell was she addressing these loathsome men with such a polite term? "You may fire at will."

Ten random metallic clicks sounded along the firing line. The first volleys cracked and zipped down range. Dust kicked up where the errant rounds struck. Very few rounds hit their targets. One board splintered, then two more split in half. Emily strode behind the group, one hand resting on her own holstered Paterson Colt pistol, the other over one ear. Terrible marksmen they were, but no problems mechanically, so far. Most of the squad exchanged cylinders and began their second round of firing.

A muffled, percussive thump erupted on her right. Not the Paterson Colt's normal sharp muzzle report, but a dull thud. Emily knew that sound. Big trouble. Either a bad percussion cap or fouled breech. She dashed toward the third militiaman down the line.

"Cease fire," Emily shouted. Shots still echoed, left and right, non-stop. "Cease fire on the line, dammit!"

A louder, ear splitting crack exploded and grew into ominous rolling echoes. The right side of her firing line disappeared into a blue-black cloud, lit with long fingers of reddish-yellow flame. Hats, caps, pistols and pistol fragments, soared into the air. The uncontrolled explosion swallowed fully one-third of the men. The rest of the squad flattened themselves in the dirt. No damned "Cease fire" with these insolent flatlanders.

Emily dashed toward the expanding cloud. Two bent and bloody militiamen, supporting each other, staggered out of the gun smoke and debris. West ran past the two as they collapsed in the sand. Smoke and dust drifted away from the explosion site. A third militiaman now visible, lay motionless on his side. Emily gripped one shoulder with both hands and rolled him onto his back. Blood pooled and soaked into the sandy soil under an open head wound. The side of his face was gone. One empty eye socket stared back at her. Broken teeth lined the bare jawbone. Brain matter, pinkish in the sunlight, bulged where the side of his skull had been. Two bad accidents already last week, and now? Well, this boy was dead for sure.

• • •

West sat in Colonel W. J. Bayley's sparse office, summoned for yet another official debriefing. The Colonel, sour-faced with a skin pallor that matched his drab gray uniform, sat with a sheaf of papers in one hand. He stopped reading and looked up at her across the rickety table. A Colt repeater pistol, the empty cylinder extracted, lay between them. So who'd get the blame? Her? Maybe Sam Colt's pistols? For certain, not the inattentive, surly bastards in the Florida militia.

"Miz West," Colonel Bayley spoke in his heavy Florida drawl, barely above a whisper. "Mo' bad news, Ah'm afraid. I simply no longer trust this here Paterson Colt." He pointed at the weapon on the table. "My boys don't neither. When the damn contraption works, ain't nothing like it." Colonel Bayley's countenance darkened. "But we got us three big misfires lately. Now we got a dead boy, too." Colonel

Bayley thrust the papers across the table. "They all yo' company's problems from bad metal or goddamn new-fangled design, I reckon."

"Colonel Bayley," Emily spoke, knowing the man wouldn't admit any culpability, "I and Mr. Colt regret the incidents. And though there's always risk, a fatality is the most serious matter." She hefted the Colt revolver and snapped the cylinder into the frame. "As I've told you, we are most familiar with the malfunction. I have been a victim myself. There's little to do with design in this case, most likely the percussion cap." She put the weapon down and spoke with authority. "I personally inspected all the weapons, the lot. The real problem though was discipline, or lack of such on the part of your men."

The Colonel wouldn't look at her. He shook his head side-to-side. What more could she say to convince Colonel Bayley that Sam Colt's invention was what he needed for the Seminole War? This venture with the Florida Militia was finished. Probably just as well. She had another idea.

"Colonel, you know as certainly as I," she weighed her next words. "Your men certainly were not blameless. Not in this last incident. My 'cease fire' command was completely ignored."

Bayley snorted and stared up at the ceiling. He crossed his arms. Emily had had to say it. Most of the Florida militiamen could neither read nor write, and none of them paid her any professional attention or respect. The boys were more interested in verbally abusing and mentally undressing her than learning to use the repeater pistol. Was any of that in the Colonel's reports?

"My men, madam," Colonel Bayley spoke, louder now, "will take their chances, single shot, against the Seminoles, rather than risk being felled by Mister Colt's mad machine. Collect your weapons and leave us be. There'll be no recompense from the Florida Territory Treasury." Colonel Bayley rose from his chair, handed her the Colt revolver and guided West by one elbow toward the door.

"Good day, Miss West." the Colonel said. "You may collect your weapons and any remaining ammunition an hour after reveille tomorrow. I'll hear no more."

The door shut behind her. Emily West walked toward the light at the end of the dank Militia Headquarters hallway and stepped into the cool humidity of winter in south Florida. Felt just like Galveston Bay this time of year, but this was definitely not Texas.

She might be leaving this assignment, but Emily was not going back to New Jersey having failed. Sam Colt needed money. She did, too. And besides, the damned pistols worked when they were properly loaded, fired and kept clean. Another few days in Florida shouldn't be a problem, not if her second plan worked.

• • •

Two days later, Emily West stood at the starboard railing of the coastal steamer and felt the comforting thump of the engine through the deck boards. Indian Key was smaller than she'd imagined, certainly not as developed as Key West had been five years back. Sweaty, dark dockhands guided the vessel to a berth alongside a small pier. The gangplank secured, she disembarked behind one other passenger, leaving the weapons crates secured in the ship's hold. Sweat beaded on her neck. Even in the winter, the sticky heat this far south in the Florida Keys was palpable.

Emily dabbed with her kerchief at the moisture and pushed her way, carpetbag in hand, past laborers bustling around the small ship. These men were either prisoners or slaves, judging from their ankle chains and filthy off-white clothes. She followed the sandy walkway through botanical gardens toward the Charles Howe Mansion, the tiny island's largest house. The mansion loomed in the distance above the vegetation. Tropical growth, green foliage with flowering reds, blues and yellows, punctuated and perfumed the stagnant air along the path. For Emily's new plan to work, her meeting with Dr. Henry Perrine must go well.

The botanist's red brick Victorian mansion dominated the jungle of plants and trees at the end of the path. Gables towered and a white-railed porch ran along three sides. The good doctor must have profited handsomely from his work since she'd first encountered him in Key West half a decade ago. Now, from what Emily had heard, the second Seminole uprising was getting in the way of Dr. Perrine growing and selling sisal. She had an answer for that.

West reached the foot of the front staircase. A manservant she remembered from years earlier greeted her and took her heavy valise, bowing without recognition. My God, André was still there. Doctor Perrine stood, hands on narrow hips on the covered veranda, peering out under an oversized straw hat. Emily lifted her skirt with one hand and climbed the stone steps.

"Doctor Perrine, I am Emily West." She smiled. "My employer, Samuel Colt and I wish to sincerely thank you for seeing me on such short notice."

The botanist shrugged and touched his hat brim, spectacles low on his nose and a sunken grin on his lips. God, the moist heat. Even in winter it was hard to breathe here. Or was it more Emily's nerves?

"I hasten to add," Emily remarked, "That my visit has nothing to do with botany, though I am intrigued by your exotic gardens."

"My passion," Doctor Perrine spoke with an elegant Northeastern accent. "Has always been to prove the commercial worth of my plantings." He wiped his brow with a white kerchief. "In the moment, though, I am hindered in my research and development by the local savages. You may be familiar with the Seminole. These simple folk have no appreciation for my work, and I cannot abide their wishes to keep these islands wild and primitive."

Perrine removed his hat and beckoned her into the mansion. Emily stepped into the cool, welcoming darkness. The botanist's office occupied one wing of the first floor. Aromatic wood paneled the walls and ceiling. Bookshelves, probably filled with reference books, stood along the wall behind his massive desk. Doctor Perrine seated her, and André positioned the valise at Emily's side. She accepted tea brought in by a second servant. The girl, probably Haitian, couldn't have been more than twelve, the age when Emily had started her own work as a servant.

West began, the cup and saucer on her lap. "You may recall hosting a dinner party for Captain James Morgan and others in his company several years ago. I attended that spectacular affair at your Key West residence."

Perrine nodded. Ah, a glimmer of recognition, then confusion, crossed his face. He took a sip of tea. The Doctor's small eyes scanned Emily from head to foot.

"Miss, uh, Miss West." Perrine scratched at stubble on his chin. "West is it now? Yes. Yes, it's coming back to me. You indeed were with Colonel Morgan and his party, headed to the wild frontier of Texas. But were you not introduced as the wife of my acquaintance at my dinner party, His Excellency, Lorenzo de Zavala?"

Emily smiled and looked down. Not up to her to go into the past. At least the doctor was ready to talk, ready to listen. She could see she'd piqued his interest.

"No matter," Doctor Perrine intoned. "Those were unusual times for us all. Though, I dare say we had quite the stormy evening, what with the weather and my friend John Houseman's untimely demise. Your party's hasty exit, too, always puzzled me. But enough of old times. What brings you to me today?"

"Good Sir. Doctor Perrine," Emily began her plea. "We all must play our part to advance the cause of liberty. So it was back then, and so it is today." Emily had to keep focused on selling pistols and not get caught up in the past. "To my point, you face the intrusion of, as you put it, Seminole savages. A considerable threat, not only to you and your enterprise, but to the liberty of Dade County itself. Perhaps a menace to the development of the entire Florida Territory."

Perrine nodded agreement. Emily West bent to one side and

opened the valise. She lifted out a Paterson Colt revolver and laid the weapon on his desk. The doctor's eyes widened, then he smiled broadly.

"You are a scientist. An inventor," Emily said, her voice earnest and direct. "My employer, Mr. Samuel Colt, is likewise an inventor. I am here at his behest to offer you and your security forces on Indian Key new weapons technology." She pointed to the pistol with an open hand. "With as few as fifty of these repeating pistols in the service of your private army, you can tip the scales of battle with the Seminoles."

Emily picked up the weapon and presented it to the Doctor. He grasped the pistol, grinned more with that strange line of a mouth. His frail thumb half-cocked the hammer. The Doctor knew pistols, liked what she'd brought. Now Emily just needed to close the deal.

She laid out wads, lead balls and percussion caps, cradled in paper, on his desk. Emily spent the next two hours demonstrating the mechanics of the pistol and its function.

"Miss West," Perrine said, waving the Colt revolver, "if this repeater works even half as well as it appears intended, I'll take it. I've gambled on far less certain matters and won."

He handed the weapon back to her, handle first. Emily smiled and put the pistol back in her valise. The trip to Florida would pay off after all, despite the failure of the Militia deal. She would demonstrate the Paterson Colt, develop a training routine for Dr. Perrine's forces and collect her payment. The look on Samuel Colt's face when she told him the story would be worth all the hassle of Florida.

"What say you, Madam?" Dr. Perrine brought Emily back to the present. "Are you willing to provide me a bit of sport?" He winked. "I am merely asking for a firing demonstration, Miss West. Then perhaps dinner with me and my Militia Commander this evening."

• • •

Emily West wondered how long she'd be in getting the good news to Samuel Colt. This wasn't the deal she'd gone to Florida to administer, but Doctor Perrine had bought the entire cache of weapons.

The training had gone well. First, she'd briefed his militia commander and two senior Haitian officers on the weapons' use and care. In less than a week on the firing range, Emily had run through drills and target practice with more than forty disciplined mercenaries. The Doctor's men, wherever he'd found them, were a far better lot than the boys she'd come across in the Florida Militia.

For Emily, this had been quite a favorable outcome. Sometimes revisiting the past indeed helped one celebrate the future. Wonder who'd said that? And what would Samuel Colt say to this latest turn of events?

She strode up the gangplank of the New York-bound coastal steamer. Emily presented her papers to the ship's captain. Minutes later, she followed the first officer to cramped but adequate quarters in a secure area of the vessel. If all went well, she'd be back in New York in a week at the most.

She nodded a silent goodbye to the Florida Keys fading in the distance over the railing of the ship. After two eventful visits in a decade, Emily had no plans to return.

Back in her quarters before dinner, Emily unlocked the sea chest at the foot of her bunk and checked the contents of her valise. Two thousand dollars in federal fifty-dollar banknotes lay in the folds of her red-and-brown carpetbag. She took her heavy leather purse from her shoulder and drew out a canvas pouch with another five-hundred dollars in Coronet Half Eagle gold coins. Those Emily secured in the chest as well. By God, now she was truly in business with Samuel Colt.

PART THREE

The Rangers

"Me and Red Wing not afraid to go to hell together. Captain Jack, he too mucho bravo. He not afraid to go to hell all by himself!"

Flacco the Younger, Lipan-Apache scout for the Texas Rangers, describing Captain Jack Hays leading a cavalry charge, his Paterson Colt revolvers blazing at a Comanche war party, while the rest of his unit struggled to keep pace.

Chapter Thirteen

Guns for the Republic - March 1840

Jack Hays sat in a cane chair in the General's office. He'd been a Captain only a week and already he was crossways with General Sam, but for what? If this was about the Council House raid in San Antone, he hadn't been involved. Hadn't even been near the place. Nor had anybody in his Ranger company. But then, General Houston knew that already.

On the other hand, Colonel William Cook, the man sitting next to Jack, had sure as hell taken part in that debacle. He'd been the senior officer in charge of the peace parley with twelve Comanche Chiefs and their families at the Council House last week. Didn't matter that Will Cook used to be head of the Texas Militia and was now President Mirabeau Lamar's Secretary of War. He was in real trouble with General Sam. So why did Jack have to be here?

"Dammit all to hell and back!" Sam Houston flung his copy of the March 24th printing of The Texas Sentinel across the room in fluttering pages. "Cook, I know I ain't President of the Republic no more," Houston pushed his x-frame military spectacles up the bridge of his nose, "but I am still a General. I'm orderin' you to tell me what the flamin' hell happened out there!"

Hays shifted his gaze to Colonel Cook, who squirmed uncomfortably in his squeaky chair. Houston poured Tennessee sour mash whiskey into a tin cup, then offered the flask to Jack. Jack waved away the pour. Colonel Cook motioned for a shot. Houston acquiesced and passed the whiskey.

Jack had read the headline article, what the Austin newspaper called "The Council House Fight." Nothing but a bloody massacre of peace seekers, if you were Comanche. Buffalo Hump and the other senior Comanche war chief, Peta Nokona, hadn't been there. Those two had refused peace talks or even any suggestions for releasing White hostages in exchange for land. So now, the devil's work would be afoot. These two Chiefs would plan some kind of revenge for all the killings of their people.

Houston eyed the Colonel and shouted, "How can a bunch of Comanche peace chiefs and their women and children end up bein' gunned down by our folks like goddamn fish in a rain barrel? I smell Mirabeau Lamar's shady doin's in all this, I reckon."

Sam Houston leaned back in his chair. The General took a deep draw from his tin. Was there any water at all in there? Probably not. Just whiskey today.

"General Sam." Colonel Cook spoke. "Now, I know your feelin's about Indians. By God, most talk is you're least half-Cherokee anyhow. Cherokee, Apache, even the damned Comanche, they all trust you. That said, it ain't a secret that you and President Lamar have your personal differences about dealin' with Redskin folk."

No reaction came from Sam Houston. Hays turned his eyes back to Colonel Cook. Comanches trusted General Sam? The Colonel took a sip of sour mash from his tin and cleared his throat. Pretty risky business, Colonel Cook saying General Sam was nothing but a lover of Indians, even if it was true.

"This Council House thing," Colonel Cook put one open

hand up. "It was all a terrible mistake. But…but that poor little girl they brought with them. Clothes ragged. Her all dirty, filthy, full of scars n' tattoos, and no nose." Cook made a slicing motion toward his face. "The savage bastards had cut her whole nose right off, Gen'ral Sam. For what reason, God in Heaven don't even know. Couldn't let 'em leave just like that, clean as a whistle."

Houston still had not moved, hadn't blinked. Goddamn, what was he thinking? What was the General going to do? No way was Colonel Cook going to get out easy. He'd lose some rank, or get a court martial. General Sam was pissed, anyone could see that.

"They had it comin'," Cook shouted. "And we lost some good men ourselves in that scrape. Don't forget that, General Sam."

Stony quiet, even now in the General's office. Jack didn't know Colonel Will very well, but the man must have had either giant balls or a real death wish, talking on like that. Reminded Jack of some of his own insubordinations. Nobody moved. Sam Houston's eyes were shut tight, like he might be praying.

"All right, Will. All right." Sam Houston opened his eyes and sighed. "Must've been truly hard seein' that girl and all. Don't envy you that." Houston stood and leaned on his cane. "But you know what the Comanche'll do now? This ain't finished, not by no means. Dammit." He waved the heavy cane at Colonel Cook. "For them, they're just gettin' started. They got to hit back, and it'll be bloody."

Houston slammed his cane down across his desk. Hays jumped, almost tipping out of his chair. Will Cook flinched and ducked.

"Our folks gonna die. Hundreds of 'em." Houston waved his cane around again. "We barely finished our fuckin' war with the Mexicans, now we got another on our hands with the Comanche, thanks to a bunch of squeamish, trigger-happy fools." He pointed the cane barely an inch from the Colonel's face. "Like you and your fuckin' man Mirabeau in Austin."

So, no respect for President Mirabeau Lamar. And Lamar had been General Sam's cavalry hero at San Jacinto, too. When – and perhaps more importantly, how – might Jack be excused from this confrontation? At least he wasn't the one riling up General Sam today.

The General sat down and leaned his cane beside the desk. Time crawled by like pouring molasses. Then Houston stood again, slow and stiff, and offered his hand to the Colonel. Now that was odd, considering the ranting and raving the General had done. And why was Jack here, seeing and hearing all this? Why hadn't General Sam done it the Army way: praise in public, chew ass in private?

"Colonel Cook. Will," Houston said. "Thanks for showin' up, even though you knew what was coming." Sam Houston leaned on his cane. "Now, in your official capacity, I need a favor. I want them 200 or so new repeater pistols, the ones we ordered for the Texas Navy a few months back, and I want 'em now."

Jack leaned forward in his chair. Repeating pistols? Navy? What the hell? He'd heard rumors of some fellow back east developing five-shot pistols. Rifles, too. Had General Sam ordered some already? And was he getting them for the fuckin' patrols against Mexicanos and common pirates in the Gulf? Why not for the Rangers going up against Indians and bandits? Now that would be a good reason for Jack being here and witnessing all this.

"I figure," Houston said, waving one hand toward Jack, "they'll be just what my boy Captain Jack here needs to beat back the Comanche and their like. I want 'em redirected and shipped to Hays and his company, pronto." Houston straightened himself and pointed the cane at Cook. "And one more thing, Will. I want you to find that goddamn Yankee, that pistol inventor, Samuel Colt. Get him the hell out here, along with his guns."

Cook nodded. A long time coming, but Jack now knew why he was at the meeting. Rangers were gonna get new pistols, and the fellow who made them was going to show him and his men how to use the damned things. About time Hays' Rangers got recognized for the tough boys he'd turned them into. More firepower was all they needed.

"Our boys'll need proper training," Houston said, glancing first at Jack, then eyeing Cook. "The last thing I want is Captain Hays here teachin' Rangers his horseshit idea of weaponry on his own." Houston turned to Jack. "That's it, Captain. You're dismissed."

Jack Hays stood, saluted both officers and headed for the door. He'd get repeater pistols, maybe at least two each. That was something the Comanche wouldn't be expecting. Wonder how they'd react? For that matter, how would he feel not needing to haul around three or four damned single-shot flintlocks? Pretty soon, he'd be carrying what amounted to ten flintlocks. Except, he'd only need two. From now on, war was going be different, maybe even a little fun.

Chapter Fourteen

The Warpath - Early June 1840

A lead-gray wall of approaching rain framed Buffalo Hump's village of beige and white tipis dotting the green plateau. Lightning streaked across the roiling thunderhead towering in the western sky. The storm was favorable medicine.

Rumbles of distant thunder from the Great Spirit's war drum overpowered the noise of hundreds of pony hooves clattering on the trail. Peta Nokona, bare-chested astride a gray Apaloosa, led his Nokoni warrior band into the sprawling Penateka village. Yellow Wolf and a band of Yamparikas trailed the last of the Nokoni war party. Iron Jacket had already arrived with his Quahadi band, more than two hundred warriors, a day earlier.

Buffalo Hump walked the path between long lines of young Comanche braves, honing the points of war lances and making arrows. He nodded to others sitting under tipi flaps, painting sacred buffalo emblems on leather and wooden shields. Women, soaked to the skin from an earlier downpour, scurried about in the mesquite bushes gathering wood for the war fire that Buffalo Hump had ordered lit when the thunderstorms passed.

He would make war. Kill White Faces. Buffalo Hump had lost his most trusted peace envoy, Chief Muragua, in the Council House Massacre. Thirty-five Comanche, among them twelve peace chiefs, had been gunned down either inside the White Faces' meeting house, or in the streets of San Antonio. They'd died like running dogs. Some thirty more Penatekas and Nokoni had later been imprisoned there. Buffalo Hump would never again talk of peace.

But could General Sam Houston have been part of this slaughter? No matter now, his people – Texas Army and Rangers – had done the evil deed.

At the last full moon, Buffalo Hump had resolved what must be done to return balance and order to his world. He had ordered the White Face hostages in his camp to be ceremonially executed. The ones he'd punished had not been the offenders, they were nothing more than surrogates. Other White Faces in San Antonio and Austin, their Paraibos, had left him no choice.

To show Buffalo Hump's deepest despair with the Council House slaughter, he'd chosen the most severe and ancient Penateka retribution, ritual death by fire. The Chief personally selected two young White Face boys and tied them to spits and roasted them alive. The Chief had forced their parents and the rest of his hostages to attend the ceremony, then had come his more merciful killing of the rest.

He'd spared one White Face woman to carry his message to Austin. Buffalo Hump gave her a fast pony. He instructed her to ride to the White Faces, tell them of the ritual deaths she had witnessed. Tell them she had seen Numunuh justice.

Still, there was no satisfaction. Even these executions did not restore equilibrium for Buffalo Hump. Chief Muragua's death and that of the other great Numunuh warriors and their families required further acts. All Comanche held by the White Faces had to be released. More intruders on Numunuh land had to die soon. Great spoils and many captives should be taken. A quiet order, peace at last, entered Buffalo Hump's thoughts. He considered the war council to come.

• • •

Buffalo Hump, Chief of the Penatekas and the Comanches' strongest war chief, sat cross-legged in front of his council fire. The oldest war chief, Iron Jacket, and the second youngest, Yellow Wolf, flanked Buffalo Hump. Peta Nokona, youngest of nine chiefs present, sat across from him. The heavy rain pelting the longhouse and constant thunder could not dampen the will and war spirit of the council. Everybody had lost family members or comrades in the San Antonio Massacre of the first Spring Moon.

No Numunuh peace chiefs were left alive to attend the conclave, nor would they have been invited. Buffalo Hump called no medicine men to the council. He would not permit talk of peace ever again, and he required no advice from shamans. Buffalo Hump's medicine was strong enough.

He addressed the gathering. "My Brothers, though we come together from separate camps, none is above the other in importance. No war chief was required to join this council. We must avenge the senseless killings of our people." Buffalo Hump made a sweeping motion with one hand. "You come here with your band to be part of a mighty war party, a great raid. Together, we will make war that Numunuh will speak of in legends to their children and grandchildren."

The Chief waited. Silence. Shifting torsos made the only sounds. Iron Jacket's coat of Spanish chain mail rustled, glistening in the light of the council fire. The oldest war chief turned to face Buffalo Hump. He nodded once, chin touching his metal-clad chest.

Eyes shut, the Chief put one hand on the shoulder of the eldest warrior's metal jacket. Now he had Immortal Iron Jacket's blessing. There would be no mercy to White Faces. Buffalo Hump opened his eyes and surveyed the circle of chiefs.

"We are fewer than before," Buffalo Hump said, determination in his voice. "White Face attacks and White Face pestilence reduce our numbers. Even so, the Great Mystery protects us who remain. He makes our medicine strong. Soon, our great fire will burn." He stood and raised his hands. "We will sing and dance to celebrate war and the victory to come."

Buffalo Hump ducked down at the door and led the war council out of his longhouse. The Comanche War Chiefs took their places near the massive pile of mesquite. Buffalo Hump positioned

Iron Jacket on the right, the place of honor. Then the Penateka Chief moved away from the group, shed his buffalo robe and gripped his war axe. Buffalo Hump would make this a celebration no Numunuh would ever forget.

The rain had passed and Buffalo Hump motioned for women to light the fire. Low drums began a barely audible beat somewhere in the gathering dusk. More than four hundred armed warriors in war paint and full battle dress danced past Buffalo Hump in one line, bowing and swaying to the rhythmic thumping. The warriors snaked around until the line joined to form a great circle around the growing flames.

Outside the circle, Buffalo Hump signaled with his war axe for more women and children and apprentice braves – boys just learning combat skills – to gather around the outer perimeter. Soon, two thousand feet propelled his Great Comanche War Party. Left and right, forward and back, bodies undulating in unison closer to the war fire and then backing away.

The drumbeat quickened and grew louder. His time had come. Buffalo Hump bent low and danced into the circle. He emerged out of the smoke east of the fire. His cobalt blue war vest trimmed in white beads and fringed in red leather covered his bare chest and back. Brown, fringed and red-beaded leggings extended to the Chief's bare feet. Four eagle feathers plaited with red and black rawhide hung in the Chief's long tails of coal black hair. Buffalo Hump's painted face, a mask of black and white, reflected the fire. The Chief of the Penatekas signaled his readiness for the battle to come.

Buffalo Hump glided with high, deliberate steps clockwise around the circle. He swung his iron war axe in a slow, menacing arc. The Chief moved first south, then west, then north in the sacred direction of the sun and moon.

He came full circle back to the east. Drums fell silent. The War Chief lifted his head and thrust the iron axe toward the low, gray clouds. Buffalo Hump let out the great war cry. The sound, like a hundred screaming eagles, echoed back from the hills and down from the clouds.

Then Buffalo Hump spread his arms and waved his war axe side-to-side. He had traced the path of sun and moon. The Penateka Chief had loosed the great war cry. His duty to make sure all were under the Great Mystery's divine protection was done.

"This time tomorrow, my brothers and sisters," Buffalo Hump rasped, his voice hardened by the ear-splitting scream. "By the Blood Moon's light, we ride to glorious battle. We do not fear the enemy's medicine. Ours is stronger. Our cause is just."

He raised his war axe again. The weapons of the assembly followed skyward in unison. Buffalo Hump stepped onto a boulder, the surface under the Chief's bare feet shone wet in the firelight.

"They are the devils. They are the cowards." Buffalo Hump warned the gathering. "We will avenge our brothers and sisters who fell in their village. We will free our captives. We will burn their dwelling places." He took a breath. "We, the Numunuh, will drive these intruders and their scourges from our land forever."

The drumbeat started again, soft and steady. Buffalo Hump vaulted from the rock and moved toward the knot of war chiefs by the fire. He began the Comanche Raid Chant. Warriors, women and children joined in with low and lyrical voices. He danced, and they followed, dancing to the drums and chanting. His Numunuh, more than a thousand strong, began their evening of war celebration around the fire.

We all go on a warpath
So let us dance and sing
We now go off to see a land
That we have never seen.
And when we've won, we all will feast
Upon a colt that's young and lean

Chapter Fifteen

Comanches and Colts - North Central Texas - June 1840

Captain Jack Hays lay propped on his elbows on a grassy slope with Chief Flacco to his side. He peered through the eyepiece of his Hicks single-draw telescope. Silhouetted in the first full moon of summer, a long line of Comanche warriors rode down the steep path and switchbacks of the escarpment. Had to be more than five, maybe six hundred of the bastards, most mounted on ponies, and most carrying lances or war clubs and axes. Several warriors held muskets that gave off telltale reflections in weak moonlight.

Earlier, Flacco and Red Wing had shadowed Peta Nokona and Iron Jacket's war parties headed to Buffalo Hump's conclave. Jack had reported the Comanche pow-wow to General Sam, and he'd ordered Jack out of garrison to their present position. Jack had force-marched his unit three nights to get here.

Hundreds of Comanche women and children made up the rear party, either on horseback or walking. At least half of them dragged travois loaded with tipis and supplies. This was no ordinary summer raid, and no, these Comanche were certainly not leaving their homeland. The bastards were on the warpath. But to where? Should he violate his "no-fire" order from General Sam and stop them? He could do it, here and now.

"This bad, Captain Jack," Chief Flacco whispered. "Comanche make war soon. Big war somewhere. We attack. Stop Buffalo Hump now."

Flacco wanted to ambush them. He did, too. Like every Texas Ranger, Jack had studied "Roger's Rules for Ranging," and he had at least three key elements of ambush going for him: surprise, cover and concealment. He also had sixty tough Rangers lying along a low ridge with weapons trained on the descending Comanche war column. All Jack had to do was fire the first shot and his men would rain lead on the Comanche. He might even prevail, despite being outnumbered ten-to-one. But even if Jack kicked their ass and lived to tell the tale, he'd be done as a Ranger captain. General Houston would either lock him up or run him off for disobeying orders.

"Maybe Captain Jack and Flacco die," his scout whispered cautiously. "But we kill Chief Erection That Not Go Down. Tonight, Comanche be finished."

Jack had to smile. Flacco despised the Comanche. He'd whispered the literal translation of Buffalo Hump's true tribal name, "Po-cha-na-quar-hip." But goddamnit, just no getting around that written order signed by General Houston about "not firing unless attacked – recon only" that was tucked away in Jack's pommel bag. He let the Indians ride on.

• • •

Captain Jack Hays stormed into General Sam Houston's office in Austin. He'd ridden the 80 miles from Ranger headquarters in San Antone hard so he could speak his mind. Hays snapped his short-billed sea cap off and slammed it down on Houston's desk. Papers fluttered off to one side in the rising dust. Houston looked up, put down his quill pen and pulled the spectacles down his nose.

"Dammit all, Gen'ral Sam," Jack screeched through his black beard and moustache. "Less'n a month ago we had Buffalo Hump in our sights. Could have hit his whole red-assed bunch in the dark before they could go anywhere." He took a breath. "Just using three Ranging Rules, me and the boys would've killed half of them before they ever knew where we was." Jack's chest heaved as he waved both arms and spoke. "Sir, that fuckin' no-fire order from you.... Observe and report." Jack took another breath and swore. "Bullshit, Sir! That's what that was. Pure bullshit."

No reaction came from the Texas Militia Commander. Jack picked up his cap and dusted it off. Damn, he'd overdone things this time. Felt a little like Colonel Cook must have felt back last March with General Sam.

So what now, the stockade? Dammit though, why have a fighting unit that didn't fight? The Comanche had gone and beat them again.

"Son," Sam Houston pointed the quill pen at him, "you best simmer down and shut that insubordinate hole in your face hair."

The General opened a drawer and laid some kind of new weapon on the desk. Never seen anything like that before. A pistol that looked like it must weigh three or four pounds at least. Was this thing the new repeater from that inventor, Colt?

"I could've shot you five times already," Houston waved the weapon in the air, "but, maybe not. My draw, I reckon it's somewhat slower'n yours." Houston used his thumb to rotate some kind of cylinder near the gun's half-cocked hammer. "Goddamnit, sit down before I break the handle on this here new Paterson Colt over your thick Tennessee skull."

Jack took a seat. Needed to keep his mouth shut, but the General had made a mistake. Jack's unit could've prevented the Victoria and Linnville attacks, even with their old flintlocks. Damn, that was indeed a fine-looking pistol, though.

"Now you listen here, boy." Houston groused. "You know well as I do, hell, everybody in Texas knows. Buffalo Hump and his bunch are on the warpath. What'd you expect after Council House? Goddamn tea and roses?" Houston took out a handkerchief and blew his nose. "You thought they'd just lick their wounds and bury dead Peace Chiefs? Then what? Go back to huntin' buffalo?"

"But sir," Jack Hays raised a hand, pleading, "that bastard Buffalo Hump roasted boys like barbecue. Gutted prisoners. Now he's killed more. Burned folks outta house and home south of here, Victoria and Linnville." Jack took a breath. "Goddamnit, sir, you saw the reports. More'n twenty dead. A thousand horses gone. Comanche linin' the levees, all dressed up in top hats n' finery they stole from the mercantiles." Jack crossed his arms on his chest. "Right shameful, I'd say."

Sam Houston stood and grabbed the pistol. Jack froze in his chair. The General darted around his desk – damn quick without that cane, too. Houston rapped Jack Hays across one knee with the long barrel of the new Colt.

"Damn you, sonny!" Houston bellowed, "I can read. I know what happened in the Great Comanche Raid." Houston stared down at him with one hand leaning on his desk. "And by the bye, I can recite all twenty-eight of Major Rogers' goddamn Rules for Ranging, you insolent little shit. Nothing more than fuckin' infantry and patrollin' tactics." Houston went back around his desk. "I'm a strategist, not a goddamn' tactician, boy. And I'm in charge of the military, if you hadn't noticed. That includes you and your bunch of misfit maniacs."

Looked like the General wasn't through with the ass chewing.

"I brought you here to clean up the Rangers," Sam Houston proclaimed as he sat again. "And by God, you've done the job. You've shown yourself a man. I'll see that you have your shot at the Comanche soon enough." Houston calmed down a little. "We wasn't ready for war with the Indians yet, Jack. But we will be." Houston waved that damned pistol at him again. "Tomorrow noon, you be at that main firin' range in San Antonio. I'm comin' there myself. Me and Colonel Cook got some folks you'll be pleased to get more acquainted with."

Jack Hays sat rubbing a painful kneecap. Hurt like hell. Was that his only punishment? At least he had a better idea about what he'd be doing come tomorrow.

• • •

Unbelievable. Jack took a deep breath. Emily West, the same woman he'd met years back at the Comanche hostage parley, had just fired five rounds into a man-sized wooden board fifty yards down range. The shot group was tighter than the diameter of Jack's field cap. His ears rang and buzzed. Emily West dropped her hands and exchanged cylinders with the Yankee from New Jersey standing next to her. She snapped the second loaded magazine into the pistol frame with a metallic thump and returned to a firing stance.

Jack Hays stood behind her on the firing line. General Sam and Colonel Cook were ten yards back in the shade. Emily West's face was partly hidden by a broad-brimmed, white straw hat. Was that the same green scarf wrapped around her graceful neck that she'd worn a couple of years back at the Comanche hostage negotiation? West's long, leather-clad arms extended to gloved hands that gripped the still-smoking, strange looking pistol. The dandy dressed fellow beside her with both fingers in his ears was the inventor General Sam had introduced, Samuel Colt.

Five more rounds hammered a second man-size wooden plank and presented pretty much the same shot pattern as before. Damn, the woman had fired ten kill shots in less time than a Comanche warrior could've launched the same number of arrows. Jack smiled, happy to get reacquainted with the woman he'd encountered three years earlier on the plains. But he was more excited to see Samuel Colt's repeating pistol in action.

"Awright, Captain Hays," Sam Houston spoke from somewhere behind Jack, "you're up, son. Let's see how you handle Mister Colt's repeater."

Why the hell had the General taken to calling him "son?" Jack was almost twenty-three now, a grown man and a Texas Ranger captain and Indian wars veteran. He frowned and took a second loaded pistol from Emily West. He waved West and Colt back from the firing line – Jack needed room.

He half-cocked the Paterson Colt and sauntered left along the firing line. Then, still pacing, Jack full-cocked the pistol, steadied the weapon across an extended forearm, and fired his first shot. The ball splintered the top of the first board. Hays cocked the hammer again and again, kept firing as he walked. Four of his rounds hit their target, head or chest shots.

Where the devil had the other round gone? Jack handed the pistol to Samuel Colt. A wisp of smoke curled from the heated barrel.

"Great shooting, Captain!" Samuel Colt shouted. "Never seen anything like that. No sir." Colt handed Jack a belted leather contraption with another pistol. "Strap this on. I call it a quick-draw holster. More practical than trying to stuff my repeater in your pants. Safer, and a lot quicker, too."

Jack smiled and buckled the heavy belt. So far, he had mixed feelings about Sam Colt. A real dandy dresser. A little woman-like. Sorta queer. And the Yankee sure was a kiss-ass. But Colt's repeater could be just what Jack needed to deal with the Comanche bastards.

A nod to the inventor, then Jack pulled the pistol from the holster several times. Damn, that felt real good. He turned his back to the target area, made sure the repeater was holstered again, and waved that he was ready.

"Come on, Captain," Sam Houston leaned on his cane. The General's gravelly voice boomed at him from the shade and echoed off the berm down range, "you gonna show off now?" Houston waved his cane at Jack. "You ain't gonna live long, showin' your backside like that to the goddamn Indians and Mexicanos. I'm buying dinner at the Menger for everybody if you hit a damn thing this time."

Jack Hays wheeled around, drew the Colt pistol, and dropped toward a prone position. He full-cocked the hammer and fired down range two-handed as he fell. The round split the top of Jack's target board before he came to rest on his forearms, the pistol still in both hands. He fired four more rounds, with his head up and body flat. The board shattered into splinters from the force of the massive forty-caliber balls.

"My God," Emily West shouted, "That display took less than ten seconds. Captain Hays, our congratulations!" She turned to face the General and Colonel Cook. "I, for one, am certainly looking forward to General Houston's dinner this evening."

. . .

Jack Hays sat at one end of the long oak table and sipped a mug of dark ale. William Menger, proprietor of the Menger Boarding House and Brewery, sat to one side of him, with Colonel Cook to his left. Emily West and Samuel Colt were seated opposite Menger and Cook, and General Sam Houston sat at the opposite end of the table, smiling at Jack and wiping his mouth with a kerchief.

General Sam was paying for dinner all around. Jack would tell his children that story some day if he ever got married and had kids. It was a simple meal of enchiladas and beans with lots of tomatoes and chili peppers, washed down with a strong ale from German immigrant William Menger's brewery next door. Jack had asked for champagne for Emily West. Instead, she chose pints of ale, same as the men.

Jack finally responded to persistent questions from General Houston, "Yes sir, I did shoot a man in a Nacogdoches saloon a few years back. Place wasn't near as nice as Mr. Menger's here, though." Jack turned to face Emily. "And it ain't true what Gen'ral Sam keeps saying. They did not make me the mayor of Nacogdoches."

Then he smiled and tried to end the story, but Sam Houston stared at him until he went through the whole thing in more detail. Jack's tale inspired everybody around the table to spout off, every damned adventure a taller tale than the one before. He had a hard time hearing though. His ears were still ringing from the test firing in the afternoon. Guess he'd need some cotton in his ears from now on, but that seemed kind of sissified.

Samuel Colt was well into describing how he'd invented the repeating pistol when Emily West gripped Jack's outstretched arm. Oh God, that felt good. Hadn't had that feeling since…since he couldn't remember when. Then she slid her hand down and left something metal in his palm. Emily smiled and moved her hand away. Jack closed his fist and took his hand off the table.

Colt frowned toward Emily West, then stared at Jack. Must not've liked whatever he saw. Too bad, Mister Inventor. She's your assistant, not your property. And I'll wager she ain't your lover, neither. Jack looked down, opened his hand, and grinned. He slid the long iron door key into his pocket.

"General Houston, Colonel Cook," a stone-faced Samuel Colt ended his tale and lifted his tankard, "Thank you for your trust in the Colt Arms Company. I and my assistant, Miss West, will take our leave tomorrow. Your hospitality has been exceptional. I appreciate your business." Then Colt took a sip of ale and offered, "My hope is to return one day, Sirs, and join your Rangers, using my weaponry in mortal combat."

Well, what a piece of pure bull crap. Would be a cold day in hell before he'd have Samuel Colt in that fine silk shirt and those shiny boots riding in his Ranger company against a bunch of savages. Wonder if Colt had even fired one of his damned guns? And had he hit anything?

• • •

Birds chirping outside the open window woke Jack Hays at dawn, dizzy and dry-mouthed. Too damn much ale and not enough sleep. He shook his head and tried to clear the cobwebs out of his brain.

What in bloody-hell was that noise in the room? Sounded like water being squeezed out of a sponge. Jack sat straight up in bed.

There she stood, bare backed and bare-assed at the hotel room wash stand. Uh-oh. Oh, shit. Emily West was naked as a jaybird and bathing herself. So Jack was in her room? Emily glanced over her shoulder and smiled at him.

"Good morning, Mad Jack." West turned fully around and whispered, her voice deep, velvety, "From now on I shall call you 'Mad Jack.' Much more appropriate than 'Captain Hays,' don't you think?" She smiled and leaned back against the wall. "And your men would agree and approve, I'm sure."

Chapter Sixteen

Guns or Roses - Winter and Spring 1841

On his way to the Menger Hotel, Jack Hays stepped from one
wet board to another, wanting to stay out of the mud in the San
Antonio streets. Damned rain had been going on since Thanksgiving.
No amount of wet was going to dampen Jack's enthusiasm, though.
Three weeks earlier, just before Christmas, he'd been issued one
hundred twenty Paterson Colt revolvers and five revolver rifles. All
his boys would get two pistols and some extra five-round cylinders.
Two of the rifles would for sure go to Flacco and Red Wing. Those
Apache boys were the best rifle shots he'd ever come across. He'd see
if his scouts liked the repeaters better than those single-shot Jaegers
they'd been so proud of.

One long stride put Jack beyond the puddle at the foot of the
Menger front entryway. He stomped his boots and shook the water
from his oilcloth duster and hat. Jack stepped into the lobby, lit by
too few candles in the massive wood chandelier over his head. The
innkeeper stood by in the gloom, ready to direct him to his dinner
guests already in the dining room.

Guests? Jack had expected only one, Emily West. She was
back in San Antonio at Sam Houston's request to help Jack train his
Rangers with the Paterson Colts. Who the hell was the second
person? Wasn't Sam Colt – the innkeeper had said Miz West had
brought another woman with her.

Ornate oil lamps on the walls and candles on the tables
brightened the Menger dining room more than the lobby. Jack peered
in and spotted Emily at a table near the back wall. A stunning, dark-
haired young woman sat across from her. Both women's profiles
reflected in soft, yellow light. They leaned toward each other in
conversation. Emily sipped ale from a tin. The other woman was

having…wait a minute. My God, sure as sure could be, that was the girl who'd been picking flowers when he did the coin trick a couple years back. He'd remember that face anywhere, hat or no hat. What was going on? Who was she, and why was she with Emily?

"Oh Jack, over here. Here we are." Emily smiled, waving him over. "It's so good to be back. So good to see you again."

She stood and grasped Jack's arm. Emily extended her hand toward the seated woman. The woman smiled. Recognition?

"May I introduce my traveling companion?" Emily said. "This is Miss Susan Calvert. We met on the steamer coming from New Orleans to Galveston. As is often the case, the world is quite small. She, like me, has seen you in action, Mad Jack."

Blood rose under Jack's collar and flushed his cheeks. Good thing he'd grown that beard. He took off his cap and nodded polite as he could to Miz Calvert, then pulled a chair back from the table and sat down. Hard to believe. Jack was about to eat dinner with the two best-looking women in San Antone, and he already knew one of them a lot better than he probably should, especially if he and Emily had to work side-by-side for the next few weeks.

But what about Miz Calvert here? All decked out in fancy clothes – pretty damn fine looking. So she'd told Emily about his trick riding shenanigans. As far as Jack knew, he was still the only rider who could snatch a silver coin out of the dust at full gallop. Now what the hell had Emily told this girl about him?

"Good evenin', Miss Emily." Jack nodded, then turned to the other woman. "And I'm pleased to meet you, Miss Calvert. Believe I must have seen you somewhere's around San Antone. Maybe a couple of years back. How you been keeping?"

"I have been well, Captain." Susan Calvert spoke a little more Texan-like than Emily. "I was visiting then from Alabama. Happily, though, I now call Seguin my home. My father's Judge Jeremiah Calvert. You've perhaps been in his courtroom?"

She looked at Jack with dark, penetrating eyes. Eyes he'd not forgotten. Jack smiled and glanced from Susan Calvert to Emily and back. He signaled the waiter to bring him an ale, then put one hand on the flintlock jammed into his shirtwaist.

"No, Ma'am, not been to Seguin," Jack replied. "Mostly just chasin' Indians these days. Not much to do with bandits and ne'er-do-wells. And we don't ever have to bring them Comanche boys in for court." He smiled and lowered his voice. "I'm confident your father's a fine judge, though. Like to make his acquaintance one of these days."

No wedding ring. Maybe no man in her life? Fact was, she had no jewelry on at all. Kind of odd for an Easterner. Even Texas women, leastways the up-bred ones, had a bracelet or a necklace or two. Emily liked silver. She almost always wore bracelets and nice earrings.

Jewelry or no, Miss Calvert was sure interesting looking. A thin scar peeked out of that scarf round her neck. Her hands were a little red and not quite as well-kept as Emily's. Anyway, he'd hear her story more another time. For now, he needed to focus on the business that had brought Emily West back to Texas; getting him and his boys trained to use the Colt pistols.

• • •

The next morning, more rain drummed overhead. Jack leaned back in his chair in the company headquarters tent. Rain or no rain, sure had been nice to see Emily again. He'd missed her. Liked the new girl, Susan, too. Last night when dinner was done, she'd promised to invite him over to Seguin soon. Didn't say a thing about Emily coming with him, neither.

Thunder erupted. No, not thunder, but a helluva noise, anyway. Somebody was stomping on the walkway boards outside like a bear in boots. Dammit, what was all the commotion? Hays moved to the entryway and threw back the wet tent flap. Water splashed, not on a grizzly bear, but on a Biblical Goliath of a man. The fellow had to be near seven foot tall, wearing a wide, dripping wet hat and covered head-to-foot in fringed, soaked-to-the-skin leather. The rain-drenched giant grinned and looked down at him.

"Cap'n Hays, are ya?" The voice was even higher pitched than Jack's. "My proper name's William A. Wallace, originally the Virginia Wallaces." One meaty hand at the end of an arm longer than Jack's leg reached out. "Most folks just call me 'Bigfoot.' Lot easier to remember. I'm reporting for duty. Orders from Colonel Will. Will Cook, that is."

So General Sam and Colonel Cook were making good on their promise to send him some seasoned Indian fighters. Two had already shown up. One, Bob Gillespie, was a Tennessee boy, a little taller than Jack, as most folks were. Bob had said he and his brothers started some kind of land speculation business over in Matagorda. He got bored and started fighting Indians for fun and eventually met up with General Sam just before San Jacinto. Gillespie must've fought pretty well if Sam Houston had personally recommended him.

The second recruit was a Marylander. Quiet fellow by the name of Sam Walker. Told Jack he'd come up against the Seminoles fighting in Florida. He'd used a Paterson Colt revolver there. To hear Sam Walker tell it, when the damned thing didn't misfire, wasn't nothing else in the world better for killin' Indians. Now, what of this giant in front of him, Bigfoot Wallace? Jack motioned the big man into the headquarters tent and sat him down.

"So, Private Wallace." Jack looked at the open, long face of his newest recruit. "What's your story? How come you showed up here in the pourin' rain, all ready to ride with Hays' Rangers?"

"Cap'n sir, like I done said," Bigfoot Wallace responded as he took off his wet hat. "I come from Virginia little while back. Had a brother'n a cousin come here before me. They was at Goliad with Fannin. Murderin' Mexican bastards kilt 'em both."

Bigfoot Wallace bowed his massive head. His mountain of a

body shivered all over. Goliad, that hell hole. Damn the memory, the sweat, death rot smell, bodies stacked high, men on the burial detail swearing and vomiting. So two of those dead boys had been Wallace's relations? No wonder the big fellow was pissed off. He had a right to be. Everybody in Texas ought to by God remember Goliad.

"I'm real sorry to hear that," Jack said, locking eyes with Bigfoot Wallace. "It was a terrible thing. I was there, too, but just for burying. One of these days, us Rangers'll give you a shot at the Mexicans."

Jack handed Wallace papers to sign, along with a pencil, and pointed to where he expected Wallace to make no more than an "X." The big man licked the pencil point and scribed "William A. Wallace" in flowing script. The new recruit was more educated than he appeared.

"For now, Private Wallace," Jack added. "Comanches are the job."

"Captain Hays." Bigfoot spoke, keeping steely-eyed contact. "I can shoot a turkey eye out at two hunnert yards with this here piece." He hoisted a well-oiled Jaeger rifle and shook it by the hand guard. "If we ain't got no Mexicans yet, I'm proud to stay on and shoot somethin' else that's useless. Goddamn Comanche'll do just fine."

• • •

Seguin wasn't all that far from San Antone, at least not when Jack had a pony that liked to run and knew the wagon trail. Jack had already been over to Judge Calvert's for dinner once since he'd met Susan back in the winter. He looked forward to his second meeting with her this afternoon and evening. He slowed the pony to a trot at the long path leading up to the Calvert estate.

Susan and her mother, Missus Priscilla, were waiting on the

steps of the big Victorian house. A taller shadow in the doorway behind them had to be the Judge. The two women smiled and waved. Jack touched his hat brim and dismounted.

Their Mexican servant boy came, just like the first time, and took Jack's horse and his pommel bag. He hoped the boy would put the bag in the same sleeping room again, the one with the high, four-poster bed. Jack had not slept better since he'd left Aunt Rachel's and President Jackson's Hermitage years ago, back in Nashville.

Jack wore his best black trousers, new boots, a silver-studded vest, and a cutaway black jacket. Cleaning up the white shirt underneath hadn't been easy. Still a little damp. He'd left the sea cap in his quarters and instead wore a new broad-brimmed, white hat. A regular western hat and the Paterson Colt strapped on his right thigh were more Ranger-like.

With all the range firing, Jack hadn't had time to trim his beard, either. Susan wouldn't mind. But her mother would comment, sooner or later. Clean shaven men were her preference, she'd said. So how could the Judge keep those hellish long and bushy white sideburns?

"An uneventful ride, I trust?" Judge Calvert surged in front of the two women on the top step. "Come on up the stairs, Captain." The man still sounded formal, courtroom-like. "You'll need to go inside and get freshened up pretty quick. Dinner's in one hour."

Susan Calvert took Jack's arm and guided him through the wide entryway. He'd best take off the hat and put it somewhere close to the door. Better unstrap the pistol, too, for politeness. The weapon could hang close-by on his chair post, even at dinner. Judge and Missus Calvert understood that Rangers needed to keep their guns ready. And damn, whatever was cooking smelled good. Sure as hell, he'd not be eating beans and tamales tonight.

• • •

After dinner, Jack sat beside Susan on the maroon velvet couch in the Calvert's parlor. Polite talk with Judge and Missus Calvert went on until the Judge and his wife went off to bed. Once he and Susan had moved out onto the moonlit porch and the cooler evening air, Jack pushed the double rocker back and forth with one foot. Susan Calvert sat close and held his arm. The broad, slatted seat swayed as the curved wooden rails creaked in a slow arc.

"A beautiful night," Susan whispered.

Jack nodded and looked up. Damn, another full moon. Comanche raiding parties were probably out somewhere, terrorizing settlers. He'd be out there soon with his company, tracking the savages, killing some off, and chasing the rest back into their camps. Wonder what the Comanche would think when they came up against his new pistols?

And what might Emily West back in San Antone be up to this evening? She might not approve of his sittin' here like this with Susan. Truth be told, Emily was the kind of woman he could have fun with – hell, even go to war with – but Jack wasn't coming home to Emily every night the rest of his life. Wouldn't want her to be the mother of his children, neither. Anyway, she probably couldn't see herself having babies and being a homebody. Now this girl, Susan here, that was another matter.

Jack turned to look at his companion swaying beside him in the rocker. She faced Jack and smiled. Her smooth skin shone in the moonlight. Dark hair fell in soft curls over her bare shoulders.

"Why, Jack Hays," Susan teased. "Whatever are you contemplating? That face is so...so dead serious."

"Aw, nothing much, Susie," Jack hedged. "The Judge was sorta hard on me at dinner tonight. All that preaching about how us Rangers are sometimes more vigilantes than lawmen. Hard to keep quiet about matters like that. He ain't right, you know. Leastways, your Pa's not right when it comes to Hays' Rangers."

Susan Calvert put her arm around Jack's shoulder, brushed

his cheek with her lips and whispered close to one ear. "You did fine, Jack. You held your tongue real civil. Daddy's just making sure that he's got the upper hand in case we get serious." She eyed Jack. "So what's next for Captain John Coffee Hays? You coming back to Seguin soon, or do I have to come over to San Antonio to see what you and my friend Emily are up to?"

Dammit all, the redness hit his face again. He'd get by with blushing this time. The moon was at Jack's back, and the beard covered his cheeks. Damn-well time to be straight up with Miss Calvert about him and women, though.

Jack wanted to sound sincere. "Susie, for sure, ain't nothin' but business, pistol training, between me and Miss Emily. Now that the training's all done, I figure she'll be leavin' soon." He shifted closer on the seat. "Then me and my boys, we'll head out after the Comanche. Probably be gone least a couple of months. Could be more."

Susan pulled away from him and tried to stand. What the hell? Jack pulled her down again onto the rocker. Susan wrestled his hand away and drew a small kerchief from her bodice, clearly upset.

"Look here, Susie. Dammit," Jack grumbled, a hand on her arm. "Why you puckerin' like that? Fightin's what I come to Texas for in the first place. I'll be back in camp soon enough. August, for sure. I'll come straight back to Seguin and see how things are with you and your folks."

Susan Calvert's mouth curled down. She jumped from the rocker and dabbed at her eyes. Uh-oh, he'd messed up now. Jack sprang up and reached for her shoulder. Susan Calvert shrugged off his hand and headed for the door, leaving him with the sound of fading sobs. Somewhere deep inside the house a door slammed. Dammit all, still a lot he needed to learn about courting.

• • •

The April sun was bright and just warm enough to bring out the buffalo clover and indian paintbrush scattered around the Ranger camp. Jack sat on a rough bench in front of his command tent, black field cap pulled down to shade his eyes. He waited for Flacco. He'd finished training his Rangers with the new Paterson Colts and life was getting simpler. Emily West, her assignment done, had gone back East. Only Susan Calvert was left for Jack to worry about. Flacco had asked for the meeting, wanted something. Serious or not, Jack could fix whatever the Apache's problem was.

"Captain Jack," Chief Flacco arrived, out of breath. "Very sorry you wait long for me. Many pony problems this morning."

"Ain't like I had somewhere else to be, Chief." Jack's mood was light. "Sit down. What's on your mind? Need more arrows? More ponies? Pistols? Hell, just name it. We'll get whatever you need."

"Flacco worry much." The scout's voice was grave. He cleared his throat. "Bad medicine, Captain Jack. Real bad. Flacco say straight. Too much woman I think for you. First, some night all night by Madam West, I know. Now, more bad. You gone every time. Ride to Miss Susan in Seguin. Long ride. Pony tired. Sweat when back. You tired, too, Captain Jack. Much, much womans make too tired fight Comanche."

"Wait a damned minute, Chief," Jack broke in. "Firstly, training's gone well. Our boys are prepared. You done said so yourself. And Miss West is gone. Second, I was only two nights over to Judge Calvert's place in Seguin."

Flacco shook his head. Didn't agree at all. Dammit, Flacco might be a great tracker, a helluva rifle shot, and loyal as a blue tick hound, but his fuckin' Apache scout needed to stay out of Jack's love life.

"Me and the womenfolk, Chief." Jack frowned. "We ain't none of your concern. Man needs a woman sometimes. Man needs to relax. Even you Apache Chiefs."

Hays winked one eye and pulled his pistol. Flacco didn't

move, didn't flinch. Jack half-cocked the new Colt repeater and waved the barrel toward the hills.

"And as for fightin' Comanche out there," Jack lectured. "I'm sure as hell prepared. How 'bout you?"

"Captain Jack," Chief Flacco spoke low, "Rangers like Colt gun. Even some bad pieces fly off, new gun kill many enemy. Wipe out Comanche. Maybe one time, devil Mexicanos, too. But much bad medicine now in your head. Lady parts make Captain Jack forget first job, kill Buffalo Hump."

"So I'm not doin' what I ought to, Chief?" Jack raised his voice and brandished the pistol. "You say them women are distracting me? Do I look wore out to you? Damn your red ass, Chief. That's pure crap. Nothing but bullshit."

Flacco bolted upright, snapped his feet together and eyed Jack. The damned Indian wasn't finished with his lecture. Jack holstered his weapon.

"Flacco say straight one time more, Captain. Leave ladies be." He touched one palm to his chest. "They bad medicine. Flacco say you no need permanent woman. Now Captain Jack have no time for smell rose. Captain Jack need smell gun smoke. Time to kill everybody we not like."

One helluva lecture he'd gotten from Chief Flacco. The Indian wasn't happy with Jack's courting. Susan was already pissy about his going off to fight all the time. Hard to see how he could lead his Rangers to Flacco's satisfaction and still keep the peace with Susan. One matter the Indian was right about, though. Out hunting Comanche for the next couple of months, he couldn't afford to have Susan Calvert or Emily West on his mind. That could get him killed.

Chapter Seventeen

Bandera Pass - June 1841

Jack woke the Ranger company before daybreak. Breakfast was hardtack, jerky and coffee. Time to break camp and mount up. Even though his men had been trained – move by night, camp by day – there had been no such order from Captain Jack Hays for this patrol. Fires for morning java were okay, just no fires at night. Comanche had to understand that he and his Rangers were coming for them. He wanted a fight.

Today he'd ride to the headwaters of the Guadalupe River and probe the small side canyons. Jack had dispatched the two Apache boys to scout the main route to Bandera Pass. He'd told them to rendezvous at tonight's campsite. By then, either his main body or they should have made some kind of contact with the enemy.

Early morning sunlight filtered through the trees. Hays led his company away from the encampment through thick underbrush, kept away from established trails, and headed for the river crossing. Late morning, now. Jack gripped his saddle horn with one hand, then waded into the river beside his pony. Sixty dismounted Rangers and their ponies came behind him, three miles upstream from the easier but more exposed fording site. Minutes later Jack and his mount led the Ranger unit up the banks of the Guadalupe to safe footing on the opposite side.

After midday, he sent forays into the blind canyons. None flushed out any Comanche. Not a big surprise. Bastards were out there, anyway, watching and waiting. There'd been that one signal fire in the hills, smoke rising straight up, then flattening out like a big mushroom. Flacco had showed him the special way Comanche made message signals with fire and smoke. Had to use just the right wind current to pancake the smoke at the top one way or the other. So one signal fire, but nothing more. Still, it was enough to convince Jack the Comanche were shadowing him.

• • •

That evening, after a cold supper deep in a mesquite thicket, Jack sat between Sam Walker and the company sniper, Bigfoot Wallace. The O'Keefe boys, along with Flacco and Red Wing, sat cross-legged facing Hays. The sun had dropped behind western hills, putting the Irishmen and the Apache scouts in shadow. A pony snorted down by the creek. Otherwise, silence all around. Jack waited for the scouting report.

"Captain Jack," Flacco spoke, animated. "We maybe not see Comanche, but Red Wing good spotter. Find much pony shit. And we both see shadow. Heads with feather, more than one, move in rocks." Flacco held his nose ceremoniously. "Red Wing and me smell bad medicine. Smell Comanche. Numunuh stink worse than pony shit."

"Yellow Wolf wait for us," Red Wing broke in. "His favorite place be right inside Bandera Mouth. He always there, they always there, every time fight. Yellow Wolf ancestor kill Red Wing grandfather same place, long time back."

So Red Wing had a score to settle with the Comanche, just like Flacco. Hard to believe that Buffalo Hump and his people thought they were entitled to keep Texas hill country for themselves. Even called the place Comancheria. Hell, they'd come here same as Jack, same as Sam Houston and all the other folks. Fought their way in, kicked out whoever got in their way, then set up camp. Even the local Apache had suffered at the hands of Comanche invaders. By God, Jack would see that the hill country and San Antone belonged only to Texas from now on.

"Boys, I know you're right," Jack responded. "Saw one of

their damned signal fires myself." He looked at Red Wing, then Flacco. "So how many? Fifty? A hundred? Any signs of squaw work, mesquite cut for fires, or travois tracks?"

The Apache scouts shook their heads. A damned sketchy report. Comanche were out there, but how many, and where? Jack knew he'd get a fight soon. Had to be. He was taking his Rangers straight into Comanche homeland, poking the ornery devils right in the eye. By God, somebody – Buffalo Hump, Yellow Wolf, he didn't care – was going to challenge Hays' Rangers. Then the Comanche would have their first taste of Jack's boys and their new Colt repeaters. His men were prepared for battle.

Preparation. Early on, Andrew Jackson had lectured Jack on the difference between a soldier being ready to fight and being truly prepared for the chaos of combat. Prepared to kill or be killed. "Son," Jackson had observed. "Ain't no good just being ready for war. Killin' people you ain't met takes preparation, and that takes good leading. The commander's responsible for that. Man's always ready to eat or drink. He's ready to fuck or fight. But a man's got to be trained, led proper, before being truly prepared to kill a stranger."

By God in Heaven, Hays' Rangers were prepared. Where, and maybe more important, when would they meet the enemy?

• • •

At mid-morning the next day, Captain Jack Hays halted his company. A sheer rock wall to the east shaded part of the trail and gave way to a yawning, u-shaped opening – the mouth of Bandera Pass was just ahead. Scrubby mesquite and boulders marked either side of the trail into the canyon. No movement at the mouth of the pass or above on the escarpment. Where the hell were the red devils? Could be anywhere. For sure, Buffalo Hump's boys were watching and waiting.

Jack waved two squads, ten men each, into the rock-strewn ground right and left of the main trail. Flacco and Red Wing fell in close behind Jack. The rest of Hays' Rangers trailed the two scouts, single file, ten yards between riders, up the main trail and into Bandera Pass. Minutes passed. Jack motioned two fresh squads to the flanks in relief of the first men on hillside patrol. Jack didn't want anybody out there exposed as targets for too long at one time.

Morning was warming up quick with the rising sun. Jack pushed his cap back and wiped his brow with a shirtsleeve. He breathed as deep as he could to slow the pounding in his chest. Thirty minutes or more climbing already, the canyon rim couldn't be more than a half-mile ahead, maybe two hundred yards above. So far, no sign of any life, other than birds and maybe a ground squirrel or two.

What the hell were the Comanche waiting for? Why hadn't they come at him and his boys in the one big switchback down below? Jack waved his pistol in a circle over his head. The two outlying squads made their way onto the trail and brought up the rear. With his full company strung out now along Bandera Pass, he signaled "forward at the gallop." After a short dash, Jack moved to one side of the narrowing trail and waved his boys on. He wanted them to pick up the pace, get up top now, on the double. Then anybody around would have to fight him in the open.

Jack's horse column sped up, snaking accordion-like, upward. The edge of the escarpment and the open plain waited less than a hundred yards above. With half the riders past, Jack turned his pony and glanced down the trail.

Soft, whirring swishes, dull thumps, then shouts and cries behind Jack signaled an incoming arrow volley. Jack pivoted in his saddle. The deadly shafts had found their marks in the middle of Jack's unit. Four bodies slumped and fell from their saddles. More shouts and cries from his troops mixed with war whoops and echoed through the canyon. Jack wheeled his mount and kicked the pony's flanks, his hand gripping his full-cocked Colt pistol.

Shrieks, eagle-like cries and war whoops increased. Eerie, almost deafening. Comanche riders thundered down the hillsides. The first wave of bareback riding, war-painted braves charged down the steep slope on both flanks. A second cloud of arrows mixed with war lances and rained into the Ranger company. Jack fired his pistol, then again. Two warriors were hit some distance out. He had to get back to the action, and quick.

Jack thundered past Flacco and Red Wing as the Apache scouts drew repeater rifles from their saddle holsters. He waved for the scouts and his two lead squads to keep riding for the upper canyon rim, while Jack rode into the middle of the scrape.

"Dismount, dismount!" Hays shouted, reining up. "Tie your ponies. We can whip 'em right here. Ain't no doubt!"

Rangers scattered into the brush, leading skittish mounts. Some ducked behind boulders and fired. Others burrowed into fallen piles and clumps of mesquite, firing and moving. Then firing again. Arrows clattered off the hardwood branches and stone in wild ricochets. Jack stayed in the saddle, ducked to one side to avoid an arrow that swished past his neck. His nervous pony jostled him, but Jack took aim and fired his pistol once more. The animal pranced and pawed.

Jack cocked and fired, cocked and fired again. He emptied his first pistol and grasped the second one. Smoke and the deafening, crackling roar of rapid fire came from twenty Paterson Colts. Walls of galena, more than a hundred of the forty caliber balls, pounded into charging Comanche warriors on both sides of the trail. Waves of Comanche riders toppled headlong, hammered by the barrage from the Colt repeaters at close range. Painted, bare bodies littered one rocky slope. Jack glanced over his shoulder. Good, the other hillside had a bunch of the red devils scattered around, too.

So far, Jack had four Rangers down, but he'd taken at least thirty goddamn Comanche out in those first volleys. Damn fine work. His rear squads could hold their own. Jack turned his mount, Colt repeater in one hand, and rode hard for the canyon rim above.

He charged the quarter-mile uphill in less than a minute, firing at Comanche on both flanks as he rode. He passed his lead squads and the Apache scouts on the plateau, waving them to follow. The rest of his Ranger company took up the attack behind him on the dead run. Jack headed for one flank of the main body of the war party.

His pony's reins were in his pistol hand. Jack reached for and fumbled another loaded cylinder in the pommel bag. Dammit, he lost his grip on the reins, too. Still held the pistol. Then all hell broke loose.

His pony took its head. The animal lunged and bounded, too quick, and straight for the Comanche flank. He had the second cylinder in hand, but struggled to stay in the saddle. Jack's fingers fiddled with the reload. No cover. Nowhere to jump, and no chance to maybe roll behind a rock or under a mesquite bush. More than a hundred Comanche were running across his path, dead ahead. He'd been spotted. They turned to attack. Nothing left to do but shoot as many of them as he could. Jack jammed the fresh cylinder into his pistol and fired, his head low alongside his pony's neck, kneeing the animal right and left. Was anybody behind him?

He emptied the revolver, aiming each shot through a hail of arrows and war spears. Three bare-chested bodies flew off bareback horses. More braves on foot – war clubs in hand – slumped over rocks or fell in bushes. Jack careened through their ranks, now trying to reload a third cylinder. By God, he couldn't have been the only Ranger firing. Too many bodies around for that.

Another loaded cylinder clicked into place, Jack bent further forward in the saddle and reached for his reins. After two more tries, he managed to grip the flying leather thong. He jerked hard, pulled the pony up short and wheeled the animal around. His eyes took in the sight. His Rangers – the whole damned bunch – were there. Impossible, yet, there they were. Flacco, Red Wing and the two squads. They'd followed Jack's lead. He'd had them with him the whole way.

The Comanche, those still alive, were now in full retreat, riding and running hard as could be away from the fight. Flacco and the boys drew up beside Jack, ponies winded, but without a scratch. The rest of his men popped up from behind boulders and out of the mesquite below. Cheers erupted, weapons and hats waved.

"Not quite time for cheering yet, boys." Jack shouted, relieved.

He rode from squad to squad, getting those down below remounted and moving his company back on line. Consolidate the position. Get reloaded. Take care of the dead and wounded. The damn Comanche couldn't be finished. After the Indians figured out what had happened, they'd be back. But he'd be ready again.

Nobody, not Flacco nor anybody else, needed to know that his flank attack hadn't been deliberate, at least not in the way he'd charged off. The good luck of war, that's what he'd been graced with. And Jack sure as hell hoped his luck would last a little longer. This had to be just the beginning.

• • •

Hours later, the sun cast long shadows across the high plain. No sign of the Comanche, other than death cries from the hills to the east. Seven of Hays' Rangers and two ponies had perished. He'd ordered the troops buried where they'd fallen and made sure his boys retrieved the new Colt weapons. Didn't want those in Comanche hands, ever. Animal carcasses and dead enemies were left, all unmolested where they lay. Comanche could have the dead horses for meat, and his Apache scouts would have to forego their scalping ritual. Too risky right now.

Flacco rode up. "Captain Jack, you order no scalps. Me and Red Wing not like order. Anyway, we honor. You be mucho bravo leader."

146

Jack eyed the canyon rim behind Flacco. Several Comanche stood, silent and unmoving, silhouetted against the afternoon sky. Was Buffalo Hump one of them? Maybe Yellow Wolf?

"Now me truly surprised." Flacco spoke low. "Damn Comanche honor Captain Jack. See you respect dead Comanche. Soon they pick up dead brothers and go village. Comanche no more fight today."

"Sure is good news, if you're right, Chief." Jack took a deep breath. "You got any idea exactly who we came up against?"

"Captain Jack," Flacco grinned and puffed out his bare chest. "I speak one laying down Comanche before I give him home in spirit world. He say they be Yellow Wolf party. Yellow Wolf sure in big trouble now with Buffalo Hump. Comanche boy say they very surprised. Ask me how come White Face now have one firestick every finger? Always before, have only one firestick each hand."

Chapter Eighteen

The Mexicans at Salado Creek - September 1842

The sun was a silver coin trying to penetrate the high, thin clouds over Mission Square. A crowd of well-dressed San Antonio citizens – the gentry – mingled in the plaza. Mexican dragoons in cobalt blue, double-breasted tunics crossed with white belts and matching white trousers maintained order with muskets at the ready. Jack Hays leaned on a porch rail of the Menger Hotel and scanned the gathering from under an old straw hat pulled low over his brow. He wore his oldest jacket and trousers, and his Paterson Colt was hidden in the frayed belt under the tail of his coat. Jack Hays' overall appearance was purposely rumpled. Spying wasn't his favorite pastime.

These Mexican bastards and a thousand or more like them were back in San Antone. General Adrián Woll's troops had gotten in because Jack had screwed up. More than a full cavalry regiment, plus infantry and artillery, had run him and Hays' Rangers out of town a couple weeks back. On the 11th of September, to be exact. So now Jack had to fix things. He knew how to deal with Comanche, so why were Mexicans such a more difficult matter?

Wait a minute, that little turncoat French bastard, Adrián Woll, the man responsible for the mess he was in, was riding up. The General pulled the reins of his white stallion, the halting animal pawing the ground and jostling the little man. Woll was about to address the crowd. The murmuring died away after one or two shouts of "Viva México"

"Citizens of San Antonio de Béxar." Woll shouted in passable Spanish. "You and your city are the jewel of Mexico del Norte. The Most Honorable Lopez de Santa Anna, el Presidente, sends his greetings to you, the residents of his most favored spot in the New

World."

Woll was a Frenchie turned Mexicano after the Pastry War. The French and the Mexicans had fought to the death for months over some little insult regarding closing a goddamn French bakery in Mexico City. These Latinos, what a bunch of hotheads and chickenshits. Here this asshole was, back again from France, but this time fighting for Santa Anna, not against him.

Jack shook his head. Woll had gone about screwing up life in Texas just because el Presidente Santa Anna woke up one morning and decided he wanted the whole damned territory back. General Sam should've killed that Mexican at San Jacinto when he'd first caught the bastard.

One thing Sam Houston had been right about, though; just as soon as they'd got the Comanche on the run last Fall, the fucking Mexicans had sprung up again. Jack had been forced out of the San Antonio garrison when Woll's boys surprised him. This little French-Mexican weasel had sneaked a whole division down a back road into town, in the dark, right under his nose. Jack and the rest of the Rangers had barely gotten out with their hides. By God, he'd have to settle that score soon.

Some of the Anglos had escaped, but he'd heard that more than fifty, including Judge Hutchinson and his clerk, had been captured and marched out of town somewhere. So now just a bunch of Mexican sympathizers and old Spanish families were left in San Antone. And this sonofabitch, General Woll, he must have six or seven hundred dragoons, plus an equal number of horse cavalry and artillerymen scattered around town. Woll might be in charge for now, but the little man looked silly sitting on that huge horse and shouting in his Frenchie Spanish.

"I, Adrián Woll, Commandante of the Army of the North," The General waved his saber. "I have been dispatched here as your protector. My sword shields you from the Comanche raiders." The general waved his blade toward the Alamo. "And we have driven the Texian interlopers from our missions once again!"

Then Woll stood in his stirrups and pointed the gleaming blade skyward. He touched the sword's hilt to his lips before sliding the weapon into his gold-festooned scabbard. Jack shook his head. What a disgusting little performance. What an act.

"I go now from this hallowed place!" The General shouted, the white horse prancing under him. "With your permission and God's blessing, I shall personally drive the rest of the Texian wolves from their bushes and dark hiding places."

The crowd stirred and cheered politely. Scattered applause echoed off the Alamo facade on the other side of the plaza. Wasn't as much commotion as Jack had reckoned there'd be. Good. Not all as friendly to Santa Anna's boys as they could've been. And outside of town, the Mexicans sure as hell had no friends.

• • •

Jack Hays led his Rangers into Seguin just after sunset on the 17th of September. Hadn't been there since Susan left for Baltimore late last year. Wonder how she was doing? Only one letter since then, and no mention that she'd forgiven him for that night on the porch. Not that he had need of Susan's forgiveness. Judge Jeremiah, her father, and the Missus Calvert were still in Texas somewhere, but with the Mexicans terrorizing everybody, they'd boarded up the big house here in Seguin and headed for Austin. Damn, was he ever going to see Susan again? An emptiness he'd not felt before washed over him.

Ewan Cameron's and A. C. Horton's Rangers showed up just after Jack and his men gathered around the campfire. They reportedly had seen nobody, Indian or Mexican, on the trail ride over from Austin. A little later, Matthew "Old Paint" Caldwell rode in with over a hundred troopers from Gonzales. Local militia volunteers, maybe fifty, had trickled in on foot and horseback all day. Everybody around Jack had a bone to pick with the Mexicanos.

Two hundred or more grim-faced Texans, all ready for some revenge, gathered around the warming fires. Nobody had ordered any of these other men to Seguin, but here they were. Tonight, somebody had to organize this mob. Get them focused. Prepared. That would not be Jack Hays. Not this time. For once he was ready to listen to somebody else's plan.

"Boys, boys," Jack put up his hand and stepped onto a crate of munitions. "I need y'all quiet for a spell. Simmer down."

The ruckus went on. Jack's voice and his presence standing on the wooden crate only seemed to increase the din. Angry men argued and shouted about what to do next and who should lead. Jack drew his pistol and fired in the air.

"Goddamnit, fellers!" Jack shouted to the shocked and now silent assembly. "No secret, San Antone is in Mexican hands again. I got to take full responsibility for the mess. Ain't no excuse I can give. That Frenchie piss-ant General Woll, the fuckin' midget just outfoxed me."

Laughter erupted. Were the men chuckling and guffawing because of what he'd called the commandante? Maybe. But he was no taller than the French General, which was likely the real reason for all the chuckles.

"Awright. Dammit, y'all," Jack yelled. "Go on. I know I'm short. Point is, Woll snuck his whole bunch through the hills and into town overnight, right past our scouts. Before we knew it, he'd kilt off the sentries. Slit the boys' goddamn throats and run us plum out of San Antone."

As good as he was, Jack had not been prepared for Woll's Mexicans. Hell, he hadn't even been awake that night. And where the hell had Flacco and Red Wing been? What about the poor Ranger sentries, their throats slit from behind? What a mess. Even now, Jack wasn't sure how Woll's attack had succeeded and how he'd come to escape. A full division of Santa Anna's army currently occupied the second largest hamlet in the Republic, so Jack and his Rangers were duty bound to do something.

"We got to get organized, pronto. Got to have a plan," Jack announced. "What we need, and what I'm looking for in this bunch is a leader. Somebody that's got a new idea. By God, that ain't me this time, boys. Anybody else? C'mon, men. Mexicans are slick, but they ain't perfect."

Jack pulled his cap off and looked into the crowd. Captain Matthew Caldwell, the tall, gaunt veteran of Mexican and Indian firefights, squatted on his haunches in the rear and drew something in the dirt with a stick. Jack waved to him.

"Ol' Paint," Jack used Caldwell's familiar nickname. "Will you lead us? I know you can do it, if you will. Hell, you can even be 'Colonel' Caldwell. I'll sure as shit follow you."

A few restless murmurs and shuffling of feet greeted Matthew Caldwell as he stood up. The grizzled Ranger had a reputation as one helluva fighter. The man scratched at his chin whiskers, then stared unblinking at Jack. He waved the stick in Jack's direction and walked with long, slow strides to the front. He motioned Jack to step off the wooden crate and move to the side. Caldwell's splotchy face and hands did look like old, sun-blistered paint now that the fellow was up close. Caldwell drew his Colt pistol and climbed onto the box where Jack had stood.

"Cap'n Jack, Gents," Caldwell bellowed, waving his pistol. "Me and my Colt here, we'd be interested in the job. And by God, I'll accept the brevet colonelship, too. Jack, if you and the rest of the boys here will have me, I'm your man."

Cheers and shouting erupted. Rifles and sabers punched the air. Caldwell waved his hat for quiet. Jack smiled. Bad as the situation in San Antone was, maybe his Rangers and these men would kick the Mexicans out after all. Only thing left was figuring out how this new Ranger Colonel proposed to get rid of Woll and his regiment.

"Awright men, 'preciate the confidence. As it happens, I got a plan that oughta work." The new Colonel looked down at him. "Captain Jack, you'll have God's redemption for bein' run outta San Antone, and the Mexicans'll get their comeuppance. Guaranteed."

• • •

Sunup the next morning, Jack led his Ranger company south and out of Seguin. Three hours later, he halted the unit on the flat open plain barely a mile east of San Antonio and pointed to Bigfoot Wallace and Bob Gillespie, setting the ambush in motion. Jack smiled as the two dismounted and their two squads followed.

Wallace's jaw and face were set in a permanent frown. Leaving San Antone in a flurry, he'd left his leather trousers and more to the Mexicans and was clad only in his leather hat, vest and long johns. Bigfoot had not only lost a brother and a cousin at Goliad, now the Mexicans had taken his identity. The huge Virginia boy had to even the score. Revenge was a valuable motivator.

Bob Gillespie, the more cheerful of the pair, followed Bigfoot's squad with his men. The two Ranger squads disappeared into the bush on foot, the lot of them hauling weapons and leading their ponies. Hays motioned the men to spread out in the mesquite and rocks near the base of a long, low hill. They faced the red roofs of San Antonio in the distance.

Jack needed to put one more piece of the ambush in place. He searched the remaining two squads and saw no fear on any faces. Some of these troops were about to help him bait the trap. The only thing left to wonder was whether or not they'd live to see the sunset.

"Hank McCulloch," Jack turned and addressed one of his newer recruits, "You damned Rutherford County flatlander, get with Sam Walker. You two pick four or five more men that ain't afraid to die and come with me. Rest of you boys head on east to the creek and tell Ol' Paint we're set."

• • •

Barely two hours after he'd set up the ambush site, Jack Hays, a field cap pulled low over his eyes, led seven dusty riders off the cattle trail and onto a cobblestoned street in San Antonio. This time, two Colt pistols were holstered on Jack's leather-clad thighs. A repeater rifle was nestled in a saddle holster near his right leg, and loaded pistol cylinders filled his pommel bag. The other seven men – McCulloch, Walker and Creed Taylor, plus four more of the best riders in the Ranger company – followed in single file.

The men wore all manner of shirts, frayed jackets, dusty trousers, pantaloons and leather. No need to look official and tip off the enemy that his Rangers were coming. Most important, every man with Jack had at least two pistols, a rifle, a saber or musket, a couple knives, and all the munitions they could carry. He'd ordered them to bring little food, only one canteen of water, and no more than a single-blanket bed roll. He didn't plan to be in San Antone long.

Hays and his boys reined up when they were close to Mission Plaza in front of the Alamo. Almost nobody, at least no civilians, were on the streets. Why? Not siesta yet. The plaza was vacant, except for a company of maybe sixty or seventy Mexican dragoons close order drilling a hundred yards away. The enemy infantry unit moved in unison and appeared impressive in their navy blue shakos and tunics with white crossed belts. Their shiny boots thumped on the cobblestones. Muskets were right-shouldered. Bayonets in scabbards slapped red-striped legs in rhythm with their steps. Their lieutenant, or whatever he was, halted the unit when he spied Jack and his nondescript band.

"Hey, Pendejo," Hays shouted and waved his cap. "Aiee. Hey, Pedro, Juan, muchachos. Pendejos. Usted tienen nada cojones." His Spanish was bad. Jack had tried to say they were little-dicked boys with no balls. Anyway, damned Mexicanos, they understood the insults.

Jack waited for a reaction. At first, stunned silence. Then, without command or direction, the dragoons made a disciplined move. The front rank un-shouldered muskets, knelt as one, cocked and took aim. Quicker, though, went the withering fire from Hays' pistol and seven more Paterson Colt revolvers that cut down the first kneeling row of Mexicans, then most of the second rank - still standing and cocking their weapons. Not a shot gotten off by the Mexicans.

Muskets clattered on the cobblestones. Red-feathered shakos flew off dark, bearded heads. Blue jackets scattered in all directions. Eleven dragoons lay dead. Another writhed in agony from a gut wound. Down and unarmed, no Ranger shot the man. Nor did Jack's boys fire at the backs of the fleeing troops. He had bigger problems. A thundering racket had erupted to his rear.

Jack Hays glanced over his shoulder, then motioned his squad to fan out. Hank McCulloch, the last rider in the spreading formation, wheeled his mount. Hundreds of horses' hooves pounded the cobblestone street. A flying column of cavalry, more than two hundred mounted dragoons, less than a quarter-mile away. They closed on Jack and his men in a heavy cloud of dust and debris. The navy blue tunics of the cavalry formed a solid background for the glint of twirling sabers and cutlasses. Scattered musket shots rang out from the front of the column. McCulloch fired down the narrow street. Fired again.

Hank's second shot dropped the lead rider and his mount. Trailing horsemen flew headlong over the tumbling pair. Jack smiled and kneed his pony around. That had bought him some time. He galloped east, down a side street at right angles to the attack. His squad rode close behind. Jack rode as hard as he could for the edge of town, needing more distance between him and the much larger body of Mexican cavalry before they had a chance to recover. He had to outrun these dragoons and lead them into the ambush. Then again, this bunch of Mexican cavalry might be too big for the trap he'd set. Time would tell.

• • •

Jack kicked his pony in the sides and rode, head down, hugging the animal's neck. He glanced back. Less than a half-mile behind his patrol, at least four hundred Mexican horsemen were now coming fast on the open plain. Damn, way too many for the rest of his company to ambush just ahead. He needed a new plan. Two minutes later, Jack thundered into the middle of his Rangers' hiding place.

"Mount up, mount up!" Jack shouted. "Whole damned regiment was waitin' on us. Get going. Too many to fight here. Get going. Now! We'll fight 'em at the creek."

Jack's pony jostled him through the thick brush. How far was Salado Creek? Maybe five miles through knee-high prairie grass. Could Jack get his Rangers to Caldwell's main force at the creek before the Mexicans caught them? Jack flailed at his mount with the reins, then looked back. Everybody had made their way out of the ambush site and closed ranks, galloping hard behind him. His lead over the Mexicans was still half-a-mile. Musket shots came from the bastards and plunked out of range into the dirt.

A quarter of an hour passed, Jack riding like there was no tomorrow. Random musket rounds hissed over his head. One or two pinged the dirt beside his pony. Four miles under his belt and Jack's boys were still with him. But damn it, so were the Mexicans. And they were gaining.

Jack felt his mount slow, getting winded. Mexicans' horses had to be feeling the chase, too. How could they still be closing in? He and his Rangers had another mile to go. Jack untied his bedroll and let it fly behind him, then tossed his canteen. Had to lighten the load. Jack looked over his shoulder. The boys followed his lead. Most of their tied-down gear wasn't needed for the fight to come. All was thrown backward through clouds of dust.

Still, the Mexicanos kept coming. The lead Mexican unit was about to outflank him on the right side. Flintlock and musket rounds hummed across Jack's path, too close for comfort. He waved Hank McCulloch and Creed Taylor out to the right for a moving screen between the enemy and his main body.

Hanging side saddle, McCulloch and Taylor took on the damned Mexicans pretty well. Their Colt's cracked and echoed in the distance. One Mexican fell, then two more. Jack counted the rounds and the bodies as he led the rest of the company closer to the creek and relative safety. By the time he was within a hundred yards of Caldwell's front line along the creek bed, McCulloch and Taylor had toppled at least seven of Woll's Finest without a scratch themselves.

Jack pulled back hard on his exhausted pony's reins and swung out of his saddle in a running dismount. He slid down through a crevasse in the steep banks of Salado Creek leading his mount. His Rangers followed, dragging their horses into the cover of the creek bed. Jack grabbed his pommel bag and repeater rifle, then slapped the pony away. He squatted low but raised two fingers on one hand to signal Colonel Caldwell he was in position.

Jack pressed his body against the creek bank and peered over the edge. The Mexican cavalry drew up and came on line more than a hundred yards away. A long wave of dust rose from their precision maneuver and drifted toward him. Despite the thick cloud he could make out a solid wall of Mexican troops in an orderly dismount. Woll's cavalry, close to four hundred men, would attack as infantry. Jack grinned and double-cocked both pistols.

Arrogant Mexican shits. They had no idea what was waiting in that creek. Jack's ambush on the prairie hadn't worked, so now he'd kill them from the creek bed. Jack took aim and pulled both triggers. His Rangers, along with Caldwell's men, opened fire almost in unison. Thunderous salvos from Colt repeaters and rifles dropped almost a quarter of the attackers. The rest, though, maintained their disciplined march toward Jack's position. All Jack had to do was stay put and wait. Just a little closer, you Mexican boys. Hope some of you were at the Alamo or Goliad. This'll be payback.

Scattered musket rounds came at him. One plinked dirt into Jack's eye as he aimed. He blinked to clear his vision, then fired his five shots and reloaded. Fired more. Ponies whinnied and rustled somewhere in one of the ravines to the rear. More incoming musket rounds zipped and hissed overhead, but not organized fire. Colt repeater fire chattered from the men on both sides of Jack. General Woll's dragoons faltered and became navy blue heaps streaked and soaked with red. Moans and cries came from bodies strewn across the field of fire.

One of Ol' Paint's boys grabbed his throat and fell a few yards up the creek from Jack, blood spewing through his hands. The first Ranger to fall, as far as Jack could tell. He shook his head, then felt in his pommel bag for more Colt cylinders. A Mexican bugler sounded "Retreat." Already? Damn, now that was a good sign.

• • •

A long stillness came with that bugle call. Jack passed the word up and down his Ranger line to let the Mexicans retrieve their dead and wounded. Must've been over two hundred in all. Hard to believe he and Caldwell's men had only the one casualty so far. Could be more up the creek, though.

The damn Mexicans. Did they know how many Rangers were with him, or how many munitions he had? Jack was pretty sure his boys hadn't used more than a third of their supplies in that first assault. Mexicans couldn't cross the creek anywhere nearby. So, for now, he was protected from the rear, but he needed to put men in the big bend of the creek to the north, pronto. Didn't want surprises from the flank. Jack turned and motioned to Bigfoot, Flacco and three others to head up the creek, north. Ol' Paint strode past him behind the line, Caldwell's skin all blotchy and ghost-like.

"Men," Colonel Caldwell shouted. "We cain't ever surrender. And make no mistake, we can whip 'em just like we did at San Jacinto."

Had the Colonel been at San Jacinto? Maybe some of these other men, too? Didn't matter none now. This was gonna be one helluva fight. Could be bigger than San Jacinto before things were done.

"Don't waste no shots!" Caldwell bellowed, turning left and right. "You see the whites of their eyes, shoot right between 'em." Caldwell pointed his pistol toward the Mexican lines. "And if you can shoot General Woll, do it! One that kills that sonofabitch, Gen'ral Houston'll pin a medal on him hisself."

That little Frenchie shit could hear Ol' Paint, for sure. Woll had to wonder just why Jack and the rest of the Rangers had picked this god-forsaken creek as the place to challenge his Mexican army. He'd know soon enough. Double lines of hundreds of mounted dragoons were forming less than two hundred yards away. Jack cupped a hand to one ear, trying to make out General Woll's orders.

"My comrades." the little general's voice carried well across the flat plain. "For this charge at the rascal Texans, I will lead you personally!" The General drew his saber and waved it to his horsemen. "There is nothing to fear from these creek rats and their puny weapons!"

Jack glanced down at his Colts and the repeater rifle leaning against the creek bank. He eyed the sweaty faces of Rangers with their mouths drawn into thin, determined lines. The General was a slow learner.

"We will massacre them where they hide," The general stretched in his saddle and turned side-to-side, "We leave none standing! No one alive to tell how they perished. My comrades, give them no quarter. Death to all!"

Jack breathed deep and steadied his nerves. He took aim and full-cocked his first pistol. Two hundred hammers on Paterson Colts and rifles snapped. Metal-on-metal echoed up and down the creek bed. The long blue-and-white line of Mexican cavalry formed up, stirring a storm of dust, set to charge.

"Steady in them ranks, fellas," Colonel Caldwell shouted, running up and down the creek bed. "Front row, ready to fire your five on Cap'n Hays' first shot, then step back. Reload while the second rank fires. Stay covered. Make all yore shots count."

Cannons rumbled somewhere behind the line of Mexican cavalry. Whistling rattles of incoming artillery passed over Jack's head. He hugged the creek bank. The ground under Jack vibrated from the impact. Dirt, bits of shale and sand peppered into the creek behind Jack. The first volley had landed well to the east, behind the Ranger lines. The second volley would land short if the Mexican gunners were any good. Trained artillerymen knew how to bracket their target.

Cannons thundered in the distance again. Jack covered his head and pressed his face against the bank. The grapeshot rounds exploded short, between him and the Mexican horsemen. Dirt and pebbles sprayed into Jack's position. Four or five Mexican horses reared and dumped their dragoons onto the hardpan.

General Woll steadied his cavalry when a third volley of cannon fire rumbled overhead and exploded in the pecan trees above Jack. Leaves, twigs and lead pellets showered down on the Ranger ranks. Jack glanced around. Still nobody hurt. Kind of gentle, like a spring rain. Not bad shooting, assholes, but grapeshot won't do much damage in that hardwood canopy. Gonna need heavier stuff than that, Generale.

General Adrián Woll raised his saber, pointed at the center of the Texan lines, and kicked his horse. Damn, here they came, the cavalry charge. In seconds, the creek bank in front of Jack shook from the force of almost two thousand hooves. He held his fire. The Mexicans needed to be closer. More cannon balls whistled and rattled overhead, landing past the creek now, just as the first salvo had done. Guess the Mexicans didn't want to cut down their own cavalry.

Finally, Jack aimed and fired his Colt, saw one Mexican fall.

Sharp, lightning-like cracks and rumbles rippled from the creek bank and all along the Texan line. A screen of blue-gray smoke stretched almost two hundred yards. Jack kept firing. The second, third and fourth volleys echoed from other Paterson Colts. More than a thousand rounds ripped into the charging cavalry, now less than a hundred yards away.

Wounded and dying dragoons and their horses stumbled. Mexicans vaulted over falling mounts and pounded into the dirt. Shakos flew into the air and randomly bounced, one rolling over the creek bank into Jack's lap as he was reloading. Jack swiped the fancy headpiece away.

A riderless horse skidded down the creek bank to his right and struggled up the far side, blood streaming from its neck. Didn't matter how many Mexicans died, their goddamned horses, neither. The ornery, useless bastards had it coming.

Jack looked left, then right. Every Ranger was keeping up the fight. Nobody else hit yet that he could see. Wonder why the Mexicans' artillery had stopped? When was their cavalry gonna break off the attack? Where the hell was that little shit, Woll? Still a lot of infantry out there waiting. Maybe somebody was still coming down the creek, too.

Remnants of the cavalry charge drew up just yards from the creek bank. No sign of General Woll. Had he had enough? Maybe dead? Screams, curses and orders shouted in Spanish followed. Moans of the many wounded and dying, whinnies of panicked horses in distress, all mixed with scattered shots from the Rangers' repeaters. Then…there he was. Woll on a black horse, that sonofabitch. His leg was bloody. Must've had the first horse shot out from under him. Tough bastard. Hard to kill.

• • •

Woll waved his sword to regroup his scattered cavalry for another charge. The Mexican commander pranced past his remaining mounted dragoons and motioned his infantry to move up. A bugle sounded behind the Mexican lines. Jack needed a clear shot at the General, but he couldn't manage one. Maybe Bigfoot could.

Jack grabbed his pommel bag and dashed up the creek to look for his company sniper. A salvo of grapeshot exploded in a grove of pecan trees on the east side, well beyond the Ranger lines. Jack ducked and kept running. Must be the next attack. Damned bugle blasted again. Jack glanced left over the creek bank.

Mexican infantry – almost a thousand of them in two wavy lines – had begun their advance toward the creek with General Woll riding in their midst. The endless waves surged forward, firing, kneeling and reloading by row as they came. Jack found Bigfoot just as the giant took aim at somebody. Unfortunately, not General Woll. Dammit. This time his sniper had shouldered his single-shot Jaeger and not the repeater rifle.

Jack tried to redirect him to Woll. Too late. Bigfoot fired. The shot hit and mushroomed the head of a tall, lanky Mexican infantryman fifty yards out. The target slumped forward and fell on his musket. Bigfoot, clutching his empty rifle, shinnied up and over the creek bank. What the hell? Jack tried to grab the giant Ranger by the long johns. Missed him. Bigfoot ran for the Mexican he'd downed.

"Cover him, boys!" Jack bellowed loud as he could down the line. "Big feller's goin' for his pants."

Jack fired both pistols and reloaded. Fired again. Bigfoot charged the enemy lines, weaving and dodging. Wounded Mexicans stumbled and fell. Others turned and retreated. Sam Walker, squatting beside Jack, cursed and threw one of his Paterson Colts into the creek and pulled a second weapon to keep firing. Guess Sam was going to suggest more damned improvements to the pistols, if he lived through all this, that is. Still didn't look like many Texans were down anywhere. No more since that first one, as far as Jack could tell.

He fired more to cover Bigfoot's charge. God, his ears were ringing like Hell's Bells.

What in blazes was going on out there? The huge boy's massive head bobbed up and down in the tall prairie grass near the Mexican lines. Bigfoot was stark, raving mad. Jack took sharp aim with one pistol resting across his forearm and fired twice. This time, he dropped two dragoons close to the big fellow. Bigfoot jabbed and swung his rifle butt to fend off and club two more Mexicans coming at him hard with fixed bayonets. Knocked 'em ass-over-teakettle, he did. Never seen the likes of that.

The huge, quiet boy from Virginia arrived at the dead Mexican's body. He laid the Jaeger rifle aside, bent and snatched off the dead man's boots, then stripped a pair of leather leggings from the body. Jack laid down more cover fire from his second pistol. Bigfoot waved the trousers high and let loose a chilling, bloody scream. He'd got his pants and his dignity back. Now the madman snatched up his rifle and raced back in a straight, headlong line toward Jack. Bigfoot tumbled over the edge and into the shallow water beside him, leather leggings in one hand and laughing like a schoolboy. Not a damn scratch to see on his huge body.

No time for a breather yet. Jack looked past the big Virginian still hooting and wallowing in the creek to his right. Colonel Caldwell was standing straight, pointing up the creek bed. Mexicans, no uniforms – irregulars – and Indians behind 'em. Not Comanche, neither. Cherokee. Comanche wouldn't be caught dead helping Mexicans. And further back, looked like more, twenty or thirty banditos.

"That's Cardova!" Caldwell screamed, "Kill that bastard! Now! Shoot!"

So Ol' Paint knew the man in the lead? Willis Randall, one of Caldwell's boys, obliged. He fired his rifle in shadow right through tree limbs, a shot under the eye of the leader from forty yards. One side of the man's face disappeared. Brains and blood spattered the three Cherokee behind him. Wasn't much left of the head, but Mr.

Cardova wasn't hurtin'. And Ol' Paint had to be pleased.

The Cherokee and some of the Mexicanos further back in the creek raised up to see what had happened. Jack cocked, aimed and fired. Then more. He emptied both Colts in their direction. More fire came from Rangers in the creek bed. Rounds thumped into heads and chests. Blood and skin bits sprayed and fell, screams and tumbling bodies. The remnants of the party turned tail up the creek and disappeared 'round the bend.

• • •

Things got real quiet again. Jack could make out a few mumbles in Spanish through the ringing in his ears. More moans and cries from the prairie. Mexicans rounded up their dead and wounded. Then silence. Nothing more. A hot stillness came like those summer evenings on the Hermitage veranda back in Nashville.

Jack eased the hammers on his Colts to half-cock and leaned against the creek bank. His shirt was soaked through to the waist under his open duster. Sweat, nothing but cold sweat. And by God, Jack's knees were rubbery. Might still be warm in Texas in September, but he couldn't stop shaking. He drew the duster tight around himself and slumped down.

Just before twilight, a bugle blew, light and lively. Not a call Jack had ever heard. He pushed his black cap bill up with his pistol muzzle and eased up to see over the berm. He squinted through the setting sun across the plain. General Woll was still stomping around on that big, black goddamn horse. El Commandante pointed his saber west, toward San Antone.

Woll's division formed up in two straggling columns. Makeshift travois loaded with wounded and dead were dragged behind mounted cavalry. Towed cannons and stumbling infantry brought up the rear. Clouds of dust rose skyward and blew toward

Jack as the Mexicans headed away from Salado Creek. Colonel Caldwell eased closer and squatted beside him.

"In case you was wonderin', Cap'n Hays," Colonel Caldwell smiled, thin lipped, "Them Mexicanos, they was blowin' the victory call." Caldwell smirked. Spit a dirty chew in the dirt. "Fuckin' Woll's sayin' he won."

Jack snorted, then burst out loud laughing. He couldn't stop laughing. After that, the tears came. Couldn't stop them, either.

Chapter Nineteen

We the Living - San Antonio - December 1842

Three months later, Jack Hays sat in the Menger's new beer hall alone near closing time, sipping his third whiskey. He'd bought Sam Walker a beer and a couple of shots after supper and listened to Sam piss and moan about Sam Houston's safe passage order for General Woll after Salado Creek. General Sam didn't like Mexicans any more than Jack did. So why the hell had he done that? The General hadn't even asked for Jack's opinion.

Jack took another sip and eyed Lilly, the good-looking new whore. She'd come from somewhere back East a few weeks ago, smiled at everybody with her full, red lips. Her olive skin, coal black hair and big, dark eyes reminded him of Emily West. He wasn't buying Lilly a drink tonight, though. Didn't seem right, what with Susan in his life now. Jack paid his tab to the barkeep, nodded to Lilly, then pushed the beer hall's double oak doors open. Outside, less than twenty quick steps brought him to the half-mile path back to the barracks and his officer's quarters.

His breath made cloud after cloud in the damp December moonlight. Jack had walked this way God only knew how many times since he'd come from Tennessee years ago. Something was different tonight, though. Maybe Jack was just tired. Needed sleep. Or maybe he should've stayed back at the Menger and bought a glass of champagne for Lilly. Just talked some.

He rounded the corner near the blacksmith's stables. A loud thump and blinding pain struck his temple. Then nothing. Blackness.

• • •

Cold water hit Jack hard in the face. Choked him. He shook his head. Oh God, what a headache right over the ear. What had done that? And now something really bad was goin' on with Jack's neck. He couldn't reach up, though, because.... Who? What in flaming hell? His hands were bound up behind his back.

"Well, look who jes' woke up in my ol' varmit trap." A familiar voice rasped. "This time I done caught me a real Tennessee shitkicker." Grit and gravel in the throat, somebody from years back? "So, Ranger Jack. Clever, clever you might be. But not so smart as a drifter like me."

Goddamn rhymes now? Who? What the devil? Ow.... Wire, or something like wire, bit into Jack's adams apple and neck. A terrible, choking tightness. Blackness. No air. Then nothingness again.

Cold. Wet. Was that water in Jack's face? He licked at his lips, then the rasping, hacking coughs came. His coughs. God, Jack's throat was killing him. What hell on God's earth had he fallen into? Not a bear trap. Maybe a Comanche snare? Couldn't breathe. Couldn't swallow.

Oh Christ, scraggly face hair and sour breath, up real close. The beard obscured a vaguely familiar ugly face on a scrawny body. One of the hands was fiddling with something around Jack's neck. A noose? Garotte, maybe? Stinking whiskey breath, hot and heavy. Shit, how had he gotten into this mess? Oh God, how to get out?

"Tojo, Theodore." Jack rasped. "Tojo Iverson, that you?"

Jack half-remembered the face now through the fog in his head. He'd spit out the name. Hard to see, but had to be the sonofabitch Flacco had caught sleeping on guard years back.

"Tojo." Jack squirmed. "Get this goddamn thing off my neck. Unhitch me. That's..." He struggled to get the words out. "An order."

Jack tried to cough again, but Iverson forced a bandana into his half-open mouth. Cold steel, the muzzle of a pistol, jammed against Hays' throbbing temple. The hammer clicked, half-cocked. Iverson pulled the metal away and showed Jack the muzzle of his own Paterson Colt. His attacker thumbed and full-cocked the hammer.

"Keep your claptrap shut," Iverson muttered. "Those was your last words, you snivelin' lil asshole." Iverson smirked. "Ranger Cap'n though you be, you jes' a speck o' shit to me."

Iverson smiled more at his own bad, childish rhyme. He twisted on the neck wire with his left hand. Jack's temples pounded. Couldn't fight back if this went on much longer. Needed to get a grip on something to whack Iverson with. But what? How? More tightness around the neck.

"Captain Jack's gonna die tonight." Iverson jammed the Colt barrel hard under Hays' chin. "He cain't scream none. Too tired to fight." Tojo was raving mad and let out high, squeaky whinnies. "Hee hee hee...."

A soft, whirring buzz ended in a dull thud that interrupted Iverson's crazed laughter and transformed his giggles into gurgles. The feathered shaft had embedded partway into his skull, jutting straight out from Iverson's left ear. Jack's pistol fell from his tormentor's hand. The cocked weapon bounced on the ground, discharged, and sent one round crackling across the wet trail into the night's blackness. Iverson's other hand eased off and slipped from the wooden turnstock at Jack's neck.

His assailant, still squatting in the darkness, faced Jack with wide, unseeing eyes. The lunatic smile faded. Then Iverson's body toppled sideways into the mud beside him.

Flacco sauntered over and leaned down to snatch the gag from Jack's mouth. The Apache scout fumbled to loosen the turnstock under his captain's ear. Hays sputtered and hacked. Holy shit, good to see Flacco, but where'd he come from? Thought he was already gone south trading for new ponies. Jack had to get that cutting wire off his neck and get the damned ropes off his wrists. He kicked, coughed, squirmed and grunted.

"Dammit! Goddamnit, Chief," Jack mumbled, hacking and spitting saliva and blood. "How'd you get here? I thought you was gone." Jack coughed again. "You sure took your time. You…you almost let the bastard kill me!"

Jack wiggled more to loosen the rope that bound his hands. His sock feet flailed at the damp grass and mud. Horses stirred and whinnied somewhere in the corral behind the blacksmith shop.

"Captain Jack," Flacco whispered, "you must be quiet. Rest some. You good safe now. Nobody but Flacco here."

Flacco glanced around while he loosened the wire on Hays' neck more, then he cut the ropes on his hands. Jack tried to stand. Flacco put one hand on his shoulder and pushed him down.

The Lipan scout handed Jack a canteen. "Captain Jack sit. Drink water now. I find boots."

Jack sat on one leg with the other outstretched and rubbed his damaged neck. Dawn slowly hinted pink in the distance. Jack straightened and took the boots Flacco had retrieved. He pulled them on with hands still raw and numb from the rope. The cap could wait till his head cleared. Jack sipped water. Hard to swallow. Hurt bad.

"Captain Jack." Flacco broke the dawn's quiet. "That cap be good for sun, maybe rain, but not save head." The Indian waved Iverson's heavy club. "You very lucky I not be gone south already, or not with one-hour wife this night." Flacco gazed at Jack, smiling. "If so, now you be with ancestors in Spirit World."

Hays let out a laugh, or more of a rattling snort. He shook his cloudy head and stared over at the crumpled body of Theodore Iverson. The man who'd almost killed him lay as if only sleeping, except for that killing arrow in his ear and the pool of blood under his head.

"Got to hand it to you Apache folks," Jack said, finally able to talk. "That there puts a whole new meanin' to the word 'earshot'."

Flacco nodded without smiling, then stood and drew his long knife. The Indian straddled Iverson's body and broke off the feathered shaft that jutted from his skull. Jack grimaced. He knew the rest. Still, the ritual turned his stomach. Flacco grasped a handful of hair and sliced away a saucer-size piece of scalp. He attached the bloody trophy to his belt. Flacco then snatched Iverson's corpse by the boots and, without farewell, dragged the body around the corner of the blacksmith shop and out of sight.

Jack would see Flacco in a week or so when the scout finished his pony trading down south. He owed his Apache scout his life, yet had no proper way to thank him. But by all that was holy, Jack was grateful.

Still shaky, Jack stood and leaned against the fence post. He bent his knees and moved his stiff, pained legs. The December air smelled fresh, cold and crisp. Good to be alive. But he had to be a lot more careful from now on.

• • •

Two weeks later, Jack felt good enough to be back at work. The cuts on his neck hadn't healed, and he had aches everywhere. He sat in the softest chair he could find around Ranger headquarters to read his mail and reports. A letter from Susan caught his eye.

One week now till Christmas, and Susan had been back in Texas since early November. Her letter promised that she'd come see him in January if Jack hadn't recovered enough to ride over to Seguin for Christmas dinner. No matter, he could do that ride in his sleep, even with his lingering injuries. He was glad Judge and Missus Calvert were back home and not still stuck in Austin, hiding from the Mexicans. Finding presents for the Calvert family though filled Jack with a sense of dread. What should he buy? And more importantly, where?

And speaking of where, where the hell was Chief Flacco? The Apache scout and two of Jack's old hands – Rusty Stimson and the Mexican, Jaime Esteban – had left for Laredo and La Vaca to trade for ponies right after the Iverson ordeal. A long ride, for sure, but they should've been back by now.

The door bolted open and banged against the wall. Jack jumped and grabbed for his pistol. A wild-eyed Red Wing stood in the doorway. What the hell could spook the Indian that much? He motioned to Jack.

"Captain Jack. You come quick," Red Wing beckoned. "I think Flacco back. Maybe Rusty-man and Esteban, too. They be in wagon."

"Wagon?" Jack blurted. He stood up and holstered his weapon, "Red Wing, what do you mean, wagon? They went for ponies. We don't need no more goddamn wagons. Besides, bustin' in here like that.... Hell, I almost shot you."

Jack limped toward the door. Didn't sound good. Never seen Red Wing so upset. He followed the young Apache out into the morning sunlight. A local rancher sat on the wagon seat, head bowed, reins in his hands. Oh God, this was bad. Maybe worse than bad. Rangers were gathered around the wagon bed, hats and caps off.

Jack pushed through the group, took off his cap and rested stiff arms on the slatted side of the wagon. Ranger Captain Jack Hays already knew what he'd see, but he didn't want to look. Three blanket-wrapped forms were laid out, side-by-side. Sam Walker climbed into the wagon and sat down next to the rancher. He reached back over the seat and peeled away one of the blankets.

Flacco's throat had been slit halfway through. Part of his cheek was gone. Probably buzzards. But God Almighty, the scalp was still there. Cherokee would've taken the scalp. Wasn't Comanche either. Comanche would have scalped him first, then hung him by his heels in a tree. Gutted him like a deer and let him bleed out. Comanche didn't like Indians scoutin' for the Rangers.

Walker stood, climbed over the seat and straddled the other two corpses in the wagon bed. He uncovered Esteban, then Stimson. Like Flacco, their throats had been slit. Esteban's wound was the worst. Slashed through to the neck bones. His head was nearly sheared from the shoulders. But the boys still had their scalps.

Horse thieves? Had to be horse thieves. But who? The smell of death stuck in Jack's nose. Three good men gone, and for what. Nothing but a bunch of horses? Jack threw his cap in the dirt. He shook his bowed head.

Horse thieves would've just shot 'em where they slept. So who the hell would've gone through the trouble of butchering these boys like this?

"How the hell these boys let this happen?" Jack muttered at the dirt. "Who could'a done this?" He raised his head and looked around. "Whoever the fuck done this deed, they'll damn sure pay."

"Found all three tied up together under that big pe-can tree out by San Pedro Springs," the rancher looked down from the wagon at Jack. "Dead as door nails and bled out, they was. No guns. Nothin' but the clothes on their backs. Lots of horse tracks around. Flock of buzzards peckin' away at these poor boys. Had to take a scatter gun to run 'em off."

Jack choked back rage. "You see anybody else? Any idea who done this? Reckon it wasn't Comanche nor Cherokee. Men still got their scalps."

"Cain't says I did, Cap'n," the wagon driver responded. "But had to be done least a couple days past. Bodies was stinkin' up already when I found 'em."

What in God's name would he tell Sam Houston? What could General Sam say to Flacco's father? After all, Houston was the one who'd talked the old Lipan Chief into letting his son work for the Texas Rangers all those years ago.

Jack would have to write sympathy letters to Esteban's brother and Stimson's wife. He'd make sure the boys got buried proper. He and Red Wing would take Flacco home to his village. God, the Iverson thing flooded back. Flacco had saved his life, but Jack hadn't been there for him. Bunch of murderin' assholes.

And now, one more problem. Somebody, for sure, had three

of his Paterson Colts. Dammit. Would he come up against his own guns again somewhere?

· · ·

Christmas Eve morning. The year 1842 had been real bad, the worst for Jack. He led the pony carrying Flacco's blanket-wrapped corpse into the Lipan Apache village twenty miles east of San Antonio. Red Wing, his face painted into a white mask, rode to the rear. An old somber Apache waiting at the edge of the village raised his open right hand in greeting. Jack waved his in return. He'd never met Flacco's father, but from Red Wing's earlier description and the man's sad face, Flacco the Elder was the one welcoming him.

The Chief wore fringed, deerskin trousers and a long, belted vest that was trimmed in white beads. Black and white paint lined his leathery cheeks and chin. Not peace paint, and not a marker of grief, either. War paint. But who would this old man make war on? Just a way of showing anger, maybe. Fathers should not outlive their sons. Not ever.

The graying hair trailing down Flacco the Elder's back was plaited with black-and-white ribbons. Women with colorful blankets and trinkets stood behind their Chief. Black-haired Apache braves with their faces painted white and dressed in fringed deerskin breeches and vests lined the path into the village.

Jack and Red Wing dismounted. Jack took off his sea cap and nodded to Flacco the Elder. He said nothing and held out the pony's reins. The Chief took them, then rested one trembling, leathery hand on Jack's shoulder. Silence.

Red Wing would stay and attend the burial ritual. Jack would not. The young scout Flacco's time with him was done. The Apache warrior had done his duty for Jack Hays and the Texas Rangers. Now he'd come home to rest.

Jack put his cap on and stepped to his pony. He grabbed the leather horn and pulled himself into the saddle. Once astride, he reached one hand inside his duster and found the thin pouch from Sam Houston. He handed the packet down to Flacco the Elder. Jack had no idea what General Sam had put in there, but where relations with Indians were concerned, the General was always damned good.

• • •

Late afternoon on Christmas Eve, Jack rode up to the Calvert's house in Seguin. Susan waved to him from the veranda and smiled. He had looked forward to Christmas with Susan for half the year. Hadn't seen her since late May. Now, dammit all, Jack just wanted to be alone. Not here, smiling and giving out gifts, talking polite and all with Susan and her family. Flacco was dead. Esteban and Stimson, too. He needed time alone to think. How to settle the score, and with whom.

Chapter Twenty

Walker's Creek - June 1844

More than a year had passed since Flacco's murder at the hands of some gutless sons-of-bitches. Jack's rage didn't boil up every day, but the anger was always there. His silent companion.

He stood in the afternoon shade of an old, twisted live oak tree on the bank of Walker's Creek. Red Wing was due back any time now. The Apache scout had better have news about the renegade band of Comanche Jack knew to be around. A good scout, that Red Wing. Loyal, too. But the Apache just wasn't the same as the man he'd replaced. Jack missed Flacco's straight talk. Missed his humor. Nobody was ever going to fill that Indian's moccasins.

Whoever the hell had killed Flacco, they were still out there, and one day, Jack would get even with them. But for now, he was after the Comanche who'd raided settlements north of San Antonio last month. They'd killed off the men and older boys, carried off women and children, and they'd taken a lot of livestock. Word was, Yellow Wolf had done the deed. Needed to prove himself to Buffalo Hump after the Bandera Pass licking Jack had given him.

Jack had brought only Ben McCulloch, Ad Gillespie, Sam Walker and eleven others on this patrol. The toughest men in his unit, all heavily armed. He'd had them out a week already, tracking Yellow Wolf's raiding party, maybe as many as a hundred warriors.

A week, ten days at the most, was all Jack could afford to be out of garrison, though. Texas was short on money. Patrols, range firing and most training had been cut back to the bare bones. Jack had heard the talk. Everybody had. The Republic might have to disband the Rangers one of these days.

Red Wing's mid-afternoon report didn't prove much. The scout had found pony dung along Walker's Creek a little further north. Otherwise, no sign of any Comanche. Jack ordered his patrol into their saddles ready to ride back to San Antonio. The only Ranger not yet mounted was Adam Cherry, one of the newer boys. He'd spotted a beehive in an old oak tree, and Jack had given Cherry time to climb up and raid some honey.

"Captain!" the boy yelled out of the tree, pointing north along the creek. "Yonder be Comanche, I swear. They's tailing us. Two or three of the bastards just run into the woods!"

Jack shouted, "Cherry, leave the goddamn honey! Shinny down and saddle up, boy." He turned his mount to face the rest, "No need for quiet now, fellers. They know we're here."

Hays let out a deep, satisfied sigh, then moved his Rangers into the open. He rode in the center with seven men on each side in a well-spaced V formation. Jack drew his pistol and led the squad straight for the tree line where Cherry had pointed. Three bare-chested warriors dashed out, black and red war painted faces glistening in the sun. No weapons. They were the bait. The Comanche waved and shouted, then bolted back into the thicket. Jack drew the squad to a halt facing the woods and Walker's Creek beyond. Not gonna fall for that crap, boys. Old Comanche trickery, for sure.

"Steady, men." Jack ordered. "Ain't gonna charge nor fire till we see how many we're up against."

Jack waited in the open, two hundred yards out from where he'd seen the Indians duck into the underbrush. Some minutes passed. Seemed longer in the sun and humidity. Then the trees and brush along the creek bank rustled. A mounted Comanche war party, at least fifty, maybe more, edged out into the open and formed one long battle line facing Jack and his Rangers. Their weapons were visible – muskets, bows and quivers filled with arrows – but none threatened. Dead quiet. Nobody moved. The afternoon heat pressed down.

"Bastard in the middle is Chief Yellow Wolf." Jack nudged his pony's sides. "Forward at a trot, men. Weapons at the ready."

Jack jostled in his saddle as he trotted toward the war party. He drew his second pistol and half-cocked, guiding his pony with his knees. The squad followed Jack's lead. Was anybody going to blink? He was barely sixty yards out when Yellow Wolf turned and motioned the war party back into the tree line. No fight today, Chief? Some cat and mouse? More Comanche bullshit.

Jack drew the squad to a halt. Time to watch and wait. He heard and saw nothing until he stretched in his saddle to peer at the far ridge-line. Comanche were moving to the crest on the other side of Walker's Creek. They dismounted and formed one long line, this time with muskets and bows at the ready. The warriors gestured, waving weapons and yelling taunts. War whoops pierced the humid Texas air. Yellow Wolf beckoned with one arm, "come on over." He was challenging Jack to come and get him, and from the front at that.

"Cain't take 'em on from here, men!" Jack shouted left and right, "Too many and too spread out. Got that creek between us, too." He turned his pony north. "Let's ease our way down the ravine along the creek and get some hill cover. See what we can come up with. Maybe they'll think we're leavin'."

One arm in the air, Jack signaled his squad into single-file and led them past the brow of the surrounding hills, away from the taunting Comanche war party. After half an hour's march, he halted his fourteen horsemen and picked his way up a low embankment onto the open plain. He should be well behind the Comanche by now. Cackles and whoops rose and fell several hundred yards away.

Jack nudged his pony forward so he could peek over the low rise ahead. The whole damned Comanche war party stood there with their bare backs to him. Hard to believe. Some still waved and shouted across the creek. Others leaned on their bows or muskets.

One or two waved buffalo horn helmets in the air. Hays hand-signaled his squad to come up the hill behind him. He full-cocked both Colts, time to deal with Yellow Wolf.

He kicked his pony in the ribs with both heels and charged. No other command needed, Jack's patrol dashed forward alongside him. He kneed his mount straight ahead and steadied the pistols' aim. The closest Comanche braves turned to face his charge, drawing arrows and snapping them to bow strings in one fluid motion. Jack fired both Colts. Two Comanche slumped into the dirt, their arrows loosed high in slow arcs well over Jack's head.

"Fire at will, men!" Jack Hays shouted as he rode on, firing. "Hit what you aim at. Kill 'em all!"

The pistol barrage crackled. Waves of lead thundered from bluish gray clouds on Jack's left and right. More braves fell. The rest turned and ran, probably heading for their ponies in the trees near Walker's Creek. Hays drew up and signaled the squad to regroup and get ready for a counter-attack, stand their ground.

As suddenly as they had vanished on foot, the Comanche reappeared on horseback. Twenty or more young warriors made a flanking move on the run and encircled Jack's party. Riding counter-clockwise, the bronzed, bareback war party fired arrow after arrow into Jack's formation. He countered, drew his Rangers tighter and signaled them into a circle where the ponies' haunches touched. Jack and his boys fired at the circling Comanche warriors and reloaded. Fired more. Reloaded again. A few braves broke off their encirclement and charged toward one side of Jack's formation, head on, moving to break his defenses.

Jack glanced toward Sam Walker, who'd been knocked from his saddle and thudded onto the rocky ground, his shoulder pierced by a through-shot arrow. Feathers showed to Sam's front, and the bloody arrow point stuck out from his upper back. Walker's pony had taken an arrow in the neck and buckled onto its forelegs. Two other Rangers fell close by.

Sam Walker struggled to his feet near some scrub brush, his

body partly shielded by his fallen pony. He kept firing both his Colt pistols from beside his wounded mount near the encirclement. Sam was alive and still fighting. The other two hadn't moved from where they'd fallen. An arrow hissed past Jack's ear, jolting him back to business. He aimed and fired off more rounds.

A lot more Comanche than Rangers were down. The rocky ground was slick with blood. Screams, curses and animal-like grunts echoed off the hills. Comanche on foot swung war axes and clubs as they came at Jack and his boys, but none were a match for the repeater pistols. Lead-filled torsos were piling up.

Somebody needed to break the feathers off that arrow in Sam Walker's shoulder and pull the goddamn shaft through once this was all over. Didn't need to have Sam die of blood poisoning. But the Comanche weren't done yet. Yellow Wolf and the rest of his gang charged again with a straight-up-the-gut move.

"Crowd 'em!" Jack shouted, kneeing his pony around. "Powder burn their red asses. Any of 'em left need to remember who they met at Walker's Creek!"

Ad Gillespie dashed out of formation in front of Jack and rode at the young charging Comanche Chief. Yellow Wolf reined in his pony barely ten yards from Gillespie's horseback lunge and hurled his lance. The steel-pointed shaft hit the galloping Ranger high up and tore through the boy's leather vest and right shoulder as he thundered past the Indian.

Jack Hays drew up further off and stayed in his saddle. Not much he could do. Gillespie wheeled his pony around to face Yellow Wolf again. The Chief reached over one shoulder for an arrow. Ad Gillespie left-shouldered his rifle and, one-handed, shot his foe in the throat. Blood spattered and sprayed forward over Yellow Wolf's pony, coating the animal's mane and neck. The Young Comanche's head bobbed, out of control. He slumped and slid off his mount, landing with a muffled thump on the rocky ground. The battle at Walker's Creek was done.

• • •

"Fine shot, Ad. How bad you hurt?" Hays asked, spurring his horse alongside his injured trooper.

"Damn spear tore my shoulder up pretty bad, Cap'n," Gillespie muttered, "But I'll live, I guess."

Ben McCulloch rode up to Hays. The man was soaked with sweat, like the rest of the men. A long arrow shaft stuck out behind McCulloch's thigh, the point lodged in the crook of his saddle. One of McCulloch's eyes was swollen shut.

"What'd you do to that eye, Ben?" Hays asked. "And what of Sam Walker? Last I saw, he'd taken an arrow, too. Damn thing knocked him right off his horse on the hillside."

"The eye's awright." McCulloch replied. "Sand or Comanche spit, I reckon. And I told Cherry to stay with Walker. Sam warn't good." Ben McCulloch shook his head. "Arrow went plum through him in the shoulder, arrowhead stickin' right out his back. Cherry had to break the feathers off and pull the fuckin' thing through."

Well, that at least was a relief. Maybe Cherry had saved Sam Walker's life. Jack looked around. Bodies were scattered all over the damn place. Who else had he lost?

"We lost Private Fohr." McCulloch said, reading Jack's thoughts. "And two more bad injured. Plus, Ad here, and Sam."

Jack Hays shook his head, cap off. "Damned shame, that's what it is. A goddamn shame. Got to be a better way to settle this."

He waved his cap at the blood-soaked ground and looked around the field. Dead Comanche everywhere. Private Fohr, his new man, tough as he'd been, lay in their midst.

"How 'bout them, the Comanche?" Jack asked, "Looks like we killed a bunch. Buffalo Hump's pride, young Chief Yellow Wolf's layin' out in the brush there, too."

"I'd say they lost more'n twenty-five dead," McCulloch

responded. "Countin' Yellow Wolf. And must have been least forty more of 'em we wounded." He grinned. "Reckon Buffalo Hump's gonna be real pissed now. Yellow Wolf's lucky his time come out here."

Chapter Twenty-One

The Nemesis - June 1844

Buffalo Hump squinted east through the dawn haze at the approaching cortege. He had prepared his village to properly receive the two riders and the sad cargo they'd slung over the back of the third pony. Iron Jacket and Peta Nokona were bringing Yellow Wolf's body to Buffalo Hump for the burial ceremony. Summer on the high plains – even at sunrise the air bore down hot and oppressive, but the Penateka Chief dared not perspire. Such an act might offend Yellow Wolf's spirit.

Eagle feathers were plaited into the long hair running over Buffalo Hump's shoulders. His leathery face was smeared with black and white stripes, and he wore new beaded deerskin trousers with an open beaded vest. The Penateka Chief sat barefoot and bareback astride a white war pony. A long pipe decorated with black feathers rested in one hand. Braves from Yellow Wolf's raiding party stood in a single rank behind Buffalo Hump. To his side, some distance away, women of Yellow Wolf's village waited with ceremonial trinkets. In front of them, heavy stones had been piled high for the grave.

A coal-black raven pumped long, glistening wings against the sunrise. The harbinger flew low toward the northeast, along the hills just beyond the burial party. Buffalo Hump tracked the bird with understanding eyes. The Tuhu Wii in flight was a strong sign from the Great Mystery. Yellow Wolf had taken an honored place in the After Life.

Iron Jacket and Peta Nokona halted close, facing Buffalo Hump. The Chief raised his right hand in greeting and, with the other, took the proffered reins of the pony bearing Yellow Wolf's remains.

"Brothers, we have sad hearts today," Buffalo Hump intoned,

"None is more sad than mine. But we should not grieve for our comrade, Yellow Wolf." He waved a tattooed arm skyward. "We all saw the sacred raven. Yellow Wolf lives with honor in the Great After Life. He lived long enough in this poor world. No pox killed him. He did not die running from the White Faces." Buffalo Hump rested his eyes on the corpse. "No more struggles will test his spirit."

The Chief turned his pony and waved his feathered pipe to the line of warriors, the signal for Yellow Wolf to be laid to rest. Four braves padded forward and pulled the blanket-wrapped body from the pony. A light breeze blew swirls of dust that trailed the braves' moccasined feet as they carried Yellow Wolf past Buffalo Hump. The Chief motioned for the body to be placed into a small alcove in the rocky hillside. He stared down at the wrapped figure from his mounted position for silent minutes. Then Buffalo Hump kneed his pony around to face the women. The time had come for them to begin their work of sealing the burial crypt against predators and grave robbers.

Buffalo Hump swung off his pony and motioned the other two Chiefs to follow. Iron Jacket and Peta Nokona slid from their animals' bare backs and followed Buffalo Hump into the heavy shade of an old pecan grove. The Chief sat down and bowed his head. Iron Jacket and Peta Nokona crossed their legs and sat, heads bowed, facing him. The only sound came from the women stacking stones to protect Yellow Wolf's corpse and the artifacts entombed with him. When the burial detail had completed the gravesite, the village women approached and bowed to Buffalo Hump. Still seated, the Chief returned their bow. He waited until the females were out of earshot, then leaned forward to address the two other Chiefs.

"My grief is broader today than simply mourning our comrade, Yellow Wolf." Buffalo Hump whispered. "His death is but an omen. This sacred plateau can be our home for now, but one day the White Face will drive us out." Buffalo Hump fingered his long, unlit pipe. "We took this land from others." He made a sweeping gesture with his outstretched pipe hand. "We made the land good for

Numunuh. But soon, White Faces will take everything from us. Our time is almost finished. Such is the way and the will of the Great Mystery."

The two Chiefs facing him remained silent. Buffalo Hump uncrossed his legs and stood. He motioned his two comrades to their feet. They rose, heads erect and faces stern. The Penateka Chief focused his dark eyes, first on Iron Jacket, then on Peta Nokona.

"We call ourselves by a plain name, 'Numunuh,' the People." Buffalo Hump spoke with a thin smile. "Yet those we have defeated give us the highest respect. They name us Ku-man-shee, the Great Enemy, the people who fight all the time."

"I say now the truth." Buffalo Hump waved his pipe south toward San Antonio. "There is one White Face who holds our destiny in his hand. Beyond he lives, in the soldier camp near their Béxar village. A Ranger man they call Captain Jack. This White Face is the lightning that brings no rain, only destruction and death. He is our nemesis. Our Ku-man-shee. Even if we take his scalp, Lightning Without Rain will come and haunt us in the Spirit World."

PART FOUR

The End of the New Republic

"The final act in this great drama is now performed, the Republic of
Texas is no more."

*Texas Republic President, Anson Jones, handing control of the newest US state
over to Texas Governor James Pickney Henderson, 9th February 1846*

Chapter Twenty-Two

A New Mission - late 1845

Jack stood in the doorway, wide-eyed. Oak-paneled walls, a
matching desk and real furniture? General Houston had sure come
up in the world since the last time Jack had been in Austin. The
graying General paced the floor along a row of bookshelves, his back
to the open door. Sam Houston's silver-handled cane was nowhere in
sight. Guess the old ankle wound had finally quit paining him.

Had General Sam read all the books on that damned wall?
Probably not. The only reading material they'd ever discussed was
Rogers' "Twenty-Eight Rules for Ranging," and even that was more a
pamphlet than a book.

Jack rapped twice on the open door frame and took off his
black hat. Sam Houston straightened and turned to the door. The
stony face brightened. A broad, open-mouthed smile broke over the
General's face.

"Captain Hays. Jack Hays," Houston shouted. "Come on in,
boy. Don't just stand there blocking the goddamn door."

Jack walked across the room and stuck out his hand. He

didn't care any more that Houston called him "boy." The General gave him a welcoming handshake with those long, bony fingers. Sam Houston leaned on one end of his desktop and motioned for Jack to take a seat, then stepped behind his cluttered desk and lowered his long frame into a massive oak chair. He looked Jack up and down.

"Sure as hell good to see you, young feller," Houston said. "And first, got to say I'm real sorry to hear about Andy Jackson's passing. Him and me, only arguments we ever had was about Indians. I admire the Red men, most of 'em, anyway. He did not. All the same, he was cut from fine cloth, that man. And he was a helluva soldier. Good President, too."

"General Sam," Jack replied, "Been too damned long since I seen you last. I appreciate the sentiments. You know, after all they done for me, I always wanted to visit Aunt Rachel and Mr. Jackson again. If I hadn't been out chasing Comanche and Mexicans, I'd have rode back to Nashville on my own."

The General spoke, more animated. "Well, son, the Bible says the dead got to bury their own. You had your priorities straight. And since you brought up Mexicans, I called you here with a new proposition. One that's gonna get you and your boys back together."

Sam Houston locked eyes with him. Jack shifted his feet and sat up straight in his chair. Hard to believe his Ranger unit had been disbanded over a year already, right after Plum Creek and the treaty. Wasn't like there was no more enemy around with the Comanche whipped. But Texas as a country had just run out of money. Owed the United States millions, too. Lately though, Jack had heard all the news and rumors. Texas was about to be a state. They'd have money for Rangerin' again.

"Few more months," the General said, "and this here Republic is goin' away. Texas will be the twenty-sixth U-nited State. Mexico ain't gonna be happy about that."

The General smiled and pulled out his whiskey flask. He screwed open the top and sniffed. A steady hand held the whiskey container straight out, a silent offer from General Sam. Jack shook his head.

Too early in the day.

"T'ween now and statehood time," Houston said, pausing for a sip, "I want you to get your Rangers back together. Round 'em all up and start trainin'. When the new governor's appointed, probably be Jim Henderson. Leastways it oughta be. You come see him here in Austin and tell him you've got your Rangers ready to go. Tell him you want to join up either with the militia or the Bluecoats, fightin' Mexico."

Jack smiled. Great news. He'd been doing land surveying since his Rangers broke up, and he'd earned quite a tidy sum partnering with another ex-Ranger, John Caperton. Wonder how, or if, he'd get paid as much for Rangering once he and the boys got going again? Maybe John would join up, too. He'd worry about that later. Jack stood up to leave. Houston put his palm up to signify he wasn't done.

"Now, a couple more matters, son," General Houston lowered his voice. "First, I ain't supposed to know this, but I'm damned certain Jim Polk's made another horseshit agreement with that little bastard, Santa Anna. Whatever it was, Santa Anna gets back in Mexico, he'll sure double-cross President Polk like he did me and Andy Jackson years ago. Only way clear is to take over Mexico. Kill off Santa Anna."

Sam Houston looked a hole through Jack and fiddled with a pen on his desk. The General was having a hard time with something that bothered him. Jack waited. Whatever was about to come had to be life-or-death.

"My private recommendation to folks here and in Washington?" The General spoke now almost in a whisper. "We attack first. Give the Mexicans all out war. Hit the bastards hard and fast, and don't stop till we take Monterrey and Mexico City. You'll be part of that, son, if I got any say."

Damn. The General's idea suited Jack just fine. In fact, he'd have volunteered on the spot to have Hays' Rangers be the lead unit going into Monterrey or Mexico City. But after the San Antonio debacle and General Woll at Salado Creek – he'd disagreed hard and loud with General Sam about chasin' that little French shit back to Mexico – Jack probably wouldn't be that lucky. Anyway, the time had come for paying back the Mexicans for the Alamo and Goliad.

• • •

A cold March hill country wind blew in Jack's face. He skipped two of the stone steps of the State House in Austin on his way up to the wide landing. Once inside the double oak and glass doors, an orderly ushered him without fanfare down the hallway and into James Pinckney Henderson's sparsely furnished office. Four months earlier, he'd sat in Sam Houston's office when Texas was a Republic. Now Jack had an appointment with the new governor of the twenty-sixth U.S. state, elected just as General Houston had predicted.

James Henderson stood near a small window overlooking the Austin town plaza and market. He turned when Jack approached. My God, the man was taller and even thinner than Jack had remembered. Still had that black bow tie pulled up tight around a high, white collar. Made his long, sour face even longer. The governor extended his hand.

"Governor Henderson." Jack shook hands. "Thanks for making time to see me. I know you got big doings to attend. President Polk's on your ass, Mexicans are stirring up trouble and folks are all nervous about us bein' a new state."

Governor Henderson motioned Jack into a chair. The man still didn't smile. What was it like to be the man running Texas right now? At least if he was being invited to sit, Jack would get to stay a spell, maybe hear what was going on and speak his mind. The governor stepped behind his desk and picked up a stack of papers.

Henderson eyed Jack. "I know when to make time for you

Ranger boys, Jack. Like you said, Mexico is the immediate problem. Stirring the war pot. Santa Anna is behaving exactly like General Sam said he would. Ever the double-dealing dictator."

The Governor stared at Hays, then glanced down at the papers in his hand. What was in all that paperwork? Orders? Guess he'd find out soon enough. Henderson took his seat behind the desk, put the papers aside and leaned forward.

"I've told President Polk." The governor's voice was low, almost secretive like Sam Houston's had been. "The Texas Militia and you Rangers will do what's needed when the war starts. Big mistake disbanding the Rangers after Plum Creek. 'No more money and other priorities,' damned politicians said. Your boys are probably scattered all over hell by now. But Jack, we need them reconstituted, pronto."

"Governor Henderson, sir," Jack interrupted. "A couple months back, Captain Walker and me already started roundin' up the troops after a talk I had with Gen'ral Sam. Didn't talk to nobody about it, though. Sir, I'd say we're ready to move out in no more'n a month, six weeks at the most."

The governor's eyebrows raised. "That's quite the pleasant surprise. Welcome news indeed, Jack. And me, I've already asked for and been granted a leave of absence. In less than a month, I'll take my military post as a Brigadier to better assist General Taylor in his conduct of the war effort."

Henderson reached for his stack of papers again and drew out a thin packet. He handed the sheets over to Jack. He was about to go to war again.

"Once your forces are ready," Henderson said. "These are your orders."

Jack stared down at the packet without reading. Damn, the governor must've already talked to General Sam and others. War planning was a lot further along than he'd guessed. So what exactly might be his orders?

"Let me be the first to congratulate you." The governor beamed. "As of now, John Coffee Hays, you are a full colonel commanding federalized Texas Rangers and reporting to me. We're part of General Zack Taylor's U.S. Army of Occupation. Get a move on, man. Form me up a mounted regiment of the meanest men that ever rode with you."

Promoted to Colonel. The commander of a full regiment of three hundred men, maybe more, attached to the United States Army. Jack had a helluva lot to digest and pass on to Sam Walker and the rest of Hays' Rangers.

"You dare not dally," the governor admonished. "We've got a whole goddamn country south of here to take over. Moreover, there's a fucking score to finally settle with that little General Lopez de Santa Anna and his ilk."

Jack stood up and almost turned over his chair. He saluted. The Governor, soon-to-be General, returned the salute then shook Jack's hand. Hays' Rangers, or whatever they were gonna be called, would be on their way to Mexico by summer.

• • •

June in Texas. The heat was barely tolerable. Hard to believe back in March there'd been a cold blue norther howling through the hill country. Jack Hays rode along the ranks of his assembled Rangers. Two cavalry squadrons, mostly veterans of Salado Creek, Bandera Pass and other skirmishes. The long line of grizzled troops was sprinkled with a few fresh-faced recruits. All were on horseback, and none wore military uniforms. A man couldn't fight in those damned heavy jackets and trousers, especially in this heat.

Getting one company back together had been easy. Rounding up more, though, a full regiment of almost three hundred men, now that had taken some doing. Jack knew most of them already, and they looked the same as always. Some, like his surveyor friend, John Caperton, stared out from under floppy, broad-brimmed hats. Others wrapped those damned fringed cotton shawls, like Texas Bedouins, around their heads and necks to keep the heat away. Most had beards and mustaches. Maybe more protection against the sun and wind. What a bunch of ruffians.

But what Jack admired most was the weaponry. Knives, Colt pistols and long, curved sabers bristled from every torso and saddle. Rifles and muskets were slung across the backs of more than half the regiment. Jack's own Colt repeaters were strapped, handles forward, on his thighs. One extra pistol and a broad knife were stuffed into his pommel bag, along with spare cylinders. A new saber he'd received as a promotion gift from Brigadier Henderson hung in a leather scabbard over Jack's saddle horn.

My God, he was a full colonel now, a regimental commander, and only twenty-eight years on God's earth. His boyish face was now tanned and rougher from the Texas wind and sun…and getting more lines. But overall, Jack still looked and felt younger than he ought to. He wore his simple black garrison cap, and he was clean-shaven. Missus Priscilla, Susan's mother, had hinted once too often about how much handsomer Jack was without that dark beard. Jack turned his pony to face his new command.

"Men, at ease and listen up." Jack spoke loud enough for the whole regiment to hear. "Most of you got real poor judgment joinin' up with Sam Walker, Ben McColluch, Ad Gillespie and me again. Rest of you new fellers? Well, either you're crazy from the heat, or you got nothin' more'n a death wish."

Laughter rippled through the ranks. A few of Hays' former Rangers tipped their hats or saluted Jack with two knuckles. Jack tried to keep a stern face, but he felt the slightest smile creep into the corners of his closed mouth. Jack's pony pawed the hardpan. He shifted in the saddle.

"No secret, I ain't keen on military falderal," Jack shouted over the din, pulling hard on his reins. "Fact is, you men are more'n Rangers these days. You have joined the First Regiment, Texas Mounted Volunteers, the pride of General Zachary Taylor's United

States Army."

Jack waved one hand in a circle over his head. Two men broke ranks and guided their mounts to one side of their regimental commander. Both turned to face the assembled troops. Now he'd introduce his command.

"Bein' attached to the Army and all," Jack shouted. "We got to have us a command structure. So we got ourselves a brand new lieutenant colonel in this regiment. Sam Walker here will be my number two man. He's also commandin' the first squadron."

Sam Walker doffed his big hat, his thinning hair blowing in the wind.

Jack stretched tall in the saddle to see past the first row of riders, to make damned sure everybody could still see and hear him. Then he pointed to the second rider who took off his short-billed field cap.

"And this here's Major Mike Chevaille." Jack announced. "If me and Sam both go down, Mikey here's your regimental commander. Right now, he's got the second squadron. Major Chevaille's also in charge of weapons and munitions."

Andrew Jackson had once told him, "When you got to say something serious, things will go better if said with a little humor." Jack took one deep breath and looked over his command, straight-faced.

"Most important, though," Jack shouted in his best command voice. "One of you shits loses his nerve or wits, tries to get out of the regiment now or on the way to Matamoros, ol' eagle-eye Mikey's got orders to shoot your yellow, lily-livered ass dead on the spot. And Mikey don't ever miss."

Louder laughter and a few whoops let loose. Jack Hays smiled, looking at the motley assembly. Some kept laughing, some just grinned back at him. No deserters here. These boys were ready for action. They'd be prepared by the time he got them to Mexico and joined up with General Henderson's command. They'd kill Mexicans.

Chapter Twenty-Three

Trouble in Monterrey - September 1846

The thin sliver of a waning moon lit the cool night. Jack Hays sat in short grass and scrub brush near the west bank of the Rio Santa Catarina. A faint rustling came in the low mesquite behind him. Should be friendly. He half-cocked the Colt repeater in his lap and looked over his shoulder into the woods. Three short, mockingbird-like chirps, the signal that Walker and Chevaille were arriving, as expected. The two Rangers nodded a greeting and squatted opposite Jack. He eased the hammer down on his pistol and stared past his two commanders. The river drifted behind them in weak moonlight.

Good thing there hadn't been a lot of rain lately. No flood crest to contend with. He needed to get the whole goddamn regiment across this river before dawn, and in silence. Jack had to have total surprise if General Henderson's plan for him to infiltrate Monterrey was going to work.

"Evening, fellas." Jack whispered. "About time y'all showed up. I was beginning to think wasn't nobody here. Damned good discipline. Ain't none of our fellers nor their mounts made so much as a peep so far."

Walker and Chevaille nodded. Jack slid closer to the pair in the weak moonlight to better keep eye contact. He fixed his unblinking stare on Sam Walker. The new lieutenant colonel stared back.

"Sam, you and your squadron's goin' in with me at first light," Jack said in his lowest voice and waved his arm toward the river. "Mike, I want you and your boys linin' the west bank. Cover us while we cross. Lay fire on anybody coming back across the river. Whoever's coming won't be us." Jack looked from Walker to Chevaille for their nods of understanding. "Then you come cross with the second squadron right at sunup, Mike."

Henderson had advised Jack that General Zachary Taylor's main force had tried twice to take the town from the East, but the Mexicans – Major General Pedro de Ampudia's stubborn bastards – had driven them off. Well, Sénor Pedro, nobody was gonna keep Hays' 1st Regiment of Texas Mounted Volunteers out of Monterrey tomorrow morning.

The day had been a long time coming. Jack Hays straightened up and stared at his squadron commanders. They were about to strike at the heart and soul of Mexico and take Monterrey. This attack was big. Texas would have retribution for the Alamo and Goliad.

"Now, both of you get this next order clear." Jack Hays demanded. "No killin' civilians, unless they shoot first. But no military prisoners. Anybody in uniform, give 'em no quarter. Not even their officers. Kill 'em all. None of Ampudia's goddamn dragoons gonna be walkin' around Monterrey when this is done."

There was no turning back now. No need to, he'd given a clear order. Jack wanted the Mexican bastards dead.

• • •

Colonel Jack Hays led his pony in the half-light down the bank and into the warm water of the Santa Catarina River. Barely three paces behind him, Sam Walker and two hundred Texas Rangers slipped into the slow-moving current, clutching the necks of their mounts. The occasional splash of swimming horses was the only sound. Within minutes, the silent unit mounted up in one long, wet line on the east side. Jack's regiment was in position. He held his breath and sensed the battle to come.

Jack twisted in his saddle and looked left and right. A soft ruffling passed all along the line as pistols and rifles were unwrapped from oilcloths. Men checked their weapons for water, and oilcloths were folded and stuffed into pommel bags. The Eastern sky showed the first hint of yellow light on Sam Walker. He waved his pistol up and down to Jack from twenty yards away. All set to go.

Jack full-cocked both his pistols and tried to breathe deeper. He nudged his pony and guided the animal with his knees, a quiet trot toward the line of low adobe houses and shops that made up the outskirts of Monterrey. Now Jack could hear the reverberation of hooves behind him, like soft thunder. His Rangers on the advance, spread out on the hardpan. The first squadron was on the attack. Headed into battle.

Who would shoot first? From where? How accurate would their aim be? He tried to slow his breathing. Jack sensed his surroundings almost as much as he saw them. Weak light reflected off metal in the tree line ahead. Some kind of structure there? Wood? A wagon?

Double-clicks of metal-on-metal just ahead. Jack ducked against his pony's neck. A muzzle flash and a sharp crack, then a second one, just to Jack's right. Both rounds hissed overhead and ricocheted off an adobe wall on his left. Shakoed heads poked up over a wagon parked in the trees. Jack fired both pistols, followed by a volley of friendly fire echoing behind him. The barrage shattered the wagon sideboards and sent shakos flying into the early morning air.

Three Mexican infantrymen in blue tunics and white trousers slumped forward into the remnants of the wagon bed. Two others dropped their muskets and dashed around the corner of the nearest adobe building. First contact with the enemy and no more than a skirmish, but Jack knew there'd be a hell of a lot more.

"Los Diablos Tejanos! Los Diablos Tejanos!" The shouts came from the two escaping dragoons. Jack reined in his pony and peered around the corner and up a dark, empty street. "The Devil Texans" was a good description. We are here, by God, and we are taking over Monterrey. Run. Run and tell that to Santa Anna, boys. Jack kicked his pony hard and turned the corner. He galloped toward where he'd last seen white pants running.

Jack knew he wasn't riding alone. Sam Walker and three squads would be close on his tail. The rest of Walker's Ranger squadron was somewhere on the flank, riding into Monterrey through the warren of side streets and crisscrossing alleyways. He'd see them all soon at their rendezvous point, the town square.

Gunfire erupted to his front and from both sides. Shadows moved in the street. Jack aimed and fired at the moving forms. Mexican fighters fell, shouting and cursing. Screams came from a house on his right. Grunts of struggle erupted in the darkness to his left, the unmistakable sound of close combat.

Jack rode over fallen bodies. A shape, a man or boy in a straw hat, ran at him from the side and grabbed at his leg. Somebody, a damned civilian maybe, trying to pull him off his pony. Jack pulled his saber and slashed downward twice. The body tumbled away screaming. Blood stained Jack's blade.

He kept the saber in one hand, ducked down and galloped on toward the town center. The sides of adobe buildings and trees along the narrow streets flickered yellow and crackled with gunfire. Shadows ran and shadows chased. More gunfire. More death. Groaning and the haunting sounds of the dying echoed all around Jack Hays. His Rangers were fully engaged. They were killing the enemy.

• • •

An eerie quiet gripped Monterrey at mid-morning. The sun hung over the high crest of the Sierra Madre Orient east of the city. Jack Hays' Rangers were in control of the west side of Monterrey. Jack dismounted and paced the grimly silent battleground, surveying the devastation with his pony trailing him toward the central plaza. Blue-coated regulars of Zachary Taylor's Army might be mopping up on the east side, but not much of that was needed here.

A few nervous civilians looked out from windows or doorways, eyes wide. Some covered their mouths with open hands. Most shops were boarded up. Women and children wailed. Other locals glared at Jack and his men. Or they raced about going nowhere in the dusty streets. Two old men bent over the lifeless bodies of scattered Mexican troops. They scraped with little effect at corpses covered with blood and dirt. One severed head, still strapped to a red shako, lay on the rough cobblestones a yard from its torso. A boy not older than ten cried, probably over a fallen relative who'd made the mistake of opposing Hays' Rangers.

Random shots echoed between Jack and the river to his back. His "no quarter" demand might have been harsh, but the Mexican army wouldn't be blowing any damned victory bugle calls today. Jack turned and touched the brim of his cap to acknowledge the arrival of Sam Walker and Mike Chevaille. Both men approached on foot, hats in hand, with their horses trailing. They slipped into step beside Jack.

Countless more Mexican dragoons and a scattering of civilians lay dead where Hays strode with Walker and Chevaille through the streets. Several victims had been scalped, many had arms or legs severed from their torsos, and all were mutilated in one fashion or another by gunshot, knife cuts, or saber slashes. Jack gingerly stepped over a cleaved hand still gripping a Mexican saber.

Jack's nervous pony snorted in protest and tried to rear up behind him. He gripped the reins and pulled the animal down, tugging him through the carnage. The mounts of Chevaille and Walker fought their reins too. The smell of spent gunpowder mixed with the stink of death. The September sun beat down on mostly blue-and-white uniformed corpses, darkening blood pooling under and around them. No breeze stirred to blow the baking stench away.

"My God," Mike Chevaille muttered, wiping his forehead with a bandana. "What the hell have we done here, Jack?"

"You weren't at Goliad, Mikey," Hays snapped. "None of us was at the fuckin' Alamo, neither. Santa Anna's boys here, they all had it comin', goddamnit. We was no more than the instrument of God's justice."

Jack turned and glared at Mike Chevaille. The Major would not look him in the eye. Jack frowned and eyed Sam Walker. His second-in-command blinked and looked down.

"How many Rangers we lose, Sam?"

"Nine. Nine dead." Walker raised his head and looked away. "None of the old boys, though, believe it or not. Ad Gillespie's gonna lose a leg. Be lucky to live through that."

Sam Walker faced Jack and looked him up and down, then turned away again. Before Jack could ask Sam what the hell he was thinking, a blue-coated rider approached and drew up short, his mount scattering dust and pebbles. Jack grabbed for the horse's reins.

"Excuse me, sirs," the young rider shouted down. "One of you Colonel Hays? Or can you tell me where to find him, quick? General wants to see him personally before nightfall. Said best not to tarry, neither. He's real pissed!"

Zachary Taylor, or "Old Rough and Ready," as many called him. General Sam had warned Jack about the man and his sensibilities, and Andrew Jackson had told stories about him years ago. "More the gentleman than the officer," he'd said.
Jack glared up at the General's messenger, then dropped the boy's reins. "I'm Jack Hays! Tell General Taylor I'll be there just as soon's we finish cleaning up this goddamn mess in the middle of town."

He gave the horse a smack on the rump and the animal bolted away with its rider clinging to the saddle horn and fumbling for the reins. Jack frowned and stepped away from his two commanders. He'd best think about this carefully. Sam Houston had confided that Zack Taylor could, for certain, be rough and ready, but deep down, the man was a stickler for rules and tradition, and he rarely lead by example. Taylor was reportedly also a strict disciplinarian, so this meeting would probably not be good. Jack took a couple of minutes to calm down, then mounted up and wordlessly knuckle-saluted Walker and Chevaille. He reined his pony around and rode in the direction of General Taylor's command headquarters.

• • •

Jack came upon the main body of the U.S. Army of Occupation fortifying their encampments in eastern Monterrey. After a delay for identification, he was allowed to pass through the lines of Colonel Worth's Maryland and District of Columbia Battalion. By sunset, he was in General Taylor's headquarters encampment set up in a grove of gnarled olive trees. Queried, a sentry pointed Jack toward a stocky, white-headed man with long bushy sideburns who was pacing the dusty trail and slapping his gray campaign hat against his thigh. Two gold stars glistened on the epaulets of General Zachary Taylor's spotless, fitted navy blue uniform. The General turned at the sound of the horse. Jack reined in his pony and saluted.

"General Taylor, sir." Jack addressed the U.S. Commander with his best military manners. "I'm Colonel Jack Hays, Texas Rangers…. Ah, s'cuse me, sir, I mean First Regiment, Texas Mounted Volunteers. I got a message this afternoon you wanted to see me just as soon as I could get here."

The General looked up. He did not smile, nor did he return Jack's salute. Zachary Taylor stared up at him as if Jack was some strange beast loose in the street – a varmint that needed killing. Jack's gut tightened.

"Hays? You're the infamous John Coffee Hays?" Zachary Taylor spoke, almost in snorting disbelief. "But then, how the hell would I know who you are? No uniform? No rank? You ride in here looking like a bloody highwayman and observe no proper dismount before addressing your commander. Mister, you are the most uncouth bit of rabble I've seen in this war. That said, I'd wager you are indeed the killer who's responsible for all the wanton death and destruction

I'm hearing about."

Jack bit his lip and dismounted. Then, silent and rigid, he faced General Taylor without a further salute. The Army Commander could say whatever he wanted, Jack would have to listen. Obeying might be another matter.

"Son," the General softened his tone. "I'm well aware of your exploits. Stand at ease, now. The United States appreciates your bravery."

Jack felt the blood drain from his face. He shifted his feet apart and locked both hands behind his back. "Parade rest," as best Jack could recall the position. This might go well after all. He kept his eyes on General Taylor, still in the midst of his comments.

"We might not have Monterrey tonight without your efforts, Colonel Hays. The Army is grateful, yet we must abhor your barbarism, your demonstrated lack of military order and discipline." The General paced. "From my reports, you've shown an abysmal ignorance of the rules of war. Fortunately for you, however, General Henderson has vouched for your worth. You do understand what I'm saying, correct?"

Jack did not respond to the General's question. Zachary Taylor stopped pacing and turned to face him. Apparently, the General was far from done. What was next? Certainly some sort of punishment, maybe even a court martial. Taylor pointed one stubby finger at Jack.

"I've called you here, Colonel," The General said, "to provide you and your rabble an opportunity. By sundown tomorrow, I expect to receive General Ampudia's unconditional surrender. He's surrounded with no way out of the city and certainly no reinforcements. You, my young friend, are to have yourself and your men in proper uniform in time for reveille two days hence. That accomplished, you will attend General Ampudia's surrender ceremony, and there you will apologize to him for your serious breach of international military protocol in this engagement."

Jack Hays could only stare at Zachary Taylor. As a practical matter, where would he find uniforms for his entire regiment? The General had to know the order was impossible to obey. But more important, why would anybody, any Texan or American, apologize to any Mexican? And for what? For balancing the scales of justice? The General had to be a madman.

"Sir." Jack cleared his throat. "You can ask General Henderson or General Houston. My men, they don't ask much. They follow my orders. The boys know their job. They keep the peace. They kill the enemy and leave the politics and ass-kissin' to the politicians. Rangers do that real well. You U.S. Army folks, you call us irregulars, and I reckon that's a suitable moniker. Good at fighting, bad at soldierin'. We just ain't regular like you. God willing, we never gonna be. By your leave, sir, Hays' Rangers will be heading back to Texas."

Jack turned on his heel without waiting for a reaction. He put one foot in his stirrup and hoisted his weary body into the saddle. This time he did not salute Zachary Taylor. If a court martial was coming, they'd have to chase him down to serve the papers. Jack Hays slapped his pony's rear and galloped west into the gathering darkness.

• • •

Two days after he'd kicked the Mexicans' asses up around their necks and pretty much took most of Monterrey before anybody knew what had happened, Colonel Jack Hays was up early, sitting under an old oak tree. He sipped at a tin of coffee and waited for the sun to come up. He hadn't slept well at all since his meeting with that weasly, blue-coated General Taylor.

Jack had fought the Mexicans like they fought everybody else. He'd given them some of their own medicine. Yet here he sat, his whole damned Ranger regiment banished to the woods west of Rio

Santa Catarina and packing up for Texas. General Taylor had sent him a stern letter of reprimand that ordered Jack and his Rangers not to get anywhere near the surrender ceremony of General Ampudia. He hadn't any intention of doing such a thing, anyway. Shit, he'd even heard Taylor had gone and let that Mexican sonofabitch and the rest of his men have safe passage out of Monterrey. Signed a six-week armistice and let Ampudia keep his cannons, too. Wonder what President Polk might have to say about all that...that was, if anybody ever dared tell him the whole truth?

Chapter Twenty-Four

Colonel Hays goes to Washington - February 1847

Bone tired, Jack Hays stepped down the gangway of the side-wheel steamship that had docked at Pittsburgh's Allegheny River port barely an hour earlier. He'd been on coastal steamers and riverboats for more than a month since boarding in Galveston just after Christmas. Jack wore his heavy canvas duffel across his back, bandolier style. A ship's porter followed Jack with his leather valise. The red-and-yellow sign on the building across the street read, "Butterfield Coach Lines, 100 Duquesne Way," Jack's next transport point.

Back in December, Governor Henderson had ordered him east for a private meeting with President James Polk and testimony before Congress. Texas needed more resources to wage the war with Mexico. To the Governor's way of thinking, Jack was a war hero, the right man to ask for the money, even though he'd gotten that ass-chewing and official reprimand from General Taylor the year before.

The wind stung Jack's cheeks and made his eyes water. He took his valise from the porter, crossed the street and pushed his way into the Butterfield Coach Lines' waiting area. Two hours later, chewing a string of beef jerky and holding a tin of strong coffee, he stepped into the cold again and boarded a chartered coach for his five-day trip from Pittsburgh to Washington. Secretary of State Burnet had arranged the private transport.

The red-lacquered Concord Celerity coach was the latest design. A thorough leather-suspended cabin, insulating curtains and wide axle stance promised stability and comfort for the rough terrain ahead. A double-layered canvas top made the coach lighter on the road than any Jack had been on in Texas. This was transportation well suited for mountain roads in winter. Jack tinkered with a seat back strap and found that the Celerity's cabin also had a fold-down pair of padded seats for sleeping. His coach ride into Washington should be a more comfortable end to the long trip than he'd expected.

• • •

Four days and nights on the Old Washington Road brought Jack to his last morning of swaying in the coach cabin. Only twenty more miles to Washington. Jack stared out the window at the passing landscape. The snow had vanished now that they were down out of the Allegheny highlands. Sunshine warmed his coach, and horses romped in a muddy pasture close to the road. Jack stretched his legs and yawned.

The easy sway of the carriage and seeing the horses caused Jack to reflect. Weeks had passed since he'd been on his pony, even longer since that confrontation with General Taylor. Had the General been right? Were Jack and his Rangers the lawless killers that Taylor had insisted they were? Was Jack Hays just another barbarian, a savage like Buffalo Hump? For that matter, was the Comanche Chief truly a savage and as evil as most Texans thought he was?

The fresh four-horse team clattered across a wooden bridge and the stagecoach jostled, tossing Jack side-to-side. The noise and abrupt movement brought back the reality that he would soon arrive in the Nation's Capital. Jack was about to romp in the mud of Washington politics and hear the clatter of the nation's politicians. His rangering experience and military expertise would probably be of little use in Congress Hall. One thing was certain. He'd know soon.

• • •

The Willard Hotel, a block from the White House, was as grand as he'd been told, even if the establishment was cobbled together out of six homes. Jack stared up at the massive lobby columns, then over to a winding, red-carpeted staircase that appeared to go nowhere. Lot of money must've gone into fixing the hotel up, but for some reason, the effect made him uneasy. No matter, the Willard was where he'd been told to stay.

Jack registered without incident, then hustled to catch up with the hotel porter and his bags. He'd need to dig into his duffel and valise as soon as he could to find the damned new clothes and the bowtie Susan had so carefully done up for him. Jack couldn't be late for his appointment with President Polk and dinner at the White House tonight.

Inside his hotel room, his nervousness grew. Dark and heavy velvet curtains blocked the light, and some kind of newfangled indoor privy with a copper bathtub loomed behind a set of towering open double doors. The bed covers were slick and shiny, and the bed was even bigger than the one in Susan Calvert's family house back in Seguin. So different. So damned fancy. Not sure he could sleep in a place so free of grit.

A big oak footlocker sat at the foot of the hotel bed. At least that thing was practical. Jack could lock his pistols and ammunition inside, even his pommel bag. Couldn't wear those Colt pistols to the White House, and he didn't need to take money along. Damn, he'd be meeting the President and the First Lady. Should he take her something? Flowers? A bottle of good champagne? A little late to be thinking of presents. Getting dressed and ready would take all his time between now and his dinner appointment. He hoped he wouldn't sweat through his clothes before even setting foot in the White House.

• • •

Two hours later, Colonel Jack Hays walked the short distance down Pennsylvania Avenue to the White House. He felt stiff as hell in his new black trousers and white shirt with bow tie, and the dark gray vest and cutaway black jacket made him feel uncomfortably decorative. Jack was bare headed, the only man on the path not wearing some kind of hat or cap for the February night. His head wasn't cold, but his feet hurt, thanks to the damned five-eyelet brogans Susan had insisted he wear. How in the hell did people walk in those things? Jack would throw 'em away when this trip was done, for certain. His old high top trail boots were a lot more comfortable.

The White House towered in front of him in the gathering darkness. Was that President Polk himself standing at the top of the steps and waving? Must be Missus Polk standing beside him. The Hermitage back in Nashville was big, but this White House? My God, what a mansion. Hard to believe the damned British had put the torch to the place when Andrew Jackson had been a general in the Army. He'd sure as hell paid them back for that deed down in New Orleans.

"Colonel Hays! John Coffee Hays," President James Polk bounded down the stone steps shouting. "Welcome to Washington and the White House. Come on up here and meet Sarah."

Jack Hays shook the President's hand and strode up the steps behind Polk onto the wide, two-story veranda. Damn, Jim Polk was about the same size and build as him. Shorter than most men. Good. But the olive-skinned woman waiting near the entrance was much taller than him and the President. Willowy and aristocratic. Even her smile was intimidating.

"Colonel Hays," the President spoke. "This is the First Lady, my wife, Sarah Childress Polk."

Jack took Sarah Polk's soft fingers and bowed just enough. Not much time in the kitchen or garden with those hands. He looked up. Sarah Polk had to be almost six feet tall and as dark as Emily

West. God, the thought of Emily had come to him again. Why was it always Emily in his head and not Susan? After all, Susan was his fiancé.

Sarah Polk had her dark hair parted in the middle and let ringlets dangle around her ears. She wore a perfectly tailored lavender evening gown. The overall effect was striking, if not a little arrogant. Sarah Childress Polk was American royalty, and Jack felt somehow common.

"Good evening, Colonel Hays." Sarah Polk's voice matched her velvet handshake. "I am honored to meet the man that James says is single-handedly taming the Western Indians and vanquishing the Mexicans. Bravo."

A familiar heat crept up under Jack's shirt collar. He simply could not abide such flattery, especially from the wife of the President. Some kind of stupid grin crossed his face before he could even consider a proper response. President Polk intervened. He ushered the First Lady and Jack through the open doors and toward a first-floor dining room.

Once inside the massive eating space, the President gestured with one hand to Jack's chair at the long table. A fancy, gold-colored, velvet-cushioned seat beckoned, but Jack stood until James Polk had helped his wife to her place.

"Please, Colonel Hays," the President said. "Be seated and welcome. Secretary of War Bill Marcy will join you and me after dinner for a brandy. But first, I wanted the three of us to have some time alone. Talk about Tennessee and Texas. Secretary Marcy can sometimes dominate an evening."

Jack nodded to the President and his wife and took his seat at James Polk's right side, across from Sarah Polk. The three sat around the end of the long table. Lots of plates, glasses and silverware in front of Jack. A big vase of mixed flowers stood far down in the middle of the linen-decked table. Could've had another nine or ten people sitting around, if they'd been invited. Jack marveled at the gold and porcelain chandelier, matching gold-trimmed white draperies, and the long, ornate mahogany sideboard where the first part of their meal was laid out. He wished he had a drink....ale, whiskey, anything to sooth his travel weary nerves.

A simple nod from James Polk brought liveried Negro waiters – must be freemen, not slaves – to the sideboard. They moved with almost military precision, bringing the evening meal to the table. An array of meats, sauces, vegetables and breads quickly spread out before Jack. A hell of a dinner. Best looking meal he'd seen since the Calverts' spread last Christmas.

The Polks offered him well water and unfermented apple cider, but no ale. No wine or whiskey, either. Sarah Childress Polk had already explained at some length that she was against people drinking alcohol. Good Presbyterian upbringing. Jack would have to wait for a real drink until the meeting with Secretary Marcy.

"Mr. President, Missus Polk," Jack said over dinner. "Texas is sure a long way from Washington. Coastal steamers and river boats and a rough coach ride. I'm proud to be invited and to make your acquaintance. Governor Henderson extends his regards. He says you ought to visit him and Miz Henderson in Austin, just as soon as we can get this pesky war with the Mexicans behind us."

Sarah Polk raised one eyebrow at the suggestion of a Texas visit. She'd probably never set foot west of the Mississippi. Just not her style. The President nodded wordlessly and waved to the chief steward for the next course. James Polk was not getting into this conversation.

• • •

President Polk didn't say a lot through the whole meal, just tried to emphasize that settling the West was the right of Americans. What God had intended. Jack had heard that argument years before from Andrew Jackson back in Nashville. Something politicians these days called Manifest Destiny. How the hell did they know what God wanted? Probably the Comanche and even the damned Mexicans had their own idea about The Almighty's intent.

Sarah Polk kept interrupting Jack's eating with questions, more of an inquisition than her husband's sparse pronouncements. She wanted to know all about San Antonio, the Rangers and the Comanche. And Sarah Polk knew a lot about the Mexicans, almost as much as Emily West did. Missus Polk was probably the kind of wife who gave her husband too many unsolicited opinions. How many of her recommendations had the President ever taken seriously? Jack, on the other hand, had welcomed advice from Emily West in tough situations. Not so much from Susan, though. Susan had little use for politics or war. What would she have to offer in matters of life and death…or Manifest Destiny, for that matter?

All in all, the damned dinner went on a little too long, but Jack did his best to be sociable. He answered questions polite as he could and smiled a lot, probably too much. Finally, the First Lady took her leave. Despite feeling the need for sleep, Jack followed the President into a drawing room for a cigar, finally some brandy and the promised meeting with William Marcy.

With his stern, ruddy countenance framed by curly black hair and well-trimmed sideburns, Bill Marcy looked every bit a Secretary of War. His round, chattering head was punctuated by a pair of well-fed chins that jiggled over a too-tight white collar and black tie. The man paced the drawing room floor on short, bowed legs, puffing at his cigar and giving a briefing on what to expect when Jack presented the Texas request for war money to the joint congressional session. President Polk sat without interrupting, smoking his cigar and sipping brandy.

"Colonel, tomorrow won't be pretty," Marcy opined through the smoke. "Whigs are against the war. We've the votes to override them, but their representatives will have their say. One in particular, Daniel Webster of Massachusetts, he'll do his best to rile you up. Let him rant, but stick to your message."

James Polk echoed the words of William Marcy at the end of the late evening meeting. Jack hadn't needed that last brandy, considering his lack of sleep and all the traveling he'd just done. Maybe the President and Secretary Marcy saw that he was beat down and needed rest. For whatever reason, they bid Jack a good night and let him take leave for the cold walk back to the Willard Hotel.

Jack's breath clouded the midnight Washington air as he stepped briskly along the gaslit path. What could he expect tomorrow? He'd be facing professional politicians. And if the national congress was anything like the Texas legislature, most of them would be loud-mouthed, ass-covering simpletons. Too bad he couldn't strap on his Colt repeaters for the session.

• • •

The next day, Jack stood nervously to one side of the massive oak-framed entryway to Congress Hall, the US House Chamber. Noisy, pale, mostly bearded, surly men in dark suits filled the room to capacity. They waved hands filled with papers and gestured, pointing fingers and pursing lips. Some shouted to be heard above the din. A haze of tobacco smoke hung heavy over the milling crowd. Jack had been with politicians before, but never with this many at once, and not in any group of sober men who were so unruly. At least not indoors. Not even in Texas.

In the midst of the commotion came a steady hammering. A repeated rapping of wood on wood from the frizzle-haired man with a gavel, Vice-President George Dallas. Jack had eaten breakfast with him earlier at the hotel. The Vice-President now stood frowning behind his desk on the raised platform behind the podium. Younger Senators and Congressmen strutted toward their seats, the older ones hobbled. The Whigs shuffled to one side of the aisle, Democrats took seats on the opposite side. The noise died down enough so Jack could hear individual voices. He recognized only one man in the crowd – a tall, sad looking young lawyer from Illinois. Everybody knew Abraham Lincoln.

President Polk stood at the podium and introduced Jack Hays with a bunch of flowery language about being a genuine hero, the man who'd built the Texas Rangers into a legend. Applause started, louder from the Democrats' side than from the Whigs. Heat flooded into his face and neck. Jack was reddening again. Damn, he hated all this attention. Why couldn't these people just pay for the guns and enough men to beat the damned Mexicans without him having to deal with all this politicking? Pretty simple, truth be told. Not worth a long trip from Texas to Washington for anybody.

After some final whistles, a few shouts and a "whoopee" or two, the applause died down. Jack Hays shook James Polk's hand and took his place behind the wooden podium. He laid out his scribbled notes, short of breath and patience. Dammit all, he needed to be calm to make his case. His nerves were on edge, but not the same sort of feeling as going into a firefight. This was different. Nobody was trying to kill him, but somehow these men were threatening all the same.

How to begin? Jack looked over the audience, still collecting his thoughts. One steely-eyed, hawk-faced congressman on the Whig side glared at him and stood up. The man pocketed his eyepiece, about to speak. The President and Secretary of War had said last night Jack had best be ready for anything. So now would he be attacked before he'd even made his case?

"Colonel Hays," the man spoke through thin lips, a glint in his eye. "I am Daniel Webster from the great state of Massachusetts. I dare say the President has directed you here to ask for more money and more men to pursue a second diabolical war against Mexico." Webster took a breath. "Though you are but the simple instrument of his perfidy, I must inform you, clearly this is an unconstitutional war of aggression begun by your Republic of Texas and now forced upon these United States."

Hoots and angry shouts erupted from the Democratic side, loud applause and stamping of feet from Whigs. Jack Hays took in the spectacle. War of aggression? How the hell would this man, Webster, know who the aggressor was? He'd probably never been west of Pennsylvania, if even that far. The enemy had attacked United States citizens in Texas. They had to be put down.

The gavel hammered behind him, the Vice President pounding for order. Quiet returned to the gathering. Jack took a couple of deep breaths and his heartbeat slowed.

"Mr. Senator...Mr. Webster, is it?" Jack said evenly and returned the senator's glare. "Smart men like us, we usually avoid saying stupid things. But we do make mistakes, sir, and you're damned-sure makin' one now."

Scattered "aye's" of approval and applause, this time from the Democrats' side, rumbled through the chamber. Whigs booed and hooted. Again the Vice President gaveled for order. Jack Hays smiled, close-mouthed, and waited. Daniel Webster, red hair matching his flushing cheeks, was not done.

"All merely a thinly-veiled disguise by this President, sir." Webster retorted, looking first at Jack, then at James Polk. "Mr. Polk would illegally maintain land seized from Mexico, subdue the native Indians and expand Negro slavery throughout the West."

Louder responses of support for Webster came now from the Whig side of the aisle. The senator remained on his feet facing Jack. The Vice President's pounding gavel cut through the din. The assembly came back to order in fits and starts. Jack pondered his next remarks. He'd had quite enough of Senator Webster already. The fight in Texas was over the issue of the United States territory being violated by a foreign power and had nothing to do with Negroes or slavery.

"Nobody," Jack objected. "Not Mexicans, not Indians... nobody's got any more right to Texas territory than we do, Senator. Comanche kicked the Apache's asses and took their homeland. And the damned Mexicans?" Jack frowned and snarled. "Hell, they just come up and invaded everybody. Whites, free Negroes, Indians, Spaniards, folks from the Canarys. Didn't matter to the Mexicans. You didn't see that stack of more'n four hundred rotted Texas men piled up on the road outside Goliad. I did. I helped bury 'em. From the Alamo and Goliad on, Santa Anna and his damned Mexicans have broken every peace. They've killed everybody that's gotten in their way, and they're still killing, too. That's why I'm here."

A shuffling of feet. Men shifted in seats, but little more. No shouts or interruptions came from the assembly. Mostly quiet now. Matters had gotten serious. Jack stared at Daniel Webster until the Senator sat down. Jack glanced down at his notes. Not much he'd written would help from here on in. These people, Webster and his lot, were comfortable in Washington and had no idea what he was up against out on the frontier.

One row away on the Whig side, another man, much older than Webster, struggled out of his chair before Jack had collected his thoughts. The congressman couldn't quite straighten up, so he rested one gnarled hand on the rail in front of him. White, thick hair topped the old man's head and ran down his jaw to his jutting chin. His jacket was rumpled, and the fellow appeared to be short of breath.

"Colonel, I...I'm John Quincy Adams," The speaker stuttered, trembling on the rail. "Are you not the grand nephew of... of Rachel Jackson," Adams coughed into a kerchief several times, "the wife of that scalawag? That slave owner? That Negro hater and murderer, Andrew Jackson?"

Adams' words brought stirrings back to the assembly. The old man coughed again into a second kerchief, then put his gnarled hands to his neck in a single, dramatic motion. Was the old man choking?

"I dare say, Colonel Hays," John Adams tried to shout, keeping his hands at his throat, "that, for many of General Jackson's and...and your reputed escapades, we'd have seen fit to hang you both in Massachusetts!"

So this was "Old JQ." Andrew Jackson had told Jack about him. He had defeated Adams when the man ran for a second term back when Jack was a boy. A goddamn pacifist was how Jackson had described John Quincy Adams, and a man who'd given too much away to the British after the War of 1812. Andrew Jackson had never forgiven Adams for that.

Jack inhaled and folded his notes. He wouldn't need them today. Instead, he'd set the record straight, once and for all. This coward, John Quincy Adams, had insulted him and the man who'd taken Jack in as an orphan, his great aunt's husband and a national hero. Not gonna let him get away with that. Besides, Jack was no stranger to ass-chewings. General Zachary Taylor had given him a fine one, but at least he'd earned that reprimand. This was quite another matter, one of honor.

"Mr. Senator. Er, President Adams, I reckon. All respect, sir." Jack kept his voice even. "Nobody told me that President Jackson or myself would be accused of being criminals when I was invited to Washington. Is that what you're saying, sir? Me and President Jackson are nothin' but common criminals?"

A stony silence fell on the Congress Hall. Jack scanned the gathering, then returned his attention to Adams. Jack pointed a finger at his adversary, who leaned more on the rail for support.

"Senator, I ain't on trial here," Jack said. "Not me, and not Andrew Jackson, neither. Even you can see that much. General Jackson fought, died and was buried with honor. He was a true patriot. And as for me, if you want me hung, you'd best come to Texas and do your goddamndest, because I got no plan to ever come up to Massachusetts."

Laughter rippled through the Democratic side. Jack even got a few smiles from silent Whigs. Not as many folks in old John Q's camp after all, it seemed. Jack relaxed some. He had enough support to go on.

"Now about Negro people and slavery," Jack still eyed John Adams. "I care not a whit about a man's color, just long as it's not yellow. Ain't no yellow cowards workin' for me. We got Reds, Whites, a few Browns, maybe a Chinaman, and a few, I-don't-know-what's' in

Hays' Rangers. But none...not a damn one of 'em is a slave or indentured servant. They all fight hard for this country, and we pay 'em all the same fair wages. Long as they still breathin'.'"

Louder chuckles came now from both sides of the legislative chamber. John Quincy Adams trembled, but remained on his feet, swaying and gripping the brass rail. He wagged one long finger in Jack's direction.

"Colonel Hays." Adams got his voice back, louder. "Andrew Jackson was a shameless slave owner and a dueler. And you," his voice quivered, "You needed no more than slight provocation, I'm told, to...to gun down a hapless drunk Norwegian in a bar fight."

Noise and shouting erupted again. Jack put up his hands. The gavel behind and above his head echoed through the legislative chambers. Hard to believe that these men, especially this old bastard, had ever been voted into office by reasonable people. And who the hell had told Adams the old Nacogdoches bar fight story anyway?

"Congressman, let me set you straight," Jack snarled, "It was a god-damned Swede I killed in Nacogdoches, not a Norwegian. And the bullying bastard had it coming. Just like the Mexicans do now."

Men stood and applauded, whistled and stamped to thunder their agreement. The Vice President pounded his gavel. Jack waited until the noise from both sides of the aisle had died down.

"You want to talk about killing?" Jack went on, pointing a finger at Adams. "I said it already, and I'll say it again. Santa Anna's the Goliad killer. He's the Alamo murderer. Santa Anna's the real criminal this body ought to bring to justice. General Houston in Texas, Andrew Jackson when he was President, maybe some of you in this room...all of you trusting that sonofabitch, Santa Anna. You made a terrible mistake! Now just give us the goddamn money and we'll finally deal with him and his whole bunch. We'll keep the great state of Texas for America."

This time the applause was disciplined, respectful, and came evenly from both sides of the aisle. Jack wiped his brow. Wasn't exactly what he'd written in his notes, but maybe he'd done the job anyway.

It was damned hot in this meeting room, especially for February. Jack mopped his forehead again and gave a quick bow to the remaining applause. The men in the room stood and echoed words of support and encouragement. Anybody in Congress that didn't want war with Mexico was overruled today.

John Adams was not up to any further sparring. He'd sat down, the only one left seated, the old geezer. It appeared as if the Rangers and the Army would get the money they needed to finish the job. Meanwhile, these congressmen could stay here, fat and happy in the Capitol, and argue shit that didn't matter none.

Jack Hays snatched up his papers and strode off the platform toward the Congress Hall doorway. Spring would probably come to Texas before he could get home, and he had a woman there who needed tending to. And by God, some unfinished business with Mexico.

President Polk hastened alongside him and pumped Jack's hand hard with a tight grip, trying to hold him fast and keep him in the meeting room. But Jack broke away with a smile and a terse farewell. He pushed past the sergeant-at-arms and into the hallway, the thunderous sounds of Congress Hall and good wishes quickly fading behind him. Jack had done all he cared to do in Washington. No reason to tarry where he didn't belong. He had to get to his hotel room and pack up.

Chapter Twenty-Five

The Bells of Seguin - April 1847

Bells? Why were all the bells clanging? And where? God, would they never stop? Jack stirred in the big four-poster bed. His mouth felt strange, full of cotton. Bedcovers tangled around him and held his legs prisoner. The ringing hurt Jack's head, right over both eyes. Where the hell was he? Not Washington. His meeting with President Polk and Congress was still fresh in his mind, but he'd been back for over a month now.

His back hurt, too. Had somebody dragged him somewhere behind his pony? And his stomach churned. Bad supper? Nope, he was shaky. Nervous. But why? Ah, yes. Last night, he and Sam Walker, along with John Caperton the surveyor and ol' Bigfoot Wallace, had tied one on with the rest of the boys at the cantina. The party had gone on till the sun came up. Then Susan's parents' house. Seguin? Yes, Seguin. That's where he was.

Getting up the stone steps hadn't been easy. Some of that incident from last night floated back. Sam Walker had helped, weaving and stumbling up and up with Jack, arm-in-arm. Somehow, right toward the end of the climb, Sam had slid off the steps into the bushes below. He might still be stuck there. Jack snortled a laugh between dry, parched lips. He'd probably made too much noise, too, laughing and singing. Now every damn thing made his head hurt. And, damn, he was thirsty.

God, still those bells. The bells and their everlasting racket. Someone end the racket. Then Jack sat up in bed, rigid. His pulse thundered against his temples. He remembered.... The bells were for him. For him and Susan. They were getting married today.

Two hours later, Jack stood as erect as he could in the Magnolia Hotel ballroom. Reverend William Blair, a tall, hook-nosed Presbyterian missionary, loomed to one side of him. He and the Reverend faced the crowd. Jack was dressed like he was going back to the White House. His head still ached, and now the damned brogans hurt his feet again.

Emily West sat in the front row beside Missus Priscilla, smiling up at him and the preacher. Susan's mother liked Emily. She'd hired her to organize this whole damned affair. Jack didn't want to know how such relations between Emily and Missus Priscilla had all come about. Susan and Emily did know each other, but were they truly friends?

The Reverend Blair had come all the way from Victoria because he'd owed Emily some kind of favor. Didn't need those details, neither. Jack was pretty sure the Reverend Blair was not, as he was, suffering the pains of far too much drink, although he'd heard that the man frequented saloons and taverns down on the Coast to do more than just preach the Gospel.

Jack glanced to his other side. His best man, Sam Walker, stood stiff and all cleaned up from last night, but whiter of face than a fresh bed sheet. Sam Walker, new Captain, U.S. Army, not Rangering any more. Too bad. Sam was the only kind of friend a man needed. Jack would miss having him around.

The fancy tie at Jack's neck was too tight and felt a little like that wire garrote Tojo Iverson had used on him years back. Hadn't been for ol' Chief Flacco that night, Jack wouldn't be standing here waiting for Susan Calvert and her father to come down the aisle. Damn, Flacco oughta be here now to see all this fuss. He'd have enjoyed seeing Jack get married and settle down.

Over to one side of the Magnolia Hotel ballroom, a fat little man in a morning coat sat on a bench and used one stubby leg to pump his melodeon pedal. With stubby fingers he somehow coaxed pleasant music from a row of black-and-white keys. The piece was something Jack recognized from listening to his Aunt Rachel play the harpsichord back in Nashville. Maybe a song from that fellow, Mozart?

By God, he'd drink no champagne or whiskey at the party after all this marrying at the altar was done. Maybe just one cleansing ale. Jack glanced over toward Sam again. His best man was looking grim, like he might throw up any minute. Wonder if Sam had remembered the ring?

A rustling passed through the ballroom. Heads turned toward the back of the hall. Susan had started down the aisle toward him, a stunning vision in white floating between the rows of guests. She held her father's arm and smiled at Jack through a veil of fancy lace. Judge Jeremiah Calvert was smiling, too. First time ever. Jack tried to smile back. God, Susan's wedding dress was so damned white. Why was everything so white today?

Jack's heart raced, his knees grew rubbery. The life he'd known was about to end, or at least change significantly. But after all, he'd been planning to marry Susan for quite awhile. He just had to get through the wedding ceremony. Then he'd address that other matter. Hopefully with a clearer head later, he could manage some urgent Ranger business.

More war with the Mexicans was on the horizon. For that, Jack needed a thousand new pistols from Samuel Colt. He and General Sam had already discussed the revolvers and how he might recruit Emily to help. So, before the day was over, wedding or no wedding, he and Sam Walker would talk to Emily about her going to see Samuel Colt. Susan would understand he had to have the meeting. At least he hoped she'd see things his way.

Susan would be shocked if she knew some deeds he'd done. Appalled. He hadn't said much to her about all his killing, of course. The Swede in Nacogdoches, Comanche at Bandera Pass, that Frenchie General Woll's boys at Salado Creek. He'd surely not brought up the bloodbath he'd led in Monterrey. General Taylor had damn well upbraided him for that one. Emily West would've understood the carnage, but Susan wouldn't. Women, at least the marrying kind, weren't supposed to.

• • •

"Quite a celebration." Emily West grasped Jack's free arm. "You and Susan are a perfect couple. My congratulations, and all the very best wishes."

Dammit, Emily was good-looking, all dressed in that white-trimmed, yellow velvet clingy thing and fancy hat. Emily West loosed her grip on Jack and raised her half-filled champagne glass. She clinked hers with Susan's. Jack lifted his ale mug, smiled and returned the toast.

He was feeling much better, now that the ceremony was over and he'd downed almost a pint of dark brew. Should've done that hours ago. Jack turned his gaze from Emily to Susan. Emily might be a fine woman, good at a lot of things, but he'd picked the right bride. Couldn't have done better if he'd looked for the rest of his life. He patted Susan's hand, resting on his arm. She gripped his arm and squeezed.

"Emily," Susan Hays shouted over the din. "Mother and I appreciate how well you organized our wedding. The flowers, Reverend Blair, the food and drink. Everyone is having the time of their lives. Father may never recover from the cost of having his daughter's wedding in his own hotel, but one marries only once, hopefully."

"The pleasure was mine, Susan," Emily responded. Then she smiled at Jack. "Good men are hard to find these days, and Colonel Jack Hays here is a good man. Yet I fear you'll need a lariat or a leash if he's to stay home long."

Damn Emily, always poking and jabbing at him, and always when he was least ready. Aw God, the heat under the collar again. Jack glared at her. He got just a one-sided smirk in return. What about Susan? Was that a frown? Susan didn't agree with Emily? Good. Anyway, Jack was glad Emily was here. She'd done well with organizing the wedding, and now he had that other business with the new Colt pistols for her to tend to back east. The talk wouldn't keep till another day, neither.

"Emily, another matter." Jack half sighed her name and motioned for Sam Walker to join them. "Sam Walker and me, we need a few minutes for some business talk. We need your help with Mr. Colt pretty quick. Got to have guns, and a lot of 'em, for the war."

Emily West stared, wide-eyed, from under her green, feathered hat. Jack glanced at Susan. Uh-oh, the new Missus gave him that evil look he already knew too well. Sam arrived, hat in hand, and kept silent. Susan turned away, shaking her head, and marched toward her mother and father, an empty champagne glass in one hand.

Bad timing probably. Jack would have to apologize to his bride later. Getting married to Susan was important, but war with Mexico wouldn't wait for him and a honeymoon. Jack put a hand on Sam's shoulder and faced Emily.

"Sam here," Jack said. "He's just been ordered to be a Captain in the US Mounted Rifles. Ain't just a Ranger no more. He's Regular US Army now. He's put together a company that's got to be in Veracruz end of next month."

Jack kept his gaze on Emily. God, those dark eyes. He needed to get on with the pistol talk. Besides, he was just married and already in the shit with Susan.

"Maybe you know already." Jack lowered his voice. "Sam here, he had that Colt feller make him a six-shot pistol a while back. Damned thing worked real well, too. Emily, now we need them new Colts. A thousand of them. And pretty quick. Ain't supposed to talk about it, but the Rangers and the Federal Army, we're going to war with Mexico."

Susan returned, an odd half-smile on her face and a fresh glass of that expensive French champagne in her hand. He'd need to finish this business with Emily and Sam pretty quick. He glanced at Sam. His friend was looking better. Probably that pint of ale he'd had.

"Emily," Jack resumed his entreaty. "We need you to go back east and get Samuel Colt to put together them six-shooters for us. We'll pay you well, a thousand dollars gold, plus your expenses. You can offer twenty-five dollars a pistol to Mr. Colt. Twenty-five thousand's a helluva lot of money. Gen'ral Houston's already seen to the finances. Will you do the thing for me and Sam Walker here? More important, will you do the deed for Sam Houston and Texas?"

Susan broke in before Emily could respond. "For God's sake, Jack. I can't believe all this talk of pistols and going to war with Mexico. And on our wedding day? Will this madness never end? Besides, Emily has done enough for Texas. And you, Jack…you have as well. No more of this nonsense, I beg you."

Poor dead Chief Flacco's words made their way back into Jack's consciousness. "No more Captain Jack smell rose, just gun smoke. Time to kill everybody we not like." So now he'd go off to war. Or should he leave the Rangers and stay with Susan? Could Jack do battle any more without worrying about coming back alive? He was a husband, a family man now. Had Jack lost his mettle?

"Earlier today," Susan stared at Jack and went on, "you stood before God and our friends and family. You pledged your love and your life only to me. Yet you would leave now? Go off and fight again? Quite unfair, Jack Hays. Most unfair. You would risk that life you promised we'd enjoy together and perhaps leave me a widow. And for what? Texas? You married me, John Coffee Hays, not Texas."

"Susan. Susan Hays." Jack took a breath and calmed a bit. "You're right. I made you and God Almighty promises today. For better, for worse and in sickness and health, till death do us part. And dammit, woman, can't you see? 'Worse' is what we got in Texas right now. Matters between us and Mexico are so bad they couldn't be worse. Men like me and Sam here, we got to go fight. Stop the Mexicans once and for all. Make life tolerable for everybody living here."

His new bride's eyes moistened. Jack reached to touch her wet cheek. Susan pulled away and dabbed her eyes with a kerchief. He glanced at Emily West, then at Sam Walker. Both stood quiet and wouldn't look at him. They weren't getting involved in his problem. Jack faced Susan and gripped her shoulders. She tried to pull away.

Jack held Susan in front of him. "But here's another promise for you, Missus Hays. No Mexican's sendin' Jack to the Great Beyond. I'll be back when I'm finished with Santa Anna and his boys. And you asked about fairness. I tell you nothing's fair in this world, Susan Hays. Fair ain't nothin' but another four-letter 'F' word."

Susan twisted out of Jack's grip. Cold wetness hit his face. Jack flinched and blinked the stinging liquid from his eyes. His bride's empty champagne flute shattered on the floor, spraying glass shards against his goddamn brogans. Susan's narrowed eyes and pursed lips reflected sadness as much as anger. Jack's bride whirled about and stormed off through the crowd.

Idle chattering and laughter died away. Susan's whimpers and footfalls became the only sounds in the silent ballroom. Her anguish pained Jack's ears more than the bells had, but he shrugged his shoulders, looked from Sam Walker to Emily West, then down at the floor. The wet, icy shock had brought back the damned Tojo Iverson incident again. Flacco had saved him then, but Jack was on his own this time. At least the drops on Jack's nose and chin were champagne, not dirty water. Jack drew a kerchief from his breast pocket and dabbed at the wetness. His wedding night sure wasn't going to be much fun if Susan wouldn't forgive him.

Chapter Twenty-Six

The New Pistol - June 1847

Emily West held her ankle-length skirt knee-high while she climbed the two flights of rickety stairs. She gripped the handle of a large leather-and-cloth valise in the same hand that held her skirt hem. Her other hand pulled at the rough wooden stair rail. Samuel Colt might have fallen on hard times since Emily had last seen him, but surely he could have afforded better living accommodations than this, and a better office than the old workspace he'd first rented years ago in this run-down part of Manhattan.

Her gloved knuckles rapped twice against the weathered door. Footfalls sounded on the other side. The handle turned and creaking hinges announced the appearance of Sam Colt. His eyes widened and the fine line of his jaw dropped. Three years of misfortune had neither spoiled his exuberant look, nor the young inventor's taste in fine clothing. Sam Colt certainly didn't match his shabby doorframe.

"Emily. My God," Samuel Colt enthused. "What a pleasant surprise. You look incredible." He took in a quick breath. "How many years has it been? How did you find me? Come in, come in."

Colt motioned her through the door and fumbled with his cravat. He ran fingers through shaggy hair, all the while glancing left and right as if to wonder what she might stumble upon or over. Emily stepped past her former employer and into the dark, dusty workplace. She was silent.

"After all this time," Sam Colt continued, "are my routines and haunts so predictable that you can track me down in a city of half-a-million people, undetected and unannounced?"

Now she responded, "Sam, come, come! I knew I had a good chance of finding you here in the old place. A simple inquiry downstairs as to your current whereabouts, and here I am. You may be a mechanical genius, but you are indeed a man of rigid habits. Creative though you may be, the Sam Colt I know abhors change."

Emily put down her valise and peered around the small room. The windows were open and sunlight fell weakly across a long worktable in the center of Sam's office. A gleaming, long-barreled pistol held down papers against the breeze from the windows, and other metal bits and parts were scattered around. Not unusual clutter for Sam.

More difficult to fathom for Emily, though, were the long wires that ran from somewhere near one window to an odd-looking, levered device on one end of the table. A tiny seesaw with wires? Emily smiled. Sam was a tinkerer. She stepped to the table and hefted the massive revolver.

"So this is your latest work," Emily said. "Quite the cannon you've made this time, Sam. But over there?" She pointed with the pistol barrel. "If that's a weapon, the thing is indeed a strange one. How does it function?"

"Emily, you are only partly correct." Colt tucked both thumbs behind his velvet coat lapels. "You'd be amazed at what magic three men named Sam can conjure up these days. The pistol you hold is my first effort at a six-shot heavier caliber revolver. Sam Walker, you remember him? He gave me that idea months ago when he was here."

Colt moved to the end of the table and held the small, wired device in one hand. He smiled with an almost giddy look. With his other hand, Sam pushed the hinged lever down several times, metal to metal. Small sparks flew and the thing made sharp, clicking noises.

"And this, my dear, is the brainchild of another Sam," he announced. "Samuel Morse, my compatriot. He calls this machine a 'talking wire.' Says the thing will revolutionize communications. Who knows whether he's truly a genius or simply a mad man. At the moment, I am only helping him waterproof the wiring for use outdoors and underwater."

"Sam, you never stop experimenting, do you?" Emily observed, shaking her head. "The pistol I understand, but... waterproofing wires? Revolutionizing communications?"

Sam Colt furrowed his brow. "The waterproof wiring, a modest product diversification in my collaboration with Sam Morse, was made possible, indeed necessary, by the cancellation of my underwater explosive mine contract with the Navy last year. I could've made thousands of dollars, but that Massachusetts Senator, that bloody pacifist John Quincy Adams, said my mines were 'immoral warfare.' The old bastard. On his say-so, the Navy's banned Sam Colt's water bombs forever."

Samuel Colt might be brilliant, and he'd definitely been gallant – her defender that first day on the train, and again on their coach ride to Connecticut – but he was manipulative and at least a little eccentric, if not plain crazy. How and, perhaps more importantly, why had she let herself get involved with this man again? Hard to discern whether he could focus on a real business opportunity long enough to be successful, but Emily had enough money in her valise to test Sam Colt's dedication to his real talent, making repeating pistols. This time for the war against Mexico.

"Samuel Colt," Emily sighed and reached for her leather case. "I've apparently come to you at the proper time, and with quite a business opportunity."

The frown on Colt's face faded. He half-smiled and slid a chair with a worn cushion into the center of the room, beckoning Emily to be seated. She put the valise down, then bent and drew out three pieces of paper. Once she'd shifted in the seat to rearrange her skirt hem, Emily shoved the heavy case to one side and began fanning herself with the sheaf. Sam Colt took a second chair opposite her and leaned in close. Good, she had his full attention, both professionally and personally. She stopped fanning and waved the papers toward Colt.

"This is a lawful Texas contract," Emily said in a flat voice. "General Houston needs one thousand Colt revolvers, the new six-shot .44 caliber versions, and quickly. They'll go to the Texas Rangers. Maybe later, a few to the Army, too."

She fixed her eyes on Samuel Colt. He had not moved or blinked. Emily had his focus for now, but was he tuned in enough to produce a thousand pistols unsupervised? Probably not.

"I am to offer you," she stated, "twenty-five dollars per pistol. No negotiation. Three-thousand paid now, and the remainder once the lot has been safely delivered. We must have everything by August's end."

Colt stared long and hard at Emily, then down at the contract he'd been handed. Did he believe her? She bent down and found the oilcloth packet next to the Paterson Colt revolver in her valise. Colt's eyes followed Emily's every move. She held the packet in the air.

"I have sixty U.S. Treasury notes in here, Sam," Emily said. "Fifty-dollar notes. They're yours as soon as you've read and signed the agreement."

"My God, Emily." Sam Colt responded. "I'm near speechless. A fair price for the pistols, for certain, and I can obviously use the money. But I have no idea how such a massive order can be accomplished, particularly in the time allotted. I'd wager, however, that a mere three thousand dollars isn't nearly enough to get things started. And I have no reserve funds to speak of myself."

"Come now, Sam." Emily countered. "You think me naive? Uninformed? After all our past history, my embarrassment at your duplicitous mess in South Carolina? You think I'd not come here prepared? I know you still have leverage with the Whitney Company. Particularly for an order this large."

Emily let the remarks settle in, then stood up. Time to get the deal done and get out. At least out of Samuel Colt's quarters. Emily wouldn't go far, though. She'd been ordered not only to get Colt's commitment, but to stay and see the deal through. Jack had told her General Houston was adamant on that point.

"So, Mr. Colt," Emily glared. "Let us save ourselves the trouble of useless give-and-take. I am already aware of your production agreement with Mr. Blake of the Whitney Weapons factory. If all goes as planned, you'll clear at least ten dollars a pistol on this deal. And sure as God made man, there's another thousand guns that'll be needed before the war's done. You'll be rich, but only if you take my deal and perform. Now sign the damned contract, sir. I have to be off."

Emily stared at a motionless Samuel Colt, then surveyed the cluttered room again. Samuel Colt needed the money, that much was certainly clear, and Texas needed the pistols. Minutes passed before he finally looked up at her.

"Well, Miss West." Colt lifted his head and nodded. "Congratulations to you and the Texas Rangers. By August, you shall indeed be equipped with the finest and most accurate pistols the world has seen." He smiled, a bit thinner than usual, then asked, "If you can alter your plans, may I invite you to dine with me this evening to celebrate the occasion? It would seem I've just come into some fresh cash."

"A kind invitation, sir." Emily smiled, lips closed. "Regrettably, I have other matters to attend this evening. Shall we instead meet for breakfast two days hence? By then you should be able to brief me on a production plan for your Whitney Weapons venture. General Houston has instructed me to remain in New York to supervise your efforts and ensure delivery on schedule. We shall be seeing a great deal more of each other."

Samuel Colt shook his head and took the papers to his desk. He moved other piles of scattered materials to one side and put his signature on the contract. Had he even bothered to read the agreement? Colt handed back the three pages. Emily retrieved her valise, stuffed the contract inside and shook a slightly overwhelmed Samuel Colt's hand before being ushered to his door.

"Until Thursday, then," Samuel Colt said. "I shall meet you at your lodging for breakfast. You are using the same lodging as always, I suppose? The Parker House, or rather the Astor, now that John Astor's bought the place."

Emily nodded. "Then I will look forward to our meeting Thursday, Sam."

She stepped through the doorway and onto the landing. After the dankness of Colt's office, the late morning sun was instantly refreshing. Emily had less than an hour to catch the northbound train, and she wanted to keep her appointment at the Thompson Bank in Thompson, Connecticut before nightfall. She was carrying another seven thousand dollars, some in gold, in her valise, and the funds had to be secured. Moreover, she needed to verify that the Thompson Bank was holding the remaining fifteen thousand dollars that had been shipped a month earlier by courier from Austin.

Last on her immediate agenda, there was the matter of a charming little cottage close-by that Emily was interested in; one on the Massachusetts coast near Sagamore Beach. Once her business with Colt was done, she wanted a place to start a new life here in the east. There'd certainly be enough money, and nothing good could come of her going back to Texas.

Chapter Twenty-Seven

On to Mexico City - October 1847

Red-streaked clouds covered the eastern horizon. "Red sky at morning, sailors take warning," Jack had always heard. Such a dawn meant an October rainy spell in Tennessee or Texas, but he wasn't sure what "red in the morning" meant down here in Veracruz. In fact, nothing seemed certain in this damned country, except for the fact that a lot of Mexicans were going to die soon, including their little General, Santa Anna. Jack and his Rangers would see to that.

Jack splashed water on his face and walked to the makeshift corral in the trees behind the long row of tents. He took his pony's reins from the duty private, put a boot in one stirrup and swung into the saddle. The young attendant saluted stiffly to Jack's nod of thanks.

Orders had arrived with the headquarters courier last night. Jack had ten miles to ride for a breakfast meeting with his new commander, General Robert Patterson.

American combat units were camped everywhere along the road leading back into Veracruz. Must've been 10,000 or more men milling around, some still bedded down. No secret to what was happening here, America was taking over and occupying Mexico. Halfway along, Jack rode past a unit of blue-coated cavalrymen and their stable boys gathered around a morning campfire. Some laughed, while a few belted out a rousing, haunting tune Jack had never heard before. Words about a "Yellow Rose" in Texas they all longed to see again. They'd need to settle the score with the enemy here before any of these boys had a chance of getting back in the arms of a pretty woman anywhere, that was certain.

Jack was a long way south of San Antone now, deeper into Mexico than he'd ever been. The song he'd heard made him think of

Susan. He missed her. And for some reason, he thought of Emily West, too. Dammit, that Comanche years ago had called her "Yellow Woman."

Less than an hour later, Jack passed the sentries for General Patterson's division lines. He wasn't sure why he'd been summoned to the meeting with the Division Commander. Probably marching orders. High time to get going.

• • •

The mess steward held the canvas flap back to let Jack Hays enter the General's command tent. Robert Patterson sat rigidly upright, sipping coffee. Two rows of gold buttons ran from his stiff collar down the front of the General's double-breasted jacket. Gold-braided epaulettes on his shoulders displayed the two matching stars of his rank. Jack stopped a couple of paces in front of the mess table and saluted.

"Colonel John Coffee Hays reporting, sir," Jack recited.

General Patterson looked up and returned the salute. He wiped his mouth with a linen napkin and motioned Jack to take the seat opposite him at the mess table. Patterson was somber, even grim.

"Colonel Hays, be at ease and welcome to Mexico." The General's distinct Irish accent rolled through each mournful syllable. "You look as though you could use some coffee and breakfast."

Jack sat on the stool opposite the General. The mess steward placed a tin of coffee and a plate of scrambled eggs in front of him. He'd never met General Patterson before, but from the man's demeanor, this was no usual assignment briefing. Had to be bad news of some kind. The General picked up his fork and examined the tines with one finger.

"Colonel," General Patterson spoke in a low, almost reverent voice. "I am certain you and your lads will make a great difference in our battle for Mexico City. We shall deal with your upcoming orders in due course, but first, sir, I'm afraid I have some regrettable news to deliver."

Somebody was dead. The blood drained from Jack's face and whatever appetite he'd had disappeared. He felt dizzy. Good men in his command had been lost before, but who the hell could he have lost so early in this campaign? Hell, he hadn't even been in a firefight yet.

The General frowned and went on. "As I'm sure you're already painfully aware, death in war has no regard for rank or friendship. I am informed that your good friend and comrade-in-arms, Army Captain Samuel Walker, was killed in action a few days past. The 9th day of October, to be precise, in the battle for Huamantla. For what it's worth, Colonel Hays, my command saw to his proper burial with full honors."

General Patterson bowed his head, muttering something about "God's peace." Hellfire, the last time Jack had seen Sam was back in April at his and Susan's wedding. Now Jack remembered Sam prone in the dirt at the Battle of Walker's Creek, a Comanche arrow sticking out of his shoulder. His friend had somehow managed to stand up and continue the attack. Jack shook his head remembering Walker's Creek, Salado Creek and Monterrey. Sam had always been there. Always had his back. Damn him. Damn them all.

Jack blinked back the image of his hung-over friend standing at the altar in the Magnolia Hotel, fishing for Susan's wedding ring somewhere in his pocket. Now he was dead? Had to be a goddamn lie. Nobody could kill Sam Walker. Jack was overwhelmed. Why hadn't General Sam and the U.S. Army folks let Sam stay with the Rangers instead of going to the Army? He'd still be alive.

"Mistake, sir," Jack managed to croak. "Got to be some mistake. Sam cain't be dead. Him and me, we been shot at by the best. Comanche couldn't kill us. Bandito's, neither. Hell, we even tried more'n once to drink ourselves to death. Don't see how fuckin' Mexicans coulda done him in. Just ain't possible."

"Colonel Hays," General Patterson responded, his cold blue eyes focused on Jack. "We are all soldiers. Killing is our business. We fight, and sometimes we die. Unfortunately, my report is quite accurate. Multiple accounts confirm Captain Walker was felled by a Mexican sniper late in the battle."

The General gripped a thin leather packet in one leathery hand. What was that? Jack's orders? Was this all he'd get? Jack tried to sit erect on the hard stool and look his commander in the eye. General Patterson apparently had more to say.

"Certainly, you and your men are entitled to your anger and righteous grief," the General remarked. "And you shall have your chance, beginning less than a fortnight hence. An engagement to avenge your gallant comrade's death. These are your orders, Colonel. Study them well. We've come too far and sacrificed too much to fail now."

General Patterson handed over the packet. Jack opened the leather envelope, unfolded the papers and blinked away the moisture in his eyes. He and his regiment would be the first unit to enter Mexico City from the south. His eyes widened as he read the details. Engage any resistance en route. Pass through with all dispatch. U.S. Infantry will mop up. No military prisoners, but no combat with civilians, unless armed. Use only necessary force. General Patterson must've heard about him and his men at Monterrey.

"A word of comfort, if I may, Colonel." The General smiled, tight-lipped. "My favorite author, Eugené Sue, recently offered a notable piece of advice in his book, *Memoirs of Matilda*. If you've not been privy to the work, I'll quote him. Mr. Sue wrote that 'Revenge is a dish best eaten cold'."

Jack Hays blinked moist eyes again and laid the orders on the mess table. He had a sip of coffee and took a few deep breaths. Jack would be prepared for the street fighting in Mexico City. Combat was dirty business. Kill-or-be-killed. Somehow, Jack would need to exercise more restraint than in Monterrey. He wasn't used to that, and neither were his men. In spite of his rage, though, he'd have to try.

General Patterson and whoever that was he'd quoted had a good point about revenge. There'd be time enough after he got to Mexico City to find Santa Anna. And when he did, the little Mexican would pay. By God, he'd see to that personally.

• • •

The next morning, Jack stood facing his men. The eyes of more than three hundred war-ready, weathered faces stared at him from under the usual sombreros, cloth head-wraps, sweat-stained field caps and high crowned, broad-brimmed hats. Most of them sat or squatted in the shade of a grove of scrub oaks. Men further back stood to better hear Jack's orders. No insignia of rank was visible. No uniforms or indication that this was an organized military unit. Jack had issued each Ranger two new six-shot Colt pistols, and, as before, his regiment bristled with all manner of additional weapons: rifles, lances, axes, knives and sabers. To a man, the face of the regiment was tight-lipped and steeled for battle.

"Men, I said some a' this already." Jack's voice wavered. "Sam Walker was a helluva loss. Bible says we all got to die to get to Heaven, but I'm damned tired of that little Mexican shit, Santa Anna, helpin' our Maker with his work."

A ripple of laughter passed through the grizzled ranks. Solemn nods came from some. Jack held up one of his Colt pistols.

"Gents," Jack shouted. "Y'all been issued these new pistols. Best damned gun I've ever seen. Ain't no ordinary piece of Ranger hardware. This here's a Walker Colt. Sam Walker's invention. This new gun is gonna help us kick some Mexican ass."

Cheers erupted. Men jumped to their feet and thrust pistols and knives into the air. Time for battle. Sam Walker's face hovered in Jack's mind.

• • •

Hays' First Regiment, Texas Mounted Volunteers had been the lead element of General Patterson's command from the time they'd left Veracruz over a month earlier. Jack rode at the head of his column into Mexico City the first week of December. Several skirmishes had erupted getting this far, but resistance had been a lot lighter than Jack had expected. Following General Patterson's orders, he'd engaged the Mexican troops he'd encountered, but just enough to punch through their defenses and ride on, leaving most as a mop-up mission for the infantry coming behind him.

Jack looked left and right at the buildings of the Mexican capital. Civilians stared out of partly boarded-up windows and barricaded side streets. Some shouted muffled curses. Not pleased to see los Diablos Tejanos? But no uniformed enemy were anywhere to be seen. No gunfire. How far would he have to ride before making contact with elements of General Winfield Scott's Army regulars? They must already occupy parts of the Mexican capital.

Less than half-a-mile further on, two gunshots broke the silence behind Jack, then screams came from both sides of the street. Jack put up one hand to halt the regiment. He wheeled his pony around and galloped down the line until he reined in where Corporal Cherry sat in his saddle with a smoking revolver in one hand. Blood streamed from a cut over his left eye and down his face. Ten yards away, a young boy lay face down in the street, unmoving. Jack's orders had been to defend when attacked, but it was apparent that this young boy had done little else than throw a stone. Mexicans lined the roadside, crying and mumbling. But no one made a move toward the corpse.

Jack Hays touched the bill of his black field cap and nodded in Cherry's direction. Corporal Cherry holstered the Walker Colt and saluted with two-fingers to his hat brim. Jack turned his pony again and galloped toward the head of his column. Seconds later, the regiment moved on. Cries of "Diablos Tejanos," came as he passed by. Were he and his men truly the "Devils from Texas?" He'd always thought himself and his men heroic. But now?

Bare minutes passed before Jack halted his regiment again. This time, a more vocal crowd pressed into the street around and in front of him, shouting insults and urging on young men armed with knives and swords. Jack turned back along the line, nudging bystanders away with his pony and signaling his men to fire only if provoked. He drew up near Bigfoot Wallace, who pointed a pistol at a particularly noisy cordon of young Mexicans. Some had rocks. One or two were armed with knives.

One of the knife wielders stepped into the street in front of Jack and hurled a short, broad-bladed weapon toward the column. The blade struck the haunch of Bigfoot Wallace's horse and sunk partway in. The rearing beast dumped gear and Bigfoot to the cobblestones in a thumping heap. As the hulking Ranger struck pavement, he flexed his knees, dropped and rolled to his right, and began firing the new Colt, first at his assailant, then emptying the weapon into the scattering crowd. The young knife thrower fell, along with three more young men.

Jack trained both his pistols on the remnants of the crowd that now screamed insults and waved arms, rocks or knives visible in most hands. Others spat their defiance. Bigfoot Wallace stood and walked to his horse. He pulled the knife from the skittering animal. Not a lot of blood came from the wound, so he grabbed the saddle horn and mounted up. Jack signaled the regiment to move on. Wasn't much Jack could do about the Mexican casualties. Bigfoot, like Corporal Cherry, had followed his orders, and a mob could be as deadly as a regiment. Best to move along quickly and not incite an outright bloodbath before ever seeing any uniformed enemy.

An hour later, Jack halted the column near a small, shaded market square on the south side of he central plaza. He'd just read a new order delivered by the Army Headquarters messenger. General

Winfield Scott had written that he should clear the least secure sector of town, a local stronghold designated in the order as "Cutthroat Barrio." He passed word down the line to his regiment to dismount for rest and water while he developed a plan to take down any remaining Mexican opposition in the barrio.

Just before supper, Jack summoned Captain Jonathan Roberts, one of his company commanders. Roberts had been a Texas Ranger less than a year, but he was already the best tactician in Jack's regiment. Fearless, too. Jack's engagement order to Roberts was simple:

"Restore order in the Cutthroat Barrio. Anybody that don't obey orders and stand down, you know what to do. No prisoners."

Within minutes, more than thirty heavily armed horsemen thundered away from the market square, headed for Cutthroat Barrio. Jack mounted up to lead the rest of his regiment east and link up with elements of Scott's army. He knew Jon Roberts, and he knew the men under Captain Roberts' command. They'd do only what they had to do to get the job done. Still, the caution in his original orders from General Patterson gave Jack pause. "Proceed without delay. Use necessary, but not excessive force." That was clearly not how he'd just told Captain Roberts to proceed.

• • •

Barely twenty-four hours after Jack had ordered Jon Roberts into Cutthroat Barrio, the young captain and his men returned. Roberts dismounted and removed his hat as he approached Jack, gripping the reins of a second horse that carried a single body wrapped in a blood-soaked blanket. Captain Roberts' grizzled company drew up to the rear of their young troop commander. His report to Jack was terse.

"Colonel," Jon Roberts spoke, waving back at the dead man.

"No sooner'n we rode into the barrio, two bastards snatched Private Allsens here off his pony and slashed his throat." Roberts stared at Jack, wide-eyed, and went on. "That put us in a bad way, Colonel. By the time we was done, we musta killed more'n eighty of 'em. Had to. We fired, and we fired some more. Hell, they just kept comin' at us. Came at us with knives, came at us with rocks, and hell, some come at us with kitchen pots. One or two flintlocks and muskets, too. When it was finished, we left them Mexicanos laying in the street where they fell. But the place is quiet now. No more throat-cuttin'."

Captain Roberts went on to tell Jack that Alan Allsens had been the only Ranger casualty. They'd seen Mexicans, young and old, picking up their dead after the fight. He'd personally counted more than fifty bodies on litters being taken off, probably to a morgue. He and his troops hadn't ridden out of the barrio until the smoke had cleared and he was sure order was restored. Damn, Roberts and his men had certainly done their job, but even during wartime, this was going to be hard to explain to General Scott.

Jack dismissed Captain Roberts with thanks. Then, facing a cold supper of beans and hardtack, he scribbled a note for his messenger to deliver to General Winfield Scott. No telling what the reaction from General Scott might be, but this was all out war. Mexico had to be brought to its knees. Santa Anna had to die. Everybody knew that.

• • •

Early the next evening, Colonel Jack Hays stood at rigid attention in the parlor of a commandeered Mexican hacienda facing the U.S. Theater Commander, Army General Winfield Scott. The General was seated at a field table in weak candlelight, grim-faced and chewing an unlit cigar butt. He did not offer Jack so much as a stool or a tin of coffee, nor did the General return Jack's salute or put him at ease. Just dabbed that ugly cigar butt into a bent tin plate.

"Fifty executions! Probably many more than that, Colonel." Winfield Scott shouted and waved a paper in the air. "Defenseless Mexican troops and unarmed civilians, murdered in cold blood by men under your command. I'll have an explanation, sir, and the story had best be credible."

Jack cleared his throat and began. "Don't know why all the fuss, Gen'ral, Sir. You wrote me yourself, 'use necessary force.' Captain Roberts' boys…when they went in, Mexicans grabbed one of our troopers right off his horse and cut his throat. Us Rangers, we don't take shit like that, Sir. We get attacked, we kill 'em. That's necessary force, sir."

His heels were together and both arms locked tight and straight against his sides. Jack stared down at the seated general. The theater commander dabbed at his cold, wet cigar butt again. He motioned for Jack to continue.

"Sir," Jack spoke evenly. "Roberts' men had to get rid of more'n fifty, maybe as many as eighty Mexicans before things quieted, before they could even pick up poor Private Allsens' corpse without getting cut up. Good thing Allsens was the only man we lost. Just two others injured. Barrio's peaceful now. No more resistance."

General Scott shifted in his chair. He ran his hands through long, silvery hair and unfastened a second collar button. Jack moved his feet apart and crossed his palms behind his back.

"Colonel," General Scott snapped. "You are to remain at attention. I've had quite enough insubordination from you and your band of military misfits. That clear?"

Jack clicked both heels back together, slapped his hands down to his side again. Straight-faced, he eyed Winfield Scott. So what came next, the 'International Rules of War' lecture? A fuckin' invitation to dine with Santa Anna? An involuntary grin crept onto Jack's tight lips.

"Dammit, Colonel Hays," Winfield Scott scowled. "Wipe that smirk, or I'll have you thrown in the stockade within the hour."

Jack took two quick breaths. He turned his thoughts first to Susan, waiting for him back in Texas. What would she think of all this war mess? She'd hate what he'd done. Susan would tell him that it was high time he found another line of work. And Emily? Well, she'd just tell him not to back down.

General Scott went on with his lecture. "Mass killings in Cutthroat Barrio occurred some distance from your personal control. But the men who did the deed, you freely admit, operated under your direct orders. Moreover, troops of your command, and in your presence, engaged in at least two other murderous acts, did they not? Civilians, no more than defenseless children, some of them, were gunned down." The General frowned, eyes narrowing. "Colonel Hays, this is the same barbaric disregard for non-combatants that General Taylor reprimanded you for back in Monterrey. You are indeed reluctant to grasp the difference between legitimate combat and the unconscionable slaughter of innocents."

Hays nodded a silent acknowledgement of the Army Commander's accusations. Was the ass-chewing done? Was Jack being relieved of his command? If not, would he act the same in situations like Cherry's and Bigfoot's again? Would he give Jon Roberts the "no prisoners" order again? He'd best calm down now and choose his words carefully. Jack took another deep breath.

"Don't know that they was all defenseless or innocent, Gen'ral." Jack's voice was low. "Seems almost everybody here's got a knife, a rock or a gun. Some of 'em was even wearin' parts of goddamn uniforms. My men defended themselves like they was ordered to do. Killed Mexicans throwin' rocks, Mexicans shootin' at 'em, Mexicans using knives and cutting throats."

Jack stared at the general. Winfield Scott leaned forward and rested his arms on the table. He waved one hand for Jack to go on.

"That said, sir, you're right," Jack admitted. "I did nothing to my men who killed those boys in the street. Might've been too easy on 'em. And I did give Cap'n Roberts the killing orders for the barrio.

That was too strong. I take full responsibility. Somebody's gotta hang in the wind for all this, it oughta be me."

"Colonel Hays, enough." Winfield Scott shook his head, then met Jack's eyes with his. "You are fortunate, sir. Doubly fortunate. First, the United States needed you and your misfits for this fight. Second, I am most assuredly a reasonable and practical man. I abhor your atrocities and your callous disregard for human life, but there'll be no court martial. Nobody's hanging anybody. That being understood, your job's finished here. You, Colonel, are to get the hell out of Mexico City. I want you and your men cleared out of here by this time tomorrow. Do you understand?"

Jack breathed easier. Not sure where the hell he and his boys were supposed to go, but he'd find out soon enough, maybe from General Scott's Adjutant. He gave the General his best effort at a proper salute, and this time, his salute was returned. But when would he be dismissed?

"There'll be no written orders, Colonel," Winfield Scott said. "But here's what I want you to do. General Joe Lane's just broken the Puebla siege and taken Huamantla from Santa Anna. He'll get a Presidential Commendation for that. You and your men are to move out and secure the route over to Lane's division, post haste. Supposedly, there are still Mexican irregulars operating east of here and Puebla. Seein' as how you and your men seem so apt to kill, put as many of those bastards in the grave as you want, I don't give a damn."

Jack smiled, relieved. This was the kind of mission his Rangers were cut out to do. He'd be back to operating on his own, clearing hostiles and securing the main road from Mexico City east back toward the coast. Jack saluted again, this time more of an informal acknowledgement, then turned on his heel ready to leave.

"Not yet, Hays," General Scott ordered without looking up. "You are not dismissed until you acknowledge my next and final order, crystal clear."

This wasn't going to be good. Jack about-faced. Winfield Scott stood and pulled his jacket tail down. Stared at him, straight-lipped.

The Theater Commander spoke with authority. "General Lane, acting on the express wishes of President Polk to me, and on my order, has granted General Lopez de Santa Anna and his entourage safe passage from Huamantla to Veracruz. From there, they will proceed by ship to Jamaica and permanent exile. Get this clear, Colonel." Scott pointed one finger at Jack. "Should you encounter the Santa Anna entourage en route, you will extend every courtesy. They are to be permitted safe passage. No impediment."

"No, dammit. No, sir." Jack interrupted. His voice cracked, high-pitched. "All respect, Gen'ral Scott, but we cain't let Santa Anna off the hook this time. All he's done to Texas over the years. Murdering people at the Alamo, at Goliad, double-crossin' General Sam, even lyin' to President Andy Jackson. I've sworn to my men I'd kill Santa Anna myself, ever I got the chance."

"Colonel Hays." The Commanding General frowned. "General Santa Anna is considered to be a prisoner of war by the United States. Our job here in Mexico is almost done. The killing part, anyway. Killing a prisoner of war, especially this one, would be murder. You will, by God, provide Santa Anna reasonable and proper military courtesies and protection, should he request passage through your regiment. If he or any of his party suffer so much as a scratch by your hand, I shall hang you myself."

The ramrod straight general had delivered an ultimatum. Jack had no doubt that Winfield Scott would have his ass, stretch his neck in a noose, should he waylay Santa Anna. Rigid and stone-faced, Jack saluted, then turned sharply and made for the door. Halfway across the parlor, he slowed and looked over his shoulder toward Winfield Scott once more.

"I'll do it, sir," he said loud.

Did Jack mean he'd grant safe passage to General Santa Anna? Or did Jack intend to defy a Presidential Order and kill the murdering sonofabitch if he encountered him? Jack wasn't sure yet himself. If Sam Houston was here, right here in Jack's spot, what would he do? General Sam had already let Santa Anna go once. Why? What made Santa Anna's life more important than his death? Jack hastened through the door and made his way to the street. He'd had enough of Winfield Scott, and he'd had more than enough of goddamn Mexico.

Chapter Twenty-Eight

The Little General - February 1848

The blue norther howled across the barren brown Mexican hills. Cold wind numbed Jack's ears and made his eyes water. Probably felt the same to his men lining both sides of the trail behind him. He shivered in his saddle, shook off the chill and blinked to better see the uniformed rider with some kind of truce flag trotting toward him. No telling who this fellow was. Mexican Army for sure, but Santa Anna? Probably not, he'd never travel alone. Even so this intruder sure had something to do with the weasly little Mexican general.

The man wore a dark blue uniform trimmed in gold braid. His high-collared tunic buttoned down the front along both sides of an ornate red chest panel. His hat was a tall navy blue cylinder with gold Mexican sunburst insignia over a short bill. A diagonal, brown leather field belt supported his saber, but no other weapons were visible. The man carried the long staff of a white flag in one hand with the bottom end anchored in one stirrup.

The rider drew up fifty yards away from Jack. He had to be high rank in the Mexican army, at least a colonel, maybe even a general. He waved the white flag side-to-side twice, then thrust the sharpened metal heel of the staff deep into the mud. Next, the Mexican officer drew his saber and, touching the hilt to his chin in salute, he stuck the weapon upright into the muddy trail beside his truce flag. The man doffed his headgear, exposing wavy black hair. He bent from the saddle and placed his blue officer's hat on the still-swaying saber hilt. A helluva lot of ceremony for who-the-hell knew what…or why. Shit, this was the worst. This had to have something to do with the little Mexican general.

Jack raised his pistol high in one hand and turned in his saddle to address his troops. Bundled Rangers lined both sides of the rutted, muddy trail. Almost three hundred scowling, weathered men waited with weapons in hand for Jack's order. He eased off his pistol hammer with one thumb and lowered the weapon, but gave no signal for his men to stand down. All this white flag business could be a diversion. Maybe this messenger was nothing more than ambush bait. He'd find out quick enough.

"Gents," Jack shouted left and right. "Today is indeed that cold day in hell. Generale Santa Anna's here to surrender. This probably ain't him, but the feller's damned well gonna tell us where to find the bastard."

Jack turned again to face the Mexican. The officer bowed from the waist and smiled. Jack did not. Damn, was this man really part of Santa Anna's entourage? What the hell should Jack do now? He had federal orders to let Santa Anna and anybody with him pass through his defenses unharmed.

"Senór, my humble apologies for the intrusion." The Mexican rider addressed Jack in excellent English. "I am Colonel Juan Almonte, Aide-de-camp to General Lopez de Santa Anna. Could you please identify yourselves that I might properly present my credentials? I am here to request safe passage to Veracruz for my commander and his distinguished party."

Hard to believe this tall, elegant fellow was the enemy. He looked friendly, maybe even cultured. Sure didn't sound like a barbarian, or look like a murderer. How could he be mixed up with somebody like General Santa Anna? And this was how such military truces and safe passage matters were supposed to work? Jack looked Colonel Almonte up and down.

"You're speaking to Jack Hays. I'm a Texas Ranger," Jack responded, squinting at the emissary. "That's all you need to know. Ride on up to me and present whatever you're carrying. But know this, one wrong move and there won't be no more presentin'. Understand?"

The Mexican nodded and nudged his horse forward. Almonte held his right hand open in the air and reined up alongside Jack. The enemy officer saluted, then unbuttoned the red chest flap of his tunic from throat to mid-chest and displayed two folded parchment sheets. He handed the papers over. Jack took the documents without saluting and holstered his pistol. A metallic rustling behind him told Jack that most of his men were easing off on their weapons.

He scanned the first page, then the second. Both were hand-written in English. No misreading all this, Santa Anna intended to pass along this very road to safety and would be escorted by his own Regimental Guard. What General Scott had warned him about earlier was coming true. But why did Santa Anna have to come his way?

So many good people dead because of this man. Crockett and Bowie at the Alamo, and Fannin and the four hundred at Goliad, all dead. And the general he was finally about to face had been responsible for the lot. Was Jack going to let the little bastard who'd done all that killing live even one more day?

Jack shook his head and handed the documents back to Colonel Almonte. The Mexican officer returned the folded papers to his tunic, then rested both hands on his saddle horn and gave a tight-lipped smile. Jack again drew and half-cocked one pistol. He lifted the weapon over his head. Hammer clicks sounded up and down the Ranger lines behind him. Jack neck-reined his pony a half turn to address his men. He glanced back at the Mexican officer. Colonel Almonte sat motionless in his silver-trimmed Spanish saddle, his open right hand raised in the cold February air. The smile was gone.

"Fellers," Jack announced. "I got reason to hate Santa Anna much as any of you do. But his time in Mexico…it's finished. Papers I just read say so. Colonel Almonte here, he's Santa Anna's messenger. His aide. The little Generale and his family's coming up this road soon's the Colonel tells 'em it's OK."

Murmurs and grumbles came from his men on both sides of the road. Ponies' hooves restlessly pawed the muddy ground. Jack inhaled the cold, damp Mexican winter air. Had he no means of bringing justice to this confrontation?

"I'm giving them my permission to come on through." Jack went on. "Here's my order. None of you's revengin' on Santa Anna, nor killing none of his party when they pass us. I want us all clear on that. Any killin's done today, I'll do the deed myself. Nobody in my command's making a move. Nobody's firin' a shot unless I fire first. Y'all got that?"

This time, no sounds came from his troops, other than the shuffling thumps of well-shod pony hooves on bare earth. Men nodded. Jack nudged his mount away from Colonel Almonte and trotted further along the road between the two lines of his Rangers. He eyed each man, then turned again and galloped up the line. He reined in his pony in front of Colonel Almonte.

"Tell your General," Jack said, loud enough for his men to hear, "he and his entourage can come on through. They'll not be harmed, so long as none a' you makes even one false move. Anybody does, you all die right here. Understand?"

The Colonel nodded, straight-faced, then rendered a stiff hand salute. Jack sat in his saddle, silent, without returning the courtesy. Almonte turned and spurred his mount. This man was a fine horseman, but could he ride as hard and shoot as well as Jack? Probably not. The Mexican officer thundered away. He snatched his hat and saber in one graceful move, leaving the fluttering white truce flag. Just like that, Santa Anna's aide disappeared over the hillock.

That damned white flag. Could Jack ignore a symbol of truce? A flag of surrender? Could the act of sparing the little General and his family's lives somehow honor the loss of his friends and thousands of others that the Mexicans had murdered?

• • •

Once again, Jack stretched in the saddle and squinted his eyes against the stiff north wind. Colonel Juan Almonte had been gone less than an hour when a thundering rumble grew in the distance. The sounds of horses and riders, a lot of them, coming closer, just as he'd been advised in Colonel Almonte's request for safe passage.

Jack spotted the lead elements. The cold February breeze fanned the tri-colored flags of a Mexican heavy cavalry unit. A full regiment of elite mounted dragoons trotted toward him. Their gold-braided, cobalt blue tunics, red plumed shakos, white cross-belts and spotless white trousers were a stark contrast to Jack's unkempt and grizzled men, but there was no question of who was the true instrument of war. These Mexican boys were just too damn clean and pretty to fight.

A single open carriage rolled in the middle of the approaching Mexican columns. The weak winter sun reflected on the black lacquered sides and lit the white truce flag still fluttering beside the path. A lone military driver sat high in the front and reined a team of four matched white horses. Heavy gold covered the coach rails, and a presidential crest embossed the carriage door. No need to guess the identity of the occupants, or to wonder any longer what they looked like.

Antonio Lopez de Santa Anna sat facing forward, his head bare and bowed. A sultry, dark-haired woman, for sure Santa Anna's much younger wife, rode at his side with head held high and proud. The enemy cavalry escort and the Mexican General's personal carriage moved between the long rows of Jack's scowling Texas Rangers, their weapons at the ready. Jack was surprised that Santa Anna made himself so openly visible. Was he wanting Jack to kill him, or was he endeavoring to show contempt?

Jack nudged his pony and galloped past Santa Anna, wedging his way in between the stately black carriage and the trotting lines of Mexican dragoons. Then Jack turned about and raced back up alongside the General's transport. This arrogant bastard needed to feel his hate.

With his full-cocked Walker Colt in one hand, Jack cantered apace with Santa Anna. He wanted the Mexican to acknowledge him and at least admit defeat. But Santa Anna made no attempt at eye contact.

Two children, a boy and a smaller girl, sat opposite the adults on rear facing, velvet seats. The family was covered from the waist down with dark blue lap blankets, but were otherwise unprotected against the chill. Santa Anna now sat stiff and straight, still staring ahead. He wore a navy blue military jacket with gold epaulets, trimmed in red. A light blue sash festooned with medals crossed his upper torso. That jacket sure-as-shit would look a lot better with a hole in the chest from one of Jack's pistol rounds.

The General's wife had a black scarf fringed with green wrapped about her shoulders. Like Santa Anna, she was bare headed, so her long, dark hair fluttered in the wind. The woman, or rather, the girl, held Santa Anna's arm and looked toward Jack. She held his stare.

Somewhere, a dog barked and growled. Then more barking that died away in the distance. Otherwise, the only real sounds belonged to the creaking wheels of the carriage and the horses' hooves on the hard dirt. A formidable, quiet procession.

Was this little weasel really worth shooting dead on the spot? Worth a bloodbath here on the road to Veracruz? The knot in Jack's gut tightened. The temptation was palpable. He nudged his pony and rode further ahead of the Mexican entourage.

What now? Killing Santa Anna with his family looking on would sure be Divine Justice. One less devil to torment people on God's Earth. Jack smirked, then realized he was wrong. If Jack put a bullet in this Mexican, there'd soon be two less devils walking the Earth. He might live through killing Santa Anna, but Winfield Scott would certainly see him hanged.

The carriage reached the end of the Ranger column. Jack reined in his pony and turned to face Santa Anna as his carriage approached. He eased off the hammer of his revolver with a double click. Jack's hand shook when he holstered the weapon. No reaction came from Santa Anna, but his wife smiled and nodded to Jack. That dark hair and olive skin.... Quite an attractive girl. Could've been Emily's younger sister.

My God, Emily again. What about Susan? His wife would never have taken part in this conflict. Emily, though, would have relished an opportunity to go at Santa Anna again after her capture by his men years ago at Morgan's Point. But even Emily wouldn't want Jack killing the man here. Not now. Not any more.

Jack kneed his mount around and followed the procession with his eyes. Galloping cavalry obscured his view of Santa Anna's carriage. Colonel Juan Almonte, the last to ride past, snatched the white truce flag from the trailside and bowed from the saddle toward him. Jack shivered then inhaled, trying to slow the pounding in his chest. Minutes later, the last of the procession disappeared over the hillock. He turned his pony and signaled to his Rangers. Stand down. Stand down, goddammit. No more would he be Zachary Taylor or Winfield Scott's scoundrel.

Chapter Twenty-Nine

Disbanded - San Antonio - August 1848

The rocker on his front porch creaked with every forward motion. Colonel Jack Hays pushed back-and-forth with one foot and read the order again. His unit, the First Regiment, Texas Mounted Volunteers, was officially disbanded. President Polk's signature on the bottom of the page said so. And George Tyler Wood, the new Texas governor, had no doubt taken pleasure in adding his dirty, scrawled signature beside Polk's.

At the Battle of Monterrey, Wood had been a colonel in the Texas Militia. He'd commanded the Second Regiment. Damn him. Colonel Wood, all prim and proper, had been one of Jack's accusers in General Taylor's investigation into the killing of civilians in Monterrey. In fact, he'd provided his opinion that Jack was an assassin, and that his men were nothing more than "bloodthirsty barbarians." Wasn't much real proof behind all that, but General Taylor had formally reprimanded Jack all the same. He'd held up George Wood and his unit as the proper example of military decorum. They had abided by the "rules of war."

Had they been right? Had Jack influenced his Texas Rangers to be nothing more than hired gunmen, mercenaries without conscience or remorse? Lawless killers unfit for a civilized society? Jack stopped his rocking. He recalled his Great Aunt Rachel years ago back in Nashville reading him the old commandment, "Thou shalt not kill." Jack shivered despite the August heat and buried his head in his hands.

Minutes passed. A metallic clang, probably pots and pans, sounded somewhere inside the house. Jack looked up and smeared his wet eyes with a rough hand. Susan's animated Spanish flowed through the screen door, along with some pungent, familiar aromas.

Manuela had apparently done or said something to set his wife off on one of her rare Spanish language cooking lectures. Whatever they were doing inside smelled fine, though.

Jack rocked some more and stared at the brown hills. Everything was dead out there. No rain around San Antone since early June. Back to war and killing.... Death.

A little over a year ago in Washington, President Polk had introduced him to Congress as a war hero. The President's wife had gushed about him being a great Indian fighter. Everybody said he and his Rangers had scared the Mexicans to death, even Santa Anna.

Jack had certainly done in more than his fair share of men, but he'd never killed anybody who hadn't threatened him or tried to come at him first. That had to count for something. Buffalo Hump, Santa Anna, even General Sam – they'd killed people, sometimes innocent people, just for punishment, or as nothing more than examples.

No turning back the clock. But Jack Hays had learned more than one lesson about life and death here in Texas. Just thirty-one years old and already Jack was a retired colonel. Now, whether he was a real hero or no more than somebody's villain, Jack was finished with war and killing. Santa Anna, Buffalo Hump, General Sam, they were all old, so they'd had a full life of killing. Here he was, barely half their age, fortunate in war, but way too young to have so much history. From here on, he'd have to be as good a surveyor as he had been a soldier.

The screen door hinges popped and Susan Hays appeared, smiling, in the doorway. Her crisp white apron covered a long blue and white gingham dress. She was still the best-looking woman around, Emily included. What would he do without Susan? Jack was lucky she loved him after all his shenanigans.

"When do you expect John to be here?" Susan Hays spoke in a soft, soothing voice. "The brisket is done. We can eat any time."

"Should've been here by now," Jack sighed. "But as I know the man, promptness ain't one of his virtues. Only thing John's truly quick to do is fight. That or run a survey chain."

Susan wiped her hands on the apron and sat next to Jack in a second rocker. Something was on her mind. She'd been happy when the Rangers disbanded, but she knew he was having trouble getting used to being home and under foot. How much did she understand about his pangs of conscience?

"Jack." Susan looked at him and smiled. "I do have a good idea why John's coming here tonight. You two have cooked up some new surveying project. One that I suspect means we won't be staying in Texas."

"There might be some truth to that, my dear." Jack touched her hand. "We need a new start. We need to go someplace where I can put all this warrin' well enough behind me. Get on with family matters. Have children. How'd that suit you, Missus Hays?"

She smiled, grasped his arm and squeezed tight. Maybe he could tell her tonight about him and John wanting to go to California. Some fellow named Marshall had discovered gold there. Jack had no intention of mining it, but opportunity might be had for surveying and organizing claim registrations in California Territory. It all depended on how much of the metal was found. Might even be money in laying out the first real trail overland from here to the Pacific coast. Whatever was out there, he'd have more freedom, surely more satisfaction, than staying here in Texas as a leftover from fighting Comanches and Mexicans. Jack had no desire to become somebody confined to the past before his time.

Noise. Horse's hooves pounding the hardpan. A rider galloped toward the house waving his hat. Jack recognized the floppy whitish headgear. Tardy or not, John Caperton was a welcome sight. Jack gripped Susan's hand and stood up to welcome their dinner guest.

$\bullet\ \bullet\ \bullet$

"Susan, this dinner's always been my favorite." Jack wiped his lower lip with a napkin and extended a hand to his wife, "There's just nothing like your old-fashioned brisket, skillet bread and gravy."

Jack's wife took his hand and smiled. John Caperton, sitting opposite Jack, dabbed at his chin with his well-used napkin and announced his stern agreement. Susan motioned for Manuela to clear the table and moved to excuse herself, but Jack kept his wife's hand clasped in his to keep her seated. Bird's Nest pudding and fresh cinnamon cream might be waiting, but now was the time to get the talk over with.

"Susie, the dessert will keep awhile." Jack slowed his breathing. "We got to talk some, the three of us."

She half-smiled. For sure, Susan knew something of what Jack had in mind. But did she know he'd been out and about already, rounding up ex-Rangers? Men to help survey, and others as security for his party on the long trek west?

"Like I said already," he started again. "Me and John here, well...we're goin' back into land surveying. You yourself agreed all along that this was a good idea. 'High time for a new direction,' you said."

No fear or anger showed on Susan's face. She knew he was done with Texas. No keeping him here. Only question was, would she make the long haul with him?

"Susie, what I ain't explained yet," Jack went on, "well, this time the surveyin' work ain't goin' to be local like the first time me and John done it. They've found gold in California, you know. A lot of gold. I'm organizin' an overland survey party." Jack spilled the rest of his words like water from a bucket. "Hopin' to head out in the next few weeks to find the fastest way from here to California. I aim to do that 'fore anybody else can."

"Jack," Susan smiled. "After all you've been through, you think I'd stand in your way? You said to me after our wedding that we'd married for better or for worse. Things in Texas have gotten worse. For you. For us. I care not a whit about Texas or what it thinks of my husband. My life is with you, Jack Hays. And, by Heaven, your life is with me. You'd best remember that."

"Excuse me, folks," John Caperton broke his silence. "It's gettin' late and I ought to be headin' on out. Maybe save that dessert for another day."

Jack turned and looked at his dinner guest. He'd almost forgotten John was still sitting across the table. Caperton stood, stuck his hat on his head, and put one weathered hand on Susan Hays' shoulder.

"Missus Hays. Susan. I sure appreciate the hospitality." Caperton smiled, crinkling his face. "One thing needs sayin' before I go, though. Jack here's not so good with smooth talkin'. I know that well enough already. I'm sure you do, too. But I promise you this. Him and me, we damned sure know what we're doing with this California plan. Nothin'll happen to him on the trail, nor when we're out there. You'll see. And you'll get there soon enough after we've settled."

Susan smiled close-mouthed at Caperton, then stood to face him. "I know what it means, John, for my husband to have you at his side...."

His wife went silent after that. Wasn't Susan going to say more? She stepped aside, still smiling thinly. Jack could only push his chair back and see John Caperton out to his horse. The man hadn't said much this evening, and Jack hadn't been much of a host, but John had sure held up his end of the evening with that last little speech to Susan. On the porch Jack waved a goodbye to his business partner, about-faced and strode back into the house. Susan stood, her arms folded, looking out the front window. Jack put one arm around her small waist. She turned and smiled, eye-to-eye. Good thing he hadn't married a tall woman.

"Susie, one more matter." Jack's voice was low. "Next week, I got to ride over to General…uh, I mean Senator Houston's place in Huntsville. He's home from Washington for a spell and wants a sit-down with me. Don't know exactly what he's got in mind. Anyway, it's something I'd best go and at least hear out. It's a long ride, but I'll be back quick as I can."

Susan shrugged and glanced out the window again. She turned back to Jack, put a hand on his arm and laid her head on his shoulder. Must be hard for Susie, all his coming and going. Been that way since the day they got married. Would it always be so?

"Jack, do as you must." She spoke and brushed his cheek, whispering more. "Go and hear General Houston out, whatever he wants to say. Just no more war. I demand that much. And my love," her voice wavered. "We have to be together. Your leavings are agony. I only exist when you're gone, waiting. But when you come back, no matter where we are, life starts again. At least for me."

The lump in his throat and tears, the big ones he wiped back now, hadn't come to Jack since Sam Walker's death. But this woman was his world. No one else. And no more thoughts of Emily. God, please.

• • •

Two hot, dry August days and two humid nights on the trail, followed by a hard ride for the better part of a third morning finally brought Jack to the front of a whitewashed, double-pen house with an inset porch where a dog run should've been. Certainly a fancy enough place for Senator Sam Houston. "Woodland" was the man's stated pride and joy, and it had been his and Missus Margaret Lea's home just outside Huntsville village for the last two years.

Jack tied his lathered pony to the hitching rail and bounded up the front steps into the welcome shade of the porch. The screen door pushed open before he could even knock. Margaret Lea Houston, Sam's third wife, eased her tall, well-dressed frame in front of him. The woman's long black hair was pulled severely to the top of her head and secured in a large bun. Her puff-sleeved maroon blouse was held shut at the neck by an ivory brooch carved with an image that might've been George Washington. Jack doffed his cap and bowed, he hoped, just enough.

"Colonel Hays, welcome to Woodland." Margaret Houston's voice was formal and airy. "Samuel has been expecting you. Go on back 'round the corner yonder. His cabin's behind the main house. I'll see to your horse." Then she frowned a bit. "He'll have refreshment enough there. God knows what, though. Difficult to keep that man from his sinful imbibing."

Margaret Lea was the daughter of a well-known Baptist circuit rider, and truth be known, General Sam had always been a heavy drinker. Maybe this new strict wife, along with his election to the US Senate, was the right direction for an aging warrior like Sam.

Jack rolled his cap brim and addressed Houston's wife. "Thank you, Ma'am. A real pleasure to meet you. I'm hoping one of these days to make you acquainted with my wife, Susan. Her father, Judge Calvert, I believe has been acquainted with your father for some time."

He got nothing more than a formal smile from Lea Houston. Time to head for Houston's cabin out back. Jack turned and strode down the front steps. Wonder why the General had wanted him to come all this way on such short notice? He'd find out pretty quick. General Sam didn't really bother mincing words.

Not more than a hundred yards behind the main residence stood a rough, square-hewn log cabin with red trimmed window sash and matching door. Sam Houston, in an open white shirt and black suspenders that held up his equally plain black trousers, leaned against a well wall just beyond the front steps. A full dipper, presumably water, hung loosely in one hand. He lifted the utensil and offered it to Jack.

"Jack Hays. Son, it's good to see you alive and prospering." Houston spoke, smiling. "After the ride you must've had the last two days, dunno if you want this inside your belly or poured over your head. Suit yourself."

Jack took the dipper and drank deeply. The water was cool and refreshing, like a spring rain, going down. He took a second dipperful from the bucket and bent over and poured the water over his bare head. Hard to believe after all these months, he was back with General, or rather, Senator Sam. Jack ran one hand through his wet hair.

"Senator Houston." Jack tried to sound reverent, slowly glancing from Houston's bushy eyebrows down to his polished boots and back again. "I'm real pleased to see you after all this time. Don't know who's been busy shining those boots, but Washington life must be agreein' with you and the missus."

"Aw, dammit." Houston wrinkled his forehead. Bushy brows lowered, "don't get goin' about me and Washington. And as for Maggie? She hates politics. Won't go east with me. Then, once I'm home, she's busy harpin' on my ass about drinkin'. That's how come I built this office out back. She's a good woman, though. I'd prob'ly be dead already without her."

Houston put one hand on Jack's shoulder and guided him toward the cabin. Good, this was no social call. The man meant to get down to business. Maybe Sam Houston understood that Jack wanted to get back to Susan just as soon as their parley was over.

• • •

Inside the cabin, Houston's office was not like any Jack had seen him occupy before. Books were scattered about, but far fewer. Some were stacked neatly on a rough bench against one log wall. The General's saber and his silver-handled cane were cross-mounted above the heavy stone fireplace mantle. Apparently, the new Texas Senator could do without both. Sam Houston sat in a rocker facing Jack, relaxed and somehow younger with his trimmed sideburns and close-cropped, graying hair. Sure was a different feeling from that day he'd first met the General at the Fanthorpe Inn. God, Jack had been nervous back then.

The polished oak bench with spindled backrest where Jack sat now was too slick in the seat and straight up for any long meeting. As such, he hoped they'd get the matters attended to quickly. Trail riding was sure easier than sitting on this contraption.

"Here's to you and your Missus, Jack." Houston raised a short tin from the low table between them and eyed him. "Don't worry, it's cider. And not the real hard stuff, neither."

Jack grabbed his tin, gave a quick salute and took a sip. Tasted a lot better than he'd expected. Maybe General Sam was indeed mellowing. So was he after all these years.

"Story I hear," Houston spoke, at once steely-eyed and serious. "Now that the Rangerin's done, you and Caperton are off on some fool mission to California Territory."

Houston stared at Jack as if he was waiting for a response. Jack knew better. General Sam, or whatever his title was these days, wasn't done with his lecturing. Besides, where the hell had he heard the California story already?

"Some folks say," Houston took a deep breath. "you're leaving 'cause you don't feel needed. No, worse than that. Leavin' because you're not wanted here in Texas no more."

"General Sam." Jack responded, then caught himself. "Hell, I cain't even say 'Senator Sam' yet. Truth be told, that's exactly how I see things. Santa Anna's gone, and between us Rangers and the pox, the Comanche are basically done for, too. You yourself left Tennessee a long time back for a better life. I figure it's time me and Susie did the same. Head further west. There's money to be made in California, Sam. Not just in minin' gold, neither."

"Jack, I was run outta goddamn Tennessee," Houston interrupted. "Even had a fistfight with a feller my first stint in Congress. If it hadn't been for that lawyer of mine, Francis Key, I might still be in jail. That boy put on one helluva show. Then there was all the fufaraw with Jim Polk over the Cherokee. He didn't treat those poor devils right. No sir, not at all. So off I went, right along with them Indians into Arkansas Territory. I reckon you know the rest. But here in Texas? Son, nobody's runnin' you out. Not even tryin' to. You're a genuine hero."

Jack stared at his old mentor. How could he tell the man that he was part of the reason for Jack's leaving? General Sam had gone soft on Santa Anna. Now he'd signed a peace treaty with Buffalo Hump and the damned Comanche. Some of them, leastways. Best he kept his mouth shut, though. At least till the General got to whatever the hell his point was going to be. Besides, maybe ol' Sam was right, the time might have come for peacemaking and politics.

Houston interrupted his thoughts. "Jack, you've damned sure helped settle Texas. But apparently, Texas ain't settled you, so you best head on to whatever's waiting on the trail between here and California. Nobody's stopping you. But before you go, there's some unfinished business here."

Sam Houston stood and walked to a small desk under one window. He took a sizable oilskin-wrapped packet from the desk and handed the heavy bundle to Jack. What the hell was this? Felt like a pistol. Jack untied the rawhide thong and peeled the oilskin covering away.

Wide-eyed, he stared down at the blue-burnished octagonal barrel, hammer and cylinder. Damn, a new design. A new six-shot pistol. The trigger guard and handle mounting were bright, beautiful brass, and the empty cylinder was engraved with some kind of naval battle scene. The handle was carved of solid ivory and highly polished, and a wolf's head had been engraved on each side of the hammer. A real thing of beauty, this weapon.

"I got this by courier from Sam Colt a few weeks ago." Houston said. "Package had a note inside. Colt wrote that Miz Emily West was supposed to deliver the pistol to you personally, but she'd told Sam Colt that she's never comin' back to Texas. She bought herself a little East Coast cottage and settled in, according to Colt. I was supposed to make up some kind of ceremony and present the damn weapon to you myself. Now, I know neither of us is big on such merry-makin', so…."

Jack hefted the handsome weapon. Switched hands with it. A well-balanced handgun, .36 caliber. Probably the finest pistol Jack had ever gripped. He'd be obliged to send Sam Colt some kind of thank you. And as for Emily not being here? She'd be just fine – better off, even – back east. Emily West was a survivor just like him.

"Now Jack," Sam Houston said. "Before you get too attached to that new Navy Colt…. That's what Sam Colt's named it…. Here's the real job I asked you here for. And on this last mission, you'd best not carry that piece with you."

Job? Mission? No weapon permitted? Jack did not like where General Sam was headed with this. He put the pistol back on the table between them and took a sip from his tin.

Houston fixed his eyes on Jack and went on. "The old Chief, Buffalo Hump, he's asked to meet with you. Needs to powwow with 'Lightning without Rain,' he told me. That's your moniker in Comanche lingo, apparently. Chief wants to bury the hatchet. And not between your shoulder blades, neither." Houston grinned. "You know, Jack, me and Buffalo Hump, we smoked the peace pipe. When we signed that Council Springs Treaty a few months back, he asked me this favor. I promised him right then and there that I'd see to it you paid your respects. That Old Indian admires you, Jack. Besides, he says he has something that rightly belongs to you. Wouldn't say what it is, though. I figure it must be pretty important."

God Almighty. First, being ordered to let Santa Anna pass. That was humbling enough. But Jack had done as ordered. Now as a civilian, him being asked to meet with Buffalo Hump? General Sam was mad. Just plain loco.

Since Jack's confrontation with Santa Anna on the road to Veracruz, that little Mexican had sure lost his mystique. And because of that, Jack had felt less urge for revenge these days. Maybe the same would be true if he met his old nemesis, Buffalo Hump. But what could that bastard possibly have that belonged to him? And how could Jack be sure this was not just some trick? Some kind of plot so Buffalo Hump could finally punish the man who had killed so many of his people? Jack stood up and stuck the heavy pistol in his belt. Enough palaver with his old mentor, he was ready to get back home.

"Gen'ral Sam," Jack sighed. "Guess I'll do the thing you're askin'. I owe you that. That Indian might not kill me if he's promised you as much. But as for goin' alone? Unarmed? Well, I'll have to think awhile on that. Anyway, can you let the old Chief know I can ride up to his village sometime later? Let's say, early next month."

Sam Houston smiled, nodded and shook Jack's hand. There'd be no invite to stay the night, no dinner with the Senator and Missus Houston at Woodland. Jack's business here was done. And anyway, he had to get back to Susan. He needed her more now than ever.

Chapter Thirty

Rain on the Ashes - Early September 1848

"My God, Jack. I thought we were done with this!" Susan yelled. "You've truly lost your senses. And the General, or Senator, or whatever that old man calls himself these days, he's crazy as well. Let him go to the Comanche. He's old. Finished. Your whole life's still ahead of you. Ahead of us. You don't owe anything to anybody in Texas."

Jack shook his head and stared across the bedroom at Susan, rocking herself into a fit in that railed, wicker chair. His wife had a right to her anger, though. He'd promised her no more war. No more killing. And he'd keep that promise. But neither of them had bargained for Jack being asked to meet alone with his old foe, the Comanche war chief. Houston's peace treaty or not, Jack would be putting himself in harm's way. In truth, Susan's fear was warranted. He was planning to go alone and unarmed. That truly was more than anyone had a right to ask of him.

Jack actually hadn't given Houston's request much more thought, what with all his California preparations. In fact he and Susan had spoken no more on the matter until the rider had shown up yesterday with General Sam's urgent message. Buffalo Hump would see him the morning after the last Summer Moon. Damn, that was barely two days from now, and the old Chief's village was at least a day's ride from San Antone.

Jack had argued a bit more with Susan. Now they'd go to bed, probably silent and back-to-back. They'd sure done that before. In the morning, he'd have to gather his pommel bag, oilcloth duster and blanket under a silent roof. One thing for sure, though; he'd test fire the new Navy Colt before he left. Sam Colt's gift would at least be with him on the trail to the meeting. And back, too, if all went as planned.

• • •

Sleep came for Jack only after midnight – fitful and disturbing, with dreams full of nothing but death, sadness and stifling heat. Visions of mutilated corpses, dead horses, blood and gore invaded his thoughts. Weeping and wailing women and children, too.

He jerked upright in bed. Cold sweat had lathered Jack's neck and soaked the collar of his nightshirt. Susan lay silent and unmoving beside him. He felt her forehead. She turned onto her back and sighed, but kept sleeping. God, the bedroom was hot. Jack breathed in, trying to slow his heartbeat.

There, the crying came again. Then low and long hissing snarls. Maybe a horse or two whinnying? Sure not his dreaming this time. What the hell? Coyotes? Wolves? No. Maybe a puma? Not likely either. Guttural cries somewhere right outside the house, or near the creek. After that, more whinnies, then silence. Jack swung his legs over the edge of the bed and put his feet on the floor.

Once he'd found and pulled on his boots, Jack snatched the new Navy Colt from his nightstand. He checked the cylinder load and scrambled through the hallway out the front door. He vaulted off the porch into the yard and headed down the path, the new pistol a perfect fit in his hand. On the run, he half-cocked the hammer and glanced left and right, expecting damn-near anything.

Jack sprinted past the lean-to that served as the barn. Chickens clucked and fluttered, awake and nervous. He sprinted on past the corral, his breath coming shorter now. Where the hell was his pony? Two others, snorting and stomping, raced around near the log fence.

Just beyond the corral corner, Jack drew up short. Full moonlight exposed some movement near a clump of swamp grass along the far creek bank. Soft, anguished snorts and moans told him he'd found his prized mount, but matters were obviously dire. Jack darted forward and peered left, then right. He reached the creek's edge on the dead run only to find his pony sprawled and writhing in the reeds and grass up against the opposite bank. One of the poor pony's forelegs jutted out at a terrible angle. The wounded animal raised its head, struggling and making nothing more than soft cries. Its leg was broken, ruined.

Jack knew what would have to come next. He waded into the shallow water, heartbreak suddenly overwhelming him. What the hell had spooked his treasured pony? A wild animal? A horse thief? Was the intruder still around? How had he gotten out of the corral? Jack reached the animal's side and squatted, partly to shield himself and partly to comfort his best trail-riding friend and proven combat veteran. Jack shook with grief. Silent for what seemed like forever, Jack stood, steadied himself and pointed the new pistol at his pony's head. Then he full cocked the weapon and fired. With one great flinch of its body, the awful deed was done.

• • •

First light came on scattered clouds to the east. Jack still sat in the dirt beside the dead pony, heartsick. Susan had come down some time ago, looking to his welfare, and Jack had sent her back to the house. In all his years, throughout all his life-or-death struggles, Jack had never felt this amount of self-loathing. He eyed the new Colt pistol lying on a log, off to his side. Might have been beautiful before, but now the sight of it sickened Jack. He bent down, grabbed the weapon by the barrel, and flung the goddamn thing as far as he could. The weapon spun end-over-end above the mesquite bushes, then landed with a dull thud and a soft splash. Good, the gun was gone. Jack was finished with killing. Finished for good.

● ● ●

"Susie, we talked all this out already." Jack called from the hallway. "You hate where I'm going, I know that well enough. But John'll be here within the hour. I talked him into ridin' with me to the foot of the escarpment. We'll camp there for the night, then I'll head up into the hill country to see the old Indian alone, soon as the sun's up. Me and John'll head home after I'm done. I ought to be back by nightfall tomorrow. Or latest, by noon the day after. You know I got to do this, Susie. Not just for Sam Houston, neither. For me. I need to finish this."

"Jack," Susan smiled. "You are indeed an idiot. But you are my idiot. And I know your heart. Now that Santa Anna's gone, one of Hays' Devils is finally vanquished. I suppose you've one more yet to face. My only prayer is that God will protect you and bring you home to me quickly."

The sound of a lone horse and rider clattered in front of the house. Susan moved to the window. Jack lifted his trail gear, stuck a hat on his head, and felt for the old Walker Colt holstered against his hip.

"It's John." Susan turned from the window and announced. "Go now. The sooner this ordeal begins, the sooner you're done. Go on. Out with you."

Jack took his wife's hand and kissed her, a light peck on one cheek. She smiled, weary with thin closed lips. Her eyes were glassy. Jack stepped out the door and was down the front steps in a few long strides. He lifted a hand in greeting to Caperton and threw his bedroll and pommel bag across his spare pony's back. Two canteens of water hung on the saddle horn. Jack took the reins from a silent stable hand

and mounted up. He swallowed hard. No fanfare. No looking back at Susan. He and John Caperton turned and started the long ride north.

• • •

Night enveloped them, cool and calm after the September sun. Now, the last full moon of summer rose in the east and filtered through the pecan trees. The ponies had been left saddled and tied to mesquite bushes down by a narrow, near-dry creek, and Jack sat quietly by a small fire. He chewed on some buffalo jerky. Those yelps and high-pitched howls up in the hills weren't coyotes. Comanche watchmen for certain. Jack knew it. No need to hide from the Indians on this trip.

"I'm beddin' down, John." Jack announced. "Big day tomorrow, then another long ride home."

"You sleep some, Colonel." Caperton replied, formal. "I'll keep an eye out for varmints. Don't matter none whether they be two or four-legged."

Jack nodded, stretched out under his trail duster and put his head on his pommel bag. Wasn't necessary to warn John not to shoot any Indians, but no telling who or what else might be wandering out there. Jack would take the second watch shortly after midnight, then he'd brew a pot of coffee at first light.

The full moon was halfway across a pitch black, star-filled sky when Jack popped one eye open. A gentle shake on one shoulder from Caperton had let him know that his turn at the watch was due. Jack stretched from a short, fitful sleep and stood up. His partner nodded and threw more mesquite on the low fire before spreading his oilskin duster on the bare ground. Caperton curled up by the glowing pile and pulled the duster around his lanky frame. Jack walked a few paces toward the creek and stretched his bones a little more. He squinted in the weak moonlight to see that the ponies were still tied. Quiet. Too quiet. They were being watched, no doubt about that. But there was nothing to do now except wait for morning and his meeting with ol' Buffalo Hump.

• • •

Low, pink and gray clouds caught the light and scurried over the escarpment to the west. Jack sat on a boulder with his back to the smoldering fire and yawned. He rubbed his eyes. Along the ridge-line, a thin column of smoke towered over the high country and flattened out against the clouds in the winds aloft. Penateka scouts were letting Buffalo Hump know that he was camped down by the creek, and that he was not alone.

A rustling stirred behind him. Jack turned to find John Caperton bent over and tossing mesquite into soft embers to stir the fire back to life. Damn, Jack had forgotten to make the coffee.

Barely half an hour later, Jack sipped the last of the dark, bitter liquid from his tin and washed down a few bites of a stone-hard biscuit. Not much appetite this morning, anyway. He put the empty tin beside his foot and stood up. Jack handed his pistol and pommel bag over to his trail companion, who leaned back against on an old log, alongside his long-barreled rifle.

"Time for me to head out, John." Jack almost whispered. "Especially won't be needing the Colt."

"You sure 'bout this, Jack?" Caperton asked, one eyebrow raised. "Two heads are better'n one in such matters. The two of us together, totin' pistols and a rifle would show the Comanche you'd not go down without taking some of 'em with you."

"General Sam knows them Indians, my friend." Jack tried to smile. "I'll be all right. I trust I ain't walkin' into danger. But if I'm not back by mid-afternoon, you'd best ride on back to San Antone without me. Tell Susan I love her."

Jack walked to his pony and threw himself into the saddle. No more talking. He looked down and tipped his hat to Caperton. Jack's one knee urged the animal around, then a soft kick in the sides sent rider and pony at a gallop toward the base of the escarpment.

• • •

Jack rocked in the saddle and let the pony pick its way through the rocks and brush on the climb up the switchback trail. He had taken off his trail duster and rolled it behind him. Almost mid-morning and a lot warmer now.

Just as a cloud came over the sun, Jack reached the crest and reined in his mount. The plain stretched westward, seemingly unending. In the distance, Buffalo Hump's camp sprawled. My God, must be a thousand tipis spread out as far as he could see, blending with the brown grass and brush. Some had wisps of smoke snaking from their tops.

The sun emerged from the fast moving overcast, and Jack squinted in the strong morning light. Closer, less than a quarter-mile away, the narrow trail leading to the edge of the Penateka village was lined on both sides with mounted warriors. Had to be more than a hundred of them. White feathers in plaited hair, all armed with bows and quivers full of arrows. Some had feathered war lances and colored, leather shields. Their faces, unpainted, were all turned to him. Every eye was focused on Jack. But no words. No gestures. Was this an honor guard, or some sort of escort to his execution? Jack nudged his mount toward the entourage and raised his bare right hand in greeting.

Minutes later, he reined into a slow trot between the two rows of silent, stern-faced Comanche. He looked right and left, then focused straight ahead and rode on. So this was how Santa Anna had felt riding through Jack's Ranger regiment on the road to Veracruz.

Santa Anna had been exiled, forced to leave Mexico. And soon, Jack would be leaving Texas, if Buffalo Hump didn't kill him first.

Like that first day back in Nacogdoches when he'd faced down that big goddamn Swede, Jack hoped he showed no fear. Time seemed to stand still, but the edge of the village crept closer.

An Indian on foot, a familiar face, blocked Jack's path at the end of the long stretch of Comanche braves. This time no blue lightning bolt was emblazoned across the warrior's forehead, and no scalping knife showed in his leather belt. But this was definitely Kablito, the Comanche negotiator from years back. He hadn't aged a bit. Kablito stood with feet apart, dressed in white deerskin moccasins and fringed leggings. His otherwise bare upper torso was partly covered by a white-beaded vest. The Indian smiled, his open mouth showing white, even teeth.

"Welcome, Colonel Hays. Greetings from Buffalo Hump." Kablito spoke with much better English than before. "Please come down and walk with me. I am honored to accompany you to my Paraibo."

His guide gestured with one open hand and motioned toward the encampment. Jack threw one leg over his saddle and slid off his pony to face Kablito. He dropped the reins, then fell into step alongside the Comanche. Jack's mount trailed the two toward the village. Horses' hooves plodded in the dirt behind them. Jack glanced over his shoulder. The Penateka warrior band was following.

The trail wound through the village. Women and children lined the way, probably curious about the White stranger now moving among them. A few smaller children smiled and tried to wave, only to be snatched up and scolded by mothers or bigger kin. No smiles came from adults, but no frowns either. Silence, except for some faint rumbles emanating from the gray anvil cloud that mushroomed far to the west.

"So, Colonel Hays." Kablito broke the silence. "You marry Yellow Woman. Have many children now, I guess."

Jack smiled and kept pace with his guide. That day when he'd first met the Indian, they'd negotiated for release of the Pierce women. Kablito had wanted Emily West as part of the trade, but Jack had protected her by saying she was his squaw-to-be. So, the Comanche warrior still thought about Emily. The damned woman certainly had that effect on people.

"No, Kablito, my warrior friend." Jack replied. "Too much woman. I married another not long ago. But no babies. Not yet."

"Children come soon enough." Kablito spoke. Jack breathed easier. "You happy now. I happy with own wife. But Yellow Woman made big mistake not to come with me. She would be good Penateka. Happier here. Too bad for her."

As quickly as the conversation had started, Kablito went silent and halted. Jack stopped in his tracks. A short, broad-chested man stood stiffly erect and gazed at him from several yards away.

Could this be the great war chief, Buffalo Hump? The fellow was no taller than Jack. His short, muscular arms were ornately tattooed and adorned with copper wrist armlets. He had severe, dark eyes, but his face held virtually no expression. Still, the overall effect was more friendly than intimidating. The Chief, if this was indeed the famous Comanche, was dressed the same as Kablito, with fringed deerskin leggings, white moccasins and a white-beaded vest. A single long plait of hair embellished with eagle feathers fell over one shoulder and down his chest. No weapon was visible. He'd positioned himself in front of a low oval structure that was framed with crisscrossed saplings stuffed with grass and earth. The small lodge was covered halfway down the walls with finely stitched hides.

"Kee Ūmaarū Ekakwitsūbaitū." The Indian's voice was deep and gravelly. He continued with a few words more, then Kablito translated.

"Colonel Hays, this is Chief Buffalo Hump. He welcomes you as 'No Rain Lightning' to his village. My Chief does not like talking English any more. Too many mistakes, so he ask me. I speak for him."

Not waiting for a response from Jack, the Chief turned and walked, gesturing with one hand toward the entryway of the lodge. He stepped through the opening and looked back over his shoulder. Jack took off his hat and and followed the Chief into the darkness, Kablito shadowed behind. Other than the doorway, the only light was provided by a small fire in the center of the room and a small smoke hole in the ceiling. Jack tried to breathe deeply. His heart pounded, but he kept his eyes focused on the Comanche Chief.

Buffalo Hump turned, crossed his legs and sat, all the while keeping his gaze on Jack. Kablito put one hand on Jack's shoulder, a signal for them to be seated opposite the Chief. Jack settled, cross-legged, but with his back to the open door. Not comfortable like this. The lodge was hot, and the pungent smell of many fires hung in the enclosed air.

A beaded pipe decorated with three white feathers lay in front of the Chief, parallel to a long-barreled German Jaeger rifle. Both pipe and weapon were cushioned by a brightly colored blanket. Buffalo Hump took a short glowing twig from the edge of the low fire and lifted it to the pipe bowl he now held in his lips. He puffed several times. More smoke wafted into the room. The Penateka Chief exhaled and took the glowing pipe in both hands. He offered it to Jack.

"You must please smoke now." Kablito spoke faintly. "There will be no more fighting between you and Buffalo Hump. He makes peace."

Jack took the beaded pipe and nodded to his host. He puffed twice. A sharp, bitter taste. Jack exhaled, then puffed twice more. He was, he supposed, being honored with this simple ritual. Jack handed the pipe over to Buffalo Hump, then stared down at the blanketed rifle's carved walnut stock and long, well-oiled barrel. The piece looked familiar. Where had he seen it before?

Wait a minute! That was Flacco's rifle. Where the hell had Buffalo Hump gotten his long-dead scout's prized weapon? Was the thing loaded and primed? What was going on here?

"So, Ranger Jack." Buffalo Hump broke his silence and Kablito continued to translate. "Too much killing. Too little peace. General Houston and Buffalo Hump make peace already. Now you and me. Soon, nobody fight any more."

The Chief stopped talking. He furrowed his broad brow and leaned toward Jack. Buffalo Hump turned the peace pipe over and tapped a few ashes from the bowl onto the toe of Jack's boot. Jack stared down but made no move to brush off the sooty residue. Years ago General Houston had declared that no Indian had ever put ashes on his boot, which meant they'd trusted Houston in all their parleys over the years. So Buffalo Hump didn't exactly trust Jack in this matter of making personal peace with his people? No matter what Buffalo Hump believed, if Jack made it out of here alive today, he'd not be fighting Comanche again.

Bright light flickered through the lodge openings. Seconds later, thunder rumbled long and low, and much closer now. A gust of wind from the roof vent scattered smoke and dust in the dark lodge.

"Chief Buffalo Hump." Jack refocused and tried to sound respectful, despite the ashes on his boot. "I am most honored that we finally meet. But more so, I am pleased we make peace."

Maybe he should've brought his old enemy some kind of peace offering. Nope, General Sam would've told him. This was all Jack would do or say. This was the Chief's parley.

Jack eyed the rifle again. The ceremony wasn't done. The Chief looked down at the weapon then turned his eyes to Jack.

"This rifle you see. Fine weapon." Kablito translated Buffalo Hump's words. "We take rifle long time back from horse thief. Mexicano hombres steal Penateka ponies. Other bandits get away. But we kill one. He have this gun."

Jack swallowed hard. This was the last thing he'd expected to learn today, yet what he'd suspected all along. Now he had the hard truth about about Flacco, Rusty Stimson and Jaime Esteban's deaths. The fuckin' Mexicans had done the deed. Just one more reason he should've killed Santa Anna when he'd had the chance.

How should he respond now? What could he say to Buffalo Hump? He looked again at the Jaeger rifle then back at his host. The Chief had gone silent, but motioned with one hand toward Kablito. Jack waited for more talk.

Smiling, Kablito put one hand to his chest. "I, Kablito, scalp this man and take rifle. I tell Chief Buffalo Hump, this gun is from your Lipan scout, Flacco the Younger. Now Buffalo Hump wants you take back what not belong to us. Give rifle to Old Flacco."

Jack gazed unblinking into the stony eyes of Buffalo Hump across from him. "Chief, I know Flacco's father.... I'm sure he'd feel same as me, that you should keep this here rifle." Jack took a deep breath while Kablito translated. Then Jack went on. "Not as many buffalo on the Plains as before, but this Jaeger's a fine buffalo gun. You'll kill your share with it, and I think Flacco the Younger would've preferred that."

The Penateka Chief smiled with white teeth showing. He waited until Kablito finished the translation. Then Buffalo Hump picked up the rifle, examined it for a spell and softly laid it on the blanket again. The Chief put one open hand in the air between them and nodded.

A bright flash washed through the lodge, followed by a deafening clap. Buffalo Hump flinched. Jack and Kablito did as well. Deep, rolling thunder echoed and shook the ground where they sat. Damn, that was close. Too damned close.

One more weaker flash was followed by softer rattling thunder. Drops of rain tapped overhead. Seconds later, a raging downpour pounded the hide roof of the lodge. Jack, straight-faced, looked at the old Comanche War Chief. What would Buffalo Hump call him now? They'd made peace, then the rain had come. He must be good medicine. Maybe no longer "Lightning without Rain?"

Jack would keep his promise of peace. He looked forward to it. Didn't really matter if the old Indian trusted him or not. And no matter what Buffalo Hump thought about Comanche spells, once Jack got outside and headed home, the rain would wash the ashes from his boot. Soon enough, he'd tell Susan the whole story. She'd be happy he was finished fighting.

EPILOGUE

Kuhtsu' on the High Plains - Spring 1849

Buffalo Hump lay stretched out on his stomach in the high grass, propped on one forearm. In his other hand, a long, familiar kuhtsu' spear. On the plain below, a rolling dust cloud glowed yellow in the afternoon sun, The ground vibrated against his prone torso. Hundreds, maybe a thousand black shapes, the sacred kuhtsu' herd, thundered past in the valley. A small hunting party of his braves had stampeded the buffalo to give them the customary advantage. Kuhtsu' deserved such notice. The Comanche and the buffalo were linked in life and death. They provided his Penetaka with everything: food, shelter and clothes. At once, the aging Chief rose and loosed the eagle's cry, thrusting his spear high into the air – his signal to commence the hunt.

A legion of young warriors on horseback appeared and stormed over the crest of the hill. They rode toward the valley below. Many had full quivers on their backs and stout hunting bows slung across their bare chests. All others rode with their heavy buffalo lances at the ready. Kablito rode hard at Buffalo Hump with the Chief's war pony in tow. The Chief broke into a run, and in a single fluid motion, he leapt astride his passing pony with his buffalo spear gripped tightly in his free hand. The First Spring Hunt was on.

The old Chief grasped his pony's mane and raced toward the herd. Closer now, he hefted his buffalo spear into a striking position. Buffalo Hump needed no arrows today, and he certainly didn't need the long, shiny firestick given him by the White Face warrior last Fall. He would never kill the sacred animal with a firestick, only the cherished kuhtsu' spear.

He jostled on his pony's back and charged toward the stampeding buffalo herd. Thoughts of his meeting long ago with the boy-man Hays pleased him. No doubt, Ranger Jack was a great White Face warrior. Buffalo Hump had lost many good braves to him and his band. But was this Hays as honorable and trustworthy in peace as General Houston had sworn? Maybe. But maybe not. Those few ashes on Jack Hays' boot toe had been the Chief's assurance. If the White Face colonel broke his vow and killed Numunuh again, the Great Mystery would bring a terrible calamity on him and his kin.

The old Chief kicked his pony in the sides and hunched closer to the animal's neck as he plunged headlong into the panicked kuhtsu' herd. He felt his heartbeat match the thunder of a thousand hooves on the bare ground. He blinked through choking dust and eyed the rippling humps of buffalo racing all around him. Buffalo Hump clung to his pony's mane with one hand and raised his kuhtsu' spear overhead in the other.

Someday he'd be too old to hunt. And someday, like him, these sacred beasts would be gone from these hallowed Plains. But today.... Today, the Chief would kill one good buffalo.

Facts and Fiction

John Coffee (Jack) Hays was born in Little Cedar Lick, Tennessee in 1817. When his parents died in 1832, Hays took a job as a surveyor's assistant and stayed for a time in Nashville at the Hermitage, taken in by his great-aunt Rachel and her husband, Andrew Jackson. His adventurous spirit, fueled by war stories from Andrew Jackson, took Hays to Texas in March 1836 to join the fight for independence. He arrived too late for that war, but he joined the Texas Rangers.

Jack Hays was fearless, a man of conscience and an example to all he led. Historical records document that he was a remarkable horseman and deadly with a pistol. Though he was the target of thousands of arrows and gunshots, he was never seriously wounded. Western historians credit Hays with making the Texas Rangers into a superb irregular combat team and a model for objective law enforcement. Both the North and the South tried to entice Jack Hays to accept a General command in the early days of the Civil War. He declined their entreaties.

There is no evidence that Jack ever met the legendary Texas heroine, Emily West. Additionally, the scene describing his peril at the hands of Theodore Iverson is fictional, as is Iverson himself.

Jack Hays' real life exploits after he left Texas for California are as impressive as those described in this book, but that's a tale for another time.

• • •

Samuel Colt was born July 19, 1814 in Hartford, Connecticut. An inventor and industrialist, he founded the Colt Patent Firearms Manufacturing Company and developed an early mass-production technique and interchangeable parts to make his five-shot revolver commercially viable, thereby changing the course of history in the American West.

Colt's early pistols, the Paterson Colts, were notoriously unreliable. Improvements to the design occurred once Colt collaborated with Samuel Walker of the Texas Rangers to produce a heavier six-shot revolver. His business expanded rapidly after 1847 when the Texas Rangers ordered 1,000 revolvers for the war with Mexico. More than 200,000 Navy Colts were eventually produced and used by notables such as Jack Hays, Wild Bill Hickok and General Robert E. Lee.

Colt died in 1862, at the time one of the wealthiest men in America.

Although the weapons dealings Samuel Colt had with South Carolina, Florida and Texas are based on historical fact, Emily West was not part of these events, nor is there any evidence that Samuel Colt ever met her.

• • •

Emily (Morgan) West was born a Free Person of Color, in or near New Haven, Connecticut around 1811, probably to a Creole mother and a Caucasian father. She traveled to Texas in 1834 and worked for James Morgan in his New Washington Hotel as the housekeeper and Morgan's Point port logistician. Emily was captured by Mexican forces when they sacked the town just prior to the Battle of San Jacinto. Her beauty and intelligence were a reputed distraction to General Santa Anna. Whatever truly happened between the two is conjecture, but Texas historians insist that her bravery had a significant impact on the outcome of the Battle of San Jacinto in April 1836.

Some Texas historians also believe that in late 1835 or early 1836, Emily West was the inspiration for a roughly penned ode titled, "Emily, Maid of Morgan's Point," said to be the original lyrics for "The Yellow Rose of Texas."

In March 1837, officially recognizing her heroism in the Battle for Texas Independence, General Sam Houston assisted West in gaining new papers as a Free Person of Color. These documents enabled Emily West to leave Texas and travel to New York City. Little is known about the rest of her life, including where she lived, her marital status, or when and where she died.

Emily's exploits in this novel are fictional in their entirety, including her familial relationship to Nathaniel Miller and his father, Phineas, Eli Whitney's business partner.

• • •

Buffalo Hump (Chief Potsūnakwahipū) was born early in the Nineteenth Century on the Edwards Plateau of Texas, where he grew into one of the most influential of the Comanche War Chiefs. In 1838, he and Sam Houston negotiated for peace and trade. Two years later, Buffalo Hump was angered by the Council House Fight where an unarmed Comanche Peace party and their families were gunned down by heavily armed Texans. In retaliation, he organized and led The Great Raid on Lynnville and Victoria, Texas.

Whether Jack Hays and Buffalo Hump ever met is doubtful. However, Buffalo Hump's gift of an engraved spoon to Jack and Susan Hays' son, John Caperton Hays, is documented in historical archives. Further, the Chief's respect for and relationship with Sam Houston is well chronicled by Western historians.

In later years, Buffalo Hump recognized the decline of the Numunuh People and reluctantly joined their resettlement, first to the Brazos Reservation in South Texas, then to a reservation near Fort Sill, Oklahoma. Buffalo Hump farmed land on the reservation and maintained cordial relations with US military officials until his death in 1870.

• • •

Susan Sophia (Calvert) Hays, the daughter of Judge Jeremiah Calvert, a descendant of Lord Calvert of Baltimore, was born February 2, 1827 in Huntsville, Alabama. The Calverts emigrated from the United States to the Texas Republic in 1842. Susan Calvert and John Coffee Hays were married on April 29, 1847 in the Magnolia Hotel, an establishment owned by her father in Seguin, Texas.

Three years later, Susan Hays joined her husband in San Francisco. The Hays family ultimately resided at Fernwood in Oakland and had six children. Only two, John Caperton Hays (1852-1911) and Elizabeth Brenham (Hays) Norris (1869-1944), survived to adulthood. After her husband's death in April 1883, Susan Hays moved to Alameda. She died on May 28, 1913 and is interred alongside Jack Hays in Mountain View Cemetery in Oakland, California.

The relationship between Susan Hays and Emily West is fictional. As far as is known, they never met.

• • •

Samuel Walker was born February 24, 1817 at Toaping Castle in Maryland. He came to Texas in 1842 and took part in the defense against the first Mexican invasion, led by General Adrian Woll. Walker joined the Texas Rangers in 1844 under the command of Captain John Coffee Hays, where he eventually led a Ranger unit in the Mexican-American war. He died October 9, 1847 while leading federal troops in the Battle of Huamantla.

Walker and Samuel Colt were co-inventors of the famous six-shot Walker Colt revolver. The new revolver was first used by the US Mounted Rifle companies in October 1847 in the Mexican-American War.

• • •

Samuel Houston was born in Virginia, March 2, 1793. He was an American statesman, politician, and soldier, best known for his leading role in bringing Texas into the United States.

Houston served a term as Governor of Tennessee and as a Congressman, then left in protest of Native American resettlement. Francis Scott Key was indeed at one time Houston's defense counsel. Sam Houston went to Arkansas Territory with the Cherokee nation on their "Trail of Tears" and was initiated into the tribe. Later,

Houston ran a trading post and took a mixed-race Cherokee woman as his first wife.

Seeing opportunity, Sam Houston eventually moved on alone to Texas to join the fight for independence from Mexico. There he was sensitive to relations between settlers and local Native American populations. His close friendship with Flacco the Elder led him to pen a condolence to the Lipan-Apache Chief when Flacco the Younger, a Scout for Hays' Rangers, was killed in a horse thievery incident.

> "My heart is sad. A cloud rests upon your Nation.
> Grief has sounded in your camp.
> The voice of Flacco is silent.
> His words are not heard in council.
> The [younger] Chief is no more.
> His life has fled to the Great Spirit,
> His eyes are closed.
> His heart no longer leaps at the sight of the buffalo.
> The voices of your camp no longer cry,
> 'Flacco has returned from the chase.'
> But grass will not grow on the path between us.
> Let your wise men give counsel of peace.
> Let your young men walk in the white path,
> While the gray-headed men of your nation teach wisdom.
> Thy Brother, Sam Houston" (1)

During his long Texas political career, Houston was, on two occasions, President of the Republic of Texas, a U.S. Senator for Texas after statehood, and lastly, Governor of Texas. He is the only person in American history to have been governor of two states and twice president of a foreign republic.

Sam Houston was evicted from his Texas Governor's office in March 1861 after refusing to take an oath of loyalty to the Confederacy. During his confrontation with the Texas Legislature over the secession issue, Houston first spoke the words later attributed to Abraham Lincoln, "A nation divided against itself cannot stand."

Houston died of pneumonia on July 26, 1863 in Huntsville, Texas.

• • •

Erasmus "Deaf" Smith, Matthew "Old Paint" Caldwell, Ewan Cameron, John Caperton, Michael Chevallie, Robert Addison "Ad" Gillespie, A. C. Horton, Henry McColluch, Willis Randolph, Creed Taylor, William "Bigfoot" Wallace and Private Cherry were real life Texas Rangers who fought alongside Jack Hays.

Rusty Stimson, Jaime Esteban, the Irish O'Keefe brothers, along with Theodore "Tojo" Iverson are fictional additions to the annals of the Texas Rangers.

• • •

Chief Flacco the Younger was the son of Chief Flacco the Elder, with whom he shared chiefdom of a Lipan-Apache band. Flacco the Younger led Lipan scouts for Jack Hays' company of Rangers and taught him the battle tactics of Native Americans, as well as how to properly track and trail. Flacco and his recruit, Red Wing, were in many of Hays' fights with Comanche from 1840 through 1842. Flacco admired his leader's apparent courage under fire, once saying,

"Me and Red Wing not afraid to go to hell together. Captain Jack not afraid to go to hell all by himself."

During a horse drive from Laredo to San Antonio in late December of 1842, Flacco and a helper were murdered in their sleep by horse thieves.

• • •

Doctor Henry Perrine, born April 5, 1797 in New Jersey, was a US envoy to Mexico and noted horticulturist credited with perfecting the use of sisal fiber to make hemp. During the Seminole Wars, by then a resident of Florida, he took refuge on Indian Key to escape the hostilities and peacefully continue his plant experiments. Seminoles attacked Indian Key on August 7, 1840, during which Perrine hid his family in a turtle crawl under their rented house. They survived, but the doctor was killed while trying to negotiate with the Indians.

Doctor Perrine did not raise an army of mercenaries to protect his Indian Key venture, nor did he meet with Emily West or purchase pistols from Samuel Colt as depicted in this novel.

• • •

Antonio de Padua María Severino López de Santa Anna y Pérez de Lebrón, more famously known as General Santa Anna, was born February 21, 1794 in Xalapa, Veracruz to a respected Spanish colonial family. He became a political leader, general, and Mexican president who greatly influenced early Mexican and Spanish politics and government. Santa Anna fought first against Mexican independence, then later for separation from Spain.

Santa Anna was president of Mexico on eleven non-consecutive occasions over a period of 22 years. As Commanding General of the Mexican Army, he ordered the massacres at the Alamo and Goliad, then was humiliated at the Battle of San Jacinto. His defeat by General Sam Houston's forces led to the independence of Texas. His military failures over the years resulted in Mexico losing just over half its territory, beginning with the Texas Revolution and ending in the Mexican Cession of 1848. Santa Anna and his family left for exile, first to Cuba, then the United States, Colombia and St. Thomas. He eventually returned to Mexico under a general amnesty in 1874 and died two years later, nearly blind from cataracts and largely ignored by those in power.

Santa Anna was near John Coffee Hays once, but not under the circumstances described in this novel. Historians record that the General was so fearful of being introduced to Colonel Hays that he remained on the other side of the meeting room, refusing to even make eye contact.

• • •

Adrián Woll was born December 2, 1795 in Saint Germain en Laye, France. He was a soldier of fortune and mercenary who served as a general in the Army of Mexico during and after the Texas Revolution. Woll's first command came in Napoleon's army in the defense of Paris in 1814. He later immigrated to the United States and, for a time, served as Field Adjutant to General Winfield Scott. Ever the mercenary, he then moved on to Mexico and served first as Aide de Camp to General Antonio López de Santa Anna.

Woll was defeated by the Texans at the Battle of Salado Creek on September 18, 1842. He did not take part in the Mexican-American War. In June 1845, he applied for a leave of absence from the Mexican Army for reasons of health and spent three years in Montauban, France, seeking treatment for osteoarthritis. He died early in 1865.

• • •

Colonel Juan Almonte, Mexican soldier and diplomat, was born in 1803 in the state of Michoacán. Almonte was educated in New Orleans, where he learned English. In January 1836, he was appointed Aide-de-Camp to Antonio López de Santa Anna and accompanied him to Texas. At the Battle of San Jacinto, Almonte led the last organized resistance of the Mexican army, and was taken prisoner along with Santa Anna after the defeat of Santa Anna's forces. Almonte traveled with the Mexican general to Washington, acting as interpreter in negotiations with President Andrew Jackson. Almonte and Santa Anna were allowed to leave the U.S. in late January 1837 to return to Mexico aboard the *USS Pioneer*. Almonte continued his diplomatic and military career by eventually rising to the rank of major general, but he ultimately fled to Europe during a coup attempt and spent his last days in exile, dying on the 21st of March, 1869 in Paris, France.

Colonel Almonte's encounter with Jack Hays and his Rangers on the trail to Veracruz is fictional.

• • •

The actions of other well-known figures as depicted in *Ashes on His Boot*, including James K. Polk, Generals Zachary Taylor, Winfield Scott and Robert Patterson, Senators John Quincy Adams and Daniel Webster, are matters of historical record, but details and dialogue are as imagined by the authors.

(1) Excerpt from documents, property of the Texas Ranger Hall of Fame and Museum, Waco, TX

www.ingramcontent.com/pod-product-compliance
Lightning Source LLC
Chambersburg PA
CBHW032209190626
46810CB00019B/2326